Elizabeth Jeffrey was born in Wivenhoe, a small water-front town near Colchester, and has lived there all her life. She began writing short stories over thirty years ago, in between bringing up her three children and caring for an elderly parent. More than 100 of her stories went on to be published or broadcast; in 1976 she won a national short story competition and her success led her onto write full-length novels for both adults and children.p

Elizabeth JEFFREY

The Weaver's Daughter

piatkus

PIATKUS

First published in Great Britain in 2003 by Judy Piatkus Publishers Ltd
This paperback edition published in 2012 by Piatkus

3 5 7 9 10 8 6 4 2

A CIP catalogue record for this book
is available from the British Library.

ISBN 978-0-7499-5808-4

Printed and bound in Great Britain by
Clays Ltd, St Ives plc

Papers used by Piatkus are from well-managed forests
and other responsible sources.

MIX
Paper from
responsible sources
FSC
www.fsc.org   FSC® C104740

Piatkus
An imprint of
Little, Brown Book Group
Carmelite House
50 Victoria Embankment
London EC4Y 0DZ

An Hachette UK Company
www.hachette.co.uk

www.piatkus.co.uk

Acknowledgements

'Flemish and Dutch Communities in Colchester in the 16th Century' by L.F. Roker

History of Colchester by Rev. Philip Morant, reprinted by S and R Publishers & Co. Ltd, 1970

East Anglia's Golden Fleece by Nigel Heard, Dutton, 1970

The Revolt of the Netherlands by Peter Geyl, Ernest Benn, 1958

Moens Register of Baptisms in the Dutch Church in Colchester, Hugenot Society, London, Vol. 12, 1905

English Home Life 1500–1800, by Christina Hole, Batsford, 1975

The Tudor Housewife, Alison Sim, Sutton Publishing, 1998

To Jeff, my husband and my friend,
for his unfailing love and support

Chapter One

Anna crept along the passage that ran the length of the house and peered through a crack in the door at the two men seated at the table in the room to the left of the front door – the best room, proving that the meeting was important. One of the men was her father, a spare, black-clad man of above average height, although this was not apparent as he sat deep in conversation with his companion, occasionally stroking his neat grey-tinged beard, his expression sombre, his eyes watchful under beetle brows. Cornelis Fromenteel found life, like his religion, a serious matter; Anna could rarely remember her father smiling, and she had never heard him laugh.

The other man was older, fatter, with a florid face and a red nose that proclaimed his love of red wine, a goblet of which stood before him, refilled at frequent intervals from the flagon at her father's elbow. But although he was mindful of his duties as a host and kept his guest's goblet full Cornelis Fromenteel drank sparingly, unwilling to be ruled by anything but his own iron will.

As Anna watched, Otto de Hane lifted his goblet and drank, a few drops of the red wine dribbling down his beard on to his ruff, to join other unidentifiable stains there. She shuddered. This was the man, a widower twice over, with daughters older than Anna herself, who was at this moment negotiating with her father for her hand in marriage. And to her utter disgust, her father was nodding agreeably at his terms. He even raised his goblet and drank to the bargain.

Anna waited no longer, but picked up her skirts and fled, her slippers making no sound on the patterned tiles of the passage, out of the door and into the early spring sunshine. As she ran she paid

1

no heed to the gardener who came twice a week and was putting the finishing touches to the complicated knot garden he had created. She ran on, slipping through the gap in the tall hedge that screened the house from the old tumbledown weaving shed, no longer in use, at the end of the garden. This weaving shed was her private domain. Nobody bothered to come here any more, although her father had plans for demolishing it and using the space for cultivating vegetables when the knot garden was finished. And when he could afford it.

There was the rub. Cornelis Fromenteel was living above his means. It required money to maintain the standing he aspired to and it was money he no longer possessed. The tall, bow-windowed house on the outskirts of the town was far larger than necessary for himself, his wife Judith, his only child Anna and Bettris their servant, but it was a good house, in a prominent position and he was reluctant to leave it for something less ostentatious. But things were difficult for the Flemish cloth merchant in the year 1580. Prices were being undercut by cheaper cloth imported from England, much of which was manufactured by Flemish people – ironically, some of them probably his own relatives – who had fled there from Flanders during the time of the worst of the religious persecutions some twenty years ago. He had been a young man of some twenty-five summers then and he had seen no need to leave the country of his birth; his religious beliefs, though firm, were adaptable and had never been allowed to get in the way of either profit or expediency. He had never regretted his decision to stay. Until now, that is, when the ship he had bought part shares in to transport his cloth to Portugal in an effort to revive his flagging fortunes had foundered in the Bay of Biscay, with the loss of all hands and the better part of his fortune.

So Cornelis had been forced to look to his only remaining asset. His eighteen-year-old daughter. Not that he would have entertained the notion that he might be regarded as selling her as he would sell a bolt of cloth; the very thought would have horrified him. He was simply anxious that she should marry well, he told himself.

It was providential that Otto de Hane was rich and looking for a young wife just at the time when Anna was young and marriageable. What more suitable than that she should marry his friend – if

2

such a term could be applied to a recent acquaintance – and prospective business associate?

The final details of the 'arrangement' were being agreed that very afternoon in a room furnished in a way that gave no hint of its owner's straightened circumstances. That is to say, the tables were of good, solid oak under the boldly figured table rugs that covered them. The floor tiles were spotless and more tiles, depicting scenes from the Bible, decorated the skirting. The wall opposite the window, carefully chosen so that it could be seen from the street, was covered in gold-tooled leather; the other three walls were hung with tapestries. The silver candlesticks and sconces about the room had been polished to a high degree by Bettris and the wine was a good, full-bodied red. Cornelis refilled his guest's goblet yet again. Things were going well.

In the weaving shed Anna leaned against the dusty framework of the one remaining loom, her eyes tightly closed, her breast heaving as much from pent-up emotion as from her flight from the house, waiting. She didn't have to wait long. A few moments later the door clicked quietly open and Jan was there. This was where they always managed to meet on the days Jan came to work in the garden.

He took her in his arms and she leaned against him, savouring the familiar smell of rich earth mingled with manly sweat and the sharp tang of the herbs he had been planting. But when he put his finger under her chin and lifted it to kiss her she started to tremble and cry.

'What is it, my love?' he asked, immediately concerned. 'What's wrong?'

'Oh, Jan. What am I going to do? The thing I most feared has come to pass. My father is making arrangements to marry me off to Mynheer Otto de Hane, that rich, ugly old man who lives in the big house on the corner of the market square.'

'What!' Jan took a step back and stared down at her.

She nodded and gulped. 'It's true. At this very moment my father is appealing to that dreadful old man's generosity with his best wine.' She gulped again. 'I had to take in another flagon half an hour ago so that he could take another look at the goods on offer. He'd have sampled them, too, if I hadn't got out of his way. His hand was halfway up my leg before I could escape.' She shuddered. 'What am I going to do, Jan?' she cried desperately. 'I *can't* marry that awful old man. I *can't!*'

3

'Of course you can't. You're going to marry me, as we've planned,' Jan said firmly, gathering her into his arms again. 'You know I've been saving as hard as I can so that I'll be able to tell your father I can offer you a respectable life . . .' He held her slightly away from him. 'You *do* want to marry me, don't you, Anna?'

'You know I do. More than anything in the world. But it's too late, Jan. He's at this very moment promising me to that old man.' She clung to him, sobbing harder than ever.

He stood silently stroking her hair, deep in thought, for a long time. Then he said simply, 'Then I'll just have to take you away.'

Her head shot up. 'But you can't . . . I mean . . . where would we go? He'll find us. He'll fetch me back and make me . . .' she shuddered, unable to even speak the words.

'Not if we go to England.'

'England!'

'Why not? There are quite a lot of our people there. They went to escape from the Spanish during the time of the Inquisition. I know it was some time ago but I'm sure we'll find a friendly face there somewhere.' He spoke with slightly more conviction than he felt.

She nodded slowly. 'Yes. I'm told my grandparents went there. But they came back after a few years.' She frowned. 'I don't think they liked England much.'

'Maybe they didn't. But a lot of people did stay, Anna,' he said, his voice urgent. 'And England can't be that bad because people are still travelling over there to live. I've heard there's a good living to be made if you're prepared to work hard. And you know I've never been afraid of that.' He gave a wicked grin. 'I'll wager your father would never think of coming to England to look for you.'

She shook her head. 'No, he wouldn't. He hates the English. He thinks they're robbing him of his trade.' She returned his smile tremulously through her tears. 'Do you think we could, Jan? Do you really think we could escape to England?'

'We can do *anything* if it's going to save you from Otto de Hane,' he said vehemently. He released her and went over to the window. It was of no consequence that it was covered in dust and cobwebs because his thoughts were turned inwards. 'We need to get to Nieuwport,' he said thoughtfully. 'If we can only get there I'm sure we'll find a ship bound for England.'

4

She came and stood beside him. 'That's quite a long way from here. How long will it take us to walk?' she asked anxiously.

'About two days . . .' he spoke absently. Then his tone changed. 'But if I could get hold of a boat . . .' He turned to her, his face alight with enthusiasm. 'Yes, that's it. We'll go by boat.'

'When?'

'No point in wasting time. We'll go tonight. Now, listen. Here's what you must do . . .'

A little later and a great deal happier, Anna went back to the house, first collecting an armful of laundry that had been laid out on the bushes to dry, then dawdling a little to see how the gardener was progressing with the knot garden. She crossed the courtyard into the big, stone-flagged kitchen, where she helped Bettris to fold the linen and lay it in the press, then she escaped to her room.

This was a large, low-ceilinged room, hung with rather faded tapestries depicting dull country scenes. It would have been a gloomy room had it not been lightened by the two latticed windows that overlooked the street below and brightened by the pale yellow curtains and bed hangings. Anna loved her room and the ornaments and pictures with which she had decorated it over the years, and she would often sit on the wide window seat watching the scenes in the street, the men striding out on their business or pausing to exchange the latest news, the women with their laden shopping baskets hurrying home from the market, the children playing with their hoops or balls. But there was no time to look out of the window today. Trying not to hurry, she began to select what she would wear for her journey across the sea; something dark and plain, Jan had suggested, so as not to attract attention; something warm but not cumbersome. She selected a dark-green woollen dress with a white lace collar. Worn with her black grosgrain cloak and without a farthingale she would look no different from any wife or servant on market day. With shaking hands she collected what little money she had and put it in a bag, together with her few pieces of jewellery, ready to tie round her waist under her petticoat.

Busy with her preparations, she was startled by a knock on her door. Hastily gathering up the things lying on the bed and shoving them into a cupboard, she opened the door.

Her father stood there, her mother just behind him. Anna stood aside and he stepped inside, ducking his head as he entered the low doorway. Her mother followed him, like a pale ghost. Judith Fromenteel had once been a beautiful woman, with golden hair and a creamy complexion, but her colour had faded and with it the exuberant manner of her youth, sapped by years of living with a man with no humour and little compassion.

Anna bobbed a slight curtsey, then stood by the bed, twisting the bed-hangings in her hands, a wary expression on her face, waiting.

Cornelis gave a satisfied nod and said in his stentorian tone, 'Anna, I have come to inform you that all is arranged. My good friend, Mynheer Otto de Hane, looks forward to taking you for his wife. He tells me he hopes for a son. I trust you will not disappoint him.' The look he gave her was not quite a glare. 'You are to visit his house next week and be married within the month. Have you anything to say?'

Anna swallowed nervously, her mouth dry. 'No, father. I have nothing to say,' she said quietly.

He raised his eyebrows. 'No word of thanks that I have arranged such a good marriage for you?'

'Thank you, father,' she said obediently.

'That's better.' He nodded. 'Good. I'm going to the Cloth Hall now. I need to be about my business. I've wasted enough time for one day.' He turned and left the room. Anna looked wordlessly at her mother. A minute later they both started as the street door slammed behind him.

Anna took a deep breath and lifted her chin. 'I'm sorry, mother but I can't do it. I *won't* do it,' she said defiantly, 'I refuse to be married to that dreadful old man.'

Judith went over to the window and watched her husband striding along the street towards the Cloth Hall. She waited a moment to make sure he didn't turn back, then turned to Anna, her eyes bright. 'Of course you can't marry Otto de Hane,' she whispered fiercely. She put her fingers to her temples. 'We must think of something. Some way out ...' She looked up. 'You'll have to leave, of course. Immediately. You can go to your Aunt Dionis in Amsterdam. She'll find some way of hiding you.'

Anna gaped. 'You mean you *agree* with me?' she said in amazement.

6

'Of course I do,' Judith said impatiently. 'Now listen. You must go tonight. I'll make arrangements . . .' She began to pace up and down the room. 'Don't worry,' she said over her shoulder. 'I'll tell Jan where to find you.'

Anna gaped. 'How did you know about Jan?'

Judith stopped her pacing and smiled gently at her daughter. 'I've got eyes in my head, child. And don't forget I was young once.' She sat down on the bed and sighed dreamily.

Anna sat down with her and took her hands. 'Then perhaps you'll understand when I say that I've no need to go to Aunt Dionis, mother,' she said eagerly. 'Because Jan is making plans to take me away.'

'Take you away? But where?' Judith asked, astonished. 'Where can you go that your father won't find you and have you brought back? You know he is a determined man and will not take lightly to being made to look a fool if you disappear.'

'We're to go to England, mother,' Anna said, her eyes shining with excitement.

'England!' Judith's face lit up. 'Oh, thank God! Go, child, with my blessing.' She planted a kiss on Anna's forehead. 'A good choice. He'll never come to look for you there, he hates the sea!' She gave Anna's hands a little shake. 'Now, tell me. What are your plans?'

'I have to meet Jan at the old fulling mill by the canal an hour after dark. He'll be there with a boat to take us to the coast. If we're lucky along the way we might be taken on board a barge carrying cloth to Nieuwport, if not we shall manage as best we can. When we get to Nieuwport we'll find a ship that's going to England. Jan says that won't be difficult because there are always ships back and forth from there.' She hesitated. 'I don't know what will happen after that but Jan says there's sure to be work in England for a gardener.'

Judith digested her daughter's words, then she nodded. 'Jan is a good man. I've watched him and seen how hard he works. I'm happy to trust you to him. I know he'll look after you.' She put her hands up to her face. 'Now, let me think. You'll need money. And food for the journey. And what will you wear?'

Anna pulled out the garments she had pushed into the cupboard earlier.

Judith nodded approvingly. 'Good. Warm but not heavy. But you'll need a change of clothing, too.'

'I can't take much. We may have to walk some distance,' Anna reminded her.

'A small bundle. Just a few caps and collars, a spare apron, some shifts and stockings. It's very important, because you must keep yourself clean at all costs. That's what creates a good impression,' Judith insisted. She pinched her lip. 'Now, I suggest you rest. You'll need all your strength for what lies ahead. You needn't come down to the meal tonight. I'll tell Cornelis you're unwell and will have something in your room.' She gave a half smile. 'I imagine you're not anxious to sit and listen to him gloating over the bargain he's made with the old man.' She clamped her lips together. 'I shall never forgive him for what he's done this day. Never.' Her mood changed again and she became quite animated. 'I'll see that the door is left unlatched tonight and I'll leave food in the hutch for your journey.'

'Thank you, mother.' Anna leaned over and kissed her. 'And thank you for being so understanding. Oh, I shall miss you,' she said, clinging to her.

'And I shall miss you, child. Always remember how much I love you.' For a moment the two women clung together weeping, then Judith released her hold a little and said, 'I realise I may never see you again, Anna. So there is something I must tell you.' She paused and blew her nose to regain her composure, then she went on, 'Perhaps I should have told you before but I lacked the courage. I'm afraid what I'm going to say may shock you.'

Anna stared at her. 'Mother, what can you mean?'

Judith plucked at the dornicle that covered the bed. 'It's because you are going to England that I think I should tell you. Because that's where he went. Of course, England is quite a big country. You might never meet. On the other hand . . .'

'Mother, what *are* you talking about?' Anna said with a frown.

Judith looked up. 'I'm talking about your father, Anna.'

Anna's jaw dropped. 'My *father*.'

'Oh, not Cornelis, my husband,' Judith said with a trace of impatience. 'No, Henrick, the man I used to meet in the same loom shed where you've been meeting your Jan.' She paused. 'Only Henrick was not a gardener, he was a weaver who worked for my husband.' Her expression softened. 'He was a fine man and

8

we had a wonderful summer, meeting whenever we could. I knew he was not happy working for Cornelis. He was ambitious and he left to go to England to seek a better life.' She paused. 'He begged me to go with him. But I was afraid. I was afraid things wouldn't work out for Henrick and that we would starve. I was afraid to leave my comfortable life with Cornelis, even though I'd never loved him. And I was afraid for the child. Henrick's child. You, my dear.' She sighed. 'I was stupid. I should have trusted him. I've often wished I'd had the courage to go with him. I still think about him.'

Anna listened, her eyes and mouth open, hardly able to take in what her mother was saying. 'But what about my . . . your husband?' she managed to croak. 'Didn't he discover . . .?'

'Oh, no. Cornelis knew nothing about Henrick and me,' Judith said, her tone almost airy. 'He was so conceited it never occurred to him I would ever look twice at another man. And he never suspected the child I carried wasn't his.' She smiled at Anna. 'You're very like your father – your real father. He was a handsome man. His hair wàs blond and he had the same deep violet-blue eyes. Eyes the same colour as yours, Anna. It was the colour of your eyes that I most feared might give me away, but Cornelis never noticed. Cornelis never notices anything except money in the bank. Not like Henrick. He noticed everything. I've often wondered what happened to him. I'd dearly love to know.' She smiled, a secret little smile. 'It is the memory of those stolen hours in the weaving shed that has sustained me through the years, Anna. That and his likeness in you.' She lifted her head and her tone became brisker. 'And that is why you have my blessing to go with Jan.' She pressed her lips together. 'I refuse to have Henrick's child sold into that old man's bed.'

She got to her feet. 'Now, rest, child. You have a long night ahead of you. May God go with you.' With a last embrace, Judith slipped from the room, before Anna could begin to ask any of the questions that were already forming in her mind.

Chapter Two

After her mother had left, Anna lay down on her bed. But she could not rest. Her mind was in too much turmoil. Not only was there the excitement, the thrill, the apprehension, not to mention the fear over her planned elopement with Jan, she was now having to come to terms with the fact that the man she had known as her father for the past twenty years was not her father at all.

Thinking back over her life, this fact troubled her less than might have been expected. She had never felt close to Cornelis, in fact he had always been something of a shadowy figure in her life, a stern, black-clad, raven-like stranger she had feared as a child and tended to avoid as she grew older. Not that he had ever been physically cruel to her; but his acid tongue had reduced her to tears more times than she could remember.

The truth was, Cornelis was a businessman; he had no idea how to relate to children, and for some reason blossoming womanhood embarrassed him. In any case, bringing up the family was women's work and he wanted no part in it. Although he would have liked a son to carry on his name he was not displeased that Judith had only brought forth one child, even though it was a girl. He wanted no more squalling brats to disturb the peace of his household. It would never have occurred to him that the one child his wife had borne might not be of his begetting.

Lying on her bed, her hands clasped behind her head, Anna tried to imagine her real father. A fair-haired man, her mother had said, with deep violet-blue eyes. Her mother had clearly loved him very much. She closed her eyes, trying to imagine her faded mother as a young woman, hurrying to the loom shed to be with her Henrick, experiencing the same feelings that she, Anna, felt for Jan. Only Henrick and Judith had been unwilling, or unable, to curb their passion . . . Anna smiled to herself. She could understand how they had felt. Her breath quickened a little as she recalled the times she and Jan had almost . . . but not quite . . .

She opened her eyes again and frowned up at the heavy yellow silk that covered the tester above her head. How could it be that although Judith had risked so much to meet with her lover, even conceiving his child, she had been afraid to take the final step and go away with him? Why had she been so afraid to leave her comfortable lifestyle, so afraid of the unknown across the sea? She gave a sigh. Even though Judith admitted she had never loved Cornelis, the truth was that he represented the safety and security that she craved, something Henrick was unable to promise.

Anna stretched her arms above her head. She didn't share her mother's fears. She wasn't afraid to go away with Jan, she was excited. She looked forward to the adventure. She searched her mind. Well, perhaps she was a little afraid. But she feared having to stay and marry Otto de Hane more. Much, much more.

Towards evening her mother brought her soup and cheese and dark bread and a mug of weak beer, insisting that she ate and drank in preparation for her journey.

'I will make sure there is food in the hutch to take with you,' she whispered. 'But you need to eat this while you can.'

'Don't go, mother,' Anna said, as she began the meal. 'There are questions – things I must ask you . . .'

Judith glanced over her shoulder. 'Then be quick, my child. I mustn't be away for too long.'

'Tell me, where did Henrick plan to go to in England? I need to know so that I can search for him.'

Judith frowned. 'As far as I can remember there were three places that took people from this area . . .' Her frown deepened. 'A place called Norwich, the town of Sandwich and somewhere else . . . Colchester? I think that may have been the name.'

'But which one did my father go to?' Anna asked urgently.

Judith smiled a little. 'It was a long time ago, child. I believe he was going to try to get to London. I don't know which would have been the nearest town for that.' She spread her hands. 'But what does it matter? He would probably have had to go to wherever a boat was going that would take him.'

'Did he never write to you?'

Judith shook her head sadly. 'Henrick couldn't read or write. If I'd gone with him I could have taught him.'

Anna finished her meal and Judith embraced her, holding her close for a long time. Then, with a whispered, 'God go with you, my child,' she left and Anna knew she would never see her again.

She lay down on her bed. All her preparations were made so she could only watch the light fade, listening to her heart beating and trying to doze a little in preparation for the long night ahead.

When the time came, she picked up her bundle and stole from her room, her slippers making no noise on the wooden stairs, gliding through the dark, silent house, like a wraith. She could hear Bettris snoring in her bed in the wall when she reached the kitchen but this didn't worry her, she needed no light to find the packet of food her mother had left in the hutch. She unlatched the door and disappeared into the night.

Although the day had been warm for late March, the night was cold, the sky hung with icily glittering stars. The moon was not quite full and shed a grey, shadowy light sufficient for Anna to see her way. She slipped through the darkened streets and alleyways, careful to keep to the shadows in case there were roaming thieves and vagabonds. Waiting until she was well past the cobbled streets she exchanged her slippers for the stout leather shoes in her bundle, but still made sure to walk where there was grass to deaden the sound of her footsteps. Every now and then she looked behind her to make sure she was not being followed.

At last, in the distance over the fields, she could see silhouetted against the skyline the shadowy bulk of the old fulling mill, its skeletal sails spread like welcoming arms. She offered up a quick prayer that Jan would be there with the boat and quickened her step, keeping to the edge of the fields against the hedgerows so that she wouldn't be seen.

She was breathless by the time she reached the mill, partly from hurrying but also from apprehension. Suppose Jan wasn't there . . .

'Anna? Over here.' Suddenly she heard Jan's voice, barely more than a whisper in the darkness.

She hurried to the water's edge behind the mill. He was there, beside a small boat tied to the rotting jetty.

She ran into his arms. 'Oh, thank God. I was afraid . . .'

'Silly. You knew I'd be here.' He held her close for a few

seconds, then released her. 'Quickly, there's no time to lose. Get in. I'll hold the boat steady,' he said.

Minutes later he was standing in the stern, poling the boat silently along while she crouched in the bow, shivering with cold and – although she wouldn't admit it, even to herself – fright.

'I can hear your teeth chattering,' he whispered and she thought she detected a trace of amusement in his voice. 'There's no need to be afraid, Anna. You're with me now and you know how much I love you. You don't have to worry, sweetheart, I've promised to look after you and I will. With luck, when we reach the river we might get picked up by a boat carrying goods to Nieuwport.'

'When will that be?' she asked in a small voice.

'Oh, before daylight. With luck we'll be in Nieuwport before dark.'

Jan was right. They were taken on board a boat carrying sheep and pigs to be slaughtered for the market, giving the boatman their small boat, which had begun to leak, in payment for the journey. Anna would have preferred a less smelly boat, away from the all-pervading stink of animals, but she realised they were lucky to be picked up at all since several other boats had simply sailed on past them. So they sat together in the bow of the boat, watching the dawn come up, accompanied by a dawn chorus of squealing and bleating from the pens behind them.

At last they reached Nieuwport, a busy, thriving port. They thanked the boatman and hurried over to the docks where they could see the tall masts of the ocean-going ships rising above the dockside buildings. Jan left Anna and went to see if he could find a ship bound for England willing to take them as passengers. Whilst he was gone she sat on a bollard and watched the feverish activity on the waterfront, cargoes being loaded and unloaded, men running up and down gangplanks with huge bales of cloth, baulks of timber, sacks of grain or coal on their shoulders, sure-footed on the narrow planks and seemingly unhampered by the weights they carried. She saw animals protesting loudly at being forced either on or off boats and couldn't help laughing when a pig escaped and created havoc among the bales and barrels on the quayside as it evaded the men chasing it. There was another commotion when a cow fell in the water. The poor thing drowned before they could haul it out so it had to be butchered on the spot, to the delight of the scavenging dogs that roamed the quayside.

She saw sailors, sure-footed as monkeys, swarming up masts and along spars at a dizzying height, checking rigging, furling or unfurling sails, shouting orders or obscenities to each other, the wind carrying their words away so that she couldn't tell which.

Once or twice she glimpsed a tall figure striding along that so resembled her father that she cowered trembling into the folds of her cloak and turned away, fearful that she might be noticed.

At last, to her great relief, she saw Jan coming back, weaving his way between the busy crowds. She went to meet him, holding out her hands. 'Oh, I'm so glad you've come back,' she said with a sigh of relief.

'Did you think I wouldn't?' he asked, surprised.

'No, but . . .' she glanced over her shoulder. 'I shan't feel safe until we've left the country. Several times while you were gone I imagined I saw my father. But he wouldn't come here to look for me would he, Jan? Surely, my mother would suggest I might have gone to Aunt Dionis in Amsterdam. He'd go there first, wouldn't he?'

'Yes, of course he would. But you won't have to be anxious for much longer, my love, because we sail at first light tomorrow,' he told her proudly. His expression changed. 'The only trouble is, it's on a boat carrying pickled herrings so it may be a bit smelly.'

She smiled. 'Surely, it won't be worse than the boat with the pigs and sheep?'

He smiled back. 'Probably not. Do you get seasick?'

She shrugged. 'I don't know. I've never been to sea before.' She looked over her shoulder again. 'But I shan't care if I am, just as long as we get away from this place.'

He smiled back and squeezed her hand. 'That's the spirit. It's going to be quite an adventure for us both.' He rummaged in his bag and brought out a small flask of brandy. He opened it. 'To our new life together,' he said, taking a swig and handing it to her.

She took it and followed suit, choking a little as the liquid burned its way down. 'To our new life together.'

Anna remembered her brave words halfway across the German Sea when the sea began to get rough and the sails cracked like thunder in the wind. Even on deck, huddled in a corner in the stern, it was impossible to get away from the smell of the pickled herrings and what with that and the heaving and pitching of the

14

boat she felt so ill that she was ready to die. And listening to the moaning and groans of other passengers she soon realised she was not the only one. She even began to feel that marriage to Otto de Hane had its attractions compared with the present hell she was suffering in trying to escape from him.

'You'll feel better when we get on dry land,' Jan tried to console her, holding her as she retched over the side of the boat and then collapsed into his arms.

'When will that be?' she whimpered.

'About noon tomorrow, if we carry on as we are now. The captain says we're making a good passage with this fresh breeze.'

'Fresh breeze! What must it be like in a gale! And we shan't arrive before noon tomorrow? I'll be dead before then.' She groaned and crawled back to the side of the boat.

A minister of the Dutch Church, known as a predikant, was sitting on a bale of rope nearby. He watched sympathetically as Jan bathed Anna's face with a cloth soaked in brackish water.

'I have made this journey several times,' he said, 'and I always carry oranges and lemons with me. I buy them at the quayside from ships that have come from Spain or Italy. I was once told that there is nothing better for seasickness and I have found this to be true.' He held out a bag of oranges. 'May I offer you one or two for your wife?'

'Anna is not yet my wife, sir,' Jan said, anxious that the predikant should know the truth. 'But I hope to marry her as soon as we reach England. And yes, I would be most grateful for anything that might give her some relief.'

Gently, he fed her with juice squeezed from an orange. At first it did little good but after a while she was able to retain it, then to eat a slice and then another. Eventually, in tiny bites she had managed to eat a whole orange without losing it over the side.

Exhausted, she put her head in Jan's lap and fell asleep.

The predikant moved over and sat beside them. 'Where are you bound for, young man?' he asked.

'We're going wherever this boat will take us,' Jan said simply and he told the man their story.

The predikant listened, shaking his head sadly as Jan told him of the arranged marriage and his determination to rescue Anna from it. When he finished speaking, the predikant stroked his beard and nodded. 'I think I may be able to help you,' he said thoughtfully. 'This boat is making for Harwich, on the Essex coast. About twenty miles inland from there is the town of Colchester. I suggest you make for that town because I know there is a Dutch community living there. I'm sure you'll find a friendly face among the Congregation of Strangers, as they're called. In fact, I'll give you a note for the predikant there, Mynheer Tobias Archer. I've no doubt he'll give you all the assistance he can, if you tell him Abraham van Migrode sent you.'

'That's most kind,' Jan said eagerly. 'I am a gardener by trade. Will I find work? And a place to live?'

'I'm sure Tobias will help you.' The predikant took paper, ink and a quill from the bag beside him and spent some time composing a letter. When it was done he dusted it with sand from a pouch and gave it to Jan. 'Can you read? And write?'

Jan flushed in the early dawn light. 'No, but Anna can do both,' he said, looking down at her and stroking her hair. 'I'm hoping she will teach me when we're settled.'

'Good. I see you have ambitions. That's commendable in a young man.' The predikant got to his feet. 'Now I must see if I can be of assistance to some of these other suffering souls. I wish you both good fortune and God speed. I myself shall be staying in Harwich for several days, but who knows? Perhaps we shall meet again one day.' He raised his hat and began to make his way among the crowds sitting or lying on the deck.

It was midday on the third day after leaving Nieuwport before they reached the port of Harwich. By that time the wind had died and points of sparkling sunlight danced on the water as the ship sailed into the harbour, a busy quayside surrounded by a cluster of buildings where cargoes of sea coal, salt, wool and fish competed for space. Beyond the rooftops towered the masts of a massive warship in for repair at the naval dockyard and another rode at anchor in the estuary, dwarfing the little craft that had just arrived from Flanders with its passengers and cargo of salt herrings.

Anna and Jan left the ship, jostling their way down the gang-plank with the rest of the passengers. They had very little food left and now that Anna was feeling better she was very hungry so Jan bought mutton pies from a pieman selling his wares on the quay-side and they ate them as they walked, washing them down with ale that Jan bought when he went into the Jolly Sailor alehouse to ask directions for Colchester.

'It's not too far. With any luck we'll get there before nightfall,' he said optimistically as they set out.

'How do you know?' Anna asked with a frown. 'How can you understand what they are saying? English sounds a very strange language to me. I don't think I shall ever learn to speak it.'

Jan laughed. 'Yes, you will. In time. But remember, this is a port. There were Dutch-speaking sailors in the alehouse and several of the English in there had a smattering of Dutch so I didn't have any trouble making myself understood.' He took another bite of his pie. 'Mm, these pies are good. Could you eat another one?'

'Yes, I could. Now I'm on dry land again I'm starving.' She smiled at him as she took another pie. She tucked her bundle more firmly under her arm. 'Now, which way do we go?'

'Through the town then along the road that goes south till we come to the crossroads, then west at the milestone.'

'Have you got the letter from the predikant?'

'Yes.' He patted his chest. 'I have it safe in my shirt.'

They walked through the little town with its half-timbered houses huddled together in higgledy-piggledy narrow streets. Gradually the houses became larger and more widely spaced, and then as they left the town there was only the odd, isolated wattle and daub cottage as they reached more rural areas and the road became little more than a cart track between high hedgerows and woodland.

As they walked, Anna revealed to Jan the secret of her birth.

'So what you're saying is that Cornelis, the man you have always called father, is not your father at all?' Jan asked incredulously.

'That's right.' She lifted her chin defiantly. 'I'm glad. Because now I can hate him for what he tried to do to me without feeling guilty.' Her mood changed and she said, her voice dreamy, 'Just think, Jan, my mother and Henrick used to meet in the old loom shed, just like we've been doing.' She smiled. 'Except that you didn't make me pregnant.'

'You don't know how near I came to it, though,' he said with a sigh.

17

She squeezed his arm. 'I think I do, Jan,' she said softly. 'And I don't think I would have stopped you, either.'

They walked on for some time, each busy with their own thoughts. Then she said, 'Wouldn't it be wonderful if my father – my real father – was living in Colchester and we found him.'

He stopped and turned to kiss her. 'It would indeed, sweetheart, but I don't think it's very likely, do you? After all, he could be almost anywhere in England. He might even be . . .'

'Dead? I know. I've thought of that. But I like to think I might find him, all the same. And you never know.'

'No. You never know.' They walked on. Suddenly, he looked down at her feet. 'What's the matter? You're limping.'

'It's nothing. I've got a stone in my shoe, that's all.'

'Then let's sit down on that grassy bank for a few minutes. We can do with a rest, we've been walking an hour or more.'

Gratefully, Anna sank down and began to unbuckle her shoes.

Jan sat down beside her and picked a blade of grass to chew. 'We can't stay too long if we want to reach Colchester before nightfall,' he warned as he leaned back on his elbows. Suddenly, he sat up, wincing, and shaking his hand. 'What was that? Something bit me.' He pointed to a flash of yellow and black slithering out of sight through the grass. 'There! There it goes. That's what bit me.'

'I didn't see. What was it?' Anna said, twisting round to look.

'I think it was a snake. Yes, I'm sure it was. Look, I've been bitten by a snake.' He held up his hand. Two small red holes punctured the fleshy part of his hand.

'Are snakes poisonous?' Anna asked.

'I think some of them are. I don't really know. I've never seen one before.' He stared at the two little holes. The skin round them was already becoming puffy.

'It doesn't look very good,' Anna said doubtfully. She took his hand. 'I'll suck it. If it's poisoned that might make it better.'

'All right. But don't swallow it, whatever you do.'

He watched her as she sucked at the wound, spitting the blood out on to the grass. After a bit she looked up. 'There, does that feel better?'

He flexed his hand and nodded. 'Yes, I think so. Come on, we've wasted enough time. We'd better get on if we want to reach

Colchester before dark.' He stood up and helped her to her feet and they began to walk.

They had only gone a few steps, as far as a bend in the track where a tiny cottage stood, when he said, 'I feel very strange, Anna.' He passed his hand across his forehead. It came away wet with sweat. 'I don't know what's the matter with me . . . My head . . . I feel dizzy . . .' His eyelids drooped as he looked at her, then suddenly he collapsed and sank to the ground.

Chapter Three

Anna knelt beside Jan, chafing his hands and calling his name, but he made no response. Panic-stricken, she covered him with her cloak then got up and ran to the cottage and hammered on the door.

A very old woman in a sacking apron and smoking a clay pipe opened the door. Anna's heart sank. What good would this old crone be? She couldn't help to lift Jan. But there was nobody else so she grasped her hand. 'Please. Please. Help,' she said.

The old woman looked blank. She didn't understand Dutch and Anna had no English.

Anna tried again. 'Please. . .' she pointed to Jan, still lying unconscious in the road. 'My friend. . .' she made a wiggling motion with her hand and then held it up, squeezing the fleshy part with her thumb and forefinger. 'He's . . .' she made as if to faint.

The old crone raised her eyebrows. 'Ah! You reckon he's bin bit by a adder, do ye. Well, I better come and take a look.' She put down her pipe and picked up a basket of leaves and herbs from a table outside the door and made off to where Jan lay, her little stick legs going so fast that Anna had difficulty in keeping up. 'Come on, then. What you waitin' for?' she called over her shoulder as Anna ran behind.

Jan hadn't moved but his face was puffy and he'd been sick.

'Ah, that was a adder, all right,' the old woman said. She took a large leaf from her basket and rubbed it between her hands to bruise it, then she laid it on the two red marks on Jan's swollen hand. 'That'll help till we can get him to the house,' she said. She turned to Anna and pointed to his shoulders. 'You take his shoulders, I'll take his feet,' she said.

Anna nodded her understanding and picked Jan up under his arms. There was no spare flesh on his bones but he was muscular and tall and it was as much as she and the old woman – who was surprisingly strong – could do to half-carry, half-drag him the few yards into the cottage. There they laid him on the old woman's bed, which was little more than a heap of straw in the corner.

Old Betty looked down at him in the dimness of the cottage. 'Look a bit far gone to me,' she said shaking her head. 'I doubt I'll be able to save him but I'll try.'

Not comprehending the old woman's words, Anna smiled at her hopefully.

As her eyes became accustomed to the light, or rather the lack of it, Anna was appalled at the squalor of the old woman's cottage. The shutters were closed on the window, so the only light came from the open door and the fire, flickering on the hearth. Smoke from the fire found its way as best it could through the hole in the roof, mostly taking a detour round the room as it went. Opposite the hearth a ladder led to a kind of open loft or gallery where a chicken sat, staring down at the scene below. Two others scratched in the dried earth of the cottage floor. Everywhere was pervaded by the smell of smoke, unwashed bodies, herbs and rotting vegetation.

If this was what all English houses were like, Anna was beginning to wish she had never set foot in the country.

She pulled her skirt more closely round her to keep it from touching anything and watched anxiously as the old woman pulled down bunches of herbs hanging from the rafters, selecting a leaf here, a root there. These she ground to a paste with evil-looking liquid from a stone jar, all the time muttering what sounded like strange incantations. She spread the paste on a rag and laid it on Jan's wounded hand, binding it carefully. Then she stood back and looked at him, her head on one side, before going to a shelf in the corner where more stone jars stood. After some deliberation she took down the smallest jar and set it on the table. Then she found a piece of rag and dipped it in the jar and moistened Jan's lips with it.

Nodding to Anna that she should do the same she handed her the jar and the rag. Anna frowned and shook her head, disgusted at the filthy rag.

'Well, you want to save him, don't you?' the old woman barked.

Anna didn't answer but rummaged in her bundle for one of her clean collars to use instead of the dirty rag.

Old Betty shrugged. 'Suit yerself,' she said, 'but keep moistenin' his lips. Get him to drink it if you can. Get as much down him as he'll take. That way we might jest save him.' She mimed directions as she spoke and Anna nodded understandingly.

Over the next hours, Anna sat patiently beside Jan in the dirty hovel. At first she moistened his lips with her once snowy white collar, dipped in Old Betty's concoction, then she squeezed it so that the liquid dripped between his lips. When she saw that he was managing to swallow this she poured the liquid a drop at a time into his mouth from a wooden spoon.

From time to time Old Betty came and watched, nodding. 'Thass it, girl, gently does it,' she said. She laid a gnarled hand on Jan's forehead then scuttled off to fetch some large fleshy leaves with which to cool his brow.

Anna had no idea how long she spent feeding Jan with drops of the herbal mixture so when the old woman pulled her away from his side and handed her some steaming broth in a chipped wooden bowl she was surprised to find it had grown dark outside. Inside the cottage the fire had been stirred so that it shed a soft light, making the place look quite cosy in spite of the baked earth floor and sparse furniture. Anna shook her head at the sight of the broth. She didn't relish eating anything cooked in the blackened cooking pot that swung from a hook over the fire, let alone out of such a grubby wooden bowl. And with Jan so ill how could she even think of food, even though she had to admit the broth smelled appetising.

Old Betty frowned. 'You must eat,' she said sternly. 'Eat!' She mimed the word, pushing the broth under Anna's nose.

To placate the old woman she took a spoonful of broth, surprised to find how tasty it was. She took another, then another, suddenly realising that she was very hungry. She looked up at the old woman. 'Eat,' she repeated carefully, taking another spoonful. It was her first English word.

'Thass right.' Old Betty nodded, grinning and showing her one blackened tooth. 'Good?' she asked, watching her.

Anna managed a smile as she nodded back. 'Good.'

The old woman nodded again, satisfied. 'Thass right, girl. You must eat to keep your strength up.' She poured herself a basin of

22

broth and joined Anna at the table, slurping it noisily from the basin.

After they had eaten, Old Betty insisted that Anna should rest, indicating that she would watch over Jan while she slept. She pointed to the ladder. 'Up there,' she said with a jerk of her thumb. 'There's plenty of straw. You'll be comfortable enough.'

Anna didn't try to argue, although she looked askance at the chicken, still sitting up there. But she decided it was easier to do as the old woman commanded. She could always come down after a few minutes saying she couldn't rest. So she climbed the ladder to the loft and, wrapping herself in her cloak, lay down on the straw which covered the floor, trying not to think of what might be crawling or jumping about in it.

It was daylight when she woke. The door was open and Old Betty had mended the fire and was putting the blackened pot on to boil again.

'Ah, you're awake, are ye,' she said, giving Anna her one-toothed grin as she descended from the loft. She nodded towards Jan. 'He'll do. He's over the worst now,' she said.

Anna went to where Jan lay, filled with guilt because she had slept instead of keeping watch over him. She saw that his face was ashen where the day before it had been flushed, and his eyes were sunken, with black circles under them. Although his hair was still plastered damply to his head the fever had gone and his breathing was even. A fresh, cleanish rag was wrapped round his injured hand.

Old Betty put a chunk of bread and cheese on the table. 'Come and eat your breakfast, he'll sleep for a few hours yet,' she said, resting her head on her hands and closing her eyes to try and show Anna what she was saying.

Anna looked over at Jan. 'Sleep?' she said in English, copying the old woman's mime.

'Thass right. Sleep.' Old Betty nodded. 'It'll do him more good than anything.'

Anna ate her bread and cheese thoughtfully. If she was going to live in England – and remembering some of the big houses they had passed on their way out of Harwich she realised that contrary to what she had feared last night not all houses in England were likely to resemble this hovel – it was important that she should learn the language. She already knew three words, 'eat', 'good'

23

and 'sleep', and she practised them over and over in her mind. She held up what was left of the bread and cheese and looked at Old Betty questioningly.

'Bread,' the old woman said, pointing. 'And cheese.'

'Bread. And cheese,' she enunciated carefully, holding each up in turn.

Seeing that she was eager to learn Old Betty pointed in turn to everything in the room – there wasn't much – at the same time naming each item. 'Door.' 'Table.' 'Chair.' 'Fire.' 'Mug.' 'Pitcher.' From time to time both women glanced over at Jan to make sure he was still sleeping peacefully. 'Man,' Betty nodded towards him, then pointed to Anna and herself. 'Woman.'

Anna repeated the words, then pointed to each item and named it herself.

'You're quick,' Old Betty said admiringly. 'You'll learn in no time.'

'Good?' Anna said hopefully.

'Very good,' Betty agreed.

Jan woke in the middle of the afternoon, feeling strangely light and bewildered. He gazed round the tiny cottage and whispered, 'Anna? Anna. Where are you?'

She hurried across to him. 'I'm here, Jan. I'm here.'

'Where are we? What is this place?' he asked, becoming agitated.

She took his good hand in hers and told him what had happened, keeping her voice quiet and soothing. 'You were bitten by a snake. A kind old woman took us in and she's cured you with her herbs. We were lucky to be so near to her cottage. You would have died in a very short time if she hadn't treated you. I'm sure of that.'

He digested this. Then he said, 'I remember the snake.' He was silent for a few minutes, then he said, 'I'm very thirsty, Anna.'

Anna turned to Old Betty. 'Drink?' she asked in English.

The old woman smiled happily, delighted with her pupil. 'Yes, he'll be very thirsty,' she said, handing her a mug. 'Give him this elderflower cordial. He's too weak for anything stronger.'

Anna held his head so that he could sip the sweet liquid. 'Ah,' he said, when he'd finished, 'That was good.'

Anna gave the mug back to Old Betty. 'Very good,' she said with a smile.

Old Betty came and stood over him, looking him up and down, laying her hand on his forehead and examining his injured hand. Then she nodded, satisfied. 'He'll do,' she said briefly. 'Now what he needs is rest.'

Over the next few days Anna spent a lot of time sitting on the step outside the cottage with Old Betty while Jan rested inside. By a laborious process of miming and drawing pictures on the ground with a pointed stick, she managed to make Old Betty understand where they had come from and where they had been advised to make for.

'Colchester.' Old Betty shook her head. 'Ain't never been there. Long way off, I b'lieve.' She jerked her head in the direction of Jan, now able to sit in the chair beside the fire for part of the day. 'He won't be goin' nowhere yetawhile. He's still too weak.'

'He a strong man. He get better quick.' Anna had picked up a surprising amount of English, some of it rather quaint, in the few days she had spent with Old Betty.

'Is he your man? Are you his wife?' Betty asked, peering at her.

Anna frowned. 'Wife?'

Betty pointed to her ring finger. 'Are you wed?'

Anna flushed and shook her head. 'A predikant . . . we need . . . to do . . . to. . .' She waved her arms, not knowing what to say.

'To marry you?'

She nodded, still frowning. 'Then I will be wife?' she asked uncertainly.

'Yes, then you will be wife.'

They seemed a pleasant enough young couple, Old Betty decided. She hoped things would work out right for them. Suddenly, one of her 'feelings' came over her and she stared hard at Anna, frowning.

'It will not be as you expect,' she said, shaking her head. 'You will prosper, but not . . .' She paused. Sometimes it was better not to repeat the things that she could 'see' happening in the future. 'You will prosper,' she repeated, firmly. 'Much money.'

Anna smiled happily at that.

The old woman looked away. 'Money doesn't always bring happiness,' she said, taking out her pipe and jamming it between her gums and her one tooth.

Anna looked at her quizzically. She only partially understood what Old Betty was trying to tell her and the old woman didn't elaborate further.

Jan recovered slowly, helped by a combination of Old Betty's nourishing broth and her herbal magic. To repay her for her kindness and to get back his strength he began to do a little work in her garden. At first he could only manage a few minutes, then barely half an hour, but gradually he worked for longer and longer, digging and planting, all the time regaining his strength and stamina. He even made a little knot garden of herbs for her, much to her delight.

While he did this, Anna, never happy at being idle, tried to clean up the cottage. But she fought a losing battle. Old Betty refused to shut the chickens out and the smoke from the fire blackened everything. And when Anna washed herself in the wooden bucket behind the cottage the old woman looked on in horror. 'You'll ketch your death,' she predicted with dire foreboding.

It was a day in early May when Jan finally decided that he was strong enough to continue on the journey to Colchester. Old Betty was very quiet as they made their preparations and Anna was touched to think she was sad at their leaving. It hadn't occurred to her that there might be another reason.

'You mustn't tell anyone you stayed with Old Betty' the old woman said when they finally bade her farewell.

'Why not? We want to tell how you are good,' Anna said, speaking slowly and carefully. 'You healed Jan. Made him well again.'

The old woman shook her head. 'No,' she said vehemently. 'Say nothing. Tell nobody.'

'But why?'

'Folks think I'm a witch because I have the second sight.' She gave a mirthless laugh. 'After dark they come to me to cure their ills, but in daylight they denounce me as a witch.'

'A witch! What means . . . a witch?' Anna asked with a frown.

'A witch is . . .' Old Betty waved her hand in a dismissive gesture. 'Never mind. A bad person. Wicked.'

'But you are not bad person. You are kind!' Anna was incredulous. 'I do not think you are . . . witch.'

'All the same, you must never tell anyone you've been here,'

26

Old Betty insisted. 'Tell nobody I cured Jan of a snake bite. Not many people live when they've been bitten by an adder. If folk know I cured him they'll think it was by witchcraft.'

'But I saw . . .' Anna began.

Old Betty tapped the side of her nose. 'You saw what you saw. And now your Jan is better so you can forget about it.'

Anna put her arms round the old woman. 'We not forget you, Betty. Not ever.'

'Be off with you,' the old woman said gruffly, feeling for her pipe so that they shouldn't see the tears glistening in her eyes. She had not felt the comfort of another's arms round her for as long as she could remember.

They set off for Colchester, a good lump of bread and cheese apiece in their bundles together with a stone jar of Old Betty's elderflower cordial.

'And next time be careful where you sit in the hedgerow,' she called after them before disappearing back into her cottage.

They walked all day, through woods, through little villages, beside streams and across fields. By late afternoon they could see in the distance a huddle of roofs, church spires and windmills, crowned with a castle at the top of the hill, and they knew that they must be approaching their destination, although for a long time it didn't seem to get any closer. Then they saw the rows of brightly coloured cloth stretched out on the grassy slopes below the castle.

'We've come to the right place, I was told they manufactured cloth here,' Jan said happily, giving Anna a squeeze. 'See, there are the tenter fields, where the cloth is being stretched and dried on the tenter frames to keep it in shape, just as they do at home.'

They quickened their weary steps as the road widened and more horses and wagons appeared, churning up the already muddy road. Soon they began to pass more people going about their business on foot.

They crossed the bridge over the river, where barges were tied up beside the mill, and began to climb the hill to the main street.

Anna clutched her bundle and stayed close beside Jan as they were jostled by the ever-thickening crowd.

'Have you got the letter the predikant gave you on the boat?' she asked, her voice barely above a whisper.

Jan felt inside his shirt. 'Oh, dear Lord, it's gone,' he said, feeling all around. 'It must have fallen out when I was ill and then I never thought any more about it.'

'Oh, Jan, what shall we do?' she asked, alarmed.

He put his arm round her. 'Don't worry. We'll manage without it, sweetheart.'

She stayed close within the circle of his arm, becoming more and more apprehensive as they neared the top of the hill and the remains of market day. There was still a good crowd milling round the market stalls looking for the end-of-day bargains, and the stall-holders were vying with each other to shout their wares, unwilling to return home with rotting vegetables, unsold eggs or stale bread. Shoulder to shoulder, people were pushing and shoving, craning their necks to see where the best bargains were to be had. In amongst the stalls, wherever there was a space, jugglers, acrobats, fire-eaters and the like were still practising their art, pausing exhaustedly for longer and longer to hold out a shabby hat for pennies, unwilling to leave while there was a chance of another farthing. In one corner a man was trying to encourage a mangy-looking bear on the end of a chain to dance while he played a penny whistle.

They pushed their way through the crowd until they arrived at the church of St Runwald, which stood in the middle of the market place. Here, they leaned against the wall and stared about them, exhausted.

'I never thought it would be like this,' Anna murmured, on the verge of tears. 'How will we ever find someone to direct us to the predikant among all these people? Now you've lost the letter we don't even know his name, or where he lives. Oh, Jan, what are we going to do?'

Chapter Four

Jan put his arm round Anna. 'Don't worry, sweetheart. There are some of our people here. I've seen them. They will help us.'

Anna stared at him. 'How can you tell? There are so many . . .'

'Look, over there, that man in the copotain hat. He's a Dutchman, you can tell by the way he is dressed. His dress is sober and neat and he's wearing a small neck ruff. Nobody else is wearing a ruff. And the woman with him, in the grey dress and white apron, her cap is very like the one you wear, with long strings.'

'Other people are dressed soberly and neatly,' she argued. 'And other women are wearing similar caps.'

'Similar, yes, but not quite the same. None of the other women are wearing their hair in plaits, are they. No, those two *look* different, somehow. And they're keeping themselves apart, not mixing with the crowd. Anyway, we'll soon know. I'm going to speak to them. Wait here.'

'No, I'm not staying here by myself. I'm coming with you.' She clutched his hand and followed him.

'Could you direct me to the house of the predikant, Mynheer, if you please?' Jan asked when they reached the couple.

The man turned to look at them. 'Why, yes,' he answered in the same tongue. 'He lives in Stockwell Street. You'll find it over yonder, running down beside the Moot Hall. It is the fourth house on the right, with black shutters.'

Jan inclined his head. 'Thank you, Mynheer, you've been most kind.' He turned to go.

'Wait. Are you new to this town?' the man asked.

'Yes, we have but lately arrived from a small town not far from Ypres.'

'Ah,' the man nodded. 'I remember Ypres from my youth. I wish you well. And your good lady.'

'Thank you, Mynheer.'

As they turned to go the man's wife touched Anna's arm. 'Be brave,' she said. 'You may find this not an easy town for such as us . . .'

'Sophia!' her husband said sharply.

The woman bit her lip, then smiled briefly. 'We shall see you in church, no doubt. We of the Congregation of Strangers worship at All Saints, just over there.' She pointed to a stone-built church at the end of the road on the other side.

Anna gave a little nod of acknowledgement. 'Thank you, Mevrouw,' she said.

They made their way through the thinning crowds to Stockwell Street.

'See? I said he was one of our people,' Jan said as they walked. 'I could tell by his clothes.'

'Yes, and once you pointed it out I saw several others,' Anna agreed. 'I wonder what his wife meant about this not being an easy town?'

'No doubt we shall find out in due time. Ah, here we are. This must be the predikant's house.'

Anna slipped her hand into Jan's as he rapped on the door, whether to bolster his courage or her own she wasn't quite sure.

A servant answered the door and showed them into a dark panelled room near the front door. Over the fireplace hung a large picture of the Crucifixion, depicted in graphic detail. They were so mesmerised by it that they didn't hear Tobias Archer enter the room until he said, 'Good afternoon, my friends. Is there something I can do to help you?'

They both turned and saw a man of medium height, slightly overweight and balding, with a neat grey beard. He was dressed entirely in black except for white preaching tabs at his throat and gold buckles on his shoes.

He rubbed his hands together and looked from one to the other, his pale grey eyes taking in everything about them. 'I should be glad if you would be brief because I lead a very busy life.'

Jan cleared his throat nervously and told their story, beginning with their meeting on the boat with the predikant and only leaving out the business of the snake and Old Betty.

Tobias shook his head. 'I know of no predikant such as you describe,' he said. 'But no matter. Go on.'

'But first we would wish to marry,' Jan said when he had finished his tale.

Most of the time Jan had been speaking Tobias had been studying Anna. Now he turned his grey eyes on Jan. 'You have sufficient money to support a wife?' he asked, as if this was a fore-gone conclusion.

Jan lifted his head. 'I am a gardener. A very good gardener. I shall quickly find work and be able to support us both,' he said proudly.

'That's all very well. But what if you marry but then don't find work as easily as you expect and find yourselves with not two mouths to feed but three!' Tobias wagged a finger at him. Then, without waiting for an answer, he went on, 'No, it is out of the question. You cannot be married until you have a roof over your head and are earning enough to support a wife. It would be irre-sponsible of me to allow otherwise.'

Anna's face fell but Jan refused to be beaten and said doggedly, 'Very well, Mynheer. I am new to this town, so tell me where I can find work quickly so that I can save enough for us to be married.'

Tobias stroked his beard. 'I believe Lucas Weller, the dyer, is looking for a man . . .'

'But I am a gardener. I told you . . .'

Tobias turned cold grey eyes on him. 'You wish for work? I am telling you where it is to be found. Lucas Weller's assistant had an accident only last week, I buried him this morning. He needs another to take his place.'

Jan's shoulders sagged. 'Very well, Mynheer. I will ask the dyer for work.'

'But Jan . . .' Anna went to him, her face anguished. 'The man was killed. What about if you . . .?'

He patted her arm. 'Don't worry, I'll look after myself.' His voice dropped. 'And it won't be for long, my love. As soon as I find my way about this town I'll find myself something better,' he whispered.

'But what about me?' she cried. 'Where can I go?'

Tobias spread his hands and gave a deprecating smile. 'You

would be welcome to stay here with us, if you wish,' he said kindly.

'That's very kind,' Anna said doubtfully. 'But I've little money. I can't pay you.'

He waved her words aside. 'My wife is sickly. Another child is expected within a few weeks and she spends much of her time in bed. In truth, we could do with another pair of hands. Maria, our servant, has more than enough to do. You could help her.'

Jan's face broke into a smile and he took Anna's hands in both his. 'It would be a great comfort to me to know that you were safe, my love. And it won't be for long, I promise you that.'

Anna swallowed. She didn't want to be parted from Jan but she could see that there was no alternative to the predikant's kind offer. She smiled at Jan. 'If you are willing to work for a dyer for a few weeks, I'm sure I can stay here and help with the house.' She looked over her shoulder at Tobias, who was leaning over his desk, writing, then stood on tiptoe and kissed Jan on the lips. 'I shall be waiting for you, my love,' she whispered.

'Here is the address of Lucas Weller,' Tobias said, straightening up. 'But his house is quite easy to find. If you carry on down this road, past the stock well, until you come to the river, then bear left, you can't miss it. Tell him I sent you.'

As Anna heard the door close behind Jan, she felt more alone than she had ever done in her life.

Tobias came back, smiling. 'Now, my dear, come along and I will introduce you to my household.'

He held out his hand and she had no choice but to take it. She noticed with distaste that his palm was sweating.

First the predikant led Anna to a large room at the back of the house. This was obviously the most important room in the house as the walls were hung with tapestries depicting stories from the Old Testament. In front of the window was a long table with benches along each side and a chair at each end. Clearly, this was where the family took their meals. But the room was dominated by a large bed, obviously the family's most prized possession, which stood on a kind of dais at the other end of the room, and was draped from ceiling to floor in pale blue silk bed-curtains, caught back with tasselled cords. To Anna's surprise, reclining there, in a muddle of pillows and bedcovers, was Tobias's heavily pregnant wife, wearing a yellow brocaded bedgown, her hair falling in two untidy plaits from under a cap that was slightly askew. She was picking idly at a bunch of grapes.

'I have brought you someone to make your life a little easier, Geertruida,' he said indulgently, going over and kissing her brow, 'This is Anna, but lately arrived from our native land.'

Geertruida popped another grape into her mouth and stared at Anna, who was very conscious that her own skirt was stained from her journey and the time spent in Old Betty's hovel, although she had made sure to put on clean white cuffs and collar and a clean white cap and apron before entering the predikant's house. But Geertruida didn't appear to notice. She only said with a frown, 'She's rather thin, Tobias. I hope she's strong,' whilst eyeing Anna up and down over his shoulder. 'Help me to sit up, girl. My body aches from lying here with nobody to help me move.'

Tobias stood aside and watched as Anna went forward and struggled to heave Geertruida, who would have been overweight even without the added burden of her advanced state of pregnancy, into something resembling a sitting position. 'There, is that better, Mevrouw?' she asked breathlessly as she readjusted the enormous feather pillow behind her head.

'For a while, yes.' Geertruida leaned back wearily and closed her eyes. 'I don't know why you continue to bother me with trivial domestic matters, husband. Take her to the kitchen. Let Maria deal with her. Don't you think I have enough on my mind . . .' she sighed theatrically and reached for another grape.

'Very well, my dear.' Tobias kissed her again, making her giggle as he made a great play of adjusting the ruffles on the front of her bedgown before he straightened up.

Anna followed him out of the room and downstairs into the basement kitchen, surprised that he should have allowed her to see such an intimate moment between himself and his wife.

The kitchen was a warm, stone-flagged room with a scrubbed table in the centre and a large open fire at one end, that smelled of newly baked bread. Beyond the kitchen Anna glimpsed a brick-floored scullery, where a girl of about twelve was preparing vegetables at a bench.

'Anna is here to assist you in whatever way you wish, Maria,' Tobias said briefly to the woman standing at the table, busily dismembering a rabbit. He turned to Anna. 'You will be in Maria's charge. See that you do as she asks.' With that he left.

There was a clatter of a knife falling to the floor and the girl in the scullery rushed through, removing a voluminous apron as she came.

'That's good,' she said, as she went by. 'Now *she* can help you and I can go upstairs to be with my brothers and sisters.'

She didn't wait for an answer, but threw down the apron and left. A moment later she clattered noisily up the stairs.

'That's Helkyn,' Maria said with a sigh. 'A disagreeable child. And lazy, with it.' She nodded towards the scullery. 'Now she's gone you'd better finish off the vegetables. I'm waiting for them.' She looked at Anna, brushing a wisp of hair back from her brow with her forearm. 'So he's relented, then,' she said caustically.

Anna frowned. 'What do you mean?'

'I've been telling him there's too much for one pair of hands to manage, but all he says is that after the child is born the mistress will take over her duties again. Pah!' she threw the rabbit skin into a bucket under the table. 'As soon as she recovers from this birth she will be pregnant again. *He'll* see to that. That's how it is, all the time.' She wiped her bloody hands on an equally bloody rag. 'Well, go on, girl. Finish cutting up the carrots. Now you're here you'd better get used to the work.'

It was not until later that Anna had the chance to explain to Maria that she was not there as a servant but that the predikant had offered her temporary board and lodging in return for a little help around the house.

'Just until Jan has saved enough money for us to be married,' she finished.

Maria, a middle-aged woman of generous proportions, her face ruddy from the fire, nodded. 'That's what he said, did he?' she said dryly, her expression cynical. 'Well, we shall see. But I may as well warn you, "a little help around the house" and being a servant amounts to the same thing in this house.'

'I expect I shall manage,' Anna said cheerfully. 'Anyway, it won't be for long.'

She was a little over-optimistic on both counts.

She had always been encouraged to help in her mother's house, so she was no stranger to hard work but Anna had never worked as hard as she was expected to do in the predikant's house. The flagged floors had to be scrubbed every day, and this fell to Anna as did the sweeping, polishing and dusting of the rooms upstairs. On a level with and overlooking the street was the parlour, which doubled up as a study for Tobias, behind which was the room where Geertruida spent most of her time lying either in or on the bed. Upstairs again were the rooms where the children slept and played, when they were not running riot over the house, which seemed to Anna to be most of the time. They were an unruly lot and the nursemaid, Debora, who didn't look much older than Helkyn, the eldest child, spent most of her time trying to amuse and control them.

But Anna rarely had time to talk to Debora, there was too much else to be done. Apart from the floors to keep clean there was the water to fetch and the constant task of washing and scouring the pewter and cooking pots, either with a plant known as horsetails or else with sand or cinders. No sooner had she finished one task than there were three more waiting for her; herbs to pick and hang in bunches over the house, vegetables to prepare, bread to make. And all under Maria's eagle eye, although to be fair, Maria worked almost as hard as she did, because in addition to her other duties Maria visited the market and the butchers' shambles early every morning to ensure she got the pick of the vegetables and fruit and the best of the cheaper cuts of meat, or fish on the two compulsory fish days every week. The only task that didn't fall to Anna and Maria was the monthly wash, which the washerwoman came to do.

But even when this had been done and either spread on the bushes or hung up in the scullery to dry, it fell to Anna and Maria to iron the children's clothes, the fine linen undergarments and the bed linen, and to make sure everything was neatly put away in lavender-scented chests and presses.

At night Anna was glad to pull out the little truckle bed from under the table and fall asleep to the snores of Maria, sleeping in the box bed beside the fireplace.

On Sunday she attended church with Maria, Debora and all the children, where they sat on hard benches and listened to Tobias haranguing his congregation from the pulpit, telling them they were God's chosen people. Salvation was theirs, and they would receive their just dues in heaven as long as they followed his (Tobias's) example, dressed soberly and followed the Ten Commandments. But for those who transgressed . . . This was the crux of the sermon and for an hour and a half Tobias thumped the pulpit, waved his arms and shouted till he was hoarse of the dire penalties sinners would incur.

The congregation left, only briefly subdued. They had heard it all before. Many times.

'Hmm,' Debora said in Anna's ear as they walked through the churchyard, while the children scampered among the tombstones, glad to be out in the open air at last. 'To hear him talk you'd think he was a model of sanctity, wouldn't you.'

'What do you mean?' Anna whispered back.

'You'll find out if you're not careful,' Debora warned. 'You need to watch out for him. Don't let him catch you on the stairs or in the passage or he'll have his hand up your skirt or down your bodice before you realise what he's up to. And if you complain he'll have you dismissed. The only reason I'm still here is because I make sure I never move without at least one of the children beside me. I know he won't touch me while they're about.' She made a sound that was nearly a snort. 'He shouts loudly enough from the pulpit about keeping the Ten Commandments but he'd break the seventh one – "Thou shalt not commit adultery" – every day of the week if he had his way.'

'Thanks for the warning. I'll watch out,' Anna said gratefully. 'But I shan't be staying for long. Only until Jan and I can be married.' She craned her neck. 'I keep looking for him but there are so many people here today . . .'

'They only come because they'll be fined if they don't,' Debora told her, 'not because they want to listen to *him.*'

'I just wish I could see Jan,' Anna said, only half listening to her. 'I haven't seen him since he left me at the house to go and work for Lucas Weller, the dyer. Ah, there he is.' Suddenly, she saw his tall figure searching the crowd for her and she waved and started towards him. He waved back and pushed his way through to her.

'Are you well, my love? Are you happy at the predikant's house?' he asked anxiously, taking her hands in his. Then before she could answer. 'Your hands, Anna! What have you done to your hands? They're so rough and chapped.' He looked at her, alarmed.

'It's nothing, Jan. Only the lye soap I use for scrubbing,' she said, trying to free her hands from his.

'Scrubbing! You shouldn't have to scrub, Anna.' Shocked, he

36

put her hands to his lips. 'I understood you were staying there as the predikant's guest.'

'I have to work. I have to earn my keep, Jan,' she reminded him.

'Oh, my love. The sooner I can earn enough to take you away from there the happier I shall be.'

'The happier we shall both be,' she said, with a catch in her voice. 'I never thought it would be like this, Jan.'

'No, sweetheart, neither did I,' he sighed. 'I think about you all the time.'

'You're never far from my thoughts, either, Jan. But how are things with you at the dyer's house?'

His expression became grim. 'I manage,' he said. 'I don't like it and my master is a cruel man but I manage.' His voice dropped. 'The predikant told us that the dyer's previous assistant died, didn't he. Well, that assistant was his own ten-year-old son. He fell in a vat of boiling dye. That's the kind of man Lucas Weller is. And he docks my pay for every little thing I do wrong. He has a real hatred of the English, too, which I don't understand. After all, he chose to come here to live.' He looked round anxiously. 'I must go, or I'll have another penny docked for being late back from church. I'm trying hard to save enough for us to be married, my love, but it's very difficult at times with such a mean master and I long for the smell of the earth and the feel of plants in my hands.' He kissed her hands again and was gone.

Sadly, Anna went back to the house with Debora, Maria and the children. As soon as they opened the door her heart sank even further because she could hear Geertruida plaintively wailing from her bedroom for somebody to help her to the close stool.

As Anna went about her work the following week she remembered Debora's warning about Tobias. But as she saw the predikant about the house, dressed in his habitual black, often with his hands clasped in front, a devout, slightly tubby man, she couldn't believe there was any harm in him.

Until one day when she was kneeling down sweeping the stairs and she felt a tickling sensation at her ankle. She turned quickly to swat it, thinking it might be a flea, and saw Tobias walking along the passage beside the stairs. He didn't even spare her a glance, but it would have been very easy for him to have put his hand through the banister . . . She gave herself a mental shake. That thought would never have occurred to her if Debora hadn't spoken. She dismissed it from her mind.

But the same thing happened the following day. This time she curbed her instinctive reaction to turn immediately, but waited until the tickling reached her calf, then shot round. Tobias was passing, his face the picture of innocence, but she glimpsed his sleeve as he withdrew his hand through the banister.

He smiled at her, revealing small yellow teeth. 'I hope Maria is not making you work too hard, my dear,' he said smoothly, as if nothing had happened.

She didn't answer, but continued sweeping, determined to be on her guard in future. This was more easily said than done, she discovered, because his movements about the house were quiet, almost to the point of stealth, and in his black clerical garb it was very easy for him to disappear into the shadows. She was reaching above her head to dust a picture on the wall one morning, not realising he was even in the room until he came up behind her and cupped her breasts in his hands.

'Be careful with that picture. It's very valuable,' he whispered in her ear, then before she had time to react he was gone.

After that, she became jumpy and fidgety, always looking behind her to see if he was following, then discovering he was coming towards her, brushing too closely as he passed her in the passage, lingering as he went by, his hands always managing to 'accidentally' touch some intimate part of her. Yet his expression remained bland, as if these encounters were pure chance, and she knew that if she challenged him he would look horrified and accuse her of imagining things.

Chapter Five

Anna was relieved when one morning Maria asked her to go to the butchers' shambles in her place because it gave her the opportunity to get out of the house and away from Tobias's unwelcome attentions. 'It's time you learned to deal with the English,' Maria said, handing her the basket. 'Let's see if a pretty face will get us a better cut. They have good mutton on the stalls but I always seem to get scrag end.'

'Is that what you ask for?' Anna asked. 'Scrag end?'

'No. I ask for shoulder. But they don't seem to understand what I'm saying, even when I shout.'

'Maybe if you were to ask in English,' Anna ventured.

'I don't speak English. Don't see the need,' Maria answered perversely.

Anna took the basket and went out, for the first time since going to church on Sunday. It was a relief to get out of the oppressive atmosphere of the house, where Geertruida called orders from her bed from dawn till dusk, the children shouted and scampered about the house like mice behind the skirting boards and worst of all, Tobias stalked. She hated living there.

Although it was still early, the streets were busy. Pie-sellers were already abroad crying their wares; weavers were making their way to the cloth hall at the far end of the High Street, to get the huge bolts of cloth they carried on their backs searched and sealed with the Colchester seal of quality; housewives were hurrying to get the choicest cuts of meat; a cart piled high with fleeces was being pushed by a boy who couldn't see over the top of it and nearly ran into the water cart, where the water-carrier was selling buckets of water to those too busy or too idle to fetch it from the well. Even though it was not market day, red-faced farmers who had walked from the outlying villages with tumbrels of fresh vegetables to sell were crying their wares, together with their buxom wives, the egg-sellers. It was all noise and bustle, with dogs weaving among the crowd, cocking their legs and licking at the blood that flowed freely from the butchers' shambles.

Anna picked her way carefully to the stall that looked the most appetising and smiled at the butcher, who was hacking away at the carcass of a pig.

'Good morning,' she said, practising her English.

He raised his eyebrows, looking pleased. 'Yes, mistress, what can I do for you?' he asked pleasantly enough.

'Mutton, please,' she said carefully, having overheard what a previous customer asked for. 'Nice cut.'

'Nice bit o'leg?' He held up a leg of mutton.

'Yes. Good. Thank you.' She paid for the leg and put it in her basket. Then, by dint of watching carefully and listening to what other people asked for she managed to buy onions, carrots and a cabbage from the vegetable cart and six eggs from the egg-seller. Pleased with her purchases, she went back to the predikant's house.

Maria sniffed when she saw the basketful of vegetables with the leg of lamb sticking out of it. 'I hope you haven't spent too much,' was all she said. But after that it was always Anna's task to buy the meat and vegetables. This suited her very well because she was able to improve her English as she listened and watched the crowds and she even learned to haggle to get prices down.

She tried to be patient and make the best of things but the one bright spot in her week was seeing Jan after church on Sundays. Even so, their meetings had to be brief because he always had to get back to work.

'Lucas Weller makes sure he is seen at church, but after that Sunday is just like any other day as far as work is concerned,' he told her. 'Except that we have to work twice as hard to make up the time wasted. But how are you managing at the predikant's house, my love? Are you finding things very difficult?'

Anna made a face. 'I'm having to do all the things Bettris was paid to do for me when I lived at home,' she said with a rueful smile. Then her smile widened. 'If I ever have servants, Jan, I shall treat them well, because now I know what it's like to be at everybody's beck and call.'

'Oh, my poor love,' he said, drawing her behind a big elm tree and putting his arms round her.

'It's all right, Jan, really it is,' she said. 'Except . . .'

'Except what?'

'Except I don't like Tobias Archer much,' she said.

'Why? Isn't he kind to you? He said you would be treated as one of the family.' Jan was immediately concerned.

Anna hesitated. She couldn't tell Jan of the predikant's unwelcome attentions, because it would only infuriate him to realise that there was nothing he could do about it. So she simply shrugged and said, 'He doesn't always practise the things he preaches from the pulpit.'

'What do you mean by that?'

She laid her head on his shoulder. 'Oh, nothing. Let's not waste precious time talking about him.'

'No. You're right. I shall have to go soon, because if I don't work I don't get any money.' He released her with a sigh. 'Although, goodness knows, I get little enough when I do work. Lucas Weller is a real pinch-penny. I fear I shall never earn enough to marry you while I work for him.' He took her hand in his and squeezed it, the only sign of affection he was able to give her as they emerged from behind the tree into the crowded churchyard. 'And as I want to marry you as soon as I can I don't intend to stay with him any longer than I can help.' He turned and smiled at her and there was a wealth of love in his look.

'But what will you do, Jan?' she asked anxiously. 'Where will you find other work?'

He glanced round to make sure they were unobserved, then slid his arm round her waist and pulled her to him. 'I don't know yet. But I will, Anna. I promise you I will.'

The following Sunday was a blazing hot early June day. Even so, the Congregation of Strangers, as the Dutch people were known, still wore sober black to All Saints Church, the church they had been lent by the Colchester authorities until they could build their own. This suited both parties very well because although everyone confessed to belonging to the Christian church the people of Colchester practised a much less rigid faith, based on

41

loving thy neighbour – although this didn't always extend to the Strangers in the community – whilst the Calvinist doctrine of the Strangers concentrated on the sinfulness of men and the salvation of the Chosen. Neither congregation had any wish to be harangued by the 'other side'.

Even though everyone, of whatever denomination, wore their best clothes to church, somehow the Strangers were unmistakable in their dress. The men wore well-brushed, black Sunday suits and high copotain hats, the only relief either in small white ruffs or large white flat collars; the women wore black hats – perhaps with a discreet jewel on the brim – and black dresses with spotless white collars and cuffs and deep lace edging on the white aprons they habitually wore. They all carried bibles, even the children, who were dressed as small replicas of their parents.

Today, even in the normally cool interior of the stone church, the air was stifling and some of the women found it necessary to fan themselves with their aprons, although they tried to be as discreet as they could. As usual, Anna divided her time between helping Debora to keep the children quiet – the heat was making them even more fractious than usual – and looking for Jan, who couldn't always be there.

Her heart gave a little leap when she saw him in his usual place behind a pillar. He always hid himself there because he had no Sunday clothes and his breeches were stained with dye. Today there was an air of suppressed excitement about him and he gave her a brilliant smile when he caught her eye. Puzzled, she waited impatiently for the end of Tobias Archer's droning, finger-wagging, arm-waving sermon so that she could meet him and discover what it was that was making him so excited.

She hurried out of church when the service ended and went to where he was waiting under a large elm tree.

'I've done it!' he said exuberantly, catching her hands and doing a little dance with her behind the tree and away from disapproving eyes. 'I'm going back to my proper work, Anna. I'm going to be a gardener again.'

'Oh, Jan! That's wonderful news.' She returned his swift embrace and beamed at him.

'And I shall be well paid, too.' He kept his arm round her, not caring who saw, 'Soon I shall have saved enough for us to be married, my love. I'm determined on it.'

Her smile faded and she gave him an anxious glance as she clung to him. 'Oh, Jan, I do hope so,' she breathed fervently.

His look immediately turned to consternation. 'Is something wrong, Anna? Are you unhappy? You must tell me . . .'

'No. No, of course not.' She shook her head vehemently, annoyed with herself for allowing him to see her despair. 'Nothing is wrong. Tell me more about your new work.' She summoned up a smile as she spoke, determined not to spoil his good news.

He studied her face. She looked a little pale and drawn but she was smiling now and more like her old self. He drew her to a bench in the shade of the elm tree. 'Let's sit here while I tell you all about it. Can you spare the time or have you got to get back?'

'I'm not in a hurry. I prepared all the vegetables before church, so Maria won't be needing me for a little while.' She sat down and turned towards him. 'Come on, Jan, tell me. Don't keep me wondering.'

'Well, it was like this,' he began, his words tumbling over themselves in his eagerness to tell her. 'Have you noticed a tall man who sits near the front of church? A distinguished-looking man with grey hair and a very neat beard. Always by himself and always expensively dressed. Wears quite a wide ruff.'

She smiled. 'A lot of men wear wide ruffs. But I think I know who you mean. Wears a velvet hat with a jewel at the front?'

'That's him.'

'He's got a kind face.'

'I believe he's a kind man. His name is Samuel Hegetorne and he's a cloth merchant. He's been to the dye works several times and from what I can gather he isn't very satisfied with the cloth Lucas Weller has dyed for him but I don't know any details. Being a merchant, he sees the cloth right through from the sheep's back to the finished article so he knows what he's talking about. He must be quite rich, too, because he's just had a big house built at Lexden – that's a small village just outside Colchester on the road to London, beyond the road named Crouch Street.'

He paused and Anna shook his arm. 'Go on,' she urged. 'What does this have to do with you?'

'Patience, my love. I'm telling you as quickly as I can,' he said smiling at her. 'I heard him telling Lucas Weller about this new house the other day, so as he was leaving I plucked up the courage to go after him and ask him if the house had a garden.'

Her eyes widened with admiration. 'What did he say?'

'He said there was no garden there at the moment because the builders had only just finished. But he said he had seen the most beautiful gardens in foreign countries, Persia and Turkey, I think it was, so he was hoping to find a gardener who could make such a garden for him.'

Anna's face fell. 'But you've never been to those places, Jan.'

'No matter. Samuel Hegetorne has drawings, he knows what he wants.' He took her hands in his. 'I told him I was a gardener by profession and he asked me a lot of questions about plants and design. I had no trouble in answering any of his questions so he knew my claim was no idle boast.' He shook her hands excitedly. 'I am to begin work there tomorrow, Anna,' he said, his face shining. 'It will be hard because I shall have to clear the ground first, but Samuel says I can work at my own speed and he will pay me by the hour. He will even find lodgings for me.' He put her hands to his lips. 'It won't be long, Anna. I shall work and work and save all my money. Soon we shall be married. I promise you.'

'You mustn't starve yourself to save money, Jan,' she said quickly. 'The work will be hard, you must eat well.'

'I shall eat well when I have you to cook for me, my dearest love,' he said.

'Shouldn't you be at home helping Maria?' They both started as Tobias loomed over them and for a second Anna moved closer to Jan for protection before getting guiltily to her feet . . .

'I'm just coming, Mynheer,' she said meekly, smoothing her skirt.

'Good.' The predikant smiled at her. 'We'll walk together.'

A look of alarm crossed her face. 'No. I should run. I'm late,' she said quickly and without another word ran off down the churchyard.

Jan watched Tobias hurry after Anna. He didn't like the way the predikant had smiled at her – he could only describe it as a 'greedy' smile – and the man had looked most put out when she made an excuse not to walk with him. He remembered her look of alarm when he suggested it and he wondered why she was so anxious to avoid his presence. Walking back to the dyer's house, Jan's elation at his new work was replaced by his anxiety over Anna. Was she hiding something from him? Was she in some kind of trouble?

He would have been even more anxious if Anna had confided in him.

The truth was Tobias had been getting more and more persistent in his attentions towards her. He always seemed to be prowling about the house; it was as if he was constantly looking for opportunities to touch her, to press himself against her, to 'accidentally' stroke her breast. And however hard she tried to avoid him, however watchful she was and however careful not to linger in shadowy passages, he somehow always seemed to be there, to find an opportunity to squeeze too closely and too slowly by her. She sometimes wondered if he ever did anything else but lie in wait for her. There had been something about the man that she hadn't liked, right from the beginning, but now she knew what it was and she hated him. And as she sat every Sunday, listening to him bullying his congregation, demanding that they should live godly, righteous and sober lives and berating them for their sinfulness, she felt sick and disgusted at his pious posturing, because she knew that underneath he was the biggest sinner of them all.

She ran all the way back to the house, fearful that he might find a short cut and catch her up, such was her fear of him now. She arrived hot and breathless, only to find the household in a turmoil. Whilst Tobias had been holding forth to his congregation on the subject of self-denial, his wife had been brought to bed with a son – her ninth child – after a labour of less than two hours.

'She makes all that fuss while she's pregnant, lying in bed and making everybody wait on her hand and foot, but when it comes to the confinement she gives birth like shelling peas out of a pod,' Maria remarked, hurrying to the bedroom with more hot water. The new baby was no cause for celebration as far as she was concerned, it only meant more work, and once Geertruida was on her feet again, more interference in the kitchen, which Maria regarded as her domain.

But when Tobias arrived home his annoyance with Anna turned to delight at the birth of his new son. The whole household was summoned to view the new arrival, whilst he perched on the bed, kissing and caressing his wife, adjusting her ruffles, telling her what a clever girl she was and whispering things in her ear that made her giggle and blush like a schoolgirl. Quite disgusted at his behaviour, Anna was glad to escape to the kitchen.

'Is he always like this when his wife gives birth?' she asked Maria.

'Like what?' Maria asked, turning from tasting the stew hanging over the stove.

'Well, all that kissing and fussing over her.'

'Oh, that.' Maria put the spoon back in the stew. 'That's nothing new. He's like that all the time. Seems he can't leave her alone, the randy pig. You'll see, she'll be pregnant again before the year's out.' She took another slurp of stew. 'Mind you, she's as bad as he is.' Satisfied with the stew, she looked over her shoulder at Anna. 'Well, come on, girl, get the dishes. Don't just stand there mumchance.'

Anna digested Maria's words. The more she knew of the predikant the more she hated him and the more convinced she became that he was not fit to be a minister in the Dutch church. There was something evil about the man, something menacing behind his bland smile, something that quite frightened her. She resolved to be extra watchful and to keep well out of his way.

Yet in spite of her resolution and her watchfulness it was only two days later, when she was putting a pile of sheets in a chest on the landing, that she felt two arms round her waist and she was lifted to her feet and pushed into the nearest bedroom. He had crept up on her so quietly that she hadn't even heard his foot on the stair and she was so surprised that she had no time to scream before the door was kicked shut and Tobias half-dragged, half-carried her towards the bed, pushing her down and pinning her there with his own body.

'It's time we celebrated the birth of my new son, you and I,' he said breathlessly, his eyes alight with lascivious anticipation. 'I've been looking forward to this ever since I first saw you.' He began to fumble with her bodice with one hand, holding her hands behind her back with the other. She began to scream, but the scream was stifled by his horrible, slack mouth coming down on hers, his breath stinking of wine, nearly suffocating her as she tried to twist her head this way and that to escape his hideous embrace. This was a nightmare, far worse than anything that had gone before and she realised that struggle as she might, she was helpless, pinned beneath his weight. Now he had finished unfastening her bodice he turned his attention to her skirt, dragging it up so that he could get inside it whilst he nuzzled her breasts, almost beside himself with lust.

She was terrified and her terror gave her the strength to pull her hands free from where he was still holding them behind her back. She clawed at his face and neck, leaving great red weals, but this only served to excite him further and he shifted his weight a little so that he could unfasten his breeches. Seizing her opportunity, she brought her knee up as sharply as she could to the great bulge in his groin.

He immediately fell to his knees, doubled up with pain, and began rolling round the floor, groaning obscenities not fit to pass the lips of a man of his standing.

Anna didn't wait, but ran from the room, down the stairs and out of the house. She didn't stop running till she got to the steps of St Runwald's Church. There she crouched into a corner, laced her bodice with hands that were still shaking and straightened her cap. She remained, hugging herself and shivering even in the hot summer sunshine for a long time, trying to gather her scattered senses and decide what she should do. She realised that she had nothing but the clothes she stood up in and no money because she had run from the predikant's house, leaving behind everything she possessed in the world. One thing was certain. She could never, ever go back there again. Added to this, she didn't know a soul in the town except Jan and she had very little idea where to find him. She racked her brain, trying to remember what he had told her. A big new house at a place called Lexden was where he said he would be working. She frowned. She was sure it was called Lexden, on the road to London, beyond the road called Crouch Street, wherever that was.

She got to her feet, still trying to collect her thoughts, watching the passers-by going about their business in the crowded street. A stray dog came and sniffed her skirts but other than that nobody paid any heed to her. She had never felt so alone in the whole of her life. Then the thought came to her, what if one of those men passing by was her own father? What if he was here, in Colchester? How would she know? How could she ever find out? She had no way of knowing and the thought made her feel more alone than ever.

47

Chapter Six

Suddenly, Anna came to her senses and realised that it was dangerous to stay here on the steps of the church; it was much too near to the predikant's house. And if he should come to look for her and drag her back ... Hastily, she began to hurry along the street in what she hoped was the right direction for Lexden.

She soon reached the end of the Market Place and the Three Crowns Inn. Now she had to decide whether to go right, down the hill towards the river or left, along the road known as Head Street. Nowhere could she see a sign for Crouch Street.

As she hesitated a man came round the corner carrying a ladder. 'Please,' she said in her best English. 'Where is Crouch Street?'

He was dressed in grubby breeches and a jerkin that needed mending. He looked her up and down and gabbled something in English that was quite unintelligible to her. Then he gesticulated towards a large building on the other side of the road, spat at her feet and walked on. He was clearly very angry over what went on there.

She looked across at the building. It was quite an imposing place, half-timbered in the fashion of the day, the upper storey well overhanging the street below. It was a busy place, with men going in and out with bales of cloth on their shoulders and a tumbrel at the door being loaded with more cloth. This must be the Bay Hall she had heard talked of, where the finished cloth had to be taken to be examined to make sure it was perfect before it could be sold. She frowned and then her face cleared. Hadn't she heard that it was the Dutch community that administered the place? Was that what the man had been complaining about?

She crossed the road, holding up her skirts and picking her way through the filth that overflowed from the gutter, and dodging the horse-drawn cart loaded with cabbages. If what she had heard was right perhaps she would find someone at the Bay Hall who could understand her and give her directions to Lexden.

As soon as she stepped inside the building and before her eyes could become accustomed to the dimness after the bright sunlight outside, a man came up to her.

'What do you want?' he asked in heavily accented English. 'Have you business here in the Bay Hall, Mistress?'

She breathed a sigh of relief and said in her own language, 'No. I have come to ask the way to Crouch Street. Please, can you help me, Mynheer?'

His face broke into a smile. 'Of course,' he replied in the same tongue. He led her to the door and pointed. 'Go round the corner by the Three Crowns there into Head Street. Turn right when you reach the end and you will be in Crouch Street, the road that leads to London.'

'Thank you, Mynheer. I am told that is also the road to take for Lexden. Is that so?'

He nodded. 'Lexden is a small village about a mile beyond the town.' He smiled at her again.

He had a kind face and for a moment she thought she remembered seeing him in church so she took a chance and asked, 'Mynheer Samuel Hegetorne? He lives at Lexden?'

He nodded. 'Indeed he does. He has built a large house there. If it is his house you seek you should have no trouble in finding it.'

'Thank you, Mynheer. You've been most kind,' she said.

He patted her shoulder. 'God go with you, my daughter.'

She hurried off, anxious to get as far away as possible from Tobias Archer and thinking what a contrast there was between the man she had just met and the man she had just escaped from.

Head Street was a busy thoroughfare, being the main road through the town, with crowds of people, mostly on foot, a few on horseback, going about their business. She saw one rather ornate coach swaying along pulled by two black horses, an unusual enough sight for the passers-by to stand and stare as it went by. The occupant of the coach, a richly dressed man, seemed oblivious to the stir he was causing and continued to stare straight ahead, trying to maintain a dignified balance as the coach lurched from side to side on its huge wooden wheels.

She crossed the road and turned the corner into Crouch Street. This too was a wide road, bordered by a close huddle of houses that were separated at intervals by narrow alleys, where she could see women gossiping from upper windows that protruded so far out that they nearly met, whilst in the gutter below dogs and cats scavenged and fought and children squabbled.

But gradually the crowds thronging the street thinned, fewer alleys led to fewer courts and the houses became less tightly wedged together and then more and more widely spaced as she left the town behind. Eventually, she found herself walking beside fields bordered by hawthorn hedges with only the occasional wayside cottage tucked in a bend in the road, just like Old Betty's isolated hovel, where they had stayed whilst Jan recovered from the snake bite. The road itself was long and dusty even though, being the main route to London from as far away as Norwich and Ipswich, it was partially cobbled. But it was not well maintained and there were deep ruts on each side from the heavy carts and coaches that rumbled along it every day in all weathers.

Anna hurried along, keeping to the grass verge and breathing fresh air laden with the scent of the shepherd's purse that laced the hedgerow, relieved to get the rank smell of the town out of her nostrils, her step never flagging in her anxiety to put as much distance as possible between her and Tobias Archer. She shuddered at the very thought of him and kept glancing over her shoulder to make sure his black-clad figure wasn't following her. More than anything, she longed for Jan's comforting shoulder to lean on.

At last she saw a cluster of red roofs in the distance and her step quickened. Lexden was in sight. But just outside the village she noticed that there was a newly built house set in a field well back from the road on a slight rise. It was a solid-looking house, brick-and timber-built, two storeys high, with a tiled roof, tall, twisted chimneys and big mullioned windows. Between the windows on the ground floor was a huge studded oak door. She paused. Surely, this must be the house of Samuel Hegetorne, the clothier. The place where she would find Jan.

She branched off the road and made her way across the field, clumps of warm clover brushing her ankles and sending up a pleasant scent as she walked. There was no boundary, no driveway apart from the rough tracks of the builders' carts, simply a rubble-strewn yard in front of the house and no sign of life anywhere.

Her heart began to beat faster. Suppose Jan wasn't here? Suppose Samuel Hegetorne had decided not to employ him after all? What could she do? Where could she go? Where would she find him? She had no money. Nothing. For the first time she began to doubt the wisdom of fleeing from the predikant's house in such a hurry, leaving all her possessions behind.

She walked across the yard and round the side of the house to the back. Here, more mullioned windows glinted in the sunshine and a door stood open to a flagged passage, the only sign of occupation as far as she could see. She hesitated, then turned towards the garden, where she hoped desperately that she would see Jan working. But there was no garden, just a large expanse of rough ground with wooden pegs driven into it at intervals. A long wooden building stood adjacent to the house; stables, perhaps, or the brew house. She shaded her eyes, looking for some sign of life but everywhere was quiet. Even the landscape was empty.

Then, as she stood undecided what to do next, a door at the far end of the wooden building opened and two men came out, talking and gesticulating towards the land.

One of them was the man Jan had described to her, the man she had seen in church, a tall, grey-haired man, slightly older than she had first thought. The other was Jan. Her whole body sagged with relief and she hurried over to them.

'Anna!' There was no welcome in Jan's tone, only shock and surprise. 'What are you doing here?'

She had imagined throwing herself into his arms and sobbing out her story, but his stern expression forced her to pull herself together. 'I've nowhere else to go, Jan.' She managed to maintain a dignified tone although her voice shook.

'But you're supposed to be staying with the predikant,' he said accusingly.

'Yes, but I was forced to leave.'

'Why? What have you done? Why did you leave when you were being so well-looked after there?' His tone was still accusing.

'Something happened . . .' she lowered her gaze, he would have to take her word for it, she couldn't go into details in front of the rather serious-looking man standing with him, clearly his employer and the owner of this house. 'I had to leave in a hurry. I had no time to collect my belongings. I've got nothing. No money . . .' Jan's expression still hadn't changed. There was no pity, no compassion, no attempt to understand, only irritation and embarrassment. This was not the Jan she knew and loved; talking to this man was like addressing a stone wall.

She lifted her chin and said quietly, 'I'm sorry, Jan, I can see now that it was wrong of me to come here. But in truth I didn't know where else to go.' She turned and gave a brief curtsey to the man beside him. 'I beg your pardon for intruding on your property, Mynheer,' she said, then turned and began to walk away, her head held high, maintaining as much dignity as she could and hoping that the two men hadn't seen the tears of despair that had begun to flow.

'A moment, Juffrouw,' the owner of the house called before she had gone many steps. He turned to Jan with a frown. 'Isn't this the woman you've told me about? The woman you are hoping to marry?'

Jan nodded. 'Yes, Mynheer,' adding quickly, 'But I assure you we shall not be married until I have saved the required amount to provide for her. I have no wish to be a drain on the Congregation. She knows that.' He shot Anna an irritated glance. 'The predikant was kind enough to offer her a home to give me time to save the money.' His tone implied that he wished she had stayed there and not come here to jeopardise his chances with his new employer. 'I can't imagine why she has abused his hospitality in this way.'

Anna's eyes widened in surprise and fear. 'You don't understand, Jan. I didn't abuse his hospitality. It was . . . I can't go back there,' she whispered. This was a nightmare. It had never occurred to her that Jan wouldn't want her. She closed her eyes as the glinting windows of the house began to swing to and fro and she staggered a little to maintain her balance.

Samuel Hegetorne was watching her, the expression in his dark eyes giving nothing away. When he saw her sway he put out his hand to steady her. 'You look as pale as death, girl,' he said, not unkindly. 'When did you last eat?'

She pulled herself together and looked at him, puzzled. Food was the last thing on her mind. 'I'm not sure. I think it was the oat cake I had at breakfast this morning, sir,' she said. It seemed an age ago.

'Then you must be hungry.' He rubbed his hands together and said briskly, 'Jan, go to the kitchen. Ask Griete to give you bread and cheese and beer enough for two. You can sit and eat it in the sunshine whilst you decide what you wish to do. It's quite plain your Anna hasn't simply come here on a whim. I myself have business in the house to attend to with the builders. When I come back I'll hear what you have to say.' He turned to go, then came back and said to Anna in a gentler tone, 'You have nothing to fear from me, my dear.' He smiled as he spoke, a smile that lit up his face, making Anna wonder if she had been mistaken in thinking that he was annoyed with her.

He strode off round to the front of the house and before long Jan came back with bread and cheese and an onion on a platter and a pitcher of beer.

'Come, we'll sit over here on the grass,' he said briefly, leading the way.

She followed him but didn't sit down. 'I'm sorry I had to come here, Jan. I know you're not pleased to see me,' she said quietly, looking down at him. 'But in truth where else could I go? I don't know another soul in the whole town.' She folded her hands across her waist as if trying to hold herself together. 'But I've no wish to stay and be a burden to you. If you would be kind enough to give me a few pence so that I can find food and lodging I'll go away and not trouble you further. Perhaps Old Betty . . .'

Before she could say more he scrambled to his feet and put his arm round her and drew her down to sit on the grass beside him, quite taken aback by her words. 'Oh, Anna. It's not that I don't want you,' he said quickly. 'It's that . . . well, what do you imagine my new employer must think, you suddenly turning up like this? I only started work here two days ago and it's going to be a wonderful job. I'm really going to enjoy it. But I assured him I had no intention of marrying for some time yet, so what's he going to think now you've arrived? Is he going to think I'm a liar?' He threw a stone viciously at a mouse scurrying by. 'If he sends me packing where else will I find work that gives me such a wonderful opportunity to show what I can do? I could end up back at Lucas Weller's, dyeing cloth for the rest of my life. And all because you've decided you don't want to stay at the predikant's house.' He bit savagely into the onion.

'I do understand how you feel, Jan,' she said, not touching the

53

food he had brought. 'And I'm sorry if I've embarrassed you by coming here. I wouldn't have done it if I hadn't been desperate. But I think you should know that I didn't run away simply because I didn't like it at the predikant's house. I was quite prepared to scrub floors and scour linen and to be treated as a servant, even though, as you well know, that was not at all the life I've been used to.' She looked down at her cracked and chapped hands.

'Then why did you leave?' he asked, still not quite able to hide his irritation.

'I left because Tobias Archer tried to rape me.' She spoke quietly, watching her hands creasing and re-creasing her apron into folds as she said the words. She waited a few seconds and then looked at him. 'Would you have had me stay and let him have his way with me, Jan?'

He was staring at her, a lump of cheese halfway to his mouth. 'Tobias Archer? The predikant?' he asked, astonished.

She nodded. 'The same man who stands in the pulpit every Sunday shouting at his congregation and telling them what miserable sinners they are,' she said bitterly. 'Ever since the day I arrived he's lain in wait for me; round corners, behind doors, in dark passages, on the stairs. Anywhere where he could brush up against me and touch me in places where he shouldn't and either pretend it was an accident or that he hadn't done it at all. I did all I could to avoid him but somehow he always managed to search me out, even when I was hanging the linen on the bushes to dry.' She went on unsteadily, 'I've been so afraid, Jan. Even before Debora, the children's nurse, warned me, I could tell what was in his mind and I've tried to keep out of his way, never to be in a room alone with him. But I didn't think he'd try . . . not so soon after his wife was brought to bed with another baby.' She spread her hands. 'So, now you know. That is why I had to escape. That is why I've come to you, Jan.' She looked at him for the first time, her jaw set. 'And whatever happens to me I shall never go back there. I'll starve in the gutter first.'

Even as she finished speaking his expression changed from outrage to tenderness and he drew her to him and stroked her hair. 'Oh, my poor love,' he said, rocking her back and forth. 'Please forgive me for the selfish clod that I am. I'm so sorry for what I said. But I would never have believed . . . the predikant, of all people! Of course you can't go back there, sweetheart. We'll find a way, even if Samuel Hegetorne turns me out and refuses to employ me. We'll manage somehow. I can always go back to Lucas Weller. And if we can't afford to marry then we'll set up home without. Nobody need know. I promise I shall look after you and never leave you again.' Their tears mingled as he tilted up her face and kissed her.

It was some time before he released her, it was so long since they had had the opportunity to delight in each other's company. But at last he drew away, saying, 'Now you must eat, my darling. The food is good here but Samuel – he says I'm to call him Samuel – will not tolerate waste.' He broke off a piece of bread and fed her with it, followed by a generous lump of cheese. 'See? I told you, English cheese is very tasty, isn't it?' He smiled at her encouragingly.

She nodded, smiling back at him through her tears as she chewed. 'But what shall we do, Jan?' she asked, her anxiety returning as she finished the mouthful.

He popped more bread and cheese into her mouth. 'This is like feeding a starving bird,' he laughed without answering her question. 'I fear you'll bite off my finger.' He traced the outline of her mouth with his thumb.

When he was convinced she had eaten her fill and they had drunk the beer he said, 'I shall have to tell Samuel what you have told me. Yes, Anna, I must,' he repeated as he saw the look of consternation that crossed her face. 'He is a kind man and even if he turns me away from his employment he will perhaps be willing to help me find other work.' He stared out over the waste ground. 'It's a pity. I had such plans. I can see it all, vegetables down there, behind a hedge, lawns with shapes cut in them for flowers, a knot garden near the house.' He turned back to her. 'But no matter. As long as we're together, my love.' He kissed the tip of her nose.

'You would really give all this up for me, Jan?' she asked uncertainly.

He nodded. 'Of course. There are other gardens to be made. In other places. There's only one you.' He gave her another quick hug and they both scrambled to their feet as they saw Samuel coming round the corner of the house.

'Well, now,' he said, as he came towards them. 'Have you sorted matters out between you?' He beamed at them both. 'I hope you have. I'm anxious for Jan to get to work. His ideas for my garden are most imaginative. Not like the builder I've just been talking to. That man's a knave, if ever I saw one. I have to go behind him at every turn or he uses inferior materials and skimps the work. And the carpenter is as bad, using two by two timbers when I particularly asked for three by three.' He rubbed his hands together in a characteristic gesture. 'But no matter, that's for me to worry over. What about you?' He looked from one to the other and his smile again softened his features. 'You both look a deal happier than when I left you an hour ago, I'll say that.'

Jan put his arm protectively round Anna. 'Anna was quite right to come to me, Samuel, I realise that now she has told me her story. And whatever happens I shall keep her with me and look after her. And if that means you don't want my services here, sir, then so be it. I shall have to find work elsewhere.'

Samuel raised his eyebrows. 'Not want your services? Well, now, suppose you tell me her story before you make any more wild declarations,' he said mildly.

Jan looked at Anna and she bit her lip but nodded in agreement. 'Well, sir. . .' he began.

Samuel listened, stroking his beard, the other hand supporting his elbow.

'How much money did the predikant say you needed before you could be married?' he asked at one point, nodding sagely at Jan's answer of enough to support a wife and child.

When Jan described the attempted rape, Anna turned her head away in embarrassment so she didn't see the look of absolute horror and disgust that crossed Samuel's face.

'So, you see, Samuel,' Jan said when the story was told, 'Anna was quite right to come to me. After what she's been through she needs my love and protection. And she shall have it, whatever the cost.' He looked at her and there was a wealth of love in the smile he gave her.

'Of course. Of course.' Samuel cleared his throat, slightly embarrassed at Jan's show of affection. He was quiet for several minutes, then he said. 'There are things we must discuss. Come into the house with me. I can't talk out here in the sun, it's much too hot.'

He strode off into the house, motioning Jan and Anna to follow. They went in at the back door, along the flagged passage and into a room to the right of the big front door, where sunlight, flooding

56

in through the long windows, revealed a panelled room with a heavy oak table in the centre, and various chests and side tables standing round the walls and between the windows. Shelves on which a large amount of pewter was displayed were ranged above the side tables. In the inglenook either side of the empty fireplace stood matching high-backed settles, with brightly coloured shawls flung over them. A sound of hammering came from somewhere upstairs.

Samuel sat down on one settle and motioned Jan and Anna to sit on the other.

'Now,' he said, when they were comfortably seated. 'There are one or two things I don't understand. First of all, what's this nonsense about not being able to marry until you have enough money to support a family?'

'But that's what the predikant told us,' Jan said, surprised. 'He said I needed to have enough money to support a wife and children before I could marry Anna, so that we wouldn't be a drain on the Congregation.'

'That's nonsense. As long as you have work, you can support a family. And even if you haven't, there is no law that says you can't be married.'

'Is that really so?' Jan said eagerly.

Samuel nodded. 'Absolutely. Tobias Archer should never have told you otherwise.' He turned to Anna. 'It's quite clear to me that he only said it in order to get you into his household, my dear, so that he could . . .' He shook his head. 'I shall have a word with the church Elders. Clearly, Tobias Archer is not fit to be a minister in the Dutch church.' He was silent for a minute, then his expression lightened and he looked from Jan to Anna. 'But that's not for you to worry about. You wish to marry?' He laughed. 'I hardly need to ask that. Very well, I will arrange it. And I will find you a house. There are cottages on the edge of my property. I'm sure one of them will suit you very well . . .'

'You mean I can stay here and work for you?' Jan asked, hardly daring to believe it might be so. 'Even if Anna and I . . .?'

'Indeed you can, my boy. You have vision. You have ideas for my garden that surpass anything I could have imagined. You don't imagine I am going to let you go, do you? And I shall increase your wages now you will have a wife to support.' He got to his feet and called Griete. 'Fetch wine, my good woman. I wish to drink the health of this young couple. And bring four goblets. You shall join us.'

Jan took her hand and squeezed it and Anna couldn't stop smiling at this distinguished looking, rather autocratic man, who was making all their dreams come true. She couldn't believe that a day that had begun so badly could have ended so well.

And if a cold shiver ran down her spine as she raised the goblet to her lips she told herself that it was only because the wine was cold.

Chapter Seven

Samuel was as good as his word and arranged for Anna and Jan to be married with all possible speed. He even found lodging for Anna with Griete's parents while the wedding preparations were made.

But at last the day came and on the fifteenth of July in the year 1580, less than six months after she had left her native land, Anna Fromenteel was married to Joannes Verlender.

It was a simple wedding. Anna wore a russet dress and her fair hair fell in loose ringlets round her shoulders, capped by a circlet of myrtle and tiny rosebuds. Although it was simple, they followed custom. Samuel, Anna's only bride-man – usually there were at least two – led her to church along a path strewn with flowers and rushes to where Jan, who was dressed in smart new breeches and jacket, a shirt with a wide lace collar and buckled shoes, waited. He had been led into church by his bridesmaids, Griete and her sister Sophia, who carried branches of rosemary as a token of his love and constancy.

As his bride walked towards him Jan thought he had never seen Anna looking so lovely.

The church was full; a wedding was a welcome excuse for celebration whether or not the couple were well known and most of the people there wore brightly coloured scarves and gloves for the occasion. Maria and Debora, anxious to see Anna married, sneaked in at the last moment and hid behind a pillar where Tobias Archer wouldn't be likely to see them and dismiss them from his household.

Because, in spite of Samuel's efforts to have him removed, Tobias Archer was still predikant at the Dutch church in

Colchester so there was no choice but for him to officiate at the ceremony. He would have refused if he could. He glared at the congregation, clearly annoyed at their gaudy apparel and obvious pleasure in the young couple's happiness. The customs of the day irked him; the way the bride and groom were led in by their friends, the knots of coloured ribbon sewn on to Anna's skirt for young men to pull off after the ceremony to wear in their hats as bride favours. All this infuriated him and in a fit of pique he all but ruined the marriage ceremony, gabbling over it and hardly giving the bride and groom time to make their promises to each other, glowering at them if they hesitated and not waiting for them to finish if they didn't. He dropped the ring – or, Jan swore afterwards – threw it to the floor so that Jan had to grovel to search for it and he finished the ceremony without allowing the newly married pair and their witnesses the customary drinking of wine with sops in it. It was a disgraceful display of temper.

But nothing could spoil the day for Anna and Jan and to crown their happiness Samuel had called in extra cooks and provided a wonderful wedding feast in his new house, to which he invited all his friends and acquaintances as well as the few people Anna and Jan knew, declaring that it could serve as a housewarming party as well as the wedding celebration.

There were huge joints of mutton and beef, boiled bacon, fish in fine sauces, pies and puddings of all shapes and flavours. There were salads flavoured and coloured with borage flowers and rosemary and vegetables of all kinds: turnips, parsnips, beans and all manner of greenstuffs. To follow were sweet tarts, jellies, custards and fruit with an elaborate centrepiece on the table made of marchpane. No one was quite sure what this was supposed to represent; rumour had it that Griete had tried to mould it into an elaborate figure of some sort but something had gone wrong and it had fallen apart. However, by the time it was presented to the table everyone had eaten and drunk so well that nobody minded that it was a bit misshapen and great sport was had trying to guess what it was supposed to be.

After the feast there was music and dancing in the great hall for those who were still on their feet. Everyone was having a good time. Tomorrow they would again be the soberly dressed, abstemious, hard-working members of the Dutch Congregation going about their usual business – though perhaps some of them might be rather pale and fragile-looking – but tonight was for making merry and this they did with a will.

Most of the guests were still busily enjoying themselves when Jan took Anna's hand and they slipped quietly away from the festivities.

'They are all having a good time. It won't hurt to deny them the pleasure of bedding us and flinging the stocking,' Jan whispered as they crept secretly away to the cottage Samuel had provided for them on the edge of his land.

They walked back over the rough field that would soon be transformed into Samuel's garden. As they walked in the cool evening air Anna rested her head on Jan's shoulder.

'Tired, my love?' he asked softly.

'A little. But it's been a wonderful day. I just wish . . .'

'What do you wish?'

'I wish I knew whether my father – my real father – was living in Colchester. He could have come to our wedding. I should have liked that.' She gave a wistful sigh.

'Perhaps he was there. How could we tell? I believe Samuel had invited half the Dutch Congregation in Colchester and a good many from way beyond to the feast.'

'What a nice thought.' She smiled as she spoke.

He dropped a kiss on her hair. 'One day we'll find him, Anna. Somebody must know where he is. Ah, here we are. Home.' Proudly, he pushed open the door of the little cottage, sturdily built of wattle and daub and with a thatched roof. Then he turned to her. 'I hope you won't find it too humble, my love,' he said anxiously. 'I know it's a long way from the luxury you're used to.'

She put her arms round him. 'Luxury for me is being happy, Jan, and I wasn't happy in my father's house when I knew he intended to sell me off to Otto de Hane. I'm happy with you, Jan. As long as we're together, nothing else matters,' she assured him.

The cottage was indeed small but Samuel had made sure that it was well furnished and lacked nothing, down to the last cup and spoon. Jan knew he had sent a grumbling Griete across time and again to check that nothing had been forgotten.

Hand in hand in what was left of the daylight, they explored the comfortable living room. Brick-floored, at one end was the hearth, with a kettle and a cooking pot hanging on a trivet. Beside the chimney was a small brick oven. Opposite the door a livery cupboard hung on the wall, well-made and strong enough for the food – and it was already well stocked – to be safely out of the way of mice and rats. Plates and basins and other useful crocks stood on a set of shelves beside the hearth and mugs hung from hooks underneath. The table took up the centre of the room, with a stool either side and a chair at one end. A long shelf ran under the window, which had shutters that could be folded across to keep winter draughts out. Under the shelf stood two crocks containing water from the well and on it an assortment of pans and cooking pots. A drawer in the table contained knives and spoons.

'Samuel's thought of everything,' Anna breathed, looking round.

Jan smiled and nodded towards the corner of the room. 'We haven't finished yet. There's more, look.' He pointed to the ladder fixed to the wall, which led up to a sleeping loft up under the eaves that was almost half as big as the room below. Eagerly she went over and climbed the ladder. He lit a candle and followed her. A large bed stood under the window at the gable end. It had a strong wooden frame, and a feather mattress and pillows. The sheets were linen and the blankets and dornicle were of good quality, which was a relief to Anna because the bedding at Tobias Archer's had been uncomfortably coarse and lumpy, very different from what she had been used to at home.

A clothes press stood to one side of the bed and a coffer on the other, fitting the space where the roof sloped to within a few feet of the floor. Jan set the candle on a shelf and opened the coffer. 'Look, sweetheart,' he said, 'there are even extra rugs here to warm us in the winter.' He turned to her. 'Do you like it, darling?' he asked anxiously.

Anna nodded, her eyes shining. It was, as Jan had said, a far cry from the luxury of her father's house but it was home to her and Jan and she loved every part of it. 'It's perfect, Jan,' she said happily.

He put his arm round her. 'The daylight has almost gone now and I must be up at sunrise tomorrow to go to my work. We should go to bed.' He felt her stiffen at his words and a faint tremor ran through her. He released her gently, saying, 'I think I'll just go downstairs and lay the fire ready for the morning. I shan't be long, sweetheart.'

He knew, and so did she, that the fire was already laid, but she said nothing, suddenly and unaccountably shy at the thought of taking off her clothes in the presence of this man, even though she had already been through so much with him.

When he had gone and she could hear him moving about downstairs she took off the pretty russet dress and laid it on the chest. Then she brushed her hair and plaited it and climbed between the sweet, lavender-scented sheets, waiting for him, wanting him to come to her yet fearful because the memory of the predikant's brutal attack on her was still raw.

It was not long before Jan came upstairs again. He whistled quietly as he undressed, not in the least embarrassed at allowing her to see his nakedness before he blew out the candle, for he knew she had tended to his every need in Old Betty's cottage, when he was so ill after the snake had bitten him. But he felt her tremble as he climbed into bed and gathered her to him.

'Don't be afraid, my dearest love,' he whispered, beginning to caress her. 'I'll try not to hurt you.'

Before long, under Jan's loving touch all memories of Tobias Archer left her and her trembling ceased as she gave herself up to his love.

She slept curled up against him and woke at first light the next morning to hear him moving about downstairs, whistling quietly to the cheerful sound of the kettle singing on the hearth. She got up quickly and dressed in her old grey gown, with a clean white collar and a white cap, proudly leaving her hair hanging in its two plaits because she was now a married woman.

'I've been to the farm to fetch milk,' he said when he saw her. 'Master Pitt doesn't mind supplying us with whatever we need: milk, cream, butter, cheese . . .'

Anna frowned. 'But why should he mind? As long as we pay for it.'

'Because we're Dutch, darling. Aliens. We're not liked here in Colchester. But you know that, don't you. You must have noticed it when you've been to the market, how the English try to fob us off with stuff that isn't fresh, and try to push us out of the way.'

She nodded. 'Yes. I've seen that, many times. But I find I'm not so badly treated as most of our people because I can speak a little English. Not very well yet, but enough to make myself understood,' she added quickly.

'You must teach me. I should like to learn it, too. It seems to me quite wrong to come to a country and make no attempt to speak as they do. Samuel speaks English fluently. He says it's very useful in his dealings at the Bay Hall.'

'What do they do at the Bay Hall?' she asked, as he gave her a piece of bread and cut her a piece of the bacon he had found in the hutch.

'Oh, you'll have to ask Samuel about that,' he said. 'I'm a gardener. I don't know much about cloth-making, except that the dye gets into your clothes, your hands, your hair . . . Ugh.' He shuddered. 'I hated working for Lucas Weller, the dyer. Give me the good brown earth any day.'

She poured two mugs of creamy milk and they breakfasted happily together as the sun rose, shafting through the open door.

'I shall make bread this morning,' she announced, as he laced his boots ready for the day's work, 'So that I can bring your noon piece to you, all fresh and warm.'

'Just like you, wife,' he said wickedly, coming round the table and giving her a kiss that lingered for longer than either of them had intended.

At last she gave him a little push. 'Away with you. You'll be late for work,' she said, laughing a little breathlessly. 'Remember, I shall be coming to inspect what you've been doing, later on.'

After Jan had gone, she made the bread and put it to rise on the hearth. Then she swept and dusted the whole house, although it didn't really need it, singing to herself as she worked. When the bread was baked, filling the cottage with its sweet, homely smell, she wrapped a loaf in a napkin and put it in a basket with two pieces of cheese and two apples and walked over to where she could see Jan working in the distance.

It was a beautiful July day. A few lazy puffs of pure white cloud only seemed to emphasise the clear blue of a sky that stretched endlessly on and on in all directions as the sun blazed down. By the time she reached the shade of the outbuildings where it was comparatively cool, Anna was drenched in sweat. She waved to Jan, who, stripped to the waist and with an old straw hat perched on the back of his head, was busy with yard stick and string, marking out an intricate knot garden on ground in front of the house that had already been cleared and dug. Two men were busy clearing the next piece, digging out tree stumps and bushes, clearing away brambles and levelling the earth.

Jan made some calculations with a stone on a piece of slate, then came over to her, his body glistening with sweat. He wiped the sweat out of his eyes with his forearm and sat down beside her on the grass, with their backs against the building known as the workshop.

'I hope the bread is to your liking, Jan,' she said shyly. 'I used to make it in our kitchen at home, with Bettris, but I'm not yet used to the oven in our cottage.'

Jan took a bite. 'A little solid,' he said with a grin, 'but the flavour is good.' He kissed her cheek. 'All you need is practice. Is there any more?'

'It can't be very bad if you want more,' she said with a smile as she gave him another piece. 'More cheese, too?'

When they had eaten Jan went into the brew house and brought out two mugs of ale. 'Samuel said I could help myself. He knows that working in this heat makes a man thirsty.'

'What about the men doing the clearing?' she asked. They had left their work, too, and were sitting at the bottom of the garden in the shade of the hedge, eating their victuals.

'Samuel said I was to give them as much as I think fit. They get very thirsty, working in this heat, but if they were left to themselves they would drink themselves stupid and do no work,' he said with a laugh.

She looked round at the garden. A large patch had been dug over and there were other areas that had been staked out. Rubbish had been raked into huge piles, some of which would be taken by nearby cottagers to fuel their fires, the rest to be made into a bonfire.

'Is Samuel pleased with the progress you are making?' she asked.

'Oh, yes,' he said enthusiastically. 'Of course, there's not much to see yet, but we have it all planned out on paper and we have seeds already growing in the seed beds ready for autumn planting. By next spring you will see a great difference, I promise you.' He stood up and helped her to her feet. 'Over there, at the end of the garden, where the men are clearing the ground today, is where the vegetable garden will be. Eventually, it will be divided from the rest of the garden by a wall against which we can grow fruit trees. In front of the wall will be laid out to lawn, broken up by pathways and flower beds. The large area in front of the house, where I am working today, is where the knot garden will be.' He laughed. 'Samuel is very keen to have a knot garden; he doesn't know of anyone else in Colchester who has one. But it's quite complicated and has to be very carefully measured and worked out.' He waved his hand. 'By this time next year this whole garden should be a blaze of colour.'

'Who knows what this time next year may bring,' Anna said softly, already rocking a cradle in her mind's eye.

'It will bring very little if I don't get back to work,' he said briskly, totally missing her point. 'Ah, here comes Samuel. You must wait and speak with him or he'll think it strange.'

Samuel came striding across, carefully avoiding the area Jan had staked out. He had forsaken his coat because of the heat and his shirt was open. Yet somehow he still managed to look cool and uncrumpled.

'Ah, Mevrouw,' he said as he approached, 'Is everything well with you? Have you all that you need in the cottage?'

'Yes, Mynheer. Everything and more besides. You have been most generous. And our wedding . . .'

'Good.' He cut her off abruptly. 'I'm glad it was all to your liking, although I have spoken to the Elders about the disgraceful behaviour of Tobias Archer. They agree with me that he will have to go. And the sooner the better.' He rubbed his hands together and smiled at her. 'Now, with your permission I shall call you Anna and I would like you to call me Samuel. I know I am your husband's employer but I would like you to regard me as a friend, too.'

'Thank you . . .' She hesitated '. . . Samuel.' She blushed a little as she said his name.

He smiled at her. 'Good. Now we know where we are.' He turned to Jan. 'Is the work going according to plan?'

'I think so. Do you want to see how those alterations you asked for are going to look?'

'Yes. I'd like to see what you've made of them. Do you think it will work to have statues in the wall by the vegetable garden?'

'I don't see why not. They'll need to have their own niches built into the wall, of course.'

'Um. Depends on the kind of figures, I suppose. I haven't yet decided . . .'

66

The two men walked away leaving Anna to gather together the remains of the food and go home.

But they hadn't gone far when Samuel called back, 'I forgot to tell you, Anna. Go to the kitchen. Griete has something for you.'

Puzzled, Anna went to the house and found Griete busy in the kitchen. Despite the heat of the day and the fact that the big fire at one end was alight, the room struck pleasantly cool, facing as it did towards the north.

Griete was several years older than Anna. She had been working in kitchens ever since she was twelve, working her way up from scullery maid until now, working for Samuel Hegetorne, she ruled her own kitchen, with several girls working under her.

'Was everything to your liking at the cottage?' she asked, sitting down at the table and indicating that Anna should do the same.

'It's all perfect,' Anna said enthusiastically.

'It should be,' Griete said crisply, 'I can't tell you how many times a day the master sent me over there to make sure this or that hadn't been forgotten. Nearly wore me out, he did.'

'Nothing was forgotten, I can assure you,' Anna said. She got the feeling that Griete resented the fuss Samuel had made. She smiled at Griete. 'I'm very grateful to you for all the trouble you took,' she said.

'Yes. Well, the master likes to make sure everything is just right.' Griete said, slightly mollified. She got up and went to the scullery and drew two mugs of cool ale.

'He's very kind,' Anna said warmly, sipping her ale.

'Oh, aye. He's kind enough as long as he gets his own way. Which of course, he does, because he can pay for it.' Griete took a long draught and put her mug down.

Anna frowned. 'Don't you like him?'

Griete shrugged. 'I'm well paid and I have a comfortable place to work and sleep. That's all I care about.' She got up and went to the scullery again. She came back with a joint of beef. 'He says you're to take this home with you for your supper. Not the mutton, he said. Not the ham. Not the pork pie. But the beef. Can't see what difference it makes, myself. There's plenty enough of everything left over from the celebrations, in all conscience.'

'Why did he choose the beef, then?' Anna asked.

'That's just the way he is,' Griete said. 'Likes to organise everything.'

'Well, he's being very kind to us.'

'Yes, well, he would be, wouldn't he. He's got himself an expert gardener and he wouldn't want to lose him.'

As Anna walked back to the cottage, carrying the joint of beef that was far too big for their needs, she recalled Griete's words and wondered why it was that they made her feel a little uneasy. Surely Griete wasn't jealous of the attention Samuel was paying her and Jan?

Chapter Eight

Over the following months Samuel's garden began to take shape. By the time autumn came the ground had all been dug and levelled. Nearest to the house Jan had planted box hedging to mark the geometric shapes of the knot garden and gravel paths had been laid. Beyond the knot garden the lawn area had been prepared, the earth sifted ready for the grass to be broadcast between flower beds and borders already marked out. Beyond yet again the builders had been brought in to build a wall higher than a man's head to enclose the vegetable garden, with an arched entrance on each side.

When this was all done Jan supervised the setting out of all the plants that had been carefully nurtured from seedlings. There would be vegetables for the kitchen, herbs for the pot and flowers for the table next year, he promised his master.

Samuel was delighted with Jan's efforts and strode proprietorially about his garden, taking note of every change.

'I swear he notices if as much as a blade of grass appears overnight,' Jan told Anna humorously as he swallowed his breakfast and prepared for another day's work. But he was gratified by his employer's interest and enthusiasm.

Anna watched him sling his bag over his shoulder and stride off. He had grown even leaner over the past months and his skin was tanned to the colour of the earth he worked. In contrast, his hair was bleached almost white by the sun, despite the fact that he nearly always wore his battered old straw hat. He looked the picture of health.

But he was tired. Worn out from endless long summer days working from the time the first rays of the sun appeared until the last vestige of light had gone at night. Sometimes he was almost too tired to eat the meal she had prepared for him and she often felt that if she didn't make a point of taking his noon piece to him every day and making sure he sat down to eat it they would have hardly any conversation at all.

'You're working much too hard, my love,' she said when he came and sat beside her to eat the food she had brought. She gave him a piece of the succulent pig's brawn she had pressed herself. 'You'll make yourself ill, then where shall we be?'

'Hard work never hurt anyone, sweetheart. Especially when it's a labour of love as this garden is.' He put his arm round her. 'The sun is already beginning to rise later and set earlier and by the time winter comes with the frost and snow the garden will be resting and so shall I.' He dropped a kiss on her head.

'You? Rest? Never. You'll always find something to do,' she said with a laugh.

He looked at her, suddenly serious. 'Are you lonely, Anna? Do you regret our marriage?'

She shook her head vehemently. 'No. Not for one moment. And I'm never lonely, Jan. I have plenty to do. I have learned to make soap, and candles – my mother and Bettris would never let me do this back at home – and the beer I make is good, you'll testify to that . . .'

'Indeed I will,' he said with a smile, taking a swig of the small beer she had brought him.

' . . . And I visit the market nearly every day. Sometimes I walk there with Margery Frith. She lives in one of those cottages a little further along the road from our house. She's a spinner, although how she manages to spin her quota of wool in a week I can't imagine. Not with the brood of children she has.' She was quiet for a moment. Jan watched her under pretence of draining the last of his ale. He knew she was disappointed that she had not yet conceived and it was useless to point out that they had only been married for three months. There was plenty of time. And in the winter . . . He looked forward to the approaching winter, when days would be shorter and there would be less work to do on the garden. Then it would be dark almost before the evening had begun and they would go to bed early to save candles and get up that much later in the morning . . . He smiled a little. It wouldn't be his fault if Anna didn't get her wish and fall pregnant by the New Year!

He turned his mind back to what she was saying.

'We walk together as far as the outskirts of the town, then we have to go our separate ways because Margery mustn't be seen talking to me.'

He frowned. 'Not be seen talking to you? Why not?'

She made a little impatient noise. 'Oh, Jan, you know very well why not. Because I'm Dutch, of course. Not that Margery minds,' she added quickly. 'She likes me, I'm sure. And I'm learning more and more English every day.' She chewed thoughtfully on an apple. 'I think it's the people who don't bother, or simply refuse to learn their language that sets the English against them.'

Jan smiled at her. 'Is that what Margery says?' he asked, humouring her.

'No. She says the English don't like the Dutch because they take work from them.'

'That's nonsense. I'm sure there's plenty of work for everybody.'

'And it's because even the English cloth has to be taken to the Dutch Bay Hall to be examined. The English people don't think that's right.'

'You can't blame them for that, I suppose,' he said thoughtfully. 'After all, this is their country.' He got to his feet. 'But I must get back to work. The men are planting the spring cabbages today and the rest of the herbs have arrived for the knot garden. This is the exciting time in the garden, Anna. All these plants we're setting now will give us food and flowers next year.' He kissed her and went back to begin work again.

She began to gather up the remains of their meal, pondering on the animosity between the people of Colchester and her people, whom they had at first welcomed into their town but now called them 'Strangers' or 'Aliens', and threw things at them. It was a sad state for such a pretty town.

Still deep in thought she was just getting to her feet when Samuel appeared, immaculately dressed as always, even though he had spent the morning in the garden with Jan, albeit only watching and making suggestions, never going so far as to get his hands dirty.

71

'Ah, Anna,' he said coming over to her with a smile. 'You are well?'

She bobbed a curtsey. 'Thank you, Samuel. Yes.' For some reason, she never felt quite at ease in this man's presence. It was not that she was in awe of him because she had been quite used to meeting equally prosperous and important men at her home in Flanders. No, it was rather that she felt he regarded her as an encumbrance, a necessary irritation that had to be endured for the sake of the expertise of his gardener. She knew this feeling was irrational, because Samuel had never been other than charming to her. Indeed, he had gone out of his way to arrange her marriage to Jan and he had been kindness itself in providing them with a home that had everything in it a common man and his wife could possibly need. Sometimes she wondered what Samuel would say if he knew the kind of home in which she had been brought up, and that the man she had always called father was at least Samuel's equal in commerce. But this was not something she would ever speak to him about in case Samuel ever had dealings with Cornelis Fromenteel. She didn't want to run any risk of that man discovering her whereabouts.

Samuel talked for several minutes about the pleasure he was already finding in his garden and asked her, as he always did, if she had all she needed at the cottage.

She thanked him and assured him that she had; then, quite abruptly, he announced, 'Tobias Archer, the predikant, will be leaving the Dutch church in Colchester within days.'

She looked at him in surprise. Week after week since her marriage she had attended church with Jan, but only because to stay away would have incurred a fine and there was no other church that they could go to. Week after week she had hoped against hope that Tobias Archer would be gone and week after week she had been disappointed and had been forced to listen in disgust as he threatened and harangued his congregation with the wrath of God for their small sins whilst he was the greatest sinner of them all.

'I'm afraid it's taken much longer than I had anticipated to get him removed,' he explained. 'But he has finally been summoned to the Dutch church at Austin Friars, in London, and they will deal with him as appropriate.'

'Do they know what he did?' Anna said.

'Oh, yes. I wrote them a letter telling them what had been happening.' He lowered his voice. 'I'm afraid in the end I had to tell both the authorities at Austin Friars and the Elders here quite specifically what you had suffered at his hands. But it seemed the Elders here were already aware ... there had been other complaints ...'

Anna frowned. 'Then why had nothing been done before?' she asked sharply.

'Because nobody had sufficient ...' he hesitated '... courage ... or perhaps I might even say influence to expose him. After all, he was a highly respected minister of the Dutch church. He had a great deal of power in the community. More than that, who would believe a common serving-maid against the word of the predikant? Predictably, he denied all accusations as scurrilous and of course he was believed.'

Anna nodded. 'Of course.' She was quiet for several minutes, brooding on the injustice and the fact that if it hadn't been for Samuel the man could have gone on unhindered in his wicked ways. Then she asked, 'Has someone been found to take his place?'

'Yes. A man by the name of Abraham van Migrode. A good man, I'm told.'

Anna's face lit up. 'Oh, indeed. Jan and I met him on board the boat when we came over to England. He was very kind to us. It will be nice to see him again so that we can thank him for sending us to this place.'

He smiled. 'You are happy here in Colchester, then, Anna?'

'Oh, indeed, yes.'

'Good. I'm glad to hear it.' With a slight inclination of his head he left her.

A few days later Anna went to the market alone. Margery Frith couldn't go with her, she hadn't finished spinning her quota of yarn, which must be done before the agent came to collect it the next day so she couldn't spare the time. Instead she gave Anna a list of things she needed.

The road seemed long without Margery's chatter and her children's rhymes and games to shorten the way but at last she turned the corner into the High Street. On the north side of the street was the cloth market known as the Red Row and above it the Bay Hall, where there was so much dispute over the examination of the cloth that had been manufactured in the town. There was the usual press of carts loading and unloading the finished cloth with the accompanying shouting and arguing that always went on. Anna thought she glimpsed Samuel Hegetorne's tall figure disappearing into the building but she couldn't be sure.

The market was all hustle and bustle. Apart from the fruit and vegetable stalls there was a fire-eater, a juggler, a dancing bear and several stilt-walkers dressed in bright rags, their tall hats making them tower above the crowds. The stench of it all made her stomach turn until she became used to it and she realized how lucky she was to be living on the outskirts of the town in Lexden village, where the air was clear and pure, away from the stink of unwashed bodies, rotting vegetation and middens.

She bought eggs for Margery and fish for them both, then she stopped at a stall selling ribbons and lace, dreaming of the day when she could buy lace to trim tiny garments. She was enjoying her morning, she reflected, although so far she hadn't seen anyone she knew.

Suddenly, she felt a hand on her arm.

'Maria!' she said, surprised to see Tobias Archer's serving-maid. 'I hardly expected to see you here today.'

'Ah, you may well say that. There are great changes afoot,' Maria said mysteriously. She tapped the side of her nose.

Anna frowned. 'You mean . . .' she began, then broke off. Perhaps the news Samuel had given her was not yet common knowledge. 'What do you mean?' she asked cautiously.

Maria drew her to one side. 'Tobias Archer has gone,' she hissed importantly. 'Packed up his household and left three days ago. Wife, children, household goods, the lot.'

'Where has he gone?' Anna asked, knowing that was what was expected.

'To London, I believe. But nobody really knows. It was all done in a great hurry.' She sniffed. 'Not that I care where he's gone. Good riddance to bad rubbish is what I say. We were all glad and thankful to see the back of him.'

'So what about you, Maria? And the rest of the servants. Where will you find work?'

'That's all been taken care of,' Maria said smugly. 'The new predikant has already moved into the house and he has taken me on. And the kitchen maid, too. Debora is to be married so she was leaving, anyway.' Maria gave a little snigger. 'Just as well, really. This man has no wife so he's hardly likely to need a nursemaid.'

'Do you find him agreeable, this new predikant?' Anna asked, keeping her voice casual.

'Oh, yes. Abraham van Migrode is a real gentleman. Or so he seems,' she added quickly. 'Since he only arrived yesterday it's to soon to make a judgement.'

'His name is Abraham van Migrode?' Anna raised her eyebrows as if in surprise.

'That's right.' Maria said with a nod.

'Then I'm sure your judgement is sound. He is the predikant who was so kind to me and several others when we were ill from the boat's motion coming over from Flanders. He gave us oranges to suck to abate the sickness. And then, when I reached England with Jan and we had no idea where to go, it was he who suggested that we should come here, to this town.'

'Well, I never did,' Maria said, amazed. 'And now he himself has come here. That must be a good omen for you.'

Anna opened her mouth, but before she could reply, there was a great commotion, with everyone shouting and screaming and crash after crash as stalls were overturned by the press of people trying to get away.

'It's the bear!' 'The bear's broke free!' 'He's run amok!' Terrified people screamed as they ran hither and thither, tripping over the overturned stalls and slipping and sliding on the produce that had spilled from them and rolled over the market place, all trying to escape the huge animal that was lunging, equally terrified, through the crowds, its broken chain swinging and rattling as it lumbered along.

Maria grabbed Anna's hand and dragged her to the shelter of a pillar by the door of St Runwald's Church, where they could watch the scene in comparative safety. Suddenly, one of the butchers left the butchers' shambles and circled round to where the bear was lumbering blindly about and plunged an evil-looking knife into its side. The bear reared up in pain and the butcher seized his chance, pulled out the knife and plunged it straight into the creature's heart. It dropped like a stone.

The butcher was immediately hailed as a hero and carried

shoulder high through the crowd, waving his knife, still dripping with the bear's blood, high above his head.

Anna felt sick. She could see the bear now, lying dead on the ground amid the trampled vegetables, pots and pans, ribbons, fish and meat. It was huge but obviously very old, its eyes staring through a milky haze, its fur, where there was any left, a mangy matt. The poor thing had obviously been as terrified as the crowd fleeing from it as it lunged blindly about, not knowing what to do with its unaccustomed freedom. She turned away, saddened, looking for the bear's master. But he was busily picking up what he could scavenge from the overturned stalls and when he had filled his pockets with coins and his bag with as much as it would hold he ran off, leaving others to dispose of the carcass that had given him a living for more years than he could remember.

'Poor bear,' Anna said as four men dragged it away.

'Poor bear, nothing,' Maria said briskly. 'By tomorrow morning they'll be selling it as beef on the butchers' stalls, so if you're shopping here you'd better watch out or you'll end up with a joint you could sole your shoes with.'

'Oh, Maria, I'm sure that's not right,' Anna said sadly. Suddenly, the shock of it all had made her feel light-headed and strange.

'Then it shows what little you know,' Maria said with a sniff. She looked at Anna. 'Are you all right? You look a bit green. Why don't you come back with me? I'll make you a posset and you can have a bit of a rest before you walk home. Lexden, did you say you live? That's a long way, I believe.'

Gladly, Anna accepted Maria's invitation. 'But are you sure the new predikant won't mind?' she asked doubtfully.

'Oh, he'll be busy in his study sorting out his books and papers. He won't even know you're there.'

Gratefully, she went with Maria, back to the house where she had been so ill used by the previous predikant. Already the atmosphere was entirely different. Maria hummed to herself as she busied herself about the kitchen and there were two other servants, rosy-cheeked girls who clearly adored their master.

Maria had been wrong about the predikant not knowing Anna was there. He came to sit in the big kitchen with them while Anna recovered. Maria recounted what had happened in the market place, her story losing nothing in the telling. The two young girls listened, wide-eyed, then ran all the way up Stockwell Street to see the remains of the dancing bear before it was carted away on a tumbrel.

'Poor thing,' was the verdict of Rachell on their return.

'It looked so old and tired,' said Chrystine, 'I feel guilty now that I used to enjoy watching it dance.'

'Yes, that old man used to prod it with a stick to keep it dancing,' Rachell said. 'I wonder what he'll do now.'

'He filled his pockets with enough of the money that had spilled when the stalls were overturned to keep him going for some time, I should think,' Anna said, holding the posset Maria had made her in both hands as she put it to her lips, because she was still trembling with the shock of what she had seen.

Abraham turned to her as she spoke, deeming it was time to change the subject. 'I seem to recognise your face, Mevrouw, but I can't think from where . . .'

She smiled. 'I was very seasick the last time we met,' she told him. 'It was on the boat coming over from Nieuwport early last year. You were very kind to me and to my friend Jan. He is now my husband,' she added proudly.

Abraham's face cleared. 'Ah, yes. I remember it now. But it was small wonder I didn't recognise you at first. You have left the pale, thin, features of the girl I saw on the boat a long way behind, if I might say so.'

'Aye, she looks the picture of health and happiness,' Maria said. 'It must be the Lexden air that suits her.'

'Is that where you're living?' Abraham asked.

'Yes, my husband is gardener to Samuel Hegetorne. He has a house at Lexden.'

'Ah, I believe I remember the young man telling me on the boat that he was a gardener.'

'Yes. He designed and made the garden. I think he's quite pleased with the way it is looking. Of course, Samuel spared no expense in the making of it.'

'Your husband is rightly proud of his work. All the money in the world can't buy the flair for design he has shown.'

'You've visited Samuel?' Anna raised her eyebrows in surprise.

'Of course. There were matters to be cleared up . . . after the last predikant . . . he was not satisfactory, as you may know.'

Anna and Maria both nodded, but neither of them spoke of Anna's part in Tobias Archer's removal.

'And Samuel and I are old friends,' he explained. 'I knew him before he and his family were forced to flee to England.' He smiled slightly. 'Samuel's father was rather too outspoken for his own good against the Prince of Alva and the religious persecutions. The whole family had to leave in rather a hurry. His parents are dead now, of course. And so is . . .' He broke off. 'Are you feeling calmer now, my dear?' he asked, changing the subject so that she had no opportunity to question him further.

'Thank you, yes.' She got to her feet, gathering her belongings together. 'I should go. My friend Margery will be waiting for her eggs.'

'Margery?' He raised his eyebrows.

'She is an English spinner who lives just along the road from me. She is a good friend.'

'Ah, I'm glad to hear it. We of the Dutch Congregation should be more open to the ways of the English. It isn't good to keep ourselves to ourselves the way we do. It's no wonder we're not popular with the people of Colchester. Do you speak the language?'

'I'm learning it.'

'Good. And so am I.' He held out his hand. 'Goodbye, Mistress,' he said in English.

'Goodbye, Minister,' she replied with a smile.

Chapter Nine

The fish she had bought at the market was sizzling in the pan by the time Jan arrived home after his day's work. As Anna served it she couldn't wait to tell him about the bear at the market.

Jan was alarmed. 'Oh, my love! Were you near when it happened? Were you in danger?'

'No, not really. I was talking to Maria. We quickly hid behind a pillar and watched it all.'

'Was anybody harmed?' he asked. 'A bear could take off a man's head with one blow.'

'No, I don't think so. The poor thing was practically blind and I think it was more frightened than dangerous. I felt quite sorry for it, to tell you the truth.'

'What happened to it?'

'A butcher came along with a huge knife and killed the poor thing. Maria said it will be sold for meat. That can't be true, can it, Jan?'

'I should think it's very likely.' He looked up, a twinkle in his eye. 'Will you be buying meat there tomorrow or the next day?'

'Indeed I shall *not*!' she said emphatically.

They ate in silence for several minutes, then she said, 'I have another piece of news. Maria took me back to the house for a posset after the business with the bear, because I must admit I was feeling a bit shaky, and I saw Abraham van Migrode, the predikant we met on the boat coming to England. He's just moved in. Did you know he is to be our new predikant?'

'Yes. Samuel told me today. It will be good to see him again,' Jan said, picking a bone out of his fish. 'I never thanked him properly for his help to us on the boat and I'm sure he'll be pleased to know we are settled and happy here.'

'I told him. He's already seen the garden. Did you know that?'

'No, I didn't.'

'When he's been here a little while he may be willing to help us in our search for my father. My *real* father,' she said thoughtfully. She rested her elbows on the table and put her head on one side. 'Do you think we'll ever find him, Jan?'

Jan concentrated on cleaning his plate. After a few minutes he said, 'If he's living in Colchester I should think there's a very good chance of it. After all, Colchester isn't that big.' He shrugged. 'But he may have gone to London. Or Norwich. In which case . . .' he shrugged again.

Anna shook her head. 'No. I think he's here, in Colchester,' she said firmly. 'I have a feeling.'

'You're beginning to sound like Old Betty,' Jan said with a laugh. 'It's a good thing we don't have a cat or the witch-finder might be looking your way.'

'I think I should quite like a little cat,' Anna said resting her chin on her hand.

'It would keep the mice down,' Jan agreed.

'There aren't any mice.' Anna was immediately on the defensive.

'Sweetheart, there are *always* mice.'

As if to give weight to his words there was the sound of scrabbling in the roof. He cocked an eyebrow. 'See what I mean?'

She grinned. 'All the more reason to get ourselves a cat.'

When they had finished their meal Anna cleared the table and got out a piece of slate and some chalk whilst Jan unrolled his plan of the garden. Now that it was too dark for him to work such long hours in the garden Anna was teaching him to read and write by naming the flowers and vegetables that would be grown.

'Paigles, here and here,' he pointed on the map and Anna dipped her pen and wrote it neatly. Then he took the chalk and copied the letters laboriously on to the slate. 'Paigles,' he said with satisfaction.

He turned back to the plan. 'Roses.' They repeated the process.

But by the time the slate was half-filled with his ill-formed letters he threw it down impatiently and concentrated on the garden plan.

'I thought we might have a covered walk here,' he said with more enthusiasm, 'bordered with laburnum and ending in a rose-covered bower. And a sundial in the middle here, with grassy walks radiating from it, with flower beds between. You see, Anna, it's important to maintain the symmetry.'

'What are you going to put in the flower beds?'

'I haven't decided yet. Poppies, gillyflowers, oh, all sorts.' He made an impatient gesture as she picked up her quill. 'No, don't write it down yet.'

'You'll never learn to read and write if I don't.'

He gave her a long kiss. 'I'll learn it tomorrow,' he promised, rolling up the plan. 'Let's go to bed.'

The next morning after Jan had gone to work Anna busied herself about the cottage as she always did, humming to herself as she worked. First she made the bread and set it to rise, then looked to the beer brewing in the corner. After that she swept the floors and tidied the house before going to the farm for milk and cheese, where she waited politely at the door of the dairy until Mistress Pitt the farmer's wife invited her in.

'The mornings have a sharp nip about them now,' Mistress Pitt said as she poured milk into the pitcher Anna had brought with her. She liked the open-faced, friendly young Dutch girl and she respected the fact that Anna made the effort to speak to her in English, even if she was difficult to understand at times. But those aliens who came to her for milk and butter and didn't even bother to try to speak her language annoyed her and she pretended not to understand them even when she knew perfectly well what they were asking for. 'Winter will soon be upon us, bringing the usual crop of chilblains and chapped hands, I dare say,' she added cheerfully.

'I could bring you some salve. Is good for sore hands,' Anna said eagerly, anxious to be helpful. 'A friend told me how I make some very helping balm.'

Mistress Pitt was interested. 'I may be glad of that,' she said. 'My man gets cracks in his hands that go near down to the bone when the frosts come. Cheese, did you say?'

'Yes, please. And buttermilk.'

When Anna had made her purchases she made her way across the field back to her cottage. She didn't realise she had been followed until she opened the door and a little black kitten bounded in. It went over to the fire and sat down and began washing its paws.

'And where have you sprung from, little cat?' she asked, setting her bags on the table and squatting down beside the kitten.

It looked at her, purring, then went back to the more important business of washing its ears.

'I think you must have followed me home from the farm,' Anna said with a sigh, getting to her feet. 'And if that's where you've come from, then that's where you must go back to. I don't wish to be accused of stealing.' She picked up the kitten and kissed its nose. 'It's a good thing I have to go back anyway, to take the salve for Master Pitt's cracked hands.' She put the kitten in a basket and made her way back to the farm.

Mistress Pitt had finished in the dairy and was in the house. She opened the door, surprised to see Anna again so soon. 'The milk was fresh,' she began defensively. 'And the cheese straight out of the press.'

'Oh, I am not come to complain,' Anna assured her. 'I come to bring you the salve for your husband's hands.' She uncovered the basket to reveal the little kitten, which immediately jumped out and streaked off. 'And I bring this little cat back. She followed me home so I think she must belong here.'

The woman laughed. 'Oh, bless you, the cat's always birthing kittens. You're welcome to keep that one if you want it. We've more here than we know what to do with.' She held up the pot of salve. 'Call it payment for this, if you like.'

Anna's face lit up. 'I not want payment for the salve but I much like the little cat. Thank you, Mistress Pitt.' She looked round the yard, where rain was now beginning to fall quite heavily. 'I'll take her back with me. If I can find her again,' she added.

'Oh, she'll be around somewhere. She's probably gone back to the barn.'

Anna called and called and searched the farm buildings as far as she could but the little kitten was nowhere to be found. In the end, wet through and disappointed, she trudged back across the field to her cottage. She wished now she hadn't been in such a hurry to return the little kitten to the farm.

But to her surprise, when she got to her door the kitten was there, waiting patiently on the threshold for her to come back, her coat standing up in spikes from the drenching rain. Delighted,

Anna scooped it up in her arms. 'Oh, you got back before I did. I can see you're quite determined to come and live with us. Very well, so you shall.' She took the kitten indoors and gave her a saucer of milk, which she could hardly drink because she was purring so loudly. When she had finished she gave herself a perfunctory wash, sneezed three times then curled up in a ball on the hearth and fell asleep.

Anna laughed. 'There was no pepper in that milk to make you sneeze,' she said. She leaned down and stroked the silky fur. 'Now, what shall I call you?' She said softly. 'You're as black as night, except for your whiskers and that white spot under your chin. Shall I call you Spot? Or Blackie?'

As she said it the kitten opened one eye, yawned, sneezed again and went back to sleep.

'Very well. Blackie, it shall be.' Anna continued to stroke the silky fur, little realising what an influence this small cat would have on her life.

When Jan came home that night and saw the kitten washing herself on the hearth his eyes widened in surprise. 'How odd! And to think it was only last night that you were talking about getting a cat.' He bent down and rubbed her behind the ear, causing her to stop in her ablutions and begin to purr, the tip of a pink tongue sticking out of her mouth. 'She's certainly made herself at home.'

'Yes. And she was quite determined to come and live with us. She followed me home from the farm when I went to fetch the milk, so I took her back. I didn't want to be accused of stealing her,' she said earnestly. 'Anyway, she must have heard Mistress Pitt say I could keep her because she was back here before I was. I've named her Blackie,' Anna ladled stew and dumplings on to his plate as she spoke.

He drew his chair up to the table. 'Well, let's hope she'll do as I said last night and keep the mice down.' He also hoped, although he didn't say so, that the little kitten would take Anna's mind off the fact that after four months of marriage there was still no sign of a child.

But early in the New Year, when snow lay thick on the ground, protecting the seeds Jan and his helpers had sown in the autumn, Anna missed her monthly bleeding. Soon after she began to be sick every morning.

She was overjoyed and so was Jan, who laughed delightedly and said, 'I told you it would be so. Have you not heard the old saying, "He who goes to bed early to save his candle begets twins"?'

'Oh, Jan. We haven't been going to bed early simply to save candles,' she remonstrated, laying her hand lovingly over her still flat stomach.

'Indeed we have not,' he agreed firmly, a grin spreading across his face. 'Neither have we stayed in bed later of a morning to save lighting the fire! To tell you the truth I shall be quite sorry when the nights become shorter and the days longer because . . .'

Suddenly, not waiting to hear what he was going to say, she scrambled out of bed and began to retch into the bucket. 'But I don't like to see you suffer like this, my love,' he said anxiously, holding her head

'It will pass,' she said, leaning against him, exhausted. 'Margery says I shall feel better by the time the primroses bloom.' She pushed her hair back from her face, damp with sweat and gave a ghost of a smile. 'I just hope they'll bloom early this year.' She rested against him for a few minutes longer, then got to her feet. 'There, I'm beginning to feel better now. It quickly passes.' She smiled at him. 'Come, Blackie's mewing for her breakfast and I'm starving, too.'

Over breakfast he told her how he was beginning to clear the ground at the other side of the big house and the plans Samuel had for clearing the trees near the weaving sheds.

'I didn't know there were any weaving sheds,' Anna said, surprised.

'They are in those buildings right at the back, behind the vegetable garden. You must have seen them.'

'Yes, but I thought it was just a row of cottages.' She handed him another freshly baked oatcake.

'The trees need clearing to let in more light. There are four weavers working there and they need all the light they can get, especially as they produce some of the more expensive cloth, mockadoes, tobines and the like, so they can only work at their looms while the light is really good. When there's no sun, or when it rains, they can't work because they can't see what they're doing. It'll help a lot if those trees come down.' He got to his feet and slung his bag over his shoulder, gratified at being able to remember and repeat the names of the cloth that his master had told him.

'It's several weeks since I've been to the garden,' she said, accompanying him to the door. Jan carried his noon piece with him now that the weather was too cold for them to sit outside and eat it so she had no reason to go there. 'Are things beginning to grow?'

'Yes, I'm sure they are, but it's too soon to see them. The green shoots won't appear above the ground until the frosts have gone and the warm rain comes. But by the time the summer comes the garden will be a riot of colour and I shall find you a shady spot where you can sit and sew while you wait for our baby's birth.'

'I shall look forward to that, Jan,' she said happily.

The days passed uneventfully as the sun began to rise earlier and earlier and to shed more and more warmth on the land. As Margery had predicted Anna's sickness left her as the first primroses and paigles unfolded their creamy petals and Jan took her to walk round Samuel's garden so that she could see the pale green fuzz that was beginning to carpet the lawns and the first shoots that were appearing in the vegetable garden. A few weeks later the wallflowers began to bloom beside the primroses in the borders. In due course the lawn became a thick, springy turf and the flower beds were a riot of colour.

Samuel was delighted with the results of his gardener's efforts and he strode about, noticing every new bloom, often snipping off the faded ones himself, and insisting on tasting the first carrots straight out of the ground.

'Some things aren't quite right yet,' Jan said, as the days grew warmer and Anna again began to bring their noon piece to eat together. 'We need a bit of height in the border over there and the roses haven't done too well on the back wall. But the lawns look well, they're thick and level.' He munched happily on an onion. 'Samuel's pleased and so am I, considering this is the first year.' He turned and smiled at her. 'Now I've got things into shape I shan't have to spend quite so much time here. I have plans to make a garden behind our cottage. I can do that in the evening, when I finish work here. We'll have herbs, of course, and vegetables. And what sort of flowers would you like?' He began to sketch out his ideas in the ground with a stick and they were both engrossed in this so they didn't notice Samuel's approach until his shadow fell across them.

They both looked up and Jan quickly got to his feet. 'I was just about to begin work again,' he said, taking a last draught from the small beer Anna had brought him.

'There's no hurry. The day is too warm for too much haste.' Samuel waved his hand and sat down beside Anna on the grass. He began to fan himself with a paper he had in his hand. 'Do you not find it so, Anna?'

'It is rather hot today,' she answered, suddenly shy in the knowledge that the precious child she carried was beginning to thicken her waistline. Samuel had never spoken of it, although she was sure Jan must have told him. Or perhaps men didn't speak about these things, regarding them as women's business. She didn't know.

'I want to show you this, Jan,' Samuel went on, having exchanged polite words with Anna. 'No, sit down again, man. I can't show you while you're towering above me.' He turned back to Anna, who was gathering up her things ready to leave them. 'No, don't go. You must stay and listen, too, Anna. This is a very exciting venture and I'm sure you'll be interested.'

He spread out the paper in front of him. There were words on it that Anna could read but didn't understand the meaning of. Jan, she knew, wouldn't even be able to read them. But the drawings of the delicately shaped flowers made perfect sense to both of them.

'Tulips,' Jan said. 'I have heard of them, although I have only seen pictures and never seen one. They are to be found in Turkey, I believe.'

'They are to be found nearer to hand than Turkey,' Samuel said, his face alight with enthusiasm. 'A friend of mine has them growing in his garden near Amsterdam. I am to go over to Holland to see them. If the price is not too high . . .' he paused and a proud smile spread across his face. 'I could be the first person to grow tulips in England.'

'When do you intend to go, Samuel?' Jan asked.

'Next week. I want to see the flowers in bloom.'

'You won't be able to bring them back with you. The time won't be right. You can't dig bulbs up when they're in full flower,' Jan warned.

Samuel made an impatient gesture. 'I know that. I plan to send you to fetch them when the time comes. I wouldn't trust them to anyone else, you should know that.' He got to his feet. 'They will be the very thing for that corner where you said early colour was needed, Jan.' They discussed the tulips and where they could be planted to best advantage for several minutes, then Samuel went off to make plans for his journey across the German Sea.

Jan was quiet for some time after he had gone. Then he got to his feet. 'I must get back to work,' he said.

'You don't seem very excited at the prospect of having tulips in the garden, Jan,' Anna remarked.

'Oh, I am,' he said, nodding. 'But I rather fear that when the right time comes to go to Holland to fetch them you will be near your time.' He put his arm round her. 'I can appreciate Samuel's concern over getting good bulbs but I shan't be very happy at going away and leaving you, sweetheart.'

She took his other hand and gave it a little shake. 'Oh, Jan. You won't be gone for many weeks. I'm sure it can be arranged so that you're here when our baby is born.'

Yes,' he said. 'I'm sure it can.' But he was not convinced. Samuel was a man who liked his own way and a small thing like the birth of his gardener's baby wouldn't be allowed to get in the way of such an important thing as the collection of tulip bulbs.

Chapter Ten

Samuel returned from Amsterdam full of excitement over the tulips he had seen. He described the many different colours and shapes and even brought back coloured paintings of these wonderful flowers. But he swore Jan to secrecy, warning him never to speak of what he had seen and been told. Over the summer months, when things were growing at their best and Samuel invited his friends and business acquaintances to come and view his wonderful new garden, he himself never once mentioned the word 'tulip'.

Nevertheless, he openly basked in the admiration heaped upon him. Everyone agreed that it was the most colourful and imaginatively laid out garden in the whole of the town. However, he was not at all pleased when several people sought Jan's advice on making one of their own, afraid that he might be in danger of losing his gardener. He quietly increased Jan's wages considerably to insure against this.

Tucked away with her sewing in a shady spot that Jan had made for her in a far corner of the garden, Anna watched the comings and goings with interest. The visitors to the garden were Englishmen as well as Dutch because with his easy manner Samuel was one of the few people in the town who had managed to bridge the gap between the two communities. At times Anna was tempted to take the rich clothier into her confidence, to tell him about her father and ask for his help in finding him, but she realised that this would entail telling him her history, and betraying her mother, which she knew she could never do. There was also the risk that Samuel might know – perhaps even be friendly with – Cornelis Fromenteel, the man she had always known as her father, since they were both in the same line of business. That was a risk she was not anxious to take. So she kept her own counsel and watched the comings and goings, looking for any clues that might lead her to the man she only knew was called Henrick, who had fair hair and deep violet-blue eyes. It wasn't very much to go on.

She questioned Jan to the point of exasperation.

'Did you see anybody there today who might have been my father, Jan?' she asked as they sat just outside the door of the cottage, enjoying the last of the evening sun.

'Sweetheart, how would I know?'

'Well, did Samuel call anybody Henrick?'

'Not that I recall. Mostly, he addresses them as Mynheer. Except for his special friends, of course. He calls them by their Christian names.'

'Henrick?' she asked hopefully.

He shook his head. 'I told you . . .' He broke off. 'Come to think of it, there was a man called Henrick here last Friday. He'd come from Sudbury because he'd heard about Samuel Hegetorne's garden and he wanted to see it. Henrick van Houton, his name was. I remember it because he had a big, booming voice and the way he said his name was like the tolling of a huge bell. *Hen*rick van *Hou*ton.'

Anna laughed. Then she asked the inevitable question. 'Could he be . . .?'

Jan made a face. 'I shouldn't think so. I'd say he was much too old. He was a tiny, wizened little man, with little pig eyes. His voice was the biggest thing about him.'

She gave a sigh. 'How shall I ever find him, Jan?'

'Well, you don't have a great deal to go on, do you, my love? All you know is that his name is Henrick – or was Henrick, he could be dead, you know. And that he has deep blue, almost violet coloured eyes, like yours.' He paused and leaned over to kiss her. 'There was nobody that I saw who had eyes even remotely as beautiful as yours, Anna. If there had been I'm sure I couldn't have failed to recognise him immediately.' He spread his hands. 'We don't even know his last name.'

'Perhaps you could find that out when you go over to Amsterdam,' Anna said hopefully. 'If you could go and see my Aunt Dionis – she lives in Amsterdam – you could perhaps get a message to my mother. If only we could find out his full name we'd stand a better chance of finding him, wouldn't we.'

'I don't think I shall be there long enough to send a message to your mother and get a reply back, sweetheart. I don't intend to spend any longer than I can help away from you.'

'My mother could always write to me here. I should like to hear from her.'

'Then why don't you write to her?'

'Oh, yes, I could do that, couldn't I.' She hesitated. 'As long as my . . . Cornelis doesn't get hold of the letter and find out where I am. I don't want to see that man ever again.' She shook her head vehemently.

He put his arm round her. 'All right, my darling. Don't get agitated, you'll harm the child,' he said soothingly. 'You write to your mother and I'll see if I can smuggle the letter to her whilst I'm in Amsterdam. I promise. I'm sure you can trust her to keep it away from Cornelis's prying eyes.'

'Thank you, Jan.' She picked up his hand and kissed it. 'Do you know when you're going?'

'Towards the end of September. I told Samuel that was the latest I was prepared to go. That means I should be back a full month before our child is born.'

'Complete with tulip bulbs,' she said with a smile.

'That's right. Complete with tulip bulbs. For which Samuel is prepared to pay quite a high price, I might tell you.'

'Does anyone else in Colchester grow tulips?'

'No. Samuel intends to be the first.'

She nodded. 'Of course. Samuel always likes to be the first. Or the best, doesn't he.'

Jan frowned. 'Are you trying to say . . .?'

She leaned forward and stopped his words with a kiss. 'I'm not trying to say anything except that Samuel likes to be the first, or the best, in everything he does. I'm not saying it's a bad thing, I'm simply saying that's how it is. Don't be so touchy over your master, Jan.' She kissed him again.

He looked at her uncertainly. 'I just thought perhaps you didn't like him much. He's a good master, Anna, and very good to both of us.'

She ruffled his hair. 'I know that, silly. And I appreciate it.' She was quiet for a minute, then she added, 'As for my feelings towards him, I like him well enough, and I truly appreciate all he has done for us.' She sighed. 'But I do sometimes think he makes unreasonable demands on you . . .'

'Like what?'

'Like sending you off to Amsterdam to buy bulbs that could easily be sent over by boat.'

He shook his head. 'That's not so, Anna. Choosing bulbs is a skilled job. I have to make sure I get the ones I've chosen so that I don't get fobbed off with soft or rotten bulbs. And I need to make sure the colour is right. Samuel is very keen to have one – he showed us a picture of it, if you remember – which is red, with yellow streaks in it. Nobody seems sure how to propagate this particular colour in tulips, it seems to occur at random. They have even tried cutting a red bulb and a yellow one and tying them together in the hope that they will fuse together and produce these striped flowers but so far without success. I want to talk to the men who do this and learn more about it so that I can experiment, too.'

'Oh, I see.' She was immediately contrite. 'Then I'm sorry, Jan. I did Samuel an injustice.'

He smiled and kissed the tip of her nose. 'I do believe you're a little bit jealous of my master, Anna, if you're truthful.'

She smiled back. 'No, I'm not.' She made a face. 'Well, perhaps I am. A little. Especially when he keeps you talking after your day's work, when you are tired and I have your meal ready and waiting for you.'

'That's only because he's so enthusiastic about what I'm doing.' He pulled her to her feet. 'But let's not talk about Samuel any more. Come, I want to take you to bed. The child you carry is making you more beautiful and desirable than ever, if that's possible.'

The summer was hot and Anna spent more and more time sitting in a shady corner in Samuel's garden, sitting with her sewing or simply watching Jan at work, marvelling at his energy and strength. Often Blackie would follow her and sit on her lap, purring contentedly. She was growing into a pretty cat, jet black except for the tiny white spot under her chin. Anna sometimes felt tired and lethargic with the increasing weight of her pregnancy during those long, hot days and she began to look forward to the chill, often foggy days of November, because then Jan would be safely back from his trip to Amsterdam and their child would be born.

All too soon the time came for Jan to set off on his journey. Anna reconciled herself to his absence by writing a long letter to her mother, telling her all that had happened since she left home and asking for more details about the man who was her natural father, in the hope that Jan would somehow manage to smuggle it to her and bring back a reply.

'When we have more details we'll be able to pursue our search in earnest,' she said happily as she gave it to him. 'If she could only tell us his full name it would help.'

'I can't promise anything, sweetheart,' he said as he held her close and kissed her goodbye. 'But I'll try. Now, be mindful of yourself and the child whilst I'm gone. Don't carry anything heavy. Make two journeys to the well for water instead of one and ask Margery to shop at the market for you if you're feeling tired.' He gave a last glance round. 'I've chopped enough logs for the fire and the boys who are looking after the garden will make sure you have plenty of vegetables. I don't think there's anything else . . .' He looked round again.

She gave him a little push. 'Be off with you. Samuel is waiting to take you to the ship. Anyone would think you were going for a year instead of less than a month. I shall manage perfectly well, I promise.'

A last kiss and he dragged himself away, turning back and waving to her every few steps as he went.

When he was out of sight she stood at the door of the cottage, savouring the last of the autumn sunshine. Blackie came and threaded herself between her legs, rubbing against her and purring, her tail in the air.

Anna bent down and rubbed her ear. 'He'll soon be back, Blackie,' she said, a tear dropping on the little cat's sleek coat.

She couldn't know how wrong she was.

The days seemed long and empty after Jan had gone, even though the sun was rising later and setting earlier. Anna found herself reaching for him in the warmth of her bed, or listening for his step in the yard, storing up the little everyday things to tell him when he came home from work and then realising he wouldn't be there. They had not been apart for more than a few hours ever since they left Amsterdam nearly two years ago, except for the short time she was living in Tobias Archer's house, and she missed him dreadfully.

But she had Blackie to keep her company and the little cat was her constant companion, following her about and even negotiating the ladder up to the sleeping loft, something she had never ventured to do before, to sleep on the foot of Anna's bed.

One cold, early October day, when Jan had been gone just over a week, Margery Frith called at the door.

'I hope there's naught you need at the market, Anna. I've no time to go there today. My little one has been poorly so I'm behind with my spinning and the agent will be calling for it tomorrow,' she said, clearly agitated.

'No, I have more than enough for my needs now that Jan is away,' Anna said. 'But is there anything *you* need, Margery? I try to keep busy, but my day hangs heavy at times and I should be happy to go for you.'

'Aye. I'd be glad. The egg woman is there on Thursdays and Dickon will enjoy a fresh egg now that the sickness has left him. My hens are still off the lay. If they don't soon start again we shall have a nice chicken stew or two, for I can't afford to keep them in corn if they give me no profit. Oh, and some fish. Friday is fish day so if you could get me some herrings . . .'

'Of course I will, Margery.' Anna reached for her shawl. 'I'll get fish for myself, as well.' She smiled at her friend. 'To tell you the truth I'll be glad to get out of the house for a while. It seems empty with Jan away.'

'When will he be back?'

'Not for several days yet. He expected to be gone at least two weeks. Maybe more.'

Margery gave a mirthless laugh. 'I could bear it if my man went away and left me in peace for a bit. Thank the Lord I miscarried during the summer, but he's put another one there now.' She put her hand on her flabby stomach. 'If I carry this one it'll be five living, four I've buried and I've lost count of the times I've miscarried. But I can't stand here and gossip, I shan't get my quota done for the agent.' She hurried away and Anna prepared for her walk to the market.

As she walked the long road she smiled to herself at Jan's protective care for her. The walk to market wouldn't harm her, she

93

would enjoy it, even though her body was becoming heavy and ungainly. She laid her hand on her swollen belly. She loved this child, ever since the day she knew it was there she had loved it and been careful never to do anything that might harm it. She prayed every night for a safe delivery and was longing for the moment when she would hold him – she was convinced it was a boy – in her arms. She couldn't imagine a time when she would be like Margery Frith, glad to miscarry. On the contrary, she looked forward to having a whole brood of Jan's children.

She reached the market, filled as always with noisy, jostling people, pushing and shoving their way about, most of them ignoring the poor creature crouched grotesquely at the roadside between the stalls, whose limbs had been twisted and distorted at birth so that his parents – now long dead – could make money from him as a freak of nature. She put a copper in his cap, at which he said 'thank you, Mistress,' in a surprisingly deep and cultured voice. She stared at him in amazement and he smiled at her, his face peering out from somewhere under his armpit.

'The body is only a husk, mistress. A prison. The mind is free to roam where it will,' he said.

She made her purchases from the fish stall and the egg woman.

'Who is the man over there?' she asked the egg woman. 'The one with the twisted . . .'

'Ah, you mean Crippled Joe,' the egg woman said. 'He's often here. Haven't you seen him before?'

Anna shook her head. 'No, I haven't.'

'He lives with the monks at the house of the Crutched Friars. They care for him and feed him. He repays them in the only way he can, by showing himself off as the freak he is to earn a few coppers for them.'

'Oh, poor man,' Anna said.

'Aye, but the monks are good to him.' The egg woman turned to her next customer and Anna went off to wander round the other stalls, lingering as she always did at the stall selling ribbons and lace, finally succumbing to temptation and buying lace to trim a cap she had just made for the coming baby. Then she gave the fire-eater a farthing and made her way back to Lexden, trying to put poor Crippled Joe out of her mind.

She had never been inside Margery's cottage before. It was bigger than the one she shared with Jan, with an upstairs floor substantial enough to support the weaving loom she could hear clacking rhythmically as she approached the door.

Inside, the house was dim and seemed crowded, although when her eyes got used to the light she could see that there was little enough furniture, just a square table with benches round it and a trestle bed. A child lay on the bed and two more played in front of the hearth. Margery was busy at her distaff, several reels of yarn neatly stacked in a heap in the corner by the door.

'Oh, thank you, Anna,' she said as Anna entered, never pausing in her spinning as she spoke. 'Will you sit for a minute till I've finished this, then I'll pay you.'

Gratefully, Anna sank down on one of the benches. It had been a long walk and her back ached.

Several minutes passed, then Margery finished the length she was spinning. 'There. Now, you'll take a mug of beer with us. I'm sure you could do with it,' she said, putting the reel on the pile with the rest.

'Yes, the road seemed long without your company,' Anna confessed.

Margery poured the beer, took a mug up to her husband and then sat down opposite Anna. 'I've nearly finished my quota for the week,' she said, with satisfaction. 'I'm supposed to spin at least six pounds of yarn a week. Usually, I manage without a lot of trouble, but with Dickon being so poorly for three days I've got rather behind. That's why I couldn't spare the time to go to the market today. You see, the agent will be here later on today to collect the yarn.'

'Surely he would understand if you told him your son had been ill,' Anna said.

Margery gave a short laugh. 'The only thing that agent understands is six pounds of yarn, spun ready for him to collect. And he's as sly as a fox, like the rest of the agents; they're a crafty lot, always looking for ways to make out we've cheated them. One thing they do is try to say we dampen the yarn to make it weigh heavier.' She shrugged. 'Well, it's true that if the weather's a bit stormy you have to damp it a bit or it flies all over the place and you can't get an even yarn. But not enough to affect the weight.' She took a draught of her beer. 'One of the agents, not the one that comes to me, thank goodness, used to carry small stones in his pocket and make out he'd found them hidden in the reels to make them weigh heavier. Then he'd fine the spinner for short weight. Ah,' she shook her head. 'You have to be up to all their tricks. Dick Marsh, who comes to me, is always trying to catch me out so that he can fine me and not have to pay me my due. Then he pockets the difference, thieving rascal.' She banged the mug down on the table. 'But I've got wise to him. I see to it that he has no cause to complain about my work. I've no intention of putting my money into his pocket, it's hard-earned enough, goodness knows.' Automatically, she picked up her distaff and began working it again. 'This'll be the last reel,' she said contentedly, 'till he arrives and brings me the next lot of wool to spin.'

'Do you spin for Samuel Hegetorne?' Anna thought it quite likely as she lived nearby.

'Bless you, no. My man wouldn't work for a Dutchman and wouldn't let me, neither,' Margery laughed. 'We both work for Mr Markham. He lives in a big house on East Hill.'

'What does he look like?' Anna asked, wondering if he might have been one of the visitors to Samuel's garden.

'Bless you, I don't know. I've never seen him,' Margery said, surprised that Anna should have asked. 'He wouldn't have anything to do with the likes of us, now, would he?'

Later, as Ann walked home from Margery's she recalled those words and realised how lucky she and Jan were. Far from not knowing them or not having anything to do with them, even though he was Jan's employer, Samuel treated them as his friends. Almost as his equal.

Which, of course, she would have been in her other life, Anna thought wryly. But Samuel didn't know that and she was determined he should never find out.

Chapter Eleven

Almost as if he had realised she had been thinking about him, Samuel was waiting for her when she arrived back at the cottage. He had never been there before and she was surprised to see him.

He gave her a brief, almost embarrassed smile. 'I promised Jan I would see that you lacked nothing while he was away, Anna, so I have come to make sure you have everything you need,' he said by way of explanation.

'You're very kind. Thank you, Samuel. I assure you I have everything I could possibly want, and more. Jan saw to that before he left.' She smiled at him now. 'My husband worries too much about me, I fear.'

'That may be so. Nevertheless, I hold myself responsible for your well-being, since he has gone on an errand for me.' He was standing by the door to the cottage, some half a head taller than the doorway. He regarded her seriously for a moment, then turned to go. 'Good. I'm glad all is well with you.'

'Won't you step inside a moment?' she asked, suddenly remembering her manners. 'I made oatcakes this morning. Too many, since Jan's not here to eat them. I'd be glad if you would take a mug of my honey beer and an oatcake. They go well together.'

'Thank you, Anna, I should like that.'

'Mind your head,' she warned as he followed her into the cottage. 'Jan has got used to ducking his head as he comes in.'

She busied herself pouring the beer and buttering an oatcake for him and one for herself, noticing that Blackie had scuttled up the ladder to the sleeping loft as soon as she saw the strange man enter the house. As she went about these homely tasks an odd feeling washed over her. Never before had the smallness of the cottage, its

97

rustic meanness, its lack of all the things she had formerly been used to, bothered her. But with Samuel sitting at the table, dressed in the finest cloth, a snow-white ruff at his neck and lace at his cuff, his dark beard clipped to a point below his chin, just the kind of man her mother would have chosen as a husband for her, she felt suddenly shy and ashamed of her humble surroundings. And following on the shame was the sense of betrayal that she should have felt that way. This was the home she shared with Jan, whom she loved with all her heart and whose child she carried. She should be proud, not ashamed of what they had achieved since their arrival on English soil.

'These oatcakes are good. Better than Griete makes. Where did you learn to cook so well? May I have another?' he asked, grinning like a schoolboy.

She buttered two more and gave them to him. 'I learned to cook at home. Bettris, our . . .' she was about to say 'our servant' but pulled herself up short. 'Bettris and my mother taught me,' she finished.

'You came from near Ypres?' he asked, regarding her with his dark, deep-set eyes. 'That's where most of our people in this area have come from.'

'Yes.' She didn't enlighten him further.

'I still have several business acquaintances over there,' he said. He stroked his beard. 'Things have not settled down, you know. People are still being flung into prison, tortured and killed for their Protestant faith. It is a dreadful thing the Spanish Catholics have been and are still doing to our people. And the dreadful thing is, it's all in the name of religion. It's no wonder so many of us have left the country and escaped to England.' He glanced up and saw the frightened look on her face. 'Oh, I'm sorry, Anna, that was tactless of me,' he said quickly. 'Jan will be perfectly safe, I'm sure of it. Amsterdam is well outside the troubled area. And he has letters to my friends – important people, people with influence. They'll see he comes to no harm.'

Anna nodded but she was not convinced. She had memories of town dignitaries being hauled through the streets, dragged behind the tail of a cart in order to be made an example of. In fact, she had seen it with her own eyes when she was little more than a child. And she had heard tales of people being flung into graves and buried alive, of people being tied back to back and flung into the

Scheldt to drown. Important people were no safer than ordinary folk, she knew that. Less so if anything. But as Samuel said, Amsterdam was outside the troubled areas. 'When do you expect him back?' she asked.

'Next week, if all goes well,' Samuel said cheerfully, relieved to be on safer ground. 'His boat is due into Harwich next Thursday if the weather is favourable. I shall take the carriage and meet him.' He smiled. 'I believe I am almost as eager to see the bulbs he is bringing back with him as you are to see the man himself.'

'Then you are eager indeed,' she said, smiling back at him.

He got to his feet, and she noticed that he dwarfed the little room in a way she had never noticed Jan doing, even though Jan was just as tall and broader, in fact, than his master.

He turned as he reached the door. 'If there is anything you need, anything at all, you have only to ask,' he said. 'I should be failing in my promise to your husband if I allowed you to lack anything.' He paused. 'Is your health . . .?' he glanced at the bulge under her apron. 'Are you . . .?'

'I am very well, thank you, Samuel. I walked to the market today as I do most days. My child is not due for at least another month.' Her expression softened. 'By that time Jan will be long home.'

He nodded, smiling. 'We shall both be glad to see him home again. Even the garden misses his attention,' he added ruefully. 'The two men who assist him don't have his eye for what needs to be done to keep it looking at its best.'

After Samuel had left Anna sat down by the fire. Blackie, at ease now that the man who lived in the beautiful garden had gone, came down from the sleeping loft and jumped on to her lap, purring. Anna stared into the fire for a long time, absently stroking her soft fur. She couldn't understand the feeling that had swept over her when Samuel was in the cottage. She had never before been anything but proud of the little home she shared with Jan. She loved every stick of furniture, she loved keeping it neat and tidy and doing the ordinary housewifely things, such as making bread and beer, collecting the eggs from Dilly, their black hen, preserving some of the glut of vegetables Jan had grown so there would be plenty for the winter, putting down fresh rushes and strewing sweet-smelling herbs about. She felt disloyal to her husband in the sudden shame that had struck her when she saw the place as Samuel must have seen it; indeed, as she would have seen it herself only a few short years ago.

She felt shame when she remembered that she had had an almost irresistible urge to confess to Samuel that this was not the life she was used to, that she had been brought up to better things, that the home she had come from in Flanders was every bit as luxurious as the house he himself lived in. It was only the mention of his business acquaintances in the Ypres district that had prevented her. Because even if he didn't know Cornelis Fromenteel himself, he probably knew someone else who did. Or worse, he might even know, or know of, Otto de Hane, that dreadful man her father had been so keen to sell her to. She gave a shudder. The fewer people who knew who she was and where she had come from the better.

She counted the days until it was time for Jan's return, keeping busy, going to the market with Margery, whether she needed to buy anything or not, visiting the farm and talking to Mistress Pitt as she ladled milk into the pitcher she took with her every day for the purpose.

'He'll be home today, Blackie,' she said excitedly as she put down a bowl of fresh, warm milk for the little cat. 'I heard the carriage leave very early as Samuel left to go and fetch him. Yesterday, he very kindly came and asked me if I would like to go too, but I thought it wiser not to. The way that carriage sways and jogs over the bumps I feared it might bring on the birth of my child before time. And that would never do. So I said I would wait here quietly, with you.'

Blackie looked up, licking her whiskers and purring.

But Anna was so excited that she couldn't sit still. First she cleaned the cottage from top to bottom, then she made a mutton stew and put it to simmer over the fire. Then she made bread and some of the little floury cakes Jan was particularly fond of. When she had done all this she dragged the large wooden washing tub into the kitchen and bathed in front of the fire, washed her hair and brushed it till it shone and then braided it carefully into its two long braids under a clean white cap. Then, with a clean collar and cuffs and fresh white apron, she was ready for her husband's return. It was still only the middle of the afternoon.

Now there was nothing more to do but sit and listen for the carriage to return. As she sat, talking to Blackie, who was quite unconcernedly washing herself on the hearth, a little bubble of excitement kept welling up inside her at the thought of seeing Jan again, and she pictured how he would look as he came in at the door, tired, a little pale from the journey, perhaps, but so glad to see her again. She smiled a little in the fading light as she pictured their reunion; she could almost feel his arms round her and his kisses on her face.

Suddenly, she came to from her reverie. If she didn't soon put some light in the room he wouldn't be able to see her when he came in. She was just putting a taper to the fire ready to light the rushlights when she cocked her ear at the sound of a man's step in the yard. She hadn't heard the carriage return; she must have fallen asleep in her daydreaming.

Forgetting the taper, she rushed to the door and flung her arms wide, a look of pure delight on her face. But her expression froze when she saw that it was not Jan standing there, it was Samuel, and his face was bleak.

'Samuel?' She stood aside, as he strode in without waiting to be asked and threw himself down at the table without answering.

Clearly, something was very wrong. She stared at him, puzzled, and lowered herself slowly on to a chair on the other side of the table, a cold finger tracing its way down her spine, making her shudder.

'Jan?' she asked in a small voice. 'Where is Jan? Why hasn't he come with you? Has the boat not arrived? Or did he miss it?'

Samuel got to his feet and rescued the taper from the flames, looking round for the rushlights. She pointed absently to the sconces on the walls and he lit them, bathing the little room in soft yellow light.

He blew out the taper. 'Jan hasn't come back. He's dead.' He didn't look at her and his voice was hardly above a whisper.

She got up and went to him, shaking his arm. 'What do you mean, he's dead? He can't be dead. You went to fetch him from the boat.' She spoke the words angrily.

He shook her off and slumped down at the table. 'He's dead, I tell you,' he muttered.

She stared at him, disbelievingly. She felt as if she was floating a little way above her body, looking down on the scene. Herself, calm, in a kind of limbo, not wanting, not able to take in what

Samuel had said, Samuel with his face screwed up as if he might cry at any minute.

'How? What happened? Was it Alva's men? Was it the Spaniards? Did they kill him?' She rapped the questions out, amazed that she should feel so little. It was almost as if, deep down, she had known this would happen.

He shook his head. 'No. Nothing like that. He died on the boat on the way back. He caught plague and was dead in hours.' His eyes were tortured. 'It was my fault. I should never have sent him.'

'Did he get your tulips?' she asked, although she didn't really care.

He looked at her as if he didn't know what she was talking about. 'Tulips? Oh, yes. He got them.'

'That's good. At least you'll have them.' She nodded, still feeling strangely numb.

He shook his head and frowned at her. 'No. You don't understand. All his effects had to be cast overboard. They don't take chances with plague.' His mouth twisted. 'The tulips are at the bottom of the German Ocean, along with the body of your husband.' He reached out and took her hand. 'I'm so sorry, Anna. So dreadfully, dreadfully sorry. There are no words to tell you . . .' His voice broke.

'Thank you, Samuel. You're very kind.' Very gently, she removed her hand. She didn't want to be touched. She didn't want anybody near her. All she wanted was to curl up within herself, in a very tight ball, where nothing and nobody could reach her, not even the terrible anguish that was waiting to envelop her.

He passed his hand across his brow. 'You shouldn't be here alone,' he said, looking round helplessly. He didn't know how to deal with such calm, self-possession. It was not natural. She hadn't even shed a tear. 'I'll send someone, Griete, perhaps, to stay with you.'

'Thank you. I should rather be alone. At least for a little while.' Her voice was quiet, dignified. 'It was kind of you to come and tell me, Samuel.' She even managed to smile at him as she spoke.

He stared at her, frowning. This wasn't right. She should be weeping, tearing out her hair, railing at him for ever sending Jan on the fateful journey, although God knew he felt bad enough without that. His own distress at the dockside when the ship's captain told him of Jan's death had been almost as bad as when his wife, Alicia, had died, over twenty years ago. But Alicia had been ill whereas Jan had been in the prime of life, so this time his grief was mingled with a terrible guilt at having sent the man to his death, albeit unwittingly, and shame because it was caused by his greed for tulips. He shook himself. Now was not the time to give way to his own emotions. He tried again. 'Is there anything . . .?' He didn't know what to do. He wasn't sure he should leave her sitting there, looking like that. It reminded him of calm before a storm and he was afraid of what she might do after he was gone if he left her. He didn't realise that she was so completely shocked that her feelings were numb.

Feeling utterly helpless, he got up and took two mugs from their hooks under the shelf. Then he went into the back lean-to scullery and found the keg of beer and poured two mugs, spilling some on the floor because his hand was shaking. He took them back and pushed one across the table to her because he didn't know what else to do. He wished he had brought Griete with him, sent Griete instead of coming himself . . . no, he couldn't have done that, it was too cowardly. He took a long draught of beer – it was surprisingly good – and sat watching her.

She picked her mug up and took a sip, then put it down. It was just how Jan liked it, sweet, but with an edge to it. Sometimes, on a winter's evening, he would enjoy it so much he would drink a bit more than was good for him and she would have to help him, giggling, up the stairs, where they would both fall on the bed, laughing so much that they could hardly get their clothes off before making love.

Suddenly, at the memory of this and the realisation that it would never, ever happen again, a feeling of utter desolation swept over her and her face crumpled, she put her head down on her arms and began to cry, huge sobs that racked her body and shook the table.

Samuel got to his feet and went to her, patting her shoulder helplessly. God, this frightened him almost more than her dreadful calmness. He waited a moment, then crouched down beside her and with some reluctance put his arms awkwardly round her. She immediately turned and buried her head in his shoulder and still the sobs came, turning his stiffly starched ruff into a limp, damp rag. He felt totally helpless against such grief. All he could do was hold her, with tears streaming down his own face as they both wept for Jan.

At last, after a very long time, she pulled away from him. She was exhausted, her face red and swollen with tears. Every now and again a sobbing hiccup shook her.

Samuel got to his feet, stiff and cramped from holding her, and stretched his aching muscles. He reached over and picked up her beer mug and held it to her lips.

'Better?' he said softly, as she took a few sips, coughed and took a few more.

'Oh, Samuel, I shall never be better,' she whispered bleakly, the tears beginning to fall again, but quietly now, slipping down her cheeks in little rivulets to fall unheeded on to her collar.

He watched her closely for several minutes, his head on one side. She seemed calm enough now but he still wasn't happy at the thought of her being alone in the cottage. 'I can't leave you here, Anna. Not like this. I think perhaps . . .'

She lifted her head in surprise. 'But where else should I be? This is my home. The home I shared with Jan.' She scrubbed half-heartedly at her face with the corner of her apron. 'I'm not going to leave, Samuel. I'm going to stay here, where I belong.'

'But Anna . . .' He spread his hands. He had never felt so helpless in all his life.

'I shall be perfectly all right, Samuel. I promise you,' she said wearily. She gave a ghost of a smile. 'I shan't be alone, Blackie will be here to comfort me. Thank you for staying with me so long. You must have been here . . .' she glanced out of the window. It was pitch-black, although it seemed only minutes – horrible minutes, minutes she would give the world to wipe out – since he had arrived with the dreadful news. She swallowed hard '. . . hours. I think you should go now. I'm very tired. Tomorrow I shall . . .' She shook her head. 'No, I can't think about tomorrow. Not without Jan.' She pressed the back of her hand over her mouth. 'Please go now, Samuel.'

She got to her feet and went to open the door to let him out. As she did so a fierce pain struck her side, doubling her up. At the same time she felt a warm gush of water between her legs. 'Oh, God!' She sank weakly back on to her chair as the pain left her.

'What is it? What's the matter?' Samuel said wildly, coming to her side.

'It's the child.' She cupped her hands round her belly as if to support it. 'I think the child is coming. But it's too soon. It shouldn't come yet. It shouldn't come for another . . .' she stopped speaking as another pain knifed through her '. . . month.'

Chapter Twelve

Samuel recoiled in horror. He knew nothing of the birthing of babies, neither had he any wish to learn. This was women's work. He bit his thumb, trying to make his panic-stricken brain work as she sat there, holding her belly as if to protect the child inside her. Births happened in bed, that much he knew. He glanced up at the sleeping loft. He couldn't carry her up there, and even if he could, what then? No, there had to be some other solution.

He put his fingers to his temples and tried to think calmly. There was no other cottage within calling distance, not now darkness had fallen; every cottage would be shut and barred for the night so it was no use going to the door and shouting. The only thing to do was to leave her here and go for help. He strode to the door.

She put out her hand. 'No, don't leave me,' she begged as another pain knifed through her and doubled her up. 'Please. I'm frightened.'

'I'm only going for . . .' he began, then seeing her distress, came back and stood looking down at her. 'All right,' he said doubtfully. 'We'll go together, if you can walk. Can you walk?'

'I think so.' He helped her to her feet and with his arm supporting her they left the cottage. He guided her carefully because there was only half a moon to light the way and until he reached his own garden the way was rough. Every few steps she stopped and leaned on him as another pain washed over her, leaving her weak and exhausted. In the end, as they reached the smooth paths that told him he was in his own garden, he was half-carrying, half-dragging her, fear and panic that the child would be born before he could get her to safety giving him strength. As he neared the house he began to shout for somebody to come and help him.

The servants heard and came running, lanthorns bobbing in the darkness. Griete, quickly summing up the situation, sent the scullion for her mother. Jan's digging man, who had been having a quiet mug of ale in the kitchen with Griete, picked up the now barely conscious Anna in his arms and followed Samuel into the house and up the stairs to the big guest bedroom, where he laid her on the richly embroidered dornicle.

Samuel mopped his brow and sank down on a chair by the window, exhausted.

Griete came in and bustled around lighting candles as Anna writhed, moaning on the bed. 'I think you had better not stay here any longer, sir,' Griete said, with a quick glance at Anna. 'When I can leave her I will fetch you some wine.'

'What?' He got quickly to his feet as Anna's cries became louder. 'Ah, yes. You're right. But she mustn't be left. You stay with her, Griete. I can find my own wine.' He hurried nervously to the door, then paused. 'If there is anything . . .'

'There will be nothing for you to do, sir. This is women's work.' Griete was already busy easing the expensive bed cover from under Anna, shocked that she should have been put down on the master's best dornicle.

'I see. Yes.' He hurried away, glad to be out of the room yet reluctant to leave Anna.

But Anna neither knew nor cared. The pain in her body matched the pain in her heart and she didn't care whether she lived or died. In her more lucid moments she thought of the child, Jan's child, the child he had given her in love, her only link with Jan now, and she clutched at a thin thread of determination to hang on to life for his sake, a thread that seemed to grow stronger as the pain worsened and then weakened as it went on for hour after hour, sapping her strength as well as her determination. In the end she gave up trying and sank down into blessed oblivion.

Once, she came to and saw Jan. 'Jan!' she cried in delight, holding out her arms.

'No, sweetheart. Not yet,' he said, shaking his head. When she looked again he had gone and she sank back into the pain-filled pit.

She woke at last and found that the pain, the dreadful searing, unbearable pain, had gone, leaving her with no strength even to keep her eyes open for more than a few seconds.

'Oh, thank God. She's alive,' she heard a whisper.

With a great effort she rolled her head on the pillow and saw Sarah, Griete's mother, sitting beside her. 'Is it born?' she asked faintly through cracked lips.

'Aye. It was a girl. Now, drink this.' Gently, Sarah lifted her head and gave her a drink of something warm and sweet. Soon she was asleep again.

The next time she woke her head was clearer. A girl, they had said. It was a girl. *Was* a girl. She opened her eyes. 'The baby?' she asked. 'Where's my baby?'

Sarah was still beside her. 'She never drew breath,' she said gently. 'She came too soon and her birth was too hard for her to survive.'

Anna smiled, a sweet, contented smile. 'Good. I'm glad. Now I can die, too.' She closed her eyes and gave up the fight.

The birth had been long and difficult and had sapped almost all her resources but Anna was young and her inborn, unconscious will to survive was even stronger than her determination to die. This, together with the watchful nursing of Griete's mother, who stood over her while she ate nourishing broth and drank concoctions with healing herbs in them, meant that her tenuous hold on life strengthened day by day.

'Why didn't you let me die?' she asked weakly, as Sarah stood over her, spooning delicious soup into her unwilling mouth.

'Don't be so pathetic. It wasn't your time to die. You're not the only woman who's lost a husband, nor the only one to lose a child,' Sarah said, the sympathy in her eyes belying her harsh words.

'But both at the same time?' Anna's eyes filled with the tears that were never very far from the surface.

'Aye. I'll grant you that was a hard knock,' Sarah agreed quietly. 'Harder than most are called to bear. But I believe God makes the back to fit the burden. You'll survive, my girl, and you'll be the stronger for it.'

'I don't feel strong, Sarah,' she said woefully.

'Aye. I know, dearie. But time's young yet.' Sarah patted her hand in an unusual display of affection.

When she was strong enough, Abraham van Migrode, the

new predikant, came to see her. He was full of quiet encouragement.

'I remember seeing you on the boat coming over from Nieuwport,' he said with a gentle smile. 'I thought how courageous you were to leave all that you knew to come to this unknown country. I'm sure that courage won't desert you now.'

'I had Jan by my side then,' she said sadly. 'He gave me courage. I don't know how I shall face the years ahead without him.'

He took her hand. 'But you don't have to face the years ahead, child. Days come one at a time, not all at once. So don't try to look into the future. Just think about getting through today. And once you've got through it, then you face the next day and think about surviving that.' He put his other hand over the one he held. 'It won't be easy, Anna, I'm not trying to pretend it will. But you're young and with God's help you'll come through. God bless you, my child.'

After he had gone Anna felt strangely calmer, more at peace. When Sarah came back after seeing him out she said, 'I think I might like to sit at the window for a little. I should like to see the garden in its autumn colours.'

Sarah gave her an odd look but all she said was, 'You'll need to wrap yourself in this shawl. Even with the fire halfway up the chimney it's still cold.'

'Cold?' Anna said, surprised.

'Aye. It's a lovely crisp day, but everywhere is thick with frost.'

Anna frowned as Sarah helped her out of bed and tucked the shawl round her. 'But it's only . . .'

'It's the beginning of December. You've been lying in that bed for the best part of two months, my girl. Time you got the use of your legs back.'

Sarah helped her to a chair by the window overlooking the garden. Anna shed a few tears when she saw all Jan's designs, made even more beautiful by the tracery of the frost, but she was glad to know that there was a part of him that would never die. Every time she walked in the garden would be a reminder of him.

As she watched, Samuel came out of the house and walked through the knot garden. When he reached the end he looked up at her window and waved when he saw her sitting there.

She felt a pang of guilt. She had encroached on his hospitality for far too long. She must regain her strength quickly and return to her cottage.

But when she spoke to him of her intention his reply was surprising.

He had never visited her whilst she was in bed, regarding it as ungentlemanly, although he had questioned Griete and her mother closely every day about the state of Anna's health, demanding that she should be given the best of everything to help with her recovery.

'He's like a love-sick swain,' Sarah grumbled good-naturedly to Griete. 'Pacing up and down the landing the way he does. Do you reckon . . .' she cocked an eyebrow at her daughter.

Griete laughed. 'No, I don't think he's in love with her. Anyway, he's old enough to be her father. I think he's just concerned about her because of what happened to Jan. Maybe he even feels a bit guilty. He's a kind man, mother.'

'Aye. I know it,' Sarah said with a nod.

The kind man they spoke of was quite nervous as he prepared to visit Anna the day after he had seen her sitting by the window. He lived in a man's world and was not used to the ways of women, except for women servants, who were only there to do his bidding.

He knocked and entered the room, but not until Sarah had assured him several times that Anna was sitting by the window waiting for him.

He walked in, cleared his throat nervously and strode over to stare out of the window. 'I hope you are fully recovered from your ordeal, madam,' he said stiffly, carefully not looking at her.

She smiled, the first real smile. She had never seen Samuel at such a loss, but she understood his embarrassment and realised that even though he was her late husband's master she was in control and must put him at his ease.

'I am gaining in strength every day now, thank you, Samuel,' she replied. 'Please, won't you sit down? I confess it is giving me a crick in my neck, looking up at you. Sarah has drawn up a chair for you.'

'Thank you.' He sat down and stared at his hands as they rested on his knees.

'You've been very kind to me, Samuel,' she said quietly. 'If it hadn't been for you I should probably have died.' She gazed out of the window. 'Not that I should have minded that,' she added sadly.

His head shot up and for the first time he looked at her. 'You mustn't say that, Anna. You are young and . . .' he floundered. He had been going to say beautiful, but he was shocked to the core to see that she wasn't beautiful. Not any longer. Her hair hung lank and lifeless and her cheeks were pale and sunken. Even those huge, violet-blue eyes of her had lost their lustre. 'You are young,' he finished lamely. He looked round the room. 'You are warm enough?' he asked, his voice becoming stronger now that he felt on safer ground. 'They keep the fire well stoked for you? The weather is bitterly cold outside. You can see, the way the frost rimes the garden . . .' his voice trailed off. Perhaps it was insensitive to mention the garden. He glanced at her from under his lashes and saw that she surreptitiously wiped away a tear. He cursed himself for a fool. 'You have everything you need for your comfort?' he finished, his voice more gruff than he had intended.

'Everything. And more,' she answered. Except my husband and child, she added silently in her heart. She lifted her head. 'I can't thank you enough for your kindness, Samuel. It must have been a great burden to you to have a sick woman upsetting your household. And for so long, too. I hadn't realised how long I have been ill. Two months, they tell me.'

'Is it that long?' he said vaguely. 'No matter. As long as you are recovering.' He looked at her properly now and for the first time their eyes met. 'You've been very ill, Anna. At one time you were thought to die. It was an anxious time for all of us.'

She saw real concern in his blue-grey eyes. 'Thank you, Samuel,' she said quietly. After a few minutes' silence, companionable rather than awkward now, Anna said, 'Now that I am mending I must go back to my own cottage. I have taken advantage of your generous hospitality for far too long.'

'Nonsense. I won't hear of it.' They were the words of a man used to getting his own way. 'That cottage is damp from lack of use. You must stay here until you are stronger and the weather is warmer.'

'But Samuel . . .'

He lifted his hand to silence her but his words were gentle. 'You are hardly out of bed, Anna. You haven't been outside into the cold air. How can you think of going back to that cottage yet?'

She sighed. 'But I fear you must be anxious to be rid of me and the trouble I am causing you.'

111

He raised his eyebrows. 'Do I give the appearance of wanting to be rid of you? If I do it is entirely unintentional, I assure you.'

'No, not at all,' she said quickly, then added doubtfully, 'But the servants . . . All the extra work . . .'

'I pay them well for what they do. They've no cause to complain. Nor do they.' He cocked an eyebrow, smiling at her. 'Is there anything else, Anna?'

She couldn't help smiling back at him. 'No, Samuel. Except to thank you again for your generosity.'

He slapped his knee. 'Good, that's settled then. We'll have no more talk of going back to the cottage.'

'Will you come and see me again?' she asked tentatively. Once the ice was broken she had enjoyed talking with him.

'Every day. Until you're well enough to leave your room and come to the table and eat with me.'

'Oh, I . . .' she began in alarm.

'Until then I shall come and see you here,' he interrupted. He got up and strode to the door. There he paused. 'Never think you owe me anything for having you here, Anna,' he said quietly. 'Believe me, the debt is all mine.'

After he had left, Anna sat staring out of the window, unsure of what he had meant by his last words. Was it his guilt at having sent Jan to his death? But plague could strike anywhere. At any time. It just so happened that it had been on the voyage back from Amsterdam with the precious tulips that Jan had caught it. She wondered briefly if many others on the boat had died, because plague didn't usually strike in isolation.

She closed her eyes, too tired to think further. Samuel was right, she was still very weak. She had enjoyed his visit; she realised that it was the first time she had had a conversation with him as an equal and not as the wife of one of his workmen. It had been very enjoyable.

She fell asleep.

The New Year came in quietly at Samuel's house, the house he had named Garden House because that was how most people referred to it.

'A nice tribute to Jan, too, don't you think?' he asked Anna, smiling at her across the long polished table where they now ate together.

She nodded, smiling back at him through the tears that were still not far from the surface but which now fell a little less readily as she was becoming stronger and the grief in her heart more bearable.

He noted with satisfaction that the dreadful greenish pallor of her face that had so shocked him the first time he had visited her was now replaced by a more healthy creamy whiteness, her hair had begun to shine again under its white cap and the weight she had put on had filled out her cheeks and rounded her figure becomingly. Another good sign was that her hands no longer lay idle in her lap but were more often than not employed with a book or a piece of embroidery. Clearly, the nourishing broth Griete had made from vegetables grown in the garden, the calves foot jelly and the cream and cheese from Pitt's Farm had worked wonders. That and, he flattered himself, the hours he had spent with her, talking of matters ranging from the price of wool to the terrible persecutions in their native land.

He had been surprised at her knowledge about this. Even though the worst excesses of the infamous Duke of Alva, emissary of King Philip of Spain, had occurred before she was even born, she knew how he had taken his army to try to force the people of the Netherlands to renounce their Protestant faith and embrace Catholicism; she had even been aware of the infamous Spanish Inquisition, and the terrible tortures which those who refused to comply with Spanish demands had undergone. She had told him too, that her grandparents, like his own parents, had refused to renounce their Calvinist faith and had fled to England during the worst of the persecutions, but unlike his parents they had eventually returned to Flanders. She had made no mention of her mother and father, which surprised him, but he asked no questions, because he still considered their relationship too distant to pry into personal matters.

The whole of January was bitterly cold, with snow and ice. Anna was quite content to stay warm and dry in Samuel's house, where great fires burned, and tall screens kept the draughts at bay. The comfort of Garden House resembled the comforts she had been used to at her home in Flanders and she admitted to herself that she was in no hurry to relinquish them, although she was unhappy at continuing to impose on Samuel's hospitality and tried

113

to make amends by helping Griete with the bread-making and other not too demanding household tasks.

But when the ice melted and the sun shone again she realised that the time had come when she must go back to the cottage she had shared for all too short a time with Jan. She felt stronger now, strong enough to face the memories, bad as well as good, that the cottage held.

Samuel didn't argue at the proposed visit, much to her surprise. All he said was, 'Make sure you put on a warm cloak. Griete will find you one of mine to wear. And don't stay too long. We don't want you to catch a chill.'

Wrapped in Samuel's fur-lined cloak she walked the short distance to the cottage with some trepidation. Griete had offered to accompany her but she knew she must go alone to face her memories. Memories of happier times crowded into her mind as she approached the low door, blurring her eyes with tears to think that Jan would never pass through it again, yet at the same time causing her to smile, remembering the number of times he had bumped his head on the lintel.

She took a deep breath, pushed open the door and went inside.

Chapter Thirteen

Anna shivered as she stepped into the cottage, surprised at how very cold and dank it was. Then she realised that this was hardly surprising, since it had been empty for the better part of four months, and four months of a bitterly cold winter at that. She stood for a moment to adjust her eyes to the dimness, then looked around. The place was exactly as she had left it on the night Samuel had come to tell her of Jan's death; the beer mugs were still on the table and a chair was overturned and left where it had fallen when Samuel had rushed to her aid. The events of that terrible evening came flooding back to her as she stood there, the feeling of utter desolation, then the sudden pain and the fear as she realised her child was coming – too soon. She squeezed her eyes tightly shut to blot out the memory of that terrible night and to prevent the tears spilling over.

Suddenly, there was a scuffle up in the sleeping loft and Blackie, her little cat, leaped straight down on to the table and came to her, purring and rubbing herself against her.

'Blackie! Oh, Blackie!' Anna said in delighted amazement. 'I never expected to find you here! Have you been living here alone, all this time?' She picked her up and cuddled her in her arms. 'I thought you'd have gone back to the farm, or found yourself another home. I never expected to find you here, waiting for me.' She stroked the sleek, well-fed little body. 'But what have you been living on? Surely there aren't that many mice!'

Blackie purred loudly and rubbed her face against Anna's.

Still holding the little cat on her arm Anna made a desultory effort to tidy the room, talking to her all the time. She picked up the chair and poked half-heartedly at the long dead embers of the fire. The pan of stew she had made for Jan's return had been upturned on the hearth and its contents mostly eaten.

'By you, no doubt, Blackie,' she said, as the little cat scrambled up on to her shoulder. She opened the hutch. Everything in what had been a well-stocked larder was either crusted with mould or reduced to little more than dust.

'I suppose I shouldn't have expected anything else after all this time,' she said with a sigh. She sat down on a chair and leaned her elbows on the table. It had been a mistake to come here today. Even now, when she thought she was feeling so much stronger, she had neither the will nor the energy to begin making the place ready to return to. She couldn't even be bothered to light a fire.

With a sigh she got to her feet. 'We'll just go upstairs and find a few more clothes, Blackie,' she said to the purring little animal on her shoulder. 'Then we'll go back to Garden House. And you can come with me. I'm sure Samuel won't mind.'

She dragged herself up to the sleeping loft. Blackie had clearly been sleeping on the bed, and she jumped off Anna's shoulder and went to the little nest she had made for herself while Anna opened the clothes press. Everything in it was neatly brushed and folded; her mouth twisted wryly as she remembered putting lavender between the folds to keep it sweet-smelling, happy in her role as wife and with her impending motherhood to look forward to.

But now the overriding smell was of damp and decay. Everything she touched felt damp and was spotted with a greyish blue mould that no amount of brushing or shaking would ever remove. Even the linen bands she had sewn in preparation for swaddling the baby after it was born were stained with mould and rust marks.

With a heavy heart she went over and sat down on the bed. She wished she didn't feel so weak and listless. The way she felt now she could never tackle the four months of damp and neglect in the cottage. But soon she would have to make the effort to come back here and pick up her life – not where she had left it, she could never do that without Jan – but she would somehow have to make a life for herself.

She put her fingers to her temple in an effort to concentrate her thoughts. She would need money; she had an idea that there was a fund to help the poor and needy of the Dutch Congregation that was funded by fines incurred at the Bay Hall. She didn't want to apply for that if she could help it. The daughter of Judith Fromenteel must never stoop so low as to beg for charity! The only alternative was to find work, but what could she do? Perhaps her friend Margery Frith would teach her how to spin. It didn't look that difficult.

Slowly, she got up from the bed and began to climb down the ladder to the living room. Halfway down she paused as another, frightening thought struck her. What if she couldn't come back to the cottage? What if Samuel turned her out?

Because this cottage had been provided for the use of Samuel's gardener and Samuel's gardener was dead, lying with the expensive tulips he had gone to buy, plague-ridden at the bottom of the German Sea – she chose the stark words deliberately, twisting the hurt in her heart. So it might not be up to her to make this cottage habitable again; someone else would probably have that task. All she would have to do would be to collect her belongings and find somewhere else to live. Because although Samuel had been very kind to her during her illness, unstinting in his hospitality and anxious in his care for her, she couldn't impose on his good nature indefinitely; before long she must make her own way in the world.

She carried on down the ladder and sank down on to the chair again. Blackie had followed closely behind, unwilling to leave her, and she jumped on to her lap, rubbing her head against Anna's chin. Anna absent-mindedly stroked her, trying to think what she might do. If only she had some idea where to look for her father! Surely, if she could find him he would help her. But she had so little to go on – dark, violet-blue eyes and the name of Henrick! Jan had hoped to contact her mother and find out more about him, but any information he had gained had gone with him to the bottom of the sea. With no Jan to love and sustain her, no baby to look forward to, no home of her own and in a foreign land where she and her fellow countrymen were still regarded as 'aliens' or 'strangers', a feeling of utter hopelessness overwhelmed her. Tears of despair spilled over and fell on Blackie's coat.

She didn't know how long she had been sitting there when the door opened behind her. She glanced up and saw Samuel standing there. She scrambled to her feet.

'I was just . . .' she began, dashing the tears away with the back of her hand.

He smiled and held out his hand. 'Come along, my dear. I

think you've spent quite long enough here for one day,' he said gently.

'My little cat . . . Look, she was here, waiting for me,' Anna said trying to smile through her tears.

'Then you'd better bring her with you, hadn't you,' he said. He led her out and closed the door behind them.

'What am I going to do, Samuel?' she whispered. 'You'll need this cottage for one of your workmen, I realise that. I must clear my things out . . .' She shivered and he put an arm round her.

'You're cold. Even with my cloak on you're cold. You'll catch a chill. You shouldn't have stayed there so long,' he said sternly, not answering her question.

'I know. I'm sorry. I didn't think . . .' It would be terrible to be ill again and have to encroach further on his hospitality.

'Never mind. We'll soon have you sitting by a good fire,' he said, more cheerfully. 'And Griete is roasting a capon.'

He hurried her back to the house and settled her in front of a roaring fire in the great hall with a screen behind her to keep out the draughts, calling for one of the servants to bring a posset for her. When he was satisfied that she was comfortable he left her, saying, 'I have work to do. When I come back we must talk.'

She knew what that meant. She leaned back against the cushions and closed her eyes, Blackie purring happily on her lap. It was so warm and comfortable here, the painted cloths and tapestries on the walls, the tiles on the floor, all reminded her of her home in Flanders. The home she had left rather than marry that dreadful man Otto de Hane. The home she had left to be with Jan.

She pulled herself together. There was no use in wallowing in self-pity; whatever the future might hold it must be better than marriage to Otto de Hane. Somehow she must make a life for herself. She stared into the fire for a long time, as all kinds of wild schemes came into her mind and were rejected. At last the ghost of a smile flickered over her face. Of course. Abraham van Migrode, the predikant. He always said she could go to him if she needed help. He would help her to find work, she was sure of it. Perhaps a position as a servant or a nursemaid in one of the more wealthy households. At least that would give her a roof over her head. Her mind made up she closed her eyes and dozed by the fire, grateful for the warmth and comfort of Samuel Hegetorne's beautiful house while she could enjoy it.

Griete came in. 'The master said I was to be sure you lacked nothing,' she said good-humouredly. 'He's very anxious for your comfort. Ah, I see you've managed to bring your little cat back with you. I tried to tempt her to leave the cottage and come back with me but she wouldn't budge so all I could do was leave food outside for her. I reckon she wouldn't leave because she was waiting for you.'

'Oh, so it was you who's been feeding her, Griete,' Anna said with a smile. 'I couldn't understand why she was looking so sleek and well-fed. Thank you for looking after her for me.'

Griete shrugged. 'It was no trouble to me. I fed her on all the scraps. She's a friendly little thing. Just wouldn't leave the cottage. I never said anything to you about it because I was afraid you might worry about her.'

'That was thoughtful of you, Griete.' She fondled the little cat's ear. 'Oh, dear. Between us, I fear Blackie and I have made you and your mother a great deal of extra work these past months,' she said sadly.

'You couldn't help that, now, could you,' Griete said, her plain face full of sympathy. 'And you've been very good, never asked for much, haven't run us off our feet like some would have done. Anyway, the master's been very generous, we've been well paid for the extra work.'

'I'm glad to hear that,' Anna said, relieved. 'He's a very good man, isn't he. I don't know what I would have done without his kindness in taking me in.' She leaned her head wearily against the back of the chair.

Griete laughed. 'He didn't have much choice when it came to it, did he, unless he'd left you to birth under the hedge, and he wouldn't have done that. But, aye, you're right, he's a good master. Not many to equal him.' She pulled the screen a few inches nearer to Anna's chair. 'Now, is there anything you're wanting?'

Anna gave a little mirthless laugh. 'Nothing that you can get for me, Griete.'

'Aye, well, there's some things nobody can replace,' Griete said, understanding perfectly. She cocked her ear. 'Ah, that'll be the master, back from his business. I'd best be about serving the meal. I hope you're hungry, Anna.'

Anna said nothing. What was the point of telling Griete that she was so apprehensive about her future that even the thought of food made her feel sick.

But when it arrived at the table the capon smelled delicious and she found that it was tasty, cooked with wine and herbs, served with turnips and parsnips freshly dug from the garden, and she ate a good helping. Then there was a delicious raspberry syllabub to follow.

'I'm glad to see you're getting your appetite back, Anna,' Samuel said with a smile as she accepted a second helping.

She blushed. 'When I began the meal I didn't think I'd be able to eat a thing,' she admitted. 'I thought I was too worried to eat.'

'Why on earth should you be worried?' he asked, raising his eyebrows.

'You said we must talk.' She stole a glance at him and went on hurriedly, 'I know what it is you want to talk about and I've already thought about it a lot. I've decided what I must do. I know I can't go back to the cottage, you'll want it for . . .' her voice broke but she carried on '. . . for whoever takes Jan's place. So I shall . . .' She stopped in mid-sentence, her mouth open in surprise, as he held up his hand for silence.

'I said *we* must talk, Anna. So far, I haven't managed to say a word,' he said, his eyes twinkling.

'Oh, I'm sorry.' She kept her eyes on her bowl as she finished her syllabub.

'Have you finished?' he asked as he watched the last spoonful disappear.

She nodded.

He rinsed his fingers in the water bowl and dried them on the napkin at his side. 'Then come and sit by the fire again. Even with the shutters closed the wind finds its way through the cracks.'

She rinsed her own fingers then obediently went over to the fire and sat down opposite to him.

'Do you like it here, at Garden House?' he asked abruptly.

She looked up. 'Like it? Yes. You've been very kind to me whilst I've been ill, Samuel, and I'm really most grateful to you.'

He brushed her words aside with a gesture. 'That's not what I mean. You've recovered now.' He peered at her under dark, beetle brows. 'You are recovered, aren't you?'

'Thank you, yes, for the most part,' she answered honestly. 'I lack my former energy, but no doubt it will soon return when I . . .'

'Good,' he interrupted. 'I'm glad you like it here because I want you to stay. I want you to make this your home.'

She licked her lips. 'I don't understand . . .' she began.

He leaned forward, smiling. 'I want you to stay here, under my roof, so that I can look after you, Anna.' His smile faded. 'For Jan's sake, shall we say? After all, I am to blame for your present situation. If it hadn't been for my obsession with tulips . . .' he spread his hands in a helpless gesture.

'Plague can strike anywhere,' she said. 'You mustn't blame yourself for Jan's death.' She was surprised how calmly she could speak about it now. She went on, 'But even if you do there's no reason why you should burden yourself with my presence in your house. I should hate to become something of a hair shirt to you.' This time, it was he who opened his mouth to speak and she held up her hand to silence him. 'Let me finish. It's true I need some-where to live, but I'm sure I can find someone who will take me in. The predikant will help me to find a position, if I ask him. Perhaps I can find work as a nursemaid. Or cook. Maria taught me quite a lot and so did Bettris . . .' she bit her lip. It wouldn't do to let him know she had been used to living in a house with a servant.

'Bettris? You've mentioned her before, haven't you? Who is Bettris?'

She shrugged. 'Just someone I knew back at home.'

'I see.' He was regarding her intently. 'I'm not sure how you'd manage, my dear. I must say you have neither the look, nor the manner of a servant,' he remarked. 'I've often thought that, when I've seen you with Jan. You look far too well-bred for menial work.'

She shrugged again but said nothing.

They were both silent for some time, watching the flames lick round the large tree branch burning on the fire. After a while he said, 'Are you trying to tell me that you don't want to stay here at Garden House? That you couldn't be happy here? I should be very sorry if that were so because I enjoy your company.' He smiled wryly. 'I'm sure I could never regard you as a "hair shirt". In fact, the house would seem empty without you.'

'No, that's not what I'm saying at all. I'm very happy here, Samuel, and you've made me more than welcome. But I fear I've imposed on your hospitality for far too long. If there was anything I could do . . . any way I could repay your kindness, then I would be more than happy to stay.'

'I am amply repaid by your presence here, Anna,' he said quietly. He was quiet for several minutes, staring into the fire, then he said, 'You told me that your grandparents fled to England from Flanders but then returned home. Something similar happened to my family. We too were forced to flee from Alva's men – largely due to my father's outspokenness. Unfortunately, my parents were both very homesick and didn't survive long in England, but Alicia, my lovely wife, enjoyed the challenge and soon, due to her foresight, we were making a good living here. You see, before we left she had collected all the small items of value we possessed, plus all her jewellery, and sewn them into her garments, so we had no difficulty in raising funds to build the business that has made me such a wealthy man. Unfortunately, Alicia didn't live to enjoy our prosperity. She died three years ago. Our home had been in Boxted but I found it impossible to stay there after her death and so I had this house built. I thought a fresh start would help to erase memories, but I still miss her.' He glanced at her briefly. 'You can understand that better than most, of course.'

She nodded and said with a sigh, 'Oh, I can indeed.'

His mood lifted. 'There. I didn't intend to burden you with my history, Anna, but now perhaps you can understand why I am more than happy for you to stay here. Indeed, perhaps you would be happy to take over the running of my household? I'm far too busy to concern myself with such things as servants' grievances. Do you think you could do that?'

'Oh, yes. I'm sure I could. I used to help . . .' again she bit her lip, cursing her runaway tongue.

He looked at her intently, but when she didn't explain further he simply said, 'And I know you can read and write. I daresay my amanuensis will be glad of help at times.' He smiled broadly. 'So you see, your presence here will be neither as a hair shirt nor an ornament. I am sure you will be a great asset to my house.' Satisfied he had convinced her, he got to his feet and poured two goblets of wine. 'Come, let's drink to your happiness in your new home, Anna,' he said, handing her one and holding the other in his hand. 'And remember, this will be your home, to come and go as you please. I think we shall get along very well together.' A suspicion of a frown crossed his handsome face as he noticed she was still hesitating. He cleared his throat and continued gruffly, 'I assure you that I shall ask nothing more of you than that you grace my table and work with me as I have suggested. *Nothing more.*' He looked at her closely. 'Do I make myself clear?'

She flushed, annoyed with herself that her fears had been so transparent. 'Yes. Quite clear, Samuel,' she answered.

'Good. Now, let's drink to your long and happy stay under my roof.' He lifted his goblet and drank to her.

'Thank you, Samuel.' She smiled at him and took a draught of wine. It was very cold and made her shiver slightly. Or was it only the wine? Was it because even though she had been given the freedom of this lovely house and told she could come and go as she pleased she had the feeling deep down inside her that she was caught in a trap?

Chapter Fourteen

Anna tossed and turned in bed that night, her feelings jumbled. Before she closed her eyes she gazed round the warm, candlelit chamber, where the last embers of the fire glowed in the gloom, and felt a thrill of excitement to think that this elegantly furnished room was now hers for as long as she wanted it. Never more would she have to climb the ladder to the damp sleeping loft in the cottage, careful not to bump her head on the beam. But with that thought came a rush of guilt, a feeling of betrayal towards Jan, because she had made such an unfair comparison. She had loved the little cottage. It had been her home, with Jan, whom she had loved with all her heart. Even now she could see his tall figure bending his head as he came through the door after his day's work, his face tanned, his expression happy at the way the garden was taking shape. In her imagination she could feel his arms round her, smell the earthy scent of him and remember the passion of his kisses. But then she realised that she would never know his kisses again, she would never again see his smiling face, never hear the tuneless whistle that heralded his homecoming. At that a feeling of utter desolation swept over her and she laid her hand on her too flat stomach. She had even lost the child they had so looked forward to; at least that would have been living proof of their love for each other. Again her gaze swept the large, panelled room, the shuttered window with its heavy curtains, the carved chest, the comfortable chair by the fireplace. All these things could never replace the husband, the child, the simple way of life she had lost. She slept at last with tears on her pillow, her only consolation the little cat that was curled up at her feet.

But these thoughts were reserved for the dark hours of the

night. When daylight came she acknowledged that she was indebted to Samuel for his kindness in giving her a home and by taking the predikant's advice and never looking further ahead than the next day the time passed pleasantly enough despite the continued ache in her heart for Jan.

With the coming of spring some of her energy returned and she walked in the garden, which made her feel close to Jan, because she could enjoy the fruits of his labour, remembering how he had shared with her his plans for the knot garden, the flower borders and the kitchen garden. Now, as she walked round she recognised the gilly flowers that he had been unsure where to place, the narcissi, hepaticas and muscaris that rioted along the borders, the roses he had planted round the arbour so that she could smell them as she sat waiting for their baby; so many little memories that made her happy and sad at the same time.

Samuel left her very much to her own devices. He was continually busy, at the Bay Hall or in his counting house. But he made a point of eating supper in the evening with her.

'You are still very pale and thin, Anna,' he said one evening as they ate the succulent coney pie that Griete had baked. 'Have you not recovered from your . . .' he hrrumphed, embarrassed to speak of her confinement '. . . your illness?'

'I still suffer from a certain listlessness,' she admitted. 'But I have been to the still-room and made myself a tincture to give me added strength.' She traced the grain of the wood in the polished table with her finger. 'I enjoy working in the still-room. An old woman I once knew taught me a lot about herbs and remedies. I was glad to find I had not forgotten all she taught me.'

He watched her intently. 'Do you find that time hangs heavy, Anna?'

She looked up. 'At times,' she said honestly. 'You see, I've never been used to a life of idleness. My mother always encouraged me to help . . .' her voice trailed off. 'You asked me to run your household for you, but there is little enough for me to do in that direction because it runs very smoothly without any help or interference from me,' she said, a trifle ruefully.

They finished the meal and rinsed their fingers in the bowl on the table before moving to sit by the fire, still welcome in spite of a day of warm sunshine.

'Would you like to come to the Bay Hall with me, Anna?' he

asked, poking the log with his foot and sending sparks flying up the chimney. 'You've hardly been outside the gate for weeks. A change of scenery might do you good.'

'Would I be allowed in?' she asked, surprised.

He laughed. 'Women rarely visit the place but there's no reason why they shouldn't. As long as they don't get in the way. I'll give you a ledger to carry so that you look as if you've got business there. Then nobody will question you. But you haven't answered my question. Would you like to come with me?'

'Yes. Yes. I would,' she answered. 'I should like to see what goes on there. When I've been to the market I've noticed a lot of people coming and going. It seems a very important and busy place.'

'Yes, it is. I'll explain all about it when we get there. I have to go tomorrow. The carriage will be ready at ten. Can you be ready by then?'

'Indeed I can.' Her expression was more animated than he had seen it for a long time.

'Wear something dark,' he said as an afterthought. 'Bright colours wouldn't be appropriate.'

For the first time in a long time she laughed. 'Samuel, I have no choice. These are my only clothes. I admit they are becoming a little shabby but I keep them well darned and they are clean. I clean off any stains with soapwort every week.'

Samuel didn't laugh with her. He frowned. 'You have a cloak? Shoes?'

'Yes. But I left Flanders in a hurry. I could only bring what I could easily carry. Since I arrived in Colchester I have had neither the money nor the need for new garments.' She glanced at him, fearful that she had said too much about her past and that he would question her further.

But all he said was, 'Yes, many of our people are still fleeing from the persecution of the Spanish.' He stroked his beard. 'You must have new clothes. I will have some samples brought so that you can choose what you would like to have made up.'

'There's no need, Samuel,' she said firmly. 'You are kind enough to let me live under your roof and to feed me. I can hardly expect you to clothe me as well.'

'Then how will you buy new clothes when the ones you wear turn to rags?' he asked, a twinkle in his eye. 'And how shall I explain the fact that the woman I am escorting looks like a beggar woman whilst I wear expensive cloth on my back?'

'I shan't be noticed at the Bay Hall. This skirt is dark grey,' she said stubbornly.

'But suppose we are invited to dine with some of my friends? Suppose I entertain?'

She shrugged. 'That needn't concern me. As long as I make sure everything is in order I can keep out of the way.'

'Anna!' he exploded, thumping his hands on the arms of his chair. 'Don't be so difficult. You need new clothes. I shall provide them. And there's an end to the matter.' He leaned back in his chair. 'And if you wish to repay me you can do so by accompanying me with a good grace when I ask you to. It won't be often. I am not by nature a man who seeks a lot of company, unless it's by way of business.' He regarded her for a moment. 'Wear a hat tomorrow.'

'I haven't got a hat,' she said sulkily.

He sighed. 'Very well. Wear your cap.'

'I'll put a clean cap on. And a clean collar and cuffs and apron. I shan't disgrace you, Samuel, never fear,' she said with a lift of her chin.

Suddenly, he grinned at her. 'That's better. Do you realise you're beginning to show a bit of spirit, Anna? I like that.'

As she dressed the next morning Anna saw her skirt and stomacher through Samuel's eyes and realised how very shabby she had become. But her collar and cuffs were snowy white and her shoes were polished. And under her cloak, which was of the best quality, since Cornelis Fromenteel had always made sure the way his family dressed reflected his wealth, the shabbiness of her dress would never be seen.

Samuel raised his eyebrows as she got into the carriage but made no comment on the quality of her cloak, which was made of a thick woollen material, warm but light.

The Bay Hall, at the end of the Market Place, nearly opposite the Three Crowns, was already busy when they arrived. The carriage drew up under the eaves and Samuel handed her out and indicated that she should follow him up the stairs. The noise was deafening, with people shouting at or to each other, some of them in English, some of them in Dutch. After the peace and tranquillity of the Garden House Anna found it all a bit disconcerting.

127

'You will already know that the Bay Hall is the place where all the cloth is checked for quality,' Samuel said, when they reached the comparative quiet of a large room with long tables stretching down the centre. 'This is the raw hall, where the cloth is checked in its raw state, before it is dyed and thickened. The white hall is where it is checked again, after thickening. It is there that it is given the Colchester seal of quality.'

'I've heard of that,' Anna said. Cornelis, her father, had often spoken of it, saying that any cloth bearing the Colchester seal guaranteed its quality and no further checks were needed.

Samuel raised his eyebrows. 'Have you, indeed,' was all he said.

Suddenly, there was the sound of cloth being ripped in half, voices were raised and there was a scuffle at the far end of the room.

'What . . .?' Anna looked up at Samuel in alarm.

'Obviously there has been a fault found in the cloth,' he explained. 'The English always complain when their workmanship is questioned. Come, I have business elsewhere, I'll explain it to you later.' He hurried her along to a room behind the two halls, saying as they went, 'The trouble is, the English resent the fact that the Dutch examine the English cloth as well as their own. The English feel, and I have some sympathy with them, that they themselves should take responsibility for examining their cloth. As you can imagine, it causes a great deal of ill-feeling.'

'What happens when a fault is found?' Anna asked, fascinated.

'The weaver, or fuller, or dyer, whichever process is at fault, is fined. If it is the work of a Stranger, then the fine goes to the Dutch church for the relief of the Dutch poor. If it is the work of an Englishman then the fine goes to the English poor. It is a very fair system.'

'And what kind of faults might be found?'

He pursed his lips. 'Let me see, how best can I explain it to you. For one thing, if the weft threads on a piece are drawn too tight, then the cloth is "waisted" and will be rejected; if there are insufficient threads to the inch; if the dye is not even – oh, there are many reasons for rejection, particularly as the cloth must be examined and pronounced perfect at every stage of its manufacture or it can't be sealed.' He broke off. 'Ah, there's the man I came to see. Mynheer Crowbroke.' He raised his voice,

128

'Henrick!' He turned to Anna. 'Wait here. I shan't be long.' With that he pushed his way through the crowd to where a man in a tall copotain hat was standing by the door. As Samuel reached him, he lifted his hat to scratch his head and Anna saw that his hair, like his beard, was very fair.

Just like her own. And Samuel had called him Henrick . . .

She watched the two men for several minutes. Samuel looked to be several years younger than his friend, which would probably put Henrick at a similar age to her mother. She could see that he had been a very handsome man in his youth although his face was slightly florid now. Could she detect a faint likeness to herself in his features? The shape of his nose, perhaps? Her heart thumping with excitement, she began to edge her way round the room, anxious to get close enough to see the colour of Henrick Crowbroke's eyes.

Then she hesitated. If they were the same dark, violet blue colour as her own, what then? She could hardly go up to him and say, 'I believe I am your daughter.' What if she was mistaken? Even worse, what if she was right but the man already had a wife and other children? She realised that she had been so intent on searching out the man her mother had loved so long ago that she had never stopped to consider what the consequences might be if she found him. She had always assumed that he would be delighted to see her and eager to acknowledge her as his own.

But this might not be so. She realised that she would have to be very careful how she approached him and she resolved to bide her time until she knew more about the man. Nevertheless, she felt a warm glow to think that her search for her natural father might already have ended. If only he would look her way so that she could see his eyes, but he was intent on what Samuel was saying and never once looked in her direction. A minute later, slapping Samuel on the back, he disappeared through the door.

Disappointed, she waited for Samuel to return to her.

'I have to go to the Moot Hall,' he said when he reached her. 'There is yet another dispute between our people and the English. The English are accusing us of importing wire for carding the yarn from our own country instead of using English wire.' He made an impatient gesture. 'There's always something. They already complain that we use their mills for fulling our cloth. We can hardly do otherwise since all the mills belong to the English. Of course, they conveniently forget that we pay to use them. The root of all these problems is that they're jealous because we of the Dutch Congregation work harder that they do and therefore we prosper.' He turned to her. 'You can wait in the carriage for me. I shan't be long.'

'No, if you don't mind, I'll walk round the market, Samuel. I haven't been to the market for a long time and I shall enjoy having a look round,' she said.

'Don't tire yourself then.' He felt in his pocket and handed her some coins. 'Here's some money. You might find something that takes your fancy.'

She put her hands behind her. 'No. That's not necessary. I only want to look,' she said, her voice prim.

'Oh, for goodness sake, woman, take it. I make more than enough for my needs. Consider it payment for running my household if you must. I haven't the time to stand here arguing about it.' He thrust it into her hand. 'The carriage will be waiting by St Runwald's Church at noon. Don't be late. I have an appointment with my agents this afternoon.'

He left her and hurried away. She put the money in her pocket, intending to keep it there, and went down the stairs, passing a room where a length of deep russet-coloured cloth was spread on a long table and men with huge scissors were expertly shearing patterns into the pile. She experienced a sudden surge of homesickness as she remembered that her mother had worn a gown of such material years ago and she recalled how she had traced the pattern in the folds of her skirt with her finger when she was a child. She sighed. So much had happened since those days.

As usual the market was busy. Anna wandered among the stalls, the jugglers, the fire-eaters and stilt-walkers, noticing as never before how the Strangers kept to themselves, talking in their own language in dark-clothed huddles, buying their needs only from stalls set up by their own countrymen.

The English also bought only from their own countrymen and talked and bantered with each other, some of them making rude gestures towards the Dutch people and calling them names. She saw one man spit at a Stranger and shout out that he had taken his livelihood but the Stranger obviously didn't understand what he was saying and merely looked down his nose at the Englishman.

Deliberately, she went to a fruit stall run by an Englishwoman and bought a basket, talking to the woman in her still slightly halting English about the weather and anything else that came to mind as she paid over her money. After some initial hostility the woman began to answer her, and even managed to smile as she gave her the change. Then she went to buy some apples from another stall, doing the same thing. The woman on this fruit stall was less friendly and told her in no uncertain terms that her people weren't welcome in Colchester and should go home where they belonged.

'You don't wish to sell me your fruit?' Anna asked politely, turning away.

'You can buy if you like,' the woman said, anxious not to lose a sale.

'Thank you. I will have some of those red ones. Not the bruised ones,' as the woman began to pick out the bruised and speckled fruit. 'I'll have some of these, from the front of the stall. You have some fine fruit here, mistress, do you grow it yourself?'

'Yes. My man has fruit trees out Boxted way.' The woman couldn't keep the pride out of her voice. 'Our fruit is reckoned to be the best in the district.'

'I can see that. That's why I came to your stall. Thank you, mistress.' Anna smiled at the woman and was rewarded with a nod of approval.

As she turned away another woman caught her arm. It was one of the Stranger community. 'Best you don't have anything to do with the English, Mevrouw,' she said. 'They're only out to rob you. Best you deal only with our people.'

'I haven't been robbed,' Anna said showing her the beautiful red apples nestling in her basket. 'I have been treated very fairly at that stall. If you ask for the best apples she will sell them to you. In the past I have bought good meat from the butchers' shambles, too, so the same is true of the other stalls, I am sure.'

'But they don't understand our language.'

'Why should they? This is their country. Do you understand English?'

'No.'

'Then maybe you should learn.'

'Do you speak their language?'

'Yes. Not as well as I would like, but I'm learning. After all, we

131

have come to live in their country. If we don't bother to learn their language it's no wonder they continue to call us aliens.'

The woman gave a somewhat haughty shrug. 'We like to keep ourselves to ourselves.'

'Then they will always call you Strangers.'

Thoughtfully, she walked back to the carriage to wait for Samuel.

Chapter Fifteen

It was some time before Samuel arrived, flinging himself into the carriage with every evidence of exasperation.

'Have things not gone well, Samuel?' she asked nervously.

He shouted at the coachman to get a move on, then replied, hardly less testily, 'No, Anna, they have not. And there's precious little I can do about it while the two sides are ranged against each other as if the town was a battlefield.'

She watched him. There were a thousand questions she wanted to ask but she realised that this was not the time, so she waited for him to explain, which he did, counting off on his fingers the grievances.

'There's the business of the wire. We're not allowed to use our own imported wire for carding.

'We're not allowed to sell our goods to each other. But if we don't sell to each other who can we sell them to? The English won't buy from us.

'We are accused of keeping the goods we import until prices are favourable. Well, surely, that's good business.

'We pay higher customs duties. We pay double what the English pay for subsidies.

'We've repaired derelict houses. In God's name what more do they want!'

He was quiet for some time, then he said, 'To be fair, I have met some very nice Englishmen and we have done good business together. This is the nub of the matter, to my way of thinking. If we Strangers only deal with each other, if we all continue to live in the same area, worship only in our own church, speak only our native language, and refuse to have anything to do with the

English we can hardly complain if they accuse us of being clannish. And to cap it all, they have to bring their cloth to *our* Bay Hall, for *us* to examine and seal. No wonder there is friction.' He glanced at her. 'I'm sorry, Anna. I always get wound up when I've been to the Moot Hall. It's all so . . . unnecessary. We should be living together in harmony, not looking for trouble all the time.' He looked again at her, frowning. 'What have you got there, apples? Aren't the apples in our own orchard good enough for you?' His face broke into a smile as he spoke.

'Ah, but these are English apples,' she said, smiling back at him. 'And this is an English basket, both bought from English stalls.'

He gave a sigh. 'Oh, Anna. If only more of our people would do the same,' he said sadly.

'Language is one of the problems there,' she said thoughtfully.

'It is, indeed. But obviously, you managed because you've learned to speak English. Maybe we should practise it together. It will be good for both of us.'

A look of uncertainty crossed her face. 'Not all the time,' she pleaded.

He smiled. 'Oh, no. Most certainly not all the time.'

After supper that night, when they were sitting either side of the fire that was still needed in the hall against the evening chill, Samuel said quietly, 'I've told you my history, Anna, now I think it's time you told me who you are.'

She looked up, startled. 'What do you mean? You know who I am. I'm Jan Verlender's wife – widow,' her voice faltered slightly at the word.

He nodded. 'I know you were married to my gardener, and that he was an expert in his field. But your manner, indeed, your manners, indicate to me that you have been used to . . .' he hesitated, anxious not to offend her memory of Jan '. . . shall we say that you have been used to a less *rustic* kind of life? You have had no trouble at all in adjusting to the way I live, never once have I had to explain to you how things are done here. I noticed, too, that the cloak you were wearing today was made of expensive cloth, and that your shoes, although well worn, are of the best quality. Your husband was a fine gardener, Anna, the best I have known, and the last thing I would wish to do is to belittle him or his abilities, because I have no doubt his skills would have been widely sought after in due course and he would have become a rich man, had he lived.' He paused. 'Nevertheless, I am fairly sure that up to now his earnings could never have provided you with what you were wearing today.'

'I didn't steal them, if that's what you're thinking,' she said a trifle truculently, stalling for time as she wondered how much of her history she could safely reveal.

'Don't be ridiculous. Of course I know you didn't steal them,' he said impatiently. 'Just as I know Jan could never have afforded to buy them for you.' He leaned forward, his hands clasped loosely between his knees. 'You've told me you had to leave Flanders in a hurry, that you had to travel light. Why was that, Anna? What were you fleeing from? Religious persecution?' He shook his head. 'I think not, because in that case your parents would have fled, too. So what was it? Can't you tell me?'

She was silent for some time, weighing up the risk, then she said, staring into the fire all the while she was talking, 'I met Jan when he came to our house to make a knot garden for my father and we fell in love. We used to meet in an old loom shed at the bottom of the garden and we planned to marry when he had earned enough to keep a wife. We knew my father would never agree to us marrying, of course. Father was very proud of his position in the town, so for his only daughter to marry a humble gardener would have been a terrible humiliation.' Her expression softened. 'But my Jan was a better man than my father ever knew how to be.' Now her voice hardened. 'Then I discovered that my father was about to marry me off to a rich old clothier – I could have said *sell* me off because that's what it amounted to. Otto de Hane was going to pay off all father's debts in return for my hand in marriage.' She shuddered. 'He was a horrible old man, old enough to be my grandfather. When I told Jan he was furious and he immediately arranged for our escape to England, where we would be out of my father's reach.' She looked up. 'So that's how we came to be here and now you know my story, Samuel.'

'Why have you never told me before?' he asked quietly.

'I've thought about it, but I was afraid you might have known either my father or Otto de Hane. I didn't want to run the risk of them finding out where I was. You are all clothiers and there is a good deal of trade between the two countries, so it was quite possible.'

'So why have you told me now?'

'Partly because you asked. You've never asked before.' She gave a shrug. 'And because it doesn't matter any more. If you tell my father and he drags me back to marry that old man I shan't care. The best part of my life is over. I don't care what happens to me now that Jan and my child are both dead.' She turned bleak eyes on him.

A look of real pain crossed his face. 'Anna, you mustn't talk like that! The best part of your life is *not* over. You are – what? Twenty?'

'Nineteen,' she confessed.

'Then you have many useful years ahead of you. You'll marry again . . .'

'*Never!*'

'That's what you say now.' His voice dropped. 'I'm sorry. It was insensitive of me to even speak of it. But believe me, in a few years . . . But that's for the future.' His voice rose again. 'Now, for the present, I have ordered samples of material to be brought so that you can choose some new gowns and whatever you need to go with them.' He held up his hand as she opened her mouth to protest. 'Oh, I realise you are not in the least bit interested; all the same, I wish you to do this because on Midsummer Day, when my garden should be at its very best, I am planning to have a party so that all my friends and business acquaintances, both Dutch and English, can walk round and see the fruits of your husband's labours.' He put his head on one side and smiled at her. 'Can you think of a better memorial to Jan than the beautiful garden he created, Anna?'

She shook her head, her eyes filling with tears. 'No, Samuel. I can't.'

'And afterwards we shall refresh ourselves, either in the garden or here in the hall, with the most succulent food my kitchen can provide. Griete and the other servants will need your guidance with that, of course.'

She looked faintly alarmed. 'But I'm no . . .'

'I'm sure you'll manage very well, Anna,' he interrupted smoothly. 'But to get back to what we were saying, I shall require your presence, and looking suitably well-dressed, which is why I have ordered the samples of material to be brought. Naturally, they will be from material made on my own looms. There are two or three very nice striped tobines, a pretty russet mockadoe and a blue velvet that should suit your colouring very well. If there is anything else you need, you have only to ask. There is a very good sewing woman who lives in the town and she will be coming here to make up the material for you. That's all I have to say on the matter.'

She was silent for several minutes and he could see she was battling with herself. Finally, she managed to smile. 'Thank you, Samuel.' She dipped her head slightly. 'You're very kind to me.'

'I have good reason to be,' he replied a trifle gruffly.

They were both silent for some time, each busy with their thoughts. Then she said, 'Have you ever heard the name Otto de Hane, Samuel?'

He thought for a moment, then shook his head. 'No, it's not a name I know.'

'Cornelis Fromenteel?'

'Is that your father?'

'He's the man who was willing to sell me off to pay his debts,' she said bitterly.

He frowned. 'That's a name I believe I may have heard mentioned but I've never done business with the man,' he said. He held up his hand. 'And before you ask, your secret is quite safe with me.'

'Thank you, Samuel.' She picked up her sewing. Time enough to tell Samuel about her real father when she was certain that Henrick Crowbroke, whom she had seen at the Bay Hall, was the man. She wondered if he would be at Samuel's party.

In spite of herself Anna couldn't help being interested in the samples of material Samuel had chosen, especially as the russet cloth she had noticed being sheared at the Bay Hall was among them. She chose this one immediately. Not only because she knew the colour would suit her fair skin and hair, but rather because her mother used to wear a gown made of the same material and it would make her feel closer. And Henrick Crowbroke might recognise it? She smiled at her own naivety; surely not even Cornelis Fromenteel would force his wife to wear gowns that were that old.

Exciting, too, was the business of choosing patterns and standing still for what seemed hours while Mistress Sadler – Samuel had been careful to choose an English sempstress – pinned and tucked and offered suggestions as to what would go best with this and that. Anna had to confess that she was enjoying herself as the sewing woman held various materials up against her, saying this yellow would look well as a stomacher to go with the green and yellow striped tobine skirt, and this one, in cream and silver would be fine with the blue velvet, especially with silver lace at the sleeves and hem. Being eased into the stiff leather corset and the large semi-circular side pieces that had to be laced to it was less pleasant, but as Mistress Sadler breathlessly remarked as she tugged on the laces, firm undergarments made a gown hang so much better. So Anna submitted with as good a grace as she could muster as the laces of the stomacher were dragged in tightly at the waist, reflecting that when she left home her mother hadn't considered her old enough to be laced in like this and all she had worn under her petticoat was her chemise.

Whilst all the measuring and fitting was going on Mistress Sadler talked, her tongue moving almost as fast as her needle. All it needed was a chance remark, or a simple question from Anna and she was off. Sometimes she didn't even wait for that.

'My husband didn't want me to take on this work,' she said one morning as she pinned Anna into the first of the gowns. 'He said I shouldn't work for a Stranger. But I said a Stranger's money is as good as an Englishman's and we've got to eat.'

'He doesn't like the Dutch?' Anna asked.

'Not since our trouble.'

Anna said nothing. She knew she wouldn't have long to wait for the whole story.

'Ezra was happy enough to work for a Stranger at one time,' she said, through a mouthful of pins. 'He was a wool-comber. He used to work for Master Stowteheton, who lives in a big house in Head Street. Did all right with him, too. The Master always made sure he was paid on the dot for his work and there was always plenty of work for him to do. I often used to spin the yarn after he'd combed it.' She paused, adjusting the pins, then leaned back to survey her work. 'Bah, there's no money in spinning. I was lucky if I could earn threepence a day. I took up stitching instead. I've always been good with my needle. My mother taught me.'

'What was this trouble, you talked about?' Anna prompted.

'Our house burned down.' Her tone was quite matter-of-fact. 'We used to live down by Middle Mill.'

'Oh, how dreadful for you. How did that happen?' It was a

common enough occurrence. With a combination of thatched roofs and timber-framed houses, fire was one of the greatest hazards.

'Well, you see, wool-combing has to be done with hot combs. Makes the wool easier to untangle. The wool is hooked over a bracket on the wall of the combing shed and then these heavy combs are pulled through it to untangle and straighten it out. It's a heavy old job, skilled, too, because the combs weigh quite a bit. Of course a fire has to be kept going to heat the combs, and Ezra's was a proper brick-built one; he was fussy about it because of the danger. Anyway, he'd got the door open because it was a hot day and a draught must have caught a spark and blown it on to a bale of wool waiting to be done. By the time Ezra noticed it was well alight, too far gone for the bucket of water he kept close by to dowse it. Well, the shed was next to the house, so it didn't take long to get to the thatch and that was that. We saved what we could but Ezra got burned very bad trying to save his combs and the rest of the wool. He needn't have bothered. He's never been able to work since.'

'Oh, dear. That's terrible,' Anna said with a frown. 'But it could hardly be blamed on Mynheer Stowteheton, could it?'

'No, no. It wasn't his fault we didn't get any money. We never said it was. It was them as give out the poor money they collect in fines from the Bay Hall who were to blame. The Dutch said we were English so they shouldn't have to pay us out of their poor fund and the English said that since Ezra was working for the Strangers when the house burned down it was the Strangers who should pay. They haggled and haggled and in the end nobody paid us anything. We've never had a penny from anywhere. But Ezra still blames the Strangers; he said they ought to have been the ones who paid because he was working for one of them, that's why he didn't want me to come here. But I'm not so sure. After all, we were English poor, not Dutch, so really we should have been paid by our own people. But you could argue about it till the cows come home so it's no good complaining. I just thank the good Lord I've got enough skill in my fingers to give us food in our bellies and a roof over our heads.'

'Where do you live now?'

'We've got a place in Bull Yard, off Crouch Street. Nice little place, it is. I used to fret because I was barren but now I'm

139

thankful we haven't got a brood of children to be fed and clothed. I make enough to keep us comfortable and to pay for the poppy juice that keeps Ezra's pain at bay. We don't want for anything.' She sat back on her heels. 'There. I think that's about right. Let's get it off you and I'll start stitching.'

Anna was quite sad when the sewing was all finished and Mistress Sadler brought the finished garments to her for her approval because she had enjoyed learning about the older woman's life. Each gown she tried on she liked even better than the last and she was young enough to appreciate that Mistress Sadler's advice had been sound. As she surveyed her image in the looking glass in her chamber she saw a comely woman, with strikingly violet blue eyes and a clear complexion. Living under Samuel's roof she had put on a little weight, rounding her cheeks and her figure, which the clever seamstress had enhanced with tight lacing. A small starched ruff and an apron embroidered in the colours of the skirt it was to be worn with, completed the picture.

Samuel insisted on her putting on each dress to show him and she saw both surprise and admiration in his eyes as she stood for his inspection. But all he did was to nod coolly and say, 'That will do very well,' thus discouraging her from expressing gratitude at his generosity.

At the same time as this frenzy of fitting and sewing was taking place in one part of the house, Anna was making sure she had time to help Griete in the kitchen, where they spent hours trying to decide on the right kind of food for Samuel's party. Now that she was in charge of things Anna was anxious not to let him down, although she had never done anything quite like it before.

First she instructed Griete to ask her friends who were servants in other big houses for their favourite recipes, then she added a few ingredients that she hoped might improve the taste. Sometimes they did, in which case she stored the recipe in her mind, and sometimes they didn't, in which case it was discarded. She tried to dredge her own mind, trying to remember the kind of thing Bettris used to serve when Cornelis entertained. This wasn't much help. For one thing Cornelis didn't entertain much and for another, he was parsimonious in the extreme so meals were always simple. Nevertheless, she spent a lot of time in the kitchen, where she and Griete concocted new dishes and practised old and tried ones. Gradually, some kind of a menu emerged, mostly by trial and error.

At the same time the house had to be cleaned and polished from top to bottom in case guests wandered in and decided to explore. All the pewter was given an extra scouring with the plant known as horsetails to make it gleam and all the rooms were well-swept and strewn with wormwood to discourage fleas. Tables were polished and wall-hangings and tapestries were taken down, beaten and rehung.

'I really don't think it is necessary for you to go to these lengths, Anna,' Samuel said, as she nearly fell asleep over her supper. 'You're wearing yourself out.'

'The gardeners are busy making sure there is not a weed to be seen. I wouldn't want your house to disgrace you, Samuel.'

He gave a short, barking laugh. 'There's no danger of that. Since you've been in charge of my household the place has sparkled as never before. There are no rolls of fluff under the beds or little piles of dust in the corners any more. The cobwebs have all gone and the windows sparkle.' He inclined his head. 'I am indebted to you for your diligence, my dear.' His eyes were warm as he spoke and she coloured slightly.

'It is no more than any watchful housekeeper would do,' she said with a shrug.

'Housekeeper? Is that how you regard yourself?' he asked, raising his eyebrows.

'I . . . well, you asked me to run your household . . . isn't that what . . .?'

He waved his hand. 'No matter.' He got up from his chair. 'I have some accounts to attend to. Please excuse me.'

After he had left she remained sitting where she was for a long time. Samuel had not seemed pleased when she spoke of herself as his housekeeper. Yet in all honesty what else could she call herself?

Chapter Sixteen

As she lay in bed that night Anna reflected, not for the first time, on her position at Garden House. Samuel had seemed almost offended when she described herself as his housekeeper. She wondered why. Did he think she was being presumptuous in giving herself that title? Yet he was content to leave the running of the house more and more in her hands and he had noticed the improvements because Anna didn't tolerate slovenliness in servants. So what *was* she if not his housekeeper?

Or was that not how he saw her? Had he other ideas for her? He had hinted that she would marry again in due course. He was mistaken, of course, nobody could ever take Jan's place. But was this what he had in mind? Did he anticipate making her his wife in the fullness of time? She didn't think so. It was not likely that that a man in his position would ever consider marrying the widow of his gardener.

It was not as if he had ever shown any particular affection towards her. He had never even touched her hand except by accident, and never by so much as a look had he given her the impression that he might find her attractive, let alone that he had fallen in love with her.

On the other hand, perhaps he realised it was too soon for this, that her grief was still too raw. If that was so she could only respect him for it.

There was, of course, the other question: how did she feel about Samuel? She searched her mind carefully, frowning up into the darkness, trying to be completely honest with herself. She was very grateful to him for giving her a home in his beautiful house, that went without saying. And she enjoyed looking after things, working with his servants to make sure everything ran smoothly. Indeed, she regarded Griete as her friend rather than simply as another servant.

She was no longer in awe of him as she had been at the beginning; she liked going with him to the Bay Hall and learning about the cloth trade. And she now felt quite at ease when they sat together after supper, quietly talking over the day while she sewed and he tried the new habit of smoking tobacco in a long pipe, which made him cough. She supposed it was true to say they had become good friends. But that was all. She couldn't imagine ever wanting to take him to her bed and doing the things she had so enjoyed with Jan, things that she often ached for. This was not just a matter of age, although he must be at least twenty years her senior, it was simply that their relationship was not, and as far as she could see, never could be of such an intimate kind. In truth, she was perfectly happy for things to continue as they were, but she realised that the generosity was all on his side and that one day he might wish to extract payment.

The thought gave her no pleasure and to avoid dwelling on it she turned over and set her mind to preparations for the forthcoming party.

Midsummer's Day dawned with a haze that promised heat. The garden was at its best, the borders and flower beds bursting with colour, the lawns trimmed by the gardeners to a soft green carpet and the rose arbour a riot of yellow blooms. The box hedges that edged the herbs in the knot gardens had been cut with geometric precision and the herbs scented the air with lavender and thyme, sage and marjoram. The two gardeners who now tended the garden scuttled about, making sure there was never a weed in sight, propping a drooping flower head here, nipping off a faded bloom there. In the kitchen garden, peas and beans marched in arrow straight rows flanked by onions, carrots and turnips.

Samuel walked round the whole garden at least three times, peering minutely in every corner and under every leaf.

The gardeners both watched him with growing amusement. 'I reckon he's afraid a weed's gonna pop its head up while he's not lookin',' one said to the other.

'I'll give you a farthin' if he finds one,' the second one said with a laugh, knowing his money was safe.

Inside the house, things were less peaceful. Extra helpers had been drafted in from the town and there was much scurrying to and fro between the kitchen and the big hall, where it had been decided after much deliberation that the food should be served, rather than outside in the garden.

There was roast chine of beef, a roast pig, and a haunch of venison. There were jellied neats' tongues, baked chewits – pies made with minced meat – venison pasties and savoury puddings of all kinds. There was fish from the fish ponds, made into little patties or served whole with a sprinkling of dill. To eat with all these delicacies was manchet – the best white bread made from the finest flour and a selection of sallets – vegetables prepared in a variety of ways, from simple to exotic. There were sauces to go with all these delicacies, sharp, spicy sauces, bland sauces, thick sauces, thin sauces. Anna and Griete had experimented much with these and were pleased with both the appearance and the taste of the results.

But even more time-consuming had been the sweetmeats to follow. There were syllabubs, candied fruit, sweet wafers, ginger-bread, marchpane and a whole dish of fancy shapes made from sugar paste and garnished with rosemary dipped first in egg white and then in sugar to give it a frosted appearance.

To finish the meal were big round cheeses.

The whole feast was set out on long trestle tables in the hall, which was decorated with greenery and such flowers as could be spared from the garden.

As the guests began to arrive they were given a cup of cordial and invited to wander in the garden. Samuel wandered with them, dressed in dark blue breeches and striped jacket, with a wide ruff that had given him a few anxious moments when his manservant had had trouble fastening it. On his head he wore a soft blue velvet hat with a ruby brooch pinned to it. Anna, keeping well into the background and wearing the russet dress Mistress Sadler had finished only that morning, thought he looked very smart, although she didn't feel it her place to tell him so.

Samuel was not so reticent. 'You look charming, Anna,' he told her, his eyes warm with approval. He fingered the material of her skirt briefly. 'That mockadoe has made up well.'

'Thank you, Samuel,' she replied, slightly annoyed that his

compliment was directed towards her dress and not herself. 'I'm glad I don't disgrace the skill of your weavers.'

But her sarcasm was lost on him as he hurried off to greet his guests.

She soon forgave him when he made a speech, giving full credit to his late gardener, Jan Verlender, telling his guests how hard Jan had worked, planning and making the garden and speaking of his enthusiasm and skill in choosing plants and flowers. His voice dropped as he told how Jan had been so cruelly smitten with plague on the way back from an errand to Flanders to buy special bulbs. Anna noted that Samuel didn't mention the word 'tulip' and she smiled a little. No doubt before long someone else would be sent to buy them so that he could be the first in Colchester to grow them. Then her eyes glistened with tears as he spread his arms and announced that his beautiful garden was both a tribute and a memorial to a very special man.

Everybody clapped and murmured agreement and then continued their wanderings.

Samuel came to find her. 'Weren't you in the garden? Didn't you hear what I said about Jan?' he asked a trifle impatiently.

'I was just inside the window. I heard every word,' she said. 'Thank you, Samuel. I'm sure it would have embarrassed Jan to hear your words, but it gave me great pleasure.'

'Good. I'm glad.' He hurried off to talk to his guests.

Standing by the door, Anna had a good view of the crowd. The guests were mostly men, although a few had brought their wives. Some were English but they were mostly Dutch and it was noticeable that the two races rarely mixed. The English on the whole were dressed more brightly and extravagantly than the Strangers and appeared more ready to enjoy themselves. Anna kept an anxious eye open for Henrick Crowbroke and at last she saw him, standing at the end of the garden, looking at one of the statues that had been placed on plinths where the paths ended.

She hurried over to him. 'The feast will begin shortly, Mynheer,' she said in her native tongue.

He swung round. 'All in good time. I'm not yet ready to eat,' he said abruptly, dismissing her with a wave of his hand.

'Just as you wish, Mynheer.' She gave a little bob of a curtsey and turned away, her heart thumping. She had glimpsed the colour of Henrick Crowbroke's eyes and they were blue. Quite a dark blue. As far as she could see they didn't have the deep violent tint of her own eyes but perhaps that was because the man was older, perhaps the colour faded with age.

She walked slowly through the garden, wondering how she could engage him in conversation and find out something of his past. It would be difficult. His tone had been very abrupt, dismissive, rude, even. On first acquaintance she had to admit she didn't like the man.

She rounded a corner and walked straight into a young Englishman. She could tell he was English because he was wearing dark green breeches and a peacock-blue tunic. He had a cape over one shoulder, lined with silk of the same peacock blue and fastened with a large silver clasp. He wore a dark red velvet hat with a feather.

He swept the hat off and bowed low. 'I beg your pardon, Madam. I nearly knocked you into the hedge,' he said, his voice full of consternation. He offered her his arm. 'Can I escort you to your husband?'

She shook her head, smiling. 'Thank you, but no. I am a widow. My husband was Jan Verlender.'

'Then I am honoured to meet the wife of the man who designed such a beautiful garden,' he said with a smile. 'Will you sit here with me a few moments and tell me about him?'

'Indeed I will.' They sat down together on a stone seat at the end of a grassy walk while she told him about Jan and his skill as a gardener.

'I wish my father had come with me this afternoon. He would have been most interested,' he said when she had finished.

'He is not here, then?'

He made a face and leaned towards her conspiratorially. 'I have a confession to make. My father doesn't like your people,' he whispered. He shook his head impatiently. 'Not that I share his prejudices. But he refuses to see reason. He insists that the Strangers have taken trade from the English. He is furious that all the English cloth has to go to the Bay Hall to be examined and given the seal by the Strangers.' He shrugged. 'I can see his argument, up to a point, it would be better if the English were responsible for examining their cloth and likewise the Dutch.'

'Or even if the Dutch examined the English cloth and the

English examined the Dutch?' Anna asked with a smile. 'Would that not be fair?'

'It would be better than the way things are at the moment,' he agreed. 'It hardly seems right that it is all in the hands of the Strangers. Although in fairness to them I must say they are very thorough and as a result any bale of cloth sealed with the Colchester seal of quality is accepted without question everywhere it is sent.' He pinched his lip. 'There's another thing, too. My father gets annoyed at the babble of foreign language he hears everywhere these days. He thinks all Strangers should learn to speak English. As you have. You are learning to speak English very well, Madam, if I may say so.'

'Not as well as I should like,' she admitted. 'I find some words very difficult.'

'That's because your words come from your throat, whereas ours are on our tongue. It's a totally different way of forming words.' He paused, then went back to his former theme. 'I think my father is obstinate in his dislike of the Dutch, so when he refused to accept Mynheer Hegetorne's kind invitation I decided it would be churlish if one of us didn't come, so here I am.' His gave her a warm smile. 'I'm glad I came. I wouldn't have met you if I hadn't.'

As his gaze lingered on her, Anna felt her colour rising in pleasure. He continued to hold her gaze. 'My name is Paul Markham,' he said softly. 'I've enjoyed talking to you this afternoon and I should like to talk to you again. I'm afraid it may not be very easy with all the antagonism between our people, but I promise you I shall find a way.' He stood up and took her hand to help her to her feet. Before he released it he put it to his lips.

When he had gone she sank back on to the bench. She had only to close her eyes to see Paul Markham's warm brown eyes, the way his dark hair curled round the rim of his hat, his long straight nose and firm chin. Unlike many men he was clean-shaven, revealing a square-set jaw with a hint of stubbornness. He was the first man she had looked at, really looked at, since Jan's death and she had to admit she had liked what she had seen. She had liked it very much. She put the thought from her mind with a pang of guilt at her disloyalty to Jan's memory.

'Are you the woman who spoke to me earlier?' It was Henrick Crowbroke's voice breaking into her thoughts.

Startled, she opened her eyes and got to her feet in one movement.

'You told me the food was about to be served. Where is it?' he asked rudely.

'In the house, Mynheer. In the large hall at the front,' she answered, keeping her voice polite with difficulty. 'Would you like me to show you?'

'No, I would not. I am perfectly capable of finding my own way.' He strode off.

Anna sat down again and watched him go stalking along the path, with a feeling of dismay. Was that rude, arrogant man striding through the garden and looking neither to left nor right the man her mother had fallen in love with? Could he really be her own father? She had so little to go on. His hair was fair – flecked with grey now, but that was only to be expected – his eyes were a very dark blue and his name was Henrick. Common sense told her that there must be any number of men answering to that description. But if this was the man she was looking for she had to admit that she was disappointed. He was not at all the kind of man she had expected her father would be. She had hoped for a kindly, humorous man with a gentle manner, not someone whose behaviour resembled Cornelis Fromenteel, the man her mother had married.

Samuel came hurrying towards her, interrupting her thoughts. 'Come, Anna, the feast is about to begin. You're needed in the hall. I want to introduce you to the guests.' He held out his hand towards her.

She looked up at him, slightly alarmed. 'I don't think it would be appropriate, Samuel . . .'

'I'll decide what is and what isn't appropriate,' he cut in sharply. 'Come along.' He grabbed her hand and almost pulled her to her feet.

She managed to walk just half a step behind him as he strode up the garden and into the house but once they were inside he made sure she was at his side as he introduced her as the widow of Jan, his highly acclaimed gardener.

Anna noted with interest the way his introduction was received. A few men bowed low and said they were honoured to meet her, some hardly deigned to acknowledge her. Several eyebrows were raised as Samuel, apparently noticing nothing amiss, explained

148

that she was now looking after his house for him. One man sniggered loudly at this, saying 'And we all know what *that* means,' in a loud stage whisper, which made Anna blush but Samuel ignored.

'Ah, Henrick,' he said when he saw Henrick Crowbroke, already seated and hacking off lumps of roast pork. 'You haven't met Mistress Verlender, my esteemed gardener's widow, have you?'

'We met a little earlier, in the garden,' Anna said coolly.

The man made a great play of wiping his knife on the napkin provided. 'Did we? I don't remember,' he said gruffly.

'You asked me to direct you to the food,' she reminded him.

'Did I? Yes, I may have done.' He turned his attention back to his plate, clearly embarrassed.

'I hope the servants have provided everything to your liking,' she said, hoping he would look up so that she could make sure that his eyes really were dark blue.

'Yes. Yes. Very nice,' he muttered without taking his eyes from his plate.

Disappointed, Anna slipped away to the kitchen to make sure everything was running smoothly, leaving Samuel to take his place at the table. Then she stood by the screen, ready to call one of the serving girls to replace empty dishes or to direct the boys with the wine to empty goblets. It was interesting to note that the English sat at a table on their own and it was also interesting that although there were empty spaces at their table none of the Dutch people in the company chose to sit with them. Anna wondered whether there would ever be harmony between the two races. In such a small town as Colchester it was incredible how they could remain so separate and so unfriendly towards one another.

When the time came for the serving girls to remove the meats and savouries and to bring round bowls of water for the guests to wash their fingers before serving the sweetmeats, Samuel excused himself from the table where he was sitting and went to sit with the Englishmen.

A few eyebrows were raised at this but before long he was joined by first one and then another of his countrymen. Soon there were no seats left at the English table and Samuel had to call for more stools to be brought although the atmosphere, though polite, was far from cordial at first. But by the end of the feast tongues had been loosened by the freely flowing wine and friendships

149

were forged amid much back-slapping and camaraderie, most of which would be forgotten by the time the effects of the wine had worn off the next day.

When the guests had all gone Anna stood with Samuel and surveyed the remains of the feast, the overturned goblets, the half-eaten pies and puddings that had taken so long to decorate, the stains on the white tablecloths and the food trampled into the tiles.

'Do you think everyone enjoyed it?' Samuel asked wryly.

'It looks like it,' Anna replied with a smile. 'I'll call the servants and we'll begin clearing up.'

'Let them do it,' Samuel waved his hand impatiently. 'Come and walk in the garden with me.'

It was cool in the garden. Crickets chirped and an owl hooted in the trees. As dusk fell bats swooped and circled, scribbling a path in the rosy evening sky.

They walked in silence for a while. It was a comfortable silence and Anna was reluctant to speak and spoil it.

'I think Jan would have been pleased, don't you?' Samuel said at last.

'Yes, he would have been pleased that his garden gave so much pleasure,' Anna replied.

'Henrick Crowbroke was very impressed,' he said thoughtfully. 'He's not an easy man. Doesn't give compliments lightly.'

'He didn't bring his wife?' Anna asked tentatively, glad he had brought the name up.

'His wife died in childbirth soon after they arrived here. He never married again,' Samuel answered.

'When was that?' Anna held her breath.

'Oh, I don't know. About twenty-five years ago, I should say. He'd been here some years before I arrived.' He turned to her and gave a wry smile. 'Why do you ask? He's not looking for another wife, if that's what you're wondering.'

'And I'm not looking for another husband,' she said, her eyes flashing with temper. 'Not now. Not ever.'

He put his hand out to her. 'Oh, Anna. I'm sorry. I should never have said that.' He shook his head to clear it. 'The wine must have gone to my head and loosened my tongue. It was much stronger than I realised. Please forgive me.'

'There's nothing to forgive,' she said coldly. 'But now, if you don't mind, I'll go and see if the servants have finished clearing

the hall and then I shall go to bed. I'm very tired. Goodnight.'
Without waiting for him to reply she turned and hurried back to
the house.

One thing was certain. Henrick Crowbroke could not have been
her mother's lover. She was glad. She was sure her father,
whoever he might be, was not as rude and boorish as that man. But
where was he? Who was he? Would she ever find him?

Chapter Seventeen

'I've been elected to be one of the Governors at the Bay Hall,' Samuel announced one evening when Anna had been living at the Garden House for nearly a year. They had finished their meal and were sitting in the garden in the last of the late summer sun.

'What exactly does that mean?' Anna asked carefully, thinking perhaps that she ought to know, having visited the Bay Hall many times with him.

But Samuel was only too willing to explain. 'There are two Governors,' he began.

'One Dutch, one English?' Anna asked innocently, even though she knew this wasn't so.

'No. You know very well they are both are members of the Dutch Congregation,' he replied testily. 'Then there is a committee of twenty-two who are elected to inspect all the fabric that goes through the Bay Hall.' He held up his hand as he saw her open her mouth to speak. 'I know what you're going to say and yes, these men are Dutch, too. The reason for this is that when the scheme was first set up the new draperies, as they were called, were only just beginning to be manufactured in England although they had been made for some time in Flanders. So of course we knew more about them. And that's why the examining system in the Bay Hall was set up and run by us. It's always worked very well so the authorities have seen no need to change it.'

'The English don't like it,' Anna pointed out. 'There are always fights and riots there.'

'I know they don't like it. But they admit it is a fair system. All the fines are scrupulously allotted, English fines to the English poor, Dutch fines to our poor. But surely, I've told you all this before.'

'Yes,' she said thoughtfully, 'And you always say the system is fair. But I've noticed that the English cloth seems to get rejected more often than the Dutch cloth. The threads are uneven, the cloth is "waisted", the dye is streaky, the lengths are short, there always seems to be something that makes the English cloth inferior.'

'Then they should look to their craftsmen.' He got to his feet. 'It's getting colder. I'm going inside. I have a busy day tomorrow. My first day as Governor.' He squared his shoulders proudly.

'I hope you'll look to your examiners,' she said rashly, 'to make sure they don't favour their own people over the English.'

'Perhaps you'd like to come with me?' he asked, his tone cold, 'To make sure I do the job properly?'

'No, thank you, Samuel.' She smiled up at him. 'I'm sorry. I shouldn't have spoken like that. I know you have very good friends among the English and I'm sure you'll make a very good and fair Governor.'

He inclined his head stiffly to acknowledge her apology. 'Are you coming in?' he asked, offering her his arm.

'No, I think I'll stay out here for a little longer.' She pulled her shawl round her shoulders. 'I like the garden at this time of day. I can almost imagine Jan is just round the next corner and that he'll appear and that . . .' She broke off and glanced at him with an embarrassed smile. 'I expect you think I'm silly.'

'No, I don't think you're silly,' he said seriously. 'In fact, sometimes the same thought occurs to me, that Jan is still here, in his garden, watching, to make sure everything is as he would want it to be.' His voice softened. 'I try to make sure it is.' Suddenly, his tone changed and became brisk. 'Don't stay out here too long. We don't want you catching a chill.'

He strode off and Anna watched him go, shaking her head thoughtfully. He was a strange man. Sometimes she wondered if she knew him at all.

Blackie, who had been hiding in the bushes, emerged the moment Samuel left and jumped up on to Anna's lap. She sat for a long time in the gathering dusk, stroking the little cat, savouring the scent of the lavender that grew by the wall of the house and listening to the distant cry of a lonely owl. She was happy here, she loved this garden, just as she loved the house, but more and more she was beginning to feel uneasy about her position here.

Because she was neither wife nor servant, but something in between. Even her friendship with Griete was showing signs of strain as Samuel treated her more and more as his property and gave her more and more authority yet without giving her the official status of wife.

Not that he had ever, by the merest hint, suggested that he had any desire to take her to his bed.

Sometimes, in her more depressed moments, she would stand and look at her reflection in the window and wonder if she had lost all her attractiveness. She used to be quite pretty, she knew that, but had her looks faded so completely that she was no longer worth a second glance?

Yet she knew this was not so from the leering looks and nudges she received when she was at the Bay Hall with Samuel. It was obvious that many people there already assumed that she was Samuel's mistress. It was awkward. They wanted to treat her with the contempt they felt she deserved but were unwilling to risk Samuel's wrath if they did. Samuel, of course, didn't even appear to notice.

It was the same at the new Dutch church that had finally been built, a grand wooden building in Head Street, with a house for the predikant at the back. Samuel wanted her to sit beside him at Sunday worship but she had managed to persuade him that she would be more comfortable sitting with Griete and the other servants in the seat below. Even so, he escorted her into and out of the church, which she knew caused people to whisper behind their backs. It was a very difficult situation and made her feel very uncomfortable.

In a very few weeks it would be a year since Jan's death. Whilst he held – and would always hold – a special place in her heart and there were times when grief for him almost overwhelmed her, these times were getting fewer and easier to bear. She realised that life moved on; she couldn't stay rooted to the past; Jan wouldn't want that.

Did Samuel realise this? Was he biding his time until the year was up? Then would he begin to reveal his feelings towards her? And if he did how would she answer him?

She lifted Blackie off her lap and stood up and began to walk about the garden in the gathering gloom, pondering on the situation. She didn't love Samuel, not in the way a wife should love her husband, although a good many marriages had been based on a good deal less than the friendship and common interests that they shared. Marriage to Samuel would mean she could continue to live in his beautiful house, in fact, her lifestyle would change very little, except that there would be children . . . Her thoughts went off at a tangent as she thought of the baby she had borne but never even seen. She would dearly love to have children, she thought wistfully.

But suppose she should agree to be Samuel's wife and then fall in love with someone else?

She gave herself a little shake. That was a ridiculous idea. She would never, ever fall in love again. Then, unbidden, an image came into her mind of a man with warm brown eyes, a firm, clean-shaven chin and dark curling hair. She recognised him at once, of course. He was an Englishman and his name was Paul Markham.

He was a man it would be very easy to fall in love with.

She had seen him several times on her visits to the Bay Hall with Samuel, but always from a distance, although she rather thought he would like to come and talk to her. But she guessed that he, like most people, assumed she was Samuel's . . . what? Secretary? Mistress? Prospective wife? Housekeeper?

She sighed and turned to go into the house. How could anybody know what her position was when she didn't even know herself?

It was a month after being made Governor that Samuel invited Anna to accompany him to the Bay Hall again.

'You'll find it very interesting now and it will give you an idea of what we're up against,' he said, rubbing his hands together. He was clearly enjoying his new status.

'Oh, I can appreciate some of the difficulties, Samuel,' she said. 'And perhaps now you're Governor you'll be able to make sure that people are treated fairly.'

He gave her a sharp glance. 'What do you know of people being treated unfairly?'

She raised her eyebrows. 'Why, Mistress Sadler, who made my new gowns. Surely you know what happened to her?'

'Only that she was recommended as the best seamstress in the town.'

'She is indeed. But it was her husband who was treated unfairly. He was a wool-comber, and worked for a Dutch clothier. There was a fire at their house and he was so badly burned he couldn't work again.'

'So?'

'The Dutch wouldn't pay him from their poor fund because he was English and the English wouldn't pay him from theirs because he worked for a Stranger. So the poor man got no money from anywhere. They would have starved if Mistress Sadler hadn't been so handy with her needle.'

'I didn't know that. I must look into it.'

'The Sadlers have no need of charity but it would be well to make sure the same thing doesn't happen again,' she agreed. She was silent for several minutes, then she said doubtfully, 'I'm not sure that I should come with you to the Bay Hall, Samuel.'

He raised his eyebrows in surprise. 'Why ever not?'

She opened her mouth and then closed it again. How could she tell him she felt uncomfortable in public with him because she didn't know how he – or anybody else, for that matter – regarded her? It would be tantamount to asking him to declare himself. On the other hand, it would be too embarrassing to tell him that there were some men, Samuel's own friends among them, whose lewd comments and sweaty hands left her in no doubt as to what they thought her status was.

'Well, your new position ... A woman might not be welcome ...'

'Nonsense. You'll enjoy it.' His tone brooked no further argument.

He was right, although the morning was far from peaceful.

As usual the Bay Hall was busy and noisy. They went first to the raw hall, where the cloth was examined before it was dyed and fulled. This was a long, low room, with long trestle tables on which each piece of cloth was rolled out and examined. It was full of people, a veritable Tower of Babel, with men calling to each other and arguing, some in Dutch, some in English and some in a mixture of both in an effort to make themselves understood. Anna automatically held the bunch of lavender she had brought with her to her nose against the smell of unwashed bodies overlaid with the stifling smell of newly woven, untreated cloth.

Jonas Brand, an English weaver was accused that his cloth was of an uneven weave.

'Thass not my fault,' he argued. 'How can I make the weave even when the yarn I'm sent ain't reg'lar. You can't fine me if I'm sent bad yarn. Fine the spinner.'

Samuel strode over to where the man who had examined the cloth, known as a 'searcher', stood, looking bemused because he didn't understand English.

'What's the trouble?' Samuel asked.

The weaver told him.

'And who is your master?'

'Silas Markham, the clothier from East Hill.'

'Do you get your yarn from his spinners?'

'Aye, I do. And a lot of rogues they are. It's hard to weave a decent cloth with the yarn I'm sent. An' all because he won't pay his spinners a decent price. They still spin with the distaff an' you can't get such an even yarn spinnin' with the distaff as you can with the spinnin' wheel. But I get the blame because the cloth is uneven, not them. An' it's me that has to pay the fine. An' I don't get no help from Owd Markham, neither, though thass his fault in the first place.'

He would have gone on complaining about his master but Samuel held up his hand and cut him off. 'I'll take this up with your master,' he said briskly. 'I'll visit him tomorrow.'

'No need.' The man lifted his arm and pointed. 'You can take it up with him right now. He's in the Whitehall, makin' trouble there, I don't doubt.'

Samuel turned away. 'Not a happy worker,' he murmured to Anna. 'Come, let's go and beard the lion right away.'

Anna followed him next door to the Whitehall. This hall had a different smell although there was still the all-pervading stench of unwashed bodies as men moved among the tables, examining minutely but swiftly the rolls of cloth brought in. But the cloth here had been dyed and fulled and the mixture of urine and fullers earth which, even after washing and beating left an aroma from the fulling process, mingling with the smell of the vegetable dyes and mordants, meant the room was filled with a lingering, unidentifiable yet distinctive smell. Occasionally, there was the sound of tearing cloth and raised voices as a piece was rejected.

'Silas Markham?' Samuel called.

'In the shearing room,' someone replied.

Samuel sighed. 'This way,' he said to Anna.

She followed him into a room behind the Whitehall. Again there were long trestle tables, but here men with huge scissors trimmed off the loose ends left by the teasles that had been used to raise the nap on the cloth. At other tables men expertly sheared patterns into the cloth, cutting deep enough into the pile to make a contrast, but not too deep as to weaken the fabric.

'Silas Markham?' Samuel called again.

'Someone calls my name?' A large, rather florid Englishman called back.

'It's the Guv'nor,' Anna heard someone tell him in a loud stage whisper.

'I don't care if it's the Lord Mayor of London,' Silas Markham said truculently. He lifted his head as he strolled over to Samuel. 'What is it you want with me, sir?'

Samuel ignored his insolent manner and for several minutes they discussed Jonas Brand's grievances.

Finally, Samuel said, 'Well, since the fine can't be imposed on the spinners, for one thing they don't earn enough to pay it and for another it's hardly their fault if the distaff spins unevenly at times, and since Jonas Brand can hardly be blamed for weaving uneven cloth if his yarn is poor, I suggest that you pay the fine, Silas Markham.' He nodded. 'That seems fair to me.'

Silas Markham's jaw dropped. 'You can't make me pay for a man's bad workmanship!'

'I think I can,' Samuel replied smoothly. 'The spinner and the weaver are both in your employment. The spinner is not to blame – you could provide her with a spinning wheel, which would solve the problem of uneven yarn. The weaver is not to blame, he can't weave good cloth if the yarn is uneven. So, I think the blame rests with you, Master Markham. You can pay the Deputy, over there in the corner and he will give the money to your bailiffs to distribute among the English poor.'

'You can't do this,' Silas Markham began to bluster. 'I won't pay. I'm not being dictated to by any jumped-up Dutch spawn of the devil. English cloth should be examined by the English, not by foreigners.' He stared round him helplessly, looking for someone else to vent his spleen on. He found it. He waved his fist in the air.

'Jonas Brand will suffer for this. He'll have to find a new master. I'll have no sneak-thief in my employ.'

'I think the Governor is fair, father. I think we should pay,' a quiet voice said at his elbow. 'And Jonas Brand is one of our best weavers. We can't afford to lose him.' Paul Markham turned to Samuel. 'Never fear, I will personally see that the fine is paid, Governor.'

'Good.' Samuel turned away, satisfied that justice would be done.

Before Anna could move Paul said, 'Mistress Verlender. I've seen you here several times before but this is the first time I've had the opportunity to speak to you. Perhaps you remember me?' He raised his eyebrows hopefully. 'We met at your . . .' he hesitated, then tried again. 'We met at Mynheer Hegetorne's party. My name is Paul Markham.'

'Indeed I do remember you,' she said warmly, feeling her cheeks flush with pleasure.

'Are you well?' he asked.

She nodded. 'Thank you, yes, I'm very well. And you?'

He made a face. 'Well enough. I suffer from choler – my father's choler to be exact. He is the most bad-tempered man on God's earth, I do believe.' He sighed. 'I seem to spend half my life following after him and smoothing the feathers he has ruffled. I apologise for his behaviour just now. He . . .'

'He hates us Strangers.'

He looked at her in surprise. 'How did you know that?'

'You told me so when we spoke at Samuel's party,' she reminded him, a twinkle in her eyes.

He looked both surprised and pleased. 'You even remembered our conversation?'

She nodded. 'I have a good memory.'

'Then you will remember that I said I would like to talk to you again,' he said softly, smiling into her eyes.

'Oh, yes. I remember that, too.' She smiled back at him.

'Anna!' Samuel voice at her elbow said curtly. 'It's time for us to go. Good day, Master Markham.'

Paul inclined his head towards Samuel. 'Good day to you, Mynheer Hegetorne.' He turned to Anna, his eyes puzzled. 'And to you, Mistress Verlender.'

He watched as Samuel, his hand possessively under Anna's

elbow, hurried her to the door and down the stairs to the waiting carriage.

'To the church,' Samuel instructed the coachman. 'There are things I have to discuss with the predikant.'

'What things, Samuel?' she asked carefully as he climbed into the carriage beside her.

'What? Oh, business matters,' he said absently.

'Then perhaps the coachman can take me home. I've been away most of the morning and Griete is very busy. She needs my help.'

He frowned. 'She has plenty of help. The other servants . . .'

'Cannot always be trusted when it comes to preserving,' she said swiftly. 'The apples have to be laid out in the apple store, a pig has been killed and must be salted, the beer is ready to be barrelled, the rest of the peas and beans have to be dried. Oh, there are a hundred and one things to be done at this time of the year.'

'Griete must manage as best she may. Salting pork is not a task you should do. It will ruin your hands.'

'There are other things. Bread to make . . .'

'Stop making difficulties. We are going to see the predikant and there's an end of it.'

She knew it was useless to argue so she sat in the corner of the carriage, fuming silently.

The carriage drove round to the back of the church to a large square courtyard, open at one side, the church, the predikant's house and stables and outhouses forming the other three sides.

Abraham van Migrode came out to greet them and took them inside, calling to Maria to bring ale and cakes.

Whilst Samuel was talking to Abraham about the problems of living in a foreign country, Anna managed to slip away, murmuring that she needed Maria's advice on the best way to preserve pig's trotters.

Neither of the men took any notice and the last thing she heard was Abraham saying, 'But Samuel, there are second and third generations of our people living here now. Why are they still considered to be Strangers?'

She didn't wait to hear Samuel's reply, but hurried along to the kitchen.

Maria was delighted to see her and over cakes and ale beside the fire they talked and talked, catching up on all the news.

'So,' Maria said, when the conversation lapsed. 'Your Jan has been dead for just over a year now.'

Anna stared into the fire. 'That's right, although sometimes it seems only yesterday . . .'

'Time you wed again,' Maria cut in briskly. She leaned forward confidentially. 'Is that what Master Hegetorne has come to see the predikant about today?' She tapped the side of her nose. 'Ah, I've heard things. It's all the talk in the market place, the way he takes you around with him, to the Bay Hall and such.'

Anna's jaw dropped. 'Just what have you heard, Maria?'

'Never you mind what I've heard,' Maria said mysteriously. 'All I'm saying is, if he's come to discuss wedding plans, then it's not before time.'

Anna pushed her beer mug away. Suddenly, she felt slightly sick. Was that what Samuel had come to see the predikant about? And if so, why hadn't he told her? Was she to have no say at all in the matter?

Chapter Eighteen

'Silas Markham is an unpleasant man,' Samuel said thoughtfully as the carriage carried them home. 'Most of the Englishmen I deal with are at least civil, even if we don't always agree, but that man I find rude in the extreme.'

'His son seems very nice,' Anna ventured.

Samuel swivelled round to look at her. 'Ah, yes. I saw you talking to him. You need to be careful or people will start talking about you.'

'People are already talking about me, if what I hear is correct,' Anna said quietly, staring out of the window.

'And what do you mean by that?'

She gave a sigh. 'Nothing.'

He frowned but said no more on the subject and when they arrived home Anna hurried off to busy herself in the kitchen with Griete and the other servants.

But wherever she went and whatever she did Maria's words still worried her. As the days went on she became more and more annoyed with herself because she had missed the opportunity to speak frankly to Samuel as they were travelling home after the visit to the predikant, yet she knew that the carriage would not have been a suitable place for such a discussion. In truth it was difficult to know exactly when would be a suitable place and time.

Mealtimes became slightly strained and Anna began retiring to her room immediately after they had eaten rather than staying in the hall with Samuel because the huge log fires that the servants built up in the evening created an atmosphere of intimacy that she wished to avoid. She felt that her relationship with him had changed, had somehow reached a different level but for the life of her she couldn't decide what that level was and she shrank from discussing the matter with him in case ... In case what? She didn't know.

Of course Samuel noticed.

'Why do you scuttle off like a frightened rabbit as soon as the board is cleared?' he said one evening as she got up from the table and prepared to leave the hall.

'I'm tired. I've had a busy day.' She pretended to yawn.

'Nonsense. Your day has been no busier than mine. Come and sit here by the fire. This is the only time of day I get a chance to talk to you.'

She had no choice but to obey him.

'Now,' he said, when he had finished coughing after filling his pipe and getting it to draw. 'Something's bothering you. I want to know what it is. And don't try to pretend it isn't so because I know different.'

She was silent for some time, chewing her lip, trying to decide how best to explain, because she was reluctant even to speak of such a delicate matter. 'It's something Maria said to me the day you visited the predikant,' she admitted at last.

'Oh, and what was that?' He was watching her through a haze of smoke.

'People are talking.'

'Yes? It's not uncommon. People do talk. It's how they communicate,' he said gravely.

She knew he was gently laughing at her, trying to put her at her ease but it didn't help and she ignored his attempt at humour. 'They're talking about us.'

'Oh, yes? And what are they saying?' He took his pipe out of his mouth, examined it, tamped down the tobacco and put it back in his mouth. Then he looked up. 'Well?'

She leaned forward. 'It's all very well for you, Samuel. Your reputation isn't at stake. Nobody cares if you take a mistress. It's what men do. But it's not the same for me. If people think I'm your mistress then my reputation is ruined.' The words came out in a rush.

He raised his eyebrows. 'Ah, I see. And is that what people think?'

'Well, they think it's odd that you take me around with you all the time . . .'

'Which I wouldn't do if you were my mistress,' he pointed out.

'Perhaps not.'

'Most certainly not. What else did Maria say?'

'She thought you'd gone to see the predikant about us getting married. And she said if you had it was not before time because – because of what I just told you.'

'I see.' He was silent for a long time, frowning thoughtfully. Then he looked up. 'May I ask you something, Anna? And I want you to answer me truthfully, although I believe I know the answer. Are you in love with me?'

'I was afraid you'd ask me that,' she murmured.

He gave a half smile. 'It seems a reasonable enough question, under the circumstances, don't you think?'

She took a deep breath. 'I hate saying this, after all you've done for me because I don't want to hurt your feelings, Samuel, but no, I'm not in love with you.' She paused and looked at him for the first time. 'Please don't be offended, Samuel. I'm very fond of you as a friend but I don't love you, not like I loved . . .'

He held his hand up, cutting her words short. 'Good. That's what I thought.' He removed his pipe and examined it, then he replaced it in the rack beside his chair. He really didn't like this new idea of smoking tobacco, he couldn't get the hang of it at all. It made his clothes smell and left a nasty taste in his mouth. He couldn't understand why people made such a fuss about it. He looked at her thoughtfully. 'I hadn't realised that our friendship would cause such speculation, Anna. I'm very sorry. I wouldn't willingly harm you, you must know that.' He was quiet for several minutes, then he said, 'Would you like us to be married, Anna?'

'No!' she said sharply. Then realising this sounded abrupt and unkind, 'That is, I don't know. I hadn't thought . . .'

He gave a little chuckle. 'From the way you first answered I'm sure you had given it thought, Anna. As, indeed, I have myself. But . . .'

'I think I should go away,' she cut in quickly. 'I think I should leave your house. I'm sure that would be the best thing. I'll find a house in the town. I have skills. I'm sure I can earn enough to live on.' She realised she was prattling in her embarrassment.

'Oh, I don't think that would be a good idea at all, Anna. In fact it would make me very sad. I like having you here in my care. I like looking after you and seeing that you want for nothing.' He

164

shrugged. 'I see nothing wrong in that. You need somebody to care for you and after all, I'm old enough to be your father.'

She frowned. 'All the same . . .'

'I don't want you to leave me, Anna,' he interrupted. 'And I'm prepared to marry you if it will keep you here.' He was silent for a long time, then he said, his voice low, 'But I must warn you that we shall never live as man and wife. I shall never share your bed. You must understand I am no longer a young man and I have certain – difficulties in that direction.' He turned his head away as he spoke. He collected himself and went on in a stronger voice, 'Having said all that, I am fully prepared – indeed, I would be very happy to marry you if it will make you feel more comfortable here.'

It was a strange proposal. Her eyes filled with tears and she shook her head. 'I don't know, Samuel. I don't know how to answer you,' she whispered.

He became his old authoritative self. 'No, of course you don't. You need time to think. I shan't press you further, Anna. When you are ready you can give me your answer. I'm not in any hurry.' He smiled benignly. 'All I would ask is that you don't scurry away to your room every night as soon as we've eaten in the way you have been doing lately. I've missed your company.'

'I shall give you my answer tomorrow, Samuel,' she promised.

That night she didn't sleep at all. She went over and over in her mind the conversation she had had with Samuel.

She turned her mind to the choices that lay before her. If she were to marry Samuel life would go on just as it was now. She would continue to live in this beautiful house, she would be able to walk in the garden Jan had created, where she still felt his presence close to her; the garden she now realised – although Samuel had never actually said so – was a memorial to Alicia, his dead wife. She would continue to enjoy the kind of life she had been used to in her father's house, with servants, with warmth, with plenty of space, with lovely furniture and hangings, good food. Samuel would always treat her well, she was certain of that.

On the other hand, she would never again enjoy the intimacies she had so enjoyed with Jan, the proper consummation of married life. And she would never have children. Her eyes misted as she remembered the months she had carried Jan's child, the happiness it had brought them both, the sense of devastation when she discovered it hadn't lived.

Was she prepared to pay that price for this comfortable – luxurious, lifestyle? Or was she prepared to leave Garden House and make a life for herself elsewhere, probably in a small cottage somewhere in the heart of the town? And how would she live? What would she do for money? She had a little of her own but it wouldn't last long; she would have to find work of some sort. Could she do that in a town where she was regarded as an alien? The prospect was quite alarming.

But against that was the question: what if she married Samuel and then fell in love with someone else? Someone who given the chance might have given her a 'proper' marriage, with children?

Someone, she realised rationally as dawn broke, whom she might never meet. Was it worth throwing away all that she had with Samuel – this warm, possessive cocoon he was weaving round her – for the vain hope of something that only existed in her imagination?

She got up feeling tired and jaded and no nearer the solution to her problem. Refusing the delicious, freshly baked oatcake Griete offered her she simply took a draught of warm ale and went out into the garden – Jan's garden.

The very last of the autumn leaves were hanging by a thread on the trees and bushes and everywhere was damp with the smell of autumn decay. A gardener was sweeping dead leaves from the paths. She stopped and spoke to him.

'Are there no late-flowering trees or shrubs that could be planted to brighten the garden at this time of year,' she asked. 'I know winter is nearly here but everywhere looks so . . .' she cast her eyes round '. . . bleak, doesn't it?'

'There are shrubs, Mistress, but the master won't agree to me putting them in,' the gardener said, shaking his head. 'He won't have a thing touched. The garden mustn't be altered in any way.' He pointed to the border. 'Only the other day I asked about putting in more bulbs ready for the spring but he nearly bit my head off. He said that the garden was to stay as it was designed. Goodness knows why.'

She smiled at him. 'That must make life a bit difficult for you.'

'Not really, Mistress. It just means all I have to do is to keep it

166

tidy.' He frowned. 'Are you all right, Mistress? You look very pale.'

She noticed his eyes flick briefly to her stomach as he spoke, revealing that speculation on her relationship with Samuel was not simply confined to the Bay Hall.

'I slept badly last night,' she told him. 'I thought a walk in the garden might clear my head.'

'The chill air will certainly do that, Mistress. You shouldn't stay out too long, you'll catch a chill.'

'No. I'm going back into the house now.'

In fact, she went to the still-room. She always enjoyed working there, the smell of the herbs that hung from the ceiling never failed to soothe her as she made up the salves and balms, the potions and decoctions as Old Betty had taught her during the time she and Jan had spent at the old woman's cottage when they first came to England.

It seemed a lifetime ago.

As she worked, humming to herself as she pounded leaves and crushed flowers, Anna's mind gradually became clearer and she knew exactly what she wanted, what she must do. Once her mind was made up she wondered why it had taken her so long to reach her decision.

Samuel was very affable that evening as they ate their meal together. He told her a little about the people he had seen during the day and talked of his plans to employ more weavers. Anna listened with half an ear, her mind elsewhere, on her future.

When the meal was over she took her place by the fire and he came and sat opposite to her, the huge logs crackling on the hearth between them, giving out the sweet aroma of apple wood and sending showers of sparks up the chimney. Blackie sat washing herself on the hearthstone between them.

'I've made my decision, Samuel,' she said quietly as soon as he was settled with his pipe and tobacco.

He glanced at her and then away. 'Yes, my dear?' He was not in the habit of using terms of endearment; it was almost as if he anticipated her decision and was making it easy for her to say what was in her mind.

'I am truly honoured that you are willing to marry me . . .'

'The honour is all mine, my dear,' he interrupted.

She held up her hand. 'Please, Samuel, let me finish.'

He nodded. 'I'm sorry.'

She began again. 'I am truly honoured that you are willing to marry me but I don't think it would be right, either for you, or for me.'

His eyebrows shot up in surprise. It was not the answer he had expected. 'Oh, I'm sure we could . . .'

'No, Samuel. My mind is made up. I won't marry you.'

'Very well, my dear.' He gave a sigh that Anna interpreted as almost one of relief. 'So what would you like to do? Become my official housekeeper? That would satisfy any wagging tongues, surely? Really, we should have thought of it before.' His tone was light.

'No. I shall leave your house and take a small cottage in the town.'

'Oh, and what will you live on, may I ask?' He wasn't taking her seriously.

'I have my knowledge of herbs. I can read and write. I can speak English. I think I can make enough money to live on. I have a little money of my own which will last me for a few weeks.'

He puffed on his pipe, coughed and puffed again. 'You seem to have it all worked out,' he said at last.

'I think I have,' she replied.

'And where do you intend to live?'

'I believe there is a cottage near the Schere Gate that is empty. It has a small garden . . .'

'I'll go and see it and buy it for you.'

She pressed her lips together. 'Thank you, Samuel, but no. I don't want you to do that. I can rent it for few pence a week.'

'Nonsense. There's no need for that. I'll see about it tomorrow.'

'Oh, Samuel.' She shook her head sadly.

'What is it now?' he asked in surprise.

'Nothing.' How could she explain that her decision had been made the moment she remembered in the still-room that in her mind she had described the life she was living with Samuel as a 'warm, possessive cocoon'. He was possessive. He was trying to keep her close to him because he felt responsible for Jan's death and indirectly for the death of their child. This was not what she wanted and she knew she had to escape before she began to feel trapped and might even begin to hate him. Not that she could ever imagine that happening, he was far too kind and caring towards her. She knew he would never do anything to harm her. She gritted her teeth and smiled at him. 'Thank you, Samuel. It's very kind of you to buy the cottage for me.' The least she could do was to accept his kind offer.

'Good.' He looked pleased. 'And I shall give you an allowance. I can't risk you starving yourself.'

'Thank you, Samuel.' He needn't know she wouldn't touch the money. She stood up, grateful that he hadn't tried harder to persuade her to stay with him.

'I shall miss you, Anna,' he said sadly.

'I shall miss you, too, Samuel, but I know I'm doing the right thing.'

'You must come back sometimes and see Alicia's garden.'

'Perhaps.' She wasn't sure she wanted to because she knew it wouldn't have changed, that Samuel would keep it as a kind of shrine to her. Jan wouldn't have liked that; he knew that life couldn't stand still and he would have been full of ideas for changes and improvements. That was one of the reasons she had to move on. But move on to what? She didn't know.

And it was only much later that she realised that in leaving Samuel's house and the company he kept she was probably throwing away whatever slight chance there might have been of finding her real father. If, indeed, he lived in Colchester at all.

Chapter Nineteen

Reluctant to let her go at all, Samuel managed to persuade Anna to stay at Garden House until the Christmas festivities were over and the English Twelfth Night revelries had finished.

Secretly, she was not sorry to stay in the warmth and comfort of the big house for a little longer, fearful of the drunken rioting on the streets in the town, which Samuel assured her took place during the festive season.

But in the third week of January, when an icy wind blew flurries of snow that piled into corners and threatened to blanket the town, Anna finally took her leave of Griete and the other servants and left Garden House, careful to leave whilst Samuel was at the Bay Hall, because she knew their farewells would be tearful and he would beg her to stay, offering yet more excuses as to why she shouldn't leave.

So she wrapped herself in her warm cloak, straightened her shoulders and walked the mile or so to her new home, carrying Blackie, protesting loudly, in a covered basket. All her other possessions had been taken by one of the gardeners to the little cottage by the Schere Gate the previous day. Not that she had much. Her first task would be to furnish the cottage, which stood in its own garden, opposite a row of four.

But to her dismay, as soon as she pushed open the door she found that it had already been done. Just as the cottage she had shared with Jan had been furnished for her down to the last mug and platter, so was her new home at Schere Gate.

Only this time the furnishings were not simply to fulfil basic needs. The chair by the fire had comfortable cushions, the table was polished oak, as was the chair that was drawn up to it. A small court cupboard held enough pewter and glass for her needs and a cupboard held a stock of food that would last her for several days. It was the same upstairs. The bed had a soft feather mattress and was covered with blankets and a brightly coloured dornicle; the pillows were plump. At the foot of the bed there was a large carved chest, amply big enough to contain her gowns, and there was a chest of drawers for everything else.

She shook her head. 'Oh, Samuel,' she breathed, 'Will you never learn? What will my neighbours think?'

She let Blackie out of her basket and while she lit the fire the little cat explored the cottage, sniffing in all the corners and creeping up the stairs – real stairs this time, to a proper bedroom – not simply a ladder to a sleeping loft. When she came down again, treading lightly and delicately from stair to stair, obviously satisfied with her explorations, the fire was burning brightly so she sat down on the hearth and began to wash herself.

Anna stroked her soft fur. 'So you think you'll like it here in our new home, do you, Blackie?' she asked.

Blackie purred and continued with her ablutions.

Anna unwrapped the cheese and newly baked loaf that Griete had given her and ate her noon piece sitting by the fire. The cottage already felt like home, with the firelight playing on the whitewashed walls and as she sat in her armchair beside the fire watching the snow swirling round outside the window she quickly forgave Samuel for what she had at first regarded as his interference. Indeed, she was grateful for it, because she knew he only wanted what was best for her, just as she knew that it would have taken her months to collect together even half the things he had provided.

She finished her bread and cheese and drank a mug of small beer, then remained sitting by the fire, thinking about Samuel Hegetorne. He had always been so good to her, so kind; had she been foolish to insist that she must leave him and make a life for herself? Life at Garden House was ordered, comfortable, with no worries or cares; she had only to imagine she would like something and it appeared. Samuel spoiled her, cosseted her, tried to make her dependent on him, but she was well aware that this was because he was lonely without his wife and because he still felt guilty over Jan's death. Samuel didn't love her, didn't want her for herself, for the person she was.

171

She sighed. Maybe nobody would ever love her like that again, but at least here, alone in her little cottage, she could simply be Anna Verlender, loved or hated for herself, not because she was Jan's widow, dearly though she had loved him. She knew with absolute certainty that she had done the right thing in leaving Samuel's house.

The snow lasted nearly a week, during which time she had to brave the icy wind and the filthy slush underfoot to go to the market for vegetables and salt beef and to take her pitcher to the water carrier and carry it gingerly back to the cottage down the slippery Schere Gate steps. She smiled to herself as she realised that if she had stayed with Samuel all these things would have been done by somebody else, while she remained comfortably by the fire. But she felt no regret. In fact, returning to her own fireside after braving the elements to fetch what she needed was sweetly satisfying.

Inevitably, Samuel came to see her. He waited until the snow and the torrential rain that followed it had gone.

'Well, how do you like having to fend for yourself in the dreadful weather we've been having?' he asked, bending his head as he came through the door. Even so, the lintel knocked his hat off. He smiled at her, a rather smug smile. 'Have you had enough? Are you ready to come home?'

'I *am* home. I love it here, Samuel,' she said warmly. 'And so does Blackie. She's settled in very happily, just as I have.'

His smile died. 'Hmph. I'm surprised. It's very pokey.'

'It's bigger than the cottage at Lexden and more than adequate for my needs. It's *very* comfortable, too, thanks to you.'

'Yes. Well. I might tell you I was very tempted to leave it bare to teach you a lesson and make you realise where you were well off.' He glared at her, willing her to agree with him.

'Thank you, Samuel. I'm more than grateful for what you've done,' she said, ignoring his look. She knew as well as he did that he hadn't been able to resist furnishing the cottage for her. 'You know I shall always be indebted to you for the way you took me in and looked after me; it's a debt I can never repay. But it had to end. I can't – I won't – impose on your good will any longer. You've set me up in this cottage but from now on you must allow me to manage my own life.' Her voice was firm. 'I refuse to be a burden to you any longer.'

172

'Don't be silly, you've never been a burden to me.' He waved his hand. 'How do you think you're going to live, here on your own? What will you do for money, answer me that.' He was becoming quite belligerent.

'I have a little money, enough to keep me until I can earn my living. I need to stand on my own feet, Samuel.'

He banged his fist on the table. 'But there's no need. I can give you . . .'

'There's every need,' she said quietly. 'And you've given me quite enough. More than enough.'

'I had to do it. After Jan died and you lost your child I made it my business to look after you. It was the least I could do.'

'And now it's finished. Your debt, if debt it was, is paid. You need feel no further responsibility towards me.' Even as she spoke she knew she would miss his guiding hand, the comfort of knowing he was there, in control. At the same time she knew that this was the very thing she needed to escape from. 'Please believe me, Samuel. I know that what I am doing is right. I don't want to quarrel with you.'

He sniffed. 'Very well, if you don't want my help,' he said huffily.

She put her hand on his arm. 'Don't be like that, Samuel. Just let me lead my own life,' she said gently.

'You'll come and see me? You'll come and walk in Alicia's garden?' he asked, with almost boyish eagerness.

'Perhaps. In the summer. But I think it would be better if you didn't come here again. I don't yet know what my neighbours are like.' She smiled a little to release the tension. 'I wouldn't want them throwing rotten eggs at you.'

He made a face. 'Oh, dear me, no. Neither would I.' He bent down and peered out through the window. 'I still can't understand why you insisted on coming to live in this area, among the English. Why didn't you look for a cottage in the region of the Stock Well? That's where most of our people live. It would have been safer.'

'Because this cottage happened to be empty and because it has a garden where I can grow my herbs. And because if we keep ourselves to ourselves and never mix with the local people we shall always be regarded as Strangers and never be made welcome in the town.'

'You're very high-minded and stubborn. You'll soon realise you can't change the feelings of the town all by yourself.' He stared at her for a minute, then seeing she was quite determined, he picked up his hat and rammed it on his head. 'Very well, you must do as you please,' he said, irritable now because he wasn't getting his own way. 'I've done what I can for you. If you insist on refusing any further assistance there's nothing more to be said.'

'Thank you for your kindness and understanding, Samuel,' she said, following him to the door.

'I wasn't being kind and I don't understand,' he said a trifle petulantly. 'I thought when you'd been here a few days you'd realise where you were best off and be glad to come back with me. It seems I was wrong. Well, on your own head be it.' He swung himself up on to his horse and galloped away without a glance back.

She picked up her cat and closed the door and leaned on it, stroking Blackie's ear. This was her little house. Her home. Here now was where she belonged and here she would stay, in spite of the taunts and jeers she had already suffered as she cleaned off the mud that had been thrown at the window, the rotten egg that had hit the door. These were things she had been careful not to tell Samuel about. She hoped he wouldn't come again, it would only inflame the neighbours further.

The winter was difficult and sometimes she was lonely and wished she had stayed with Samuel until the spring. She spent a lot of her time in the little kitchen at the back of the cottage, sorting out the bundles of herbs she had brought with her, hanging them up to dry or turning them into tinctures and salves.

She got used to the jibes and shouts that followed her as she went up Schere Gate steps to the market and again when she returned. The people in the row of cottages opposite were mostly spinners and weavers and she was well aware how much they resented the Dutch living in the town. Sometimes, when the taunts were worse than usual, she realised she had been foolhardy to come and live among them and she wished she had done as Samuel suggested and gone to live in what was known as the 'Dutch Quarter'.

But she was determined not to give up and one morning, when she had made more bread than she would need for the day, she plucked up the courage to go and knock on the door of the cottage opposite. A young woman with a small boy beside her and a baby at her breast opened the door a crack. 'What do you want, Stranger? You know you're not welcome in these parts.'

'I don't want anything from you, Mistress,' Anna said, noticing the look of surprise when she answered the woman in her own language. 'I have made more bread than I need this morning so I've brought you a loaf.' She held it out and she could see the little boy's mouth watering at the succulent smell.

'I don't take nothin' from Strangers,' the woman said, but Anna could hear the reluctance in her voice.

'Perhaps I might give the little one a crust?' Anna tore off the end of the loaf and gave it to the boy. It was gone before his mother could protest. 'More?' he asked, tugging at Anna's skirt.

'I'll give the rest of it to your mammy. She'll give you more.' Anna held the loaf out to the woman.

'What do you want for it?' she asked suspiciously.

'A smile and a "good day" when I sweep my step in the morning. Nothing more than that,' Anna said wistfully. 'It's lonely at times with nobody to talk to.' She tousled the little boy's fair curls. 'Do you like oatcakes?'

He nodded, turning big blue eyes on her.

'Then if your mammy will let you, you can knock on my door when you smell them tomorrow and I shall give you one for your breakfast.' She smiled at the woman. 'I give you "good day", Mistress.'

The woman nodded in acknowledgement. 'My name's Martha,' she mumbled reluctantly. 'Thank you for the loaf.'

'And mine is Anna.' She went back across the road and into her cottage, where she leaned on the door, her heart beating fast. For weeks she had been trying to pluck up the courage to do that and now it was done. It was a beginning.

But she was over-optimistic.

The next morning there was a knock on the door as she took the oatcakes from the fire. She smiled to herself and opened the door.

Martha stood there, the baby in her arms and the boy beside her.

'My man says I'm not to take anything from you,' she said, clearly embarrassed. 'He says I'm to give you this back.' She handed Anna half the loaf she had given her the day before. Her voice dropped. 'I had a piece of it. It was very good. I wish you could show me how . . . Dick, here, liked it too. I'm sorry, Anna.'

'I understand. It would be wrong to go against your husband, but I'm sorry, too.' She gave a wry smile. 'It took me several weeks before I could even pluck up the courage to knock on your door. But at least we've spoken and you know I mean you no harm.'

Martha nodded. She glanced nervously over her shoulder. 'I must go. I have spinning to finish. I shall have the agent here later today to fetch my reels.'

'Who do you work for?'

'Master Nightingale. He's a good master, looks after his weavers and spinners well. My husband weaves for him.' She nodded in the direction of her cottage, where the clacking of the loom could be heard. 'Master Nightingale lives in a big house at the bottom of North Hill.' Her voice dropped. 'The Fentons – they live in the cottage next to mine – they work for old Markham, on East Hill. He's a dreadful man, got a terrible temper, too. If the work's not done on time they get fined, and they get fined if there's a flaw in the cloth so it isn't passed at the Bay Hall – and that's on top of the fines imposed by the searchers there. He's so mean he'll find any means he can to dock their money.'

'Do you mean Silas Markham?'

'That's right. You know him?'

'Not really.' Anna felt her colour rise. 'I've met his son, Paul.'

'Ah, he's a nice man, from what I've heard. Not a bit like his father.'

Surreptitiously, while they had been talking Anna had slipped an oatcake into Dick's little hand. When he finished it she gave him another one, more openly this time. 'Will you try one, too, Martha?' she asked casually.

'No, I must be going.' Martha looked over her shoulder. 'Well, perhaps just one, since they smell so good. Mmm. It's delicious.'

'I could make you some,' Anna offered.

'I'd have to pay you. My man doesn't like charity. And I couldn't tell him they came from you.'

'Then I won't make them for you. I don't want you to go behind his back. It wouldn't be right.'

A puzzled frown appeared between Martha's eyes. 'They always say the Dutch are out for all they can get but you don't seem like that, Anna. Mind you, I've never spoken to a Stranger before. But you don't seem much different to what I am.'

176

Anna smiled. 'We're all sisters under the skin.'

'Oh, I don't know about that.'

Anna watched from her doorway as Martha crossed the road to the row of small thatched cottages where she and three other families lived. She saw the doors open on two of the cottages and the women came out, their distaffs hanging at their belts, their fingers busy, trying to look casual as they went towards Martha. Martha paused and spoke to them and Anna could see from the glances that came in the direction of her cottage that she was the subject of their conversation. She was very tempted to go out and join them but she knew that if she did they would melt away, back to their own houses.

But at least the looks that came her way were curious rather than hostile. She smiled at them, then went in and closed her door.

Chapter Twenty

Anna continued to attend church on Sundays, just as she had when she lived in Samuel's house. But now she sat towards the back, alone, instead of with Griete and the rest of Samuel's servants, who were watched over by Samuel, sitting in the tall pew above them.

Each Sunday she eagerly scanned the faces of the people, all dressed in their sombre Sunday best, to see if she could detect a fair-haired man whose features might conceivably bear some slight resemblance to her own; or maybe a tall man whose dark, violet eyes were a distinguishing feature. It was a forlorn hope, she realised that, because she had no way of knowing whether her mother's lover had ever reached Colchester when he came to England, and if he had reached the place whether he had remained there. He might even be dead. But yet she felt compelled to continue her search, driven on by the conviction that somehow, somewhere, she would find the man who was her natural father.

In the end, after the service one Sunday, when the rest of the congregation had dispersed, she went to see the predikant at his house behind the church. This was a low, wooden building, built in the same style as the church, sparsely furnished, with the bare necessities but little else. It was functional, but lacked the air of homeliness a woman's touch might have added.

Abraham van Migrode didn't appear to notice the lack of comfort. He took her into his study and sat her down on a hard, high-backed chair and listened carefully from a similar chair placed behind his desk as she told him her story. Every now and then he nodded thoughtfully.

'And you say that his name is Henrick,' he said when she had finished. 'But you have no other name?'

She shook her head. 'Jan, my husband, may have found out more when he went back to Flanders, he was hoping to see my mother and ask her, but whatever he discovered – if anything – went to the bottom of the sea with him. Plague victims were thrown overboard with all their possessions, I'm told.' Her mouth twisted bitterly as she spoke these last words.

'Understandably so,' he said sadly. 'Plague is a terrible scourge.' He steepled his fingers. 'I could look in the register of the Dutch church,' he said after a long pause. 'But I'm not sure how much it would help because Henrick is a common enough name. When did you say he arrived here?'

'I'm not really sure. It would be something like twenty years ago. That is, if he came to Colchester at all,' she said with a rueful smile. She frowned and then said firmly, 'But I'm sure he did. Something tells me that this is the place he came to. Why else would I have chanced up here in this town if it was not meant for us to find each other? You know, because you were on the boat with Jan and me, that we had no idea where we were heading when we left Nieuwport. And even when we reached Harwich we had no thought of coming to Colchester until you suggested it. So there must have been a purpose.'

He stood up and patted her arm. 'God moves in a mysterious way, my child, and things don't always work out in the way we expect. Nevertheless, I will look in the register and see what I can discover, but I must warn you not to hope for too much.' He took a step back and regarded her, pinching his lip. 'Has it occurred to you, Anna, that even if your father is here in Colchester he might now be married, with a family? In which case he would most certainly not welcome a spectre from his past to appear and upset his domestic harmony.'

'Yes, I had thought of it and if I discover that to be the case I wouldn't dream of making myself known to him.' She smiled. 'But *I* would know. And that would be enough.'

'That's what you say now, my child. I fear, when the time came you might find yourself thinking differently,' he warned. His voice became brisk. 'However, I will see what I can uncover and I will let you know. What you do with any information I impart will be between you and your conscience. Of course, I may not find out anything at all.'

'Thank you for trying, anyway.'

She left him to make her way out into Church Walk, across Head Street into Gutter Street and thence to her cottage by the Schere Gate. The rest of the Dutch Congregation had long gone to their homes and the roads were full of English people leaving the Church of St Mary at the Walls nearby, where the morning service ended later.

As she crossed Head Street she heard a voice at her elbow.

'Mistress Verlender, good day to you.'

She turned and saw Paul Markham smiling down at her.

'This is an unexpected pleasure,' he said. 'May a walk a little way with you?'

'Of course you may,' she said warmly. 'I shall be glad of your company.'

'But aren't you going the wrong way?' he said in surprise as she made to turn into Gutter Street. 'Master Hegetorne . . .'

'I have my own house now,' she said proudly. 'I no longer live in Samuel's house.'

'Well, that is a surprise. I thought Master Hegetorne . . . that is, I thought you . . .' He smiled down at her, slightly embarrassed. 'To tell you the truth I don't really know what I thought, except that the arrangement was permanent and you would be staying there.'

'Indeed, no. That was never my intention, although Samuel wanted me to stay. But I felt I had taken advantage of his hospitality for too long and it was time to stand on my own feet. I have taken a cottage by Schere Gate steps.'

His frowned. 'We – that is, my father, has spinners and weavers living in Schere Gate Alley. As far as I know there are no Dutch people living anywhere near. Don't you find yourself somewhat isolated with none of your countrymen nearby?'

'I do well enough, although the cottagers in Schere Gate Alley don't trust me because my cottage is bigger and stands alone. No,' a note of bitterness crept into her voice. 'It's not just because of that. It's because I'm a Stranger.' She looked up at him and gave a little laugh. 'I've tried very hard to be friendly but it's no use. They have this idea that my people only want to take away their livelihood. They don't seem to understand that I'm no threat to them since I can neither spin nor weave.'

'I think you're very brave to choose to live there.'

She shrugged. 'It happened to be the only cottage available that had a garden.' She was quiet for a moment, then she said, 'But I didn't want to live in the area that's becoming known as the "Dutch Quarter". It's no wonder my people are labelled clannish, the way they huddle together in a few streets near the Stock Well. It must be some thirty years, maybe more, since the first people came over from Flanders. Then they were welcomed into your town and encouraged to settle here. I don't know what went wrong that there should be so much animosity now.'

'It's a long story and all tied up with the new draperies that the Dutch introduced,' he said. 'I believe the method of manufacture was different, I don't remember all the details now because it was a long time ago and I wasn't very old. Apparently – I don't remember this, of course – my grandfather was very eager to try out the new methods but my father wanted to stick with the old. There were terrible arguments between them but of course the old ways had to give way to the new in the end.' He glanced down at Anna. 'I'm afraid my father has never forgiven my grandfather for being willing to work with the Aliens, although the business has prospered over the years. I suppose that's the crux of the matter, my father never likes to admit he might be wrong.'

'Does your father employ Dutch workers?'

'Dear me, no. Grandfather used to but when he became ill father took over the business and got rid of most of them. We only have English workers now, which is a pity because we could all learn so much from each other if only we mixed more.'

'I agree with you,' she said enthusiastically. 'I think it's time we all lived together in harmony, instead of in two separate communities. I dread to think what would happen if two people . . .' She bit her tongue. She had been about to say if two people from the two communities fell in love. But walking beside this young, handsome Englishman, she realised that those words were too close to home to be spoken.

But he had read her thoughts. 'It will happen,' he said quietly. He paused, then added, even more quietly, 'In fact, you might say it already has.'

They reached the little wicket gate to her cottage. 'I shall see you again, Anna Verlender,' he said softly, then before she could answer he turned and took the Schere Gate steps two at a time.

Anna went into her cottage and sat down, absently stroking Blackie, who had immediately staked claim to her lap. Paul Markham's words were still ringing in her ears, softly though they had been spoken, giving her a warm glow inside. He would never have uttered them while she was still under Samuel's roof, she knew that without any shadow of doubt. She smiled to herself. Whatever problems or troubles might lie ahead she was glad she had left Samuel's house.

But life was far from easy. Martha was understandably influenced by her neighbours and didn't speak when she saw her, even though Dick tugged at her skirts and demanded 'oatcake from de nice lady'. Her windows were continually daubed with mud and worse and the children were not checked when they chanted rude rhymes at her gate. But if she left a basket of eggs from her chickens at the gate they quickly disappeared, with only the odd one or two flung at her door and there was never a crumb left from the plates of oatcakes she put out for passers-by.

Although the children called her names and made faces at her when she went out she managed to hold her head high, smiling at them and greeting them by name as she learned what they were called. She could see that it puzzled them that they couldn't annoy her and after a while they left her alone.

But she wasn't lonely. Most days when she went to the market she saw Maria or Griete.

'The master still won't accept that you have left,' Griete told her one day. 'He's convinced you'll miss the comforts of his house and come back. He's even told us how to behave when you return. We're to welcome you as if you'd never been away.'

Anna shook her head sadly. 'I'm sorry he won't accept that I'm not coming back, Griete. Because I shall never return to Garden House. I'm happy where I am, even though the neighbours aren't very friendly.'

'Do they call you names?'

'Yes, but don't tell Samuel that. Tell him I'm quite happy. Because I am.' She nearly said 'I'm enjoying my freedom,' but she realised that it would upset Samuel to hear that and she couldn't rely on Griete not to repeat it.

When the spring came Anna planted vegetables and herbs in

182

her garden, remembering Jan as she dug and hoed and weeded. It was almost as if he was at her elbow, saying, 'Dig a little deeper, sweetheart.' 'Ah, that's good, black soil, the plants will grow well there.' 'Plant them a hand span apart, give them room to grow.'

She hoped the plants would grow well because she intended to sell some at the market. As she had told Samuel, she had a little money of her own, but even with careful budgeting it was running low now and she refused to touch the bag of coins that Samuel's servants brought to her every month. She had augmented her little store of money with selling a few eggs at the market and now and again Maria and her friends asked her for remedies. But not many people were aware of her knowledge of herbs and she was not anxious to let it be known too widely.

She was thinking along these lines as she finished weeding the patch at the front of the cottage one day. As she straightened up she thought she saw smoke coming from the door of the end cottage in Schere Gate Alley opposite. She turned away. Clearly, somebody had made up the fire with wet wood and filled the room with smoke.

Then she looked again and saw a lick of flame curling ominously round the chimney towards the thatch and realised that it wasn't wet wood that was making the smoke, the chimney was on fire! Another minute and the whole roof would be alight. She threw down her fork and ran across the road, shouting, 'Fire! Fire! The chimney is alight! Quick, somebody help!'

She ran to the open cottage door from which black smoke was belching. Inside, the room was filled with choking smoke and the stink of burning soot, which had fallen down the chimney and out across the hearth into the room, starting small fires wherever it fell. Suddenly, she heard a choking sound coming from the corner by the ladder to the sleeping loft. Throwing her apron up to cover her nose and mouth she began to crawl on her hands and knees through the burning, acrid smoke towards the sound, knocking over a smouldering stool and burning her arm on some yarn that was well alight as she went. As she groped her way across the floor she came to a small child choking and crying in the corner. Quickly she gathered him to her and putting her apron over his head to shield him crawled back outside, by this time hardly able to breathe herself.

'Peter,' the child was crying and choking, struggling to point back the way he had come. 'Peter's still in there.'

She laid the child on the dirt, making sure he could breathe. Then she took several deep breaths to clear her own lungs and turned to go back into the cottage after the other child. But by this time the other cottagers had all come out, men who had been at their looms, women at their distaffs, and they stood watching in horror as the wind took the sparks from the roof of the end house, which was now well alight, setting off the thatch of the other cottages.

Someone caught her arm as she reached the door of the cottage. 'It's all right, Mistress, John's already gone in to fetch the other little one.'

Anna gave the man a grateful smile as she pushed her hair back with her arm and turned back to the little boy, who was still choking spasmodically and shivering with fright. 'Was it just you and Peter?' Anna asked him gently.

'No,' Martha said from behind her. 'Sal, his mother, has just been brought to bed with another. They'll still be there, in the sleeping loft.' Even as she spoke a figure appeared at the small upstairs window under the burning thatch.

'Lower the child down first, then jump yourself,' someone in the crowd called. 'It's not far. We'll catch him. Never fear.'

But Sal wasn't listening. The floor was already burning under her feet so she scrambled out of the lattice and stood petrified for a few seconds then jumped, with the child still in her arms. There was a cry of alarm from those watching, but quick as thought, one of the men stepped forward and caught them both in his strong arms and carried them to safety.

By this time the thatch from two of the cottages was well alight. Men with besoms were desperately trying to beat out the flames, standing on ladders or stools, even on each other's shoulders, anything to give them a longer reach. Meanwhile, the women and older children had made a long chain to pass wooden buckets of water from the well some distance away in an effort to douse it.

Everyone worked with a will because fire was the thing everyone dreaded. With houses huddled closely together and mostly roofed with thatch, a spark from a chimney or a spilled taper could wreak havoc and destroy whole rows of cottages. But at last the flames were put out, the damage less than it might have

184

been if Anna hadn't raised the alarm so quickly, although all that remained of the end cottage was a heap of blackened ashes. The next cottage fared slightly better in that although the roof was gone the cottage, blackened and smoke-filled, remained standing. The other cottages were scorched but still habitable, the end one, where Martha lived, hardly damaged at all.

Everybody stood together talking, garrulous with a mixture of shock and relief; counting the members of their families to make sure nobody had died in the fire, assuring themselves and each other that things could have been much worse if the alarm hadn't been raised. Nobody could remember who had given the first warning.

Martha's husband, John, had been badly burned about the hands and face helping to beat out the fire and several of the other men were burned, although less severely. There were numerous suggestions as to the best cure as John was laid on the ground with a pillow at his head, only half-conscious.

Anna, her face black with smoke, had slipped home to her cottage. Now she came back with some paste in a wooden bowl.

'Lay this gently on his skin to keep out the air,' she said to Martha.

Martha looked at her in horror. 'I can't do that!' she said. 'It might kill him.'

'No. It will soothe the burning. Look, I have smeared some on my arm where it was burned.' She showed Martha where she had smoothed the paste on her arm from the elbow to the wrist.

Martha looked at it suspiciously, then at her husband, barely conscious but moaning with pain. 'Are you sure?'

'Quite sure,' Anna said firmly. 'Would I use it on my own skin if I doubted its goodness?'

'Will you do it?'

'Of course.' Anna knelt by the man and very gently smoothed the paste on the raw skin of his face and neck and then on the backs of his strong, weaver's hands and arms. After that, she gently lifted his head and gave him tiny sips from the little bottle she took from her pocket. Then she got to her feet.

'Make his bed ready, Martha. Then two strong men can carry him to it. He'll sleep till morning. If he wakes before, just call me and I'll come.' Anna looked round. 'Is anyone else in need of help?'

185

Everybody took a step back, pretending not to hear. Then a woman tried to drag her husband forward. 'Abel's hands and arms are burned. Look!'

'Let it be, Jenny,' the man said. 'I want no Stranger's salve.' He turned away.

One of the other men said, 'I'll take your cure, Stranger, for my hands are burning and full of pain and I need to get back to my loom.'

'Aye, so will I,' another said. 'I have a roof to mend and I can't do that with hands like lumps of raw beef.'

When Anna had finished smoothing on the soothing balm a woman sidled up to her with a small girl. 'Letty here has got bad eyes. Look, they're all red and itchy. Hev you got anythin' for that?'

'Not now, Lizzie,' a voice said. 'You don't want no Stranger meddlin' with Letty's eyes. She'll send her blind.'

'I can give you something to bathe her eyes, if you wish,' Anna said with a smile. 'I'll fetch it for you.'

It was dark by the time Anna finally returned to her cottage. She washed herself thoroughly to get rid of the stink of smoke and changed all her clothes. Then she put more salve on her burns and sat down to eat the meat and vegetables that had been gently stewing over the fire all day. But she had hardly taken a mouthful when there was an urgent knock at the door.

When she opened it she recognised the woman they had called Jenny. She stood on the step, twisting her apron in her hands.

'Could you . . .? I mean, my man is in mortal pain with his burns. Have you got some of that stuff you gave the others? He wouldn't take it when you offered it before but he's that bad now I think he'd be glad of anything to ease his pain.'

Anna smiled. 'Of course. Would you like me to come and . . .?'

'Oh, no. That would never do. What I mean is, he wouldn't let you . . . If you could let me have it and tell me what to do I'll do it.'

'It's all right. I understand,' Anna said gently. She fetched more of the salve and gave it to Jenny. 'There, that should ease his pain,' she said.

Jenny put her head on one side and said in a puzzled voice,

'You're very kind. Not a bit like I expected, considering you're a Stranger. Was it you who first raised the alarm?'

Anna nodded. 'I was in my garden and I saw the flames.'

'We've got a lot to thank you for, then.'

'Just give me "good day" and a smile when you see me,' Anna replied with a hint of sadness. 'That's all I ask.'

Chapter Twenty-One

Two days after the fire Silas Markham came to look at the burned-out end cottage because Sal, who had jumped from the window with her newborn child, was one of his spinners. Beside herself with worry over the loss of her quota of yarn, which amounted to several pounds in weight, she had sent her husband to tell him that it had gone up in smoke.

'House burned down! Whatever next!' Silas said as he and his son rode up the hill side by side on their horses. 'You can't believe half these people tell you. They'll make up any excuse to keep back yarn so they can sell it for their own profit. And I don't doubt the woman thought that if she sent her husband I'd be more likely to believe their cock and bull story. I'll wager she won't be expecting me this morning to check up on her tale!'

'You're being unfair, father. Of course the woman's husband was telling the truth, it's not the kind of story anyone would invent,' Paul said, keeping his temper with difficulty. 'She had to ask him to come and tell you what had happened because she couldn't come herself. She has just been brought to bed with another child. You could see from the state of the man's arms and hands that he'd been in a fire.'

'Well, if it's true and the yarn has gone up in smoke it's money wasted and she'll have to pay for it,' Silas snapped. 'I can't have . . .' He broke off as they turned into Schere Gate Alley and reined up. He could see for himself the extent of the damage.

Paul said nothing for several minutes, watching his father absorb the scene. 'She lived in the end cottage,' he said at last. 'That heap of ash and charred timber.'

Silas remained silent, so Paul continued, 'Her husband is a

butcher and they have two children, well, three now, with the new baby.'

Silas turned in his saddle and looked at his son in surprise. 'How do you know all that?'

'I make it my business to know about all the people who work for us, father.'

'Hmph.' Silas turned back and surveyed the ruined cottage. 'Where has she gone?' he asked, more shocked than he cared to admit. 'Do you know that?'

The carpenter who lived next door to the burned-out cottage was already busily rebuilding his roof, although he was hampered by the rags wrapped round his hands. He had heard the conversation and now he leaned down from his ladder. 'Her man has taken her and the children to her mother's house, Master. She's like to die, I shouldn't wonder, what with the shock of the fire and then jumping out of the window like she did with the babe in her arms.'

'Hmph. That's a pity. Good spinners are hard to come by,' Silas said, turning away.

'If you tell me where she has gone I'll visit her and see if there is anything she needs,' Paul said to the man on the roof.

'Grub Street. That's where her mother lives.' The man came down the ladder. 'That was a powerful fire,' he said, anxious to tell all he knew. 'The chimley caught light. Sal was lucky she didn't die in her bed. She would have done, I don't doubt, if it hadn't been for the young Stranger woman who lives over the road.' He nodded in the direction of Anna's cottage. 'She saw what was happening and ran across and raised the alarm. *And* she ran in and fetched young Tommy out. She's a rare brave little wench.' He held out his bandaged hands. 'An' another thing. See these hands? They were burned that bad I didn't know where to put them for the pain. But the young Stranger woman,' again he nodded towards Anna's cottage, 'she put some wonderful salve on them and it took all the fire out. They're still painful, that I'll not deny, but it was powerful stuff, it means I can work today, as long as I'm careful.'

Silas spat. 'A Stranger woman, was it? Ah, then you'll need to be careful of more than your hands, friend. You never know what witches brew these Aliens cook up. Next thing you know she'll have turned you into a toad.'

'I think not, my Master,' the man said seriously. 'We have much to be grateful to that young woman for and I for one will never say a word against the Stranger community again. As I told you, she was the one who raised the alarm. If it hadn't been for her the whole row could have burned down.'

'Ha! Don't be misled. These Strangers are a cunning lot. She probably put the evil eye on the place to set it alight in the first place,' Silas said with a smirk. 'So it would make her look good when she raised the alarm.'

Paul rounded on his father. 'That's a vile thing to say,' he said hotly. 'Anna . . . Mistress Verlender would never do such a thing.'

Silas swung round in his saddle and stared at his son. 'Anna, is it? Mistress Verlender, is it?' he sneered. 'Am I to understand that you're acquainted with this Stranger woman?'

Paul flushed. 'We've met. Yes. She used to live at Master Hegetorne's house on the Lexden Road. Her husband was his gardener until he died. You would have met her, too, if you had attended the party Master Hegetorne held to show off the garden Jan Verlender had created.'

'I want nothing to do with Strangers. They take our trade. They're nothing but trouble in the town' Silas said pettishly. 'Come, we've spent quite long enough here. There's work to be done.' He turned his horse and dug his spurs into its side. 'Are you coming?'

'No, father. I still have business to attend to here.'

Paul narrowed his eyes as he watched his father canter up the road. He was a hard, unforgiving man, not a bit like his own father, Josiah, whose business Silas had inherited. Paul loved his grandfather, now too ill to work after the seizure that robbed him of most of the use of one arm and leg, but still full of wit and wisdom, and he knew that Josiah often shook his head in despair at the way his son treated his workers.

Paul waited until his father was out of sight, then he dismounted and went across to Anna's house and knocked on the door.

'Forgive me, Anna . . . Mistress Verlender, but I've just been told of your bravery in the fire the other day and I've come to make sure you have not suffered any ill effects,' he said awkwardly when she opened the door. 'Is all well with you?' He noticed the binding on her arm. 'Ah, I see you didn't escape unscathed.'

'It's nothing. It will soon mend,' she said. She smiled at him. 'I am just making some broth for the families in the cottages. There 'is so much clearing up to do that they'll have no time for making meals, even those who have a hearth left,' she added ruefully.

'It smells delicious. I'm sure they'll be very grateful,' Paul said warmly. He would have liked to say more, he would have liked to tell her how much he admired her courage and fortitude, how he longed to know her better, to care for her and protect her from the animosity of bigoted Englishmen like his father, but he was afraid of offending her. Yet she looked so tired, so vulnerable, so lonely, that he couldn't bear to simply walk away and leave her. He stood irresolutely by the door.

'Would you care to come in and take a mug of ale with me?' she asked shyly, seeing that he was reluctant to leave.

His face broke into a smile. 'Thank you, I'd like that.' He came in and sat down at the table, watching as she took down mugs from their hooks and poured ale from the jug. She was unconsciously graceful in her movements, as well as being so honest and kind-hearted. Just the kind of woman he could happily spend the rest of his life with, the woman he would like to bear his children. No, he thought with something of a shock, not simply the *kind* of woman, Anna *was* the woman he wanted for his wife. The realisation made his head reel. After all, he hardly knew her . . .

Anna sat down opposite to him, savouring his presence in her house, wishing she could lean on him and feel the strength and comfort of his arms round her, loving her, protecting her against an unfriendly world. She knew that here was a man she could love, a man she could happily spend the rest of her life with.

Meanwhile, he complimented her on her ale and they discussed the fate of the people in the cottages. They spoke, but only briefly, about the problems between the English and the Dutch and they both deplored the animosity between the two communities. Then, reluctantly, he left and equally reluctantly, she watched him go, neither of them having revealed what was in their hearts.

Life became a little better for Anna after the fire. The people from the cottages greeted her cheerfully, smiling and wishing her good day when they saw her, and they didn't discourage their children from talking to her or accepting her gingerbread men. She was in demand, too, for more of her burn salve. Even Jenny's husband grudgingly admitted that it was soothing and effective.

Inevitably, Samuel heard of the fire and Anna's part in it and he came to see her, bursting in without even knocking.

'Are you hurt, Anna? I heard you were burned near to death,' he said, impatiently picking up his hat, which had been knocked off on the low lintel as he came through the door.

'Tales never lose anything in the telling, Samuel,' she said with a laugh. 'I am quite well except for a slight burn on my arm which is pretty nigh healed now. But it was nothing compared with what some of the cottagers suffered.'

'Are you sure? You look pale.' He peered at her face.

'I have not slept well. I keep dreaming of what might have happened if I hadn't seen the smoke. The children could have been burned to death and their mother with them.'

'That's nothing for you to concern yourself with, Anna. They are only poor English folk. You a woman alone, shouldn't even be living near them. Come, enough of this nonsense. You've had a taste of trying to build bridges between the two communities and it's brought you nothing but anguish. I'm going to take you back to my house where I can look after you and give you the life you were used to in your father's house.'

She got to her feet.

'That's right.' He smiled encouragingly. 'Come with me now. You don't need to bring anything from this hovel. I can provide you with everything you could possibly want.'

She didn't speak but went to the door and held it open. 'Thank you for your concern over my welfare, Samuel,' she said quietly. 'But as I've told you before I am quite contented with my life here. The "poor English folk" you speak of are kind and friendly towards me and would never see me want for anything that they could give me, little enough though they have. My life is not always easy but at least it is my own. I am free to do as I please and I value that. I value it above all else.'

He shook his head and a look that was half-sad, half-puzzled, crossed his face. 'I don't know what your Jan would say, hearing you talk like that, Anna,' he said reproachfully.

'Oh, you have no need to fear, Samuel. I shall never forget that I am Jan's widow,' she said. 'I loved my Jan, I still love him and I value his memory, but I am still a young woman. I can't spend the rest of my life locked in grief. I can only be grateful for the love that I shared with him and move on, as I know he would wish me to.'

'I don't know whether to think you are brave woman or a

foolish one,' he said, scratching his head. 'I've never met anyone quite like you, Anna.'

She smiled and put her hand on his arm. 'I don't think I'm either of those things, Samuel. I just want to make my own way in the world. Thank you for all you have ever done for me. I am truly grateful and I would never want you to think otherwise. But it must stop now. I must make my own way.' She stood on tiptoe and kissed his cheek. 'Thank you for coming to see me, Samuel, I appreciate your concern but as you can see I am quite contented with my lot.'

'I can see your mind is made up.' He picked up his hat and put it on. 'But if you ever need anything . . .'

'I know. And I'm grateful, Samuel.'

'Hmph.'

After he had gone Anna closed the door and leaned on it. She hoped she hadn't upset him too much but she knew she had done the right thing in asserting her independence.

One afternoon late in spring, when she was busy in her garden planting beans, the predikant visited Anna.

'I've been through the registers,' he said when she had taken him into the cottage and given him beer and oatcakes. He smiled. 'It took me some time. Henrick is a common name.'

'But surely some could be quickly discounted. Those who were already married; those who were too old or too young . . .?'

'Even so, there are still some fifteen or twenty left.' He unrolled a paper. 'Of course, it might have made my task a little easier if you had told me his occupation,' he said thoughtfully. 'I have two glaziers, a carpenter, three wire-drawers, two clothiers . . .'

'My father was a weaver,' she broke in quickly. 'I am a weaver's daughter.'

'Ah, well now, that narrows it down a good deal.' He ran his finger down the list. 'Let's have a look. There are one, two, three, four weavers here registered by the name of Henrick. There's Henrick Lucas – he came to Colchester when he was twenty-four and moved to London within a few weeks.' He looked up. 'I've no record of what happened to him after that, you'd have to get in touch with the Dutch Church at Austin Friars if you wanted to find out more.' He went back to his list. 'Henrick Tayspill . . .' he shook his head. 'He's about the right age, but I'm afraid if he's your man it's too late. He never married but he died last year and is buried in St Martin's churchyard. I could show you his grave,' he added quickly as he saw her face fall.

She nodded, chewing her lip. 'I think I might like that.'

'But it might not be the right man,' he warned her. 'There are two more. Henrick Grenrice. He was twenty-five when he came here but there's no record of what happened to him, so I guess he didn't stay long. And Henrick Rebow, but I hardly think he's likely to be the man you're looking for. He's in the marriage register a year after arriving here as having married Clara Stowtehetten.' He looked up. 'I know them, they live in Stockwell Street, they've got three grown-up sons, all weavers. A very moral and upright family. Clara is a good wife and he's devoted to her. They're in church every Sunday.'

'Would you point him out to me?' Anna asked eagerly.

The predikant looked dounbtful. 'I'm not sure whether that would be wise . . .'

'Oh, I wouldn't dream of saying anything that might upset him or his wife. In fact, I wouldn't even speak to him if you thought I shouldn't. It's just that . . . well, I'd like to see the man my mother loved so much, the man who fathered me. Is that so very wrong?'

'No, my child. I can't believe it is,' he said with a sigh.

Anna dressed with extra care for church the following Sunday. She paid scant attention to the service because her mind was on the man who might be her father. She longed to be able to tell her mother in one of the letters they exchanged from time to time through the good offices of Aunt Dionis that she had found Henrick. She had never dared to ask for more details about him in case Cornelis intercepted the letters and Judith had frustratingly never offered any, but as she sat through the service she composed an innocent enough few words in her mind, saying she had met a weaver named Henrick Rebow who might have once worked for Cornelis, did mother or father remember him? She smiled to herself at the pleasure those words would bring to Judith and she scanned the congregation anxiously, looking for a mother and father and three sons. But the nearest she could see was a husband and wife of about the right age with three sons and a daughter. That was no good, and anyway the father's hair under his soft black cap was grey. She waited impatiently for the end of the service; obviously the Rebow family were not here today.

Samuel saw her as he walked out of church and gave her a wave but didn't stop. This saddened her a little because before the fire at the cottages he always used to stop and ask her how she was, obviously biding his time, expecting her to return to his house when she was tired of what he privately considered 'the nonsense of trying to be independent'. But her refusal to return to him after the fire had clearly upset him. She felt guilty about this; the last thing she wanted to do was to offend him after his unstinting kindness to her and Jan when they first came to Colchester; and after Jan's death she would have been lost without his support. She was grateful for this and she had told him so, many times, but she couldn't live her life burdened by a debt of gratitude. She had to move on.

Griete stopped for a word with her. 'Are you well?' she asked anxiously. 'The Master fears you may have lost your senses, staying in that hovel when you could be living in luxury with us.'

Anna laughed. 'No, I have not lost my senses, Griete. I am perfectly happy. I go where I please and do what I choose. And I don't live in a hovel. Samuel in his goodness has furnished my cottage very comfortably.'

Griete nodded sagely. 'He can't let go, can he,' she said. 'He likes to control everything. Everybody. There's the garden, too. Do you know, he'll hardly have a weed pulled!' She leaned closer to Anna. 'That garden is a shrine to his wife. Did you know that? Alicia's garden he calls it.'

Anna nodded. 'Yes, I know.'

'But he's the kindest man in the world when he gets his own way. When he doesn't he's . . . well, you know what he's like. He doesn't like to be thwarted.' She chuckled. 'And you've thwarted him. Good luck, Anna.' She hurried off, still chuckling.

The predikant was standing at the door as the congregation streamed out into the spring sunlight.

When Anna reached him he put his hand on her arm. 'Anna,' he said, 'I'd like you to meet Master Rebow and his wife,' he laid a very slight emphasis on the last word. He turned to the man at his elbow. 'Mistress Verlender is the widow of the man who designed Master Hegetorne's garden,' he said smoothly.

'Ah. I have heard it is a work of art although I have never seen it,' the man said. 'My sons and I all work for him, Jacob is a dyer,

Hans and Wouter are both weavers, like me. Wouter's wife is a spinner.'

Anna smiled. So that explained the daughter she had seen with the family. 'You are a lucky man. You have a fine, industrious family, Master,' she said, gazing into his eyes. 'I wish you all well.'

As they moved off she shook her head and answered even before the predikant spoke.

'No, that man is not my father. That man has brown eyes,' she said sadly.

Chapter Twenty-Two

Paul fell into step beside Anna as she walked home from church. He nearly always waited for her now, saying it was hardly out of his way at all to walk that way, and since he was kind enough to walk with her she felt it was only polite to offer him a cool mug of ale to help him on his way as the days grew warmer. If, for any reason, Paul couldn't be there, Anna felt a keen sense of disappointment, but this rarely happened, Paul saw to that.

On this warm Sunday in June she was wearing a practically new dress she had bought from the second-hand clothes woman at the market. It was a creamy tobine, a light, summery material, with pale green stripes embroidered in darker green. The matching stomacher was pale green with similar embroidery and dark green lacing. With it she wore a tiny green hat tipped over one eye. It had caught her eye as she walked round the market and she had bought it because the weather was getting warmer and the dresses she had were too thick and heavy. Or so she told herself.

But as she walked with Paul along the road to Schere Gate she knew that the real reason she had bought the dress was because she wanted to look nice in his eyes.

His look of admiration told her that her efforts had not been wasted. But there was concern mixed with the admiration in his eyes. 'You are sad, Anna, I can tell from the droop of your shoulders. Can you tell me what's troubling you?'

She was silent for a moment. It would be comforting to tell Paul of her unsuccessful search for her father, but something, perhaps it was that she didn't want him to think ill of her mother because she had taken a lover, prevented her. 'It's nothing really,' she said with a shrug. 'It's just that I thought I had met someone my mother might have known years ago, but it was a mistake.'

'What a disappointment for you,' he said. He looked down at her. 'Do you miss your home very much, Anna?'

'No, not very much, although of course I miss my mother,' she said honestly. 'But life is so very different here.'

'Would you like to go back?'

She shook her head vehemently. 'No. Never.'

'That's good,' he said quietly.

She stole a glance at him but he said nothing more until they reached her house, their steps gradually slowing as they neared it. Then he said, 'It's a shame to waste such a beautiful day. Will you walk in the woods beyond the Abbey with me, Anna?'

'Yes, I should like that very much,' she answered, trying not to sound too eager. 'If you wait I'll fetch some bread and cheese and beer and we can take it with us to eat in the sunshine.'

'And *I* should like *that* very much,' he said with a smile.

A little later they found themselves in the cool, dappled shade of the woods, the tall oaks spreading a canopy over the fresh, springy turf, deadening their footsteps so that they felt they were alone in a vast green world, the song of the birds only adding to the utter tranquillity.

They found a fallen log near a stream and sat down to eat the food Anna had provided. As they ate they talked. Anna told him about her escape to England with Jan to avoid marriage to Otto de Hane, of her marriage to Jan, of Jan's death and the death of their baby.

'You loved him very much,' Paul said. It was a statement rather than a question.

'Yes. He was my first love and he will always have a place in my heart.'

'I understand that,' Paul said quietly. 'Two years ago I was betrothed to a sweet girl. We were to be married but she took the sweating sickness and was dead within a week.' He closed his eyes briefly. 'I thought I should die, too, at first. When people told me that time is a great healer I was ready to strike them dead with my bare hands. Mouthing their stupid platitudes, how could they know the hurt in me? But I've found their words to be true. Time does heal. The hurt does grow less.' He looked into her eyes. 'And

I've discovered that it's possible to love again.' As he spoke he covered her hand with his own.

She nodded. 'Yes. I've discovered that, too,' she said softly.

Very gently, he pulled her to him and kissed her on the lips. 'Is it true? Can you love me as I love you, Anna?' he whispered.

'Yes, my dearest Paul, I do,' she replied.

Heady with the declaration of their love, they stayed in the green sunlight for a long time, content to be together, heedless of the problems that would lie ahead for an Englishman to marry a Stranger.

'I expect my father will disown me,' he said carelessly, as he kissed her eyelids, her cheeks, and nibbled her ear.

She sat up. 'Oh, Paul, what will you do?'

'Go to my grandfather. He has always said the two communities should live side by side without all the antagonism. In fact, he foresees the day when English and Dutch in Colchester will be totally integrated as one people, but I think perhaps he's being a bit over-optimistic in saying that.'

'He's very modern in his thinking, your grandfather,' Anna said. 'I've never heard anyone else speak like that.'

'No, he and my father have continual arguments on the subject.'

'Yes, I know your father hates my people.' She turned anxious eyes to Paul. 'Oh, Paul what shall we do?'

'Don't worry, sweetheart. We'll find a way.' He began to kiss her again. 'Shall you mind being poor?' he said, his voice muffled in her neck.

She giggled. 'I'm not exactly rich now, am I?'

He leaned away from her, surprised. 'But I thought Samuel Hegetorne provided for you. That is, I've never been quite sure . . . At one time I was afraid that you and he might marry . . . but then again, he's rather old for you . . .'

'He did suggest it,' she said slowly, 'But I couldn't marry a man I didn't love and his terms were not . . .' she hesitated, then went on. 'In truth, all Samuel wanted was to keep me under his wing. You see, he feels guilty because Jan died on an errand for him so he feels responsible for me. When I refused to marry him and insisted on leaving his house he furnished the cottage for me – against my will – and he sends money for me every week, which I never touch. He doesn't know it, but I give it to the poor.' She sighed. 'I wish he wouldn't do these things. I'd much rather he left me to make my own way, yet he has been so good to me, so kind, that I hate to upset him. It's very hard.'

'What will he say when he knows we are to be married? Because we are to be married, aren't we?'

'Oh, yes, please.' She kissed him as he held her close. After a while, safe in the crook of his arm, she said sadly, 'I'm afraid Samuel will accuse me of being a traitor to Jan's memory. And he won't like the idea of me marrying an Englishman.'

'But I thought he was all for Dutch and English integrating.'

'Yes, he is. Up to a point. But I don't think it would include me marrying an Englishman. I told you, he still feels rather proprietorial towards me.'

He frowned. 'What do you mean?'

She shook her head, tired of talking about Samuel. 'Nothing. It's not important.' She turned her face up to be kissed again. 'I love you, Paul and I pray nothing will ever come between us.'

'Amen to that,' he said fervently, thinking of his father.

His apprehension was fully justified. He waited until after supper, when his father was mellow with good wine and a full stomach before he spoke, but it made no difference.

'What, marry some Dutch whore? Never!' Silas stormed up and down the room. 'What can you be thinking of!'

'Silas,' his wife remonstrated from her chair by the window. 'Calm yourself. You'll have apoplexy. Your face is already purple.'

'Be quiet, Eleanor. This has nothing to do with you.'

'Paul is my son, too,' she reminded him.

'Then perhaps you can make him see sense, woman.'

'Anna is no Dutch whore. She is a respectable woman and I won't have you speak ill of her, father,' Paul said, when he could get a word in.

'Respectable woman, my arse! If she was a respectable woman she'd be back where she belongs, over the German Sea, not taking a living from decent English people.'

'I'm not going to enter into an argument with you, father. I'm of age, I can marry whom I choose and I choose to marry Anna.'

'I shall disown you.'

'So be it. Although you will be hard pressed to run the business without me. Grandfather taught me well.' Paul didn't raise his voice as he spoke.

'I should like to know more about this Anna,' his mother put in quietly.

Silas rounded on her. 'Silence, woman. You need to know nothing about her.'

'But if Paul is to marry her . . .'

'Paul is *not* to marry her. I shall see to that.'

Paul turned to his mother, ignoring his father. 'Anna is the woman who raised the alarm when there was a fire in father's row of cottages in Schere Gate Alley, mother. You may remember I told you how the people in the cottages praised her for her courage and the help she gave them.'

His mother nodded. 'Ah, yes, I remember. A good, brave woman, I heard.'

'Rubbish,' Silas said. He sat down in his chair with a bump and thumped the arms. 'I will not have the woman in my house, nor any member of her tribe!'

'Very well, father. Then I shall leave.' Paul turned to go but his mother laid a hand on his arm.

'Don't be hasty, my son,' Eleanor said quietly. 'I shall speak to your father. He is hot-tempered and often he says things he doesn't mean. Leave it to me.'

Paul kissed her. 'Thank you, mother, but I fear even your gentle persuasion will have little effect this time. But my course is set, I am determined that I shall have Anna for my bride, with or without my father's blessing.'

Silas snorted. 'You'll get no blessing from me. You can go to hell and take the wench with you.'

Anna knew nothing of this. Secure in Paul's love, her step was light as she went about her daily work, tending her garden, working in her little still-room at the back of her cottage, or shopping at the market. People there knew her now and both English and Dutch smiled and wished her good day; the poor cripple from the house of the Crutched Friars, the fire-eater, the man on stilts, they all waved and called to her, and the stall-holders made sure she had the best cuts of meat and the fresh-est vegetables.

Of course she knew there would be difficulties ahead. A

Stranger had never married an Englishman and although this first joining together of the two communities would be popular with some – like the predikant, who thought there should be complete integration between them – others would find it totally abhorrent. Like Paul's father. He would never welcome a Dutch wife for his son. She wondered if Paul had told him yet of his plans to marry.

She finished her shopping at the market and turned for home. Then she hesitated. The predikant had offered to show her the grave of Henrick Tayspill, but he was a busy man and the grave-yard of St Martin's Church was only a few steps away in Stockwell Street. Surely it shouldn't be difficult to find.

She bought a small bunch of flowers from the flower-seller and made her way there, shifting her basket from arm to arm, wishing she had thought to visit the graveyard before she had burdened herself with vegetables and fruit. It was cool and quiet in the little graveyard, the gravestones standing sentinel among the butter-cups and daisies, guarding the church. She walked slowly round, reading the inscriptions carved into the stone, sad that so many of them recorded the death of young women in childbirth and of young children. Then she came on the name she was looking for, Henrick Tayspill, a weaver, who died at the age of forty-nine. It was only a small headstone and it said nothing more.

She stared at it for a very long time. There was no way of being sure that this was the man her mother had loved but she had a feeling deep inside her that she had come to the right place. Carefully, almost reverently, she placed the small bunch of flowers she had bought for the purpose on the grave.

'I shall bring flowers to you every week, papa,' she whispered. Then she left, glad that she had at last found her father, but sad because she had found him too late.

The market seemed noisier and busier than ever after the quiet solitude of the graveyard; people seemed to be shouting and jostling even more than usual and carts were being driven through with never a care for who was in the way.

She stood on the steps of St Runwald's Church, trying to get used to the din, shading her eyes against the bright sunlight.

Then as her ears became accustomed to the cacophony she heard the cry, 'Witch! Witch! Witch!', getting louder and louder as a tumbrel rumbled through the market with three women in it, tied together back to back so they shouldn't escape, stumbling and swaying with the movement of the cart, trying as best they could to hold each other up.

Horrified, Anna stared in disbelief. She had heard of witch-hunts but she had never seen evidence of one before. And the three women on the tumbrel looked harmless enough, one of them had a small child with her and another was old and bent. She looked again at the old woman. It was Old Betty, the woman who had saved Jan's life and befriended them when they first arrived in England.

She ran forward, waving her arms. 'Stop! Stop! Old Betty is no witch! She's a wise woman. She cures people!' she called at the top of her voice.

The witch-finder, a man dressed all in black, with a tall black hat and a whip in his hand, was sitting with the driver on the cart and looking very pleased with his morning's work. He turned and craned his neck to see who had shouted. When he saw Anna he made the driver stop the cart and he got down.

'Are you a friend of the old crone?' he asked, his voice silky.

'Yes. Yes, I am,' she said eagerly. 'Old Betty befriended me when I first came here.'

He smiled, baring wolfish teeth. 'A Stranger, too, I hear by your Stranger's sounding voice.' His voice hardened. 'So mayhap you too are a witch,' he said.

'No, of course I'm not a witch.' She brushed off his statement as the nonsense she knew it to be. 'And neither is Old Betty, so let her go free and I'll look after her. I can't vouch for the others but I know Old Betty to be a good woman. She cured my man of a snake bite.'

'By magic, no doubt,' the witch-finder sneered, and the crowd laughed.

'No. With herbs . . .'

'Leave it be!' Old Betty's voice rang out, surprisingly strong for an old woman. 'Tell him no more, Anna.'

'Ha!' the witchfinder turned to Old Betty and then to Anna. 'So you are two witches together, brewing up your potions and evil spells.'

Suddenly, the crowd parted for a man on a black horse. 'You're right, sir. This woman is as black as the old crone. I've seen the potions she brews up. And she put the evil eye on some cottages where my spinners and weavers live and set fire to them.'

Anna turned and her face turned deathly white as she recognised the man denouncing her as Paul's father, Silas Markham.

'It's not true!' she cried. 'I helped to save . . .'

'You! You in the crowd there, what's your name?' Silas Markham pointed his whip at a woman in the crowd. 'You know I speak true. You were there. You saw what she did. Come, woman, speak up. Tell what you know or it will be the worse for you.'

Anna turned pleading eyes towards the woman. It was Jenny, who had been so grateful for the salve she had given her to ease her husband's burns. Anna smiled at her.

The women's eyes slid away. She was clearly terrified. 'What my master says is true,' she muttered. 'There was a fire. She lives opposite. With her little cat.' She slunk away into the crowd before she could be questioned further.

'There! What did I tell you! You heard what the woman said. *And* she has a cat as her familiar,' Silas Markham shouted triumphantly. 'If you were to strip her I don't doubt you would find she has the three nipples of a witch into the bargain.'

'Take her. Tie her on the cart with the others,' the witch-finder said, pleased at finding another victim so easily. 'We'll strip her later when we get her to the castle.'

Anna couldn't believe what was happening. She was so shocked and surprised that she didn't even struggle as the two men who had been walking behind the tumbrel caught her and deftly tied her hands behind her back and almost threw her on to the cart with the others. The last thing she saw was all her apples and carrots being trampled underfoot as the crowd surged forward to follow the cart, jeering and pelting it with rotten fruit and eggs.

And the look of naked triumph on Silas Markham's face.

'Ah, child, you did yourself no favours there,' Old Betty said, as they were thrown into a dank cell together. 'You should have let things be.'

'But I couldn't do that, Betty,' Anna said. She was weeping with fear and frustration. 'I wanted to save you. You were so good to Jan and me when we first came to England. How could I not speak up for you?'

'Because I am old and you are young,' Betty said sadly. 'My life is nearly over. If I'm not hanged for a witch I shall soon die of old age, so what matter? My Maker knows I've never practised witchcraft and it is to Him I shall answer on the Dreadful Day of

Judgement. I care nothing for witch-finders. They will rot in hell and with luck I shall watch them burn.'

'But it is wrong. You are no witch. And I will not have them call you so.'

Old Betty laid a scrawny arm round Anna's shoulders. 'Nobody has ever bothered about me before and it warms my heart to know that you cared enough to speak up for me. But you should never have done it, child, because now they will hang you, too. And you are young.' As she spoke, a tear trickled down the deep wrinkles in the old woman's face.

Chapter Twenty-Three

Anna had no idea how many days and nights passed in the misery of the castle dungeon. She had been thrown with Old Betty into a tiny, dank, evil-smelling cell, the only light coming from a grating high up in the wall. What had happened to the other women they weren't told. Now and again they were thrown a few crusts of mouldy bread and some brackish water.

'You're gonna die so you don't need much,' the turnkey said bluntly, jangling his keys. 'Thass on'y because I like to see a good hangin' that I'm botherin' to feed you at all.'

'You eat it, dearie,' Betty said as she picked it up and gave it to Anna. 'He's right. I shall die. I'm ill with more than I've cure for so it matters little to me whether I die slowly or with my head in a noose. But you'll need all your strength to get out of here.'

'I can't get out. There's no escape,' Anna said on a sob, trying to force down the coarse, evil-tasting loaf. 'I've been all round the walls and all I can feel is slime and rusty chains – at least we're not chained up, we have that to be thankful for, I suppose. The door is thick and barred and that grating is so high up and so small that I couldn't get out of it even if I could reach it.' She spoke wearily. She had beaten on the door in fury, she had screamed in denial and terror, and she had shed tears till she was drained, tears of frustration and utter despair, and all the time Old Betty had held her and whispered words that had eventually soothed and calmed her.

'I thought I was saving you, Betty,' she moaned over and over again. 'I wanted them to know you were my friend, that you were good and kind, that you would never do evil to anybody. Why didn't they listen to me?' Her tears had flowed anew at the dreadful plight they were in.

She hadn't given a thought to her own danger when she spoke up for Old Betty. She had spoken out because of the injustice of the accusation and she had never even considered the possibility that she might end up joining her.

But Silas Markham, Paul's father, had been all too ready to condemn her, she recalled bitterly. He was an important clothier in the town so his word was listened to. He had happened to be riding through the market place as the witchfinder drove through and had heard Anna's cries of protest. Realising who she was, he had grasped his chance to take his revenge on her and stop her marrying his son. It was all down to chance, she thought miserably. If Silas Markham hadn't ridden through just at that time then things might have been very different and both she and Old Betty might now be free.

She slid down on to the stone floor with her back against a wall that was running with water and forming a pool where she sat. Her hair was a tangled mass, she had lost her cap and her clothes stank. But she didn't care. What did it matter? Her future with Paul, loving him, bearing his children, being his companion as they grew old, a future they had both so looked forward to, was gone. It was breaking her heart. And even worse, it would break Paul's heart. That was what she couldn't even bear to think about, breaking Paul's heart. A sob broke in her throat.

Betty felt for her with a claw-like hand. 'Don't give up, my pretty, you're not finished yet,' she said sternly. 'You've got friends. They'll speak up for you, won't they?'

'How can they? Nobody knows I'm here except the man who denounced me and he's not likely to tell anybody.' She swallowed. 'How long have we been here, Betty?'

'About four days, by my reckoning. But I'm only guessing. With the only light we get coming through that grating up there you can't tell whether it's daylight or moonlight. But we've had four lots of bread and water thrown in at us.'

'Have we? I can't tell. I'm not hungry. The stench in here turns my stomach.' Suddenly, she began to cry again, great despairing sobs. 'Oh, why don't they just take us out of this dreadful hole and hang us and let that be an end of it. I shall go mad if I have to stay here much longer.'

'There, there, my pretty. Old Betty's got you.' The old woman said, groping until she had her arms round her. 'Sit quiet and I'll tell you my story,' she crooned. 'It'll help pass the time.' Her voice droned on, quiet and calming. 'I didn't always live in a hovel by the side of the road, you know. My father was a farmer. But after my mother died he lost heart and didn't work so he had his land taken from him. We were on the road for several years, the two of us, and I made a living for us as best I could from my herbs and such. Then he died of a fever and I was alone. I walked for several days, sleeping under hedges and in haystacks and then I found a little empty cottage by the roadside so I thought I'd stay there till somebody turned me out. Well, nobody did, in fact nobody seemed to bother that I was there so I just stayed on. I've been there ever since and that's where you found me.'

'Haven't you been lonely sometimes?' Anna asked, soothed by Old Betty stroking her forehead.

'No. I've always had the birds and the animals for company. I've often thought of you and your man, since you left, though. I enjoyed the time you were with me.'

'Jan's dead.' Anna told her the story.

'Life goes on, child. You'll be happy again,' Betty said sagely when she had finished.

Anna burst into tears again. 'How can you say that! My life isn't going on! How can I be happy again? I'm going to be hanged for a witch, with you,' she sobbed.

'Don't be afraid, my pretty. I shall . . .' Betty's words were drowned as the door suddenly burst open with the clanking of keys.

'Come on, you two. Time to find out what the magistrate's got in store for you. I'spect you'll both hang,' the turnkey said and they could hear the glee in his voice. He fastened ropes round their waists to keep them together and dragged them out of the cell.

They both stumbled out into a passage, with Anna supporting Betty, and up to the court room in the castle.

It was full of people jostling for the best position. There was not much room for public viewing so they were all crushed together, a stinking, heaving mass of humanity, eager for the excitement of the trial.

There were four women up for trial and they stood in a row

before the magistrate, a large, florid man holding a bunch of herbs to his nose from time to time.

The first case was quickly over. The woman was obviously pregnant and so she was acquitted. In the second case, Alice Furnival, the woman with a small child, was charged with prescribing a cure for her neighbour's colic. But the woman had died two days later in agony and Furnival was now cohabiting with the woman's husband. The charge had been brought by the dead woman's sister out of jealousy, the husband attested, because she herself wanted to come and live with him. He further claimed that his wife had died of the bloody flux and had been too far gone for Furnival's cure to do more than ease the pain for a short time. After some deliberation the case was dismissed.

Then it was Anna's turn.

'Widow Verlender?' the magistrate asked, scowling at her.

'Yes. My name is Anna Verlender,' she replied, her voice shaking.

'I see you are of the Stranger community.'

'Yes.'

He looked up. 'Who brings these charges?'

'I do.' The witchfinder, in his black coat and hat, looking for all the world like a great black crow, stepped forward. 'This woman is in league with that old woman, the witch known as Old Betty, standing there beside her.'

'On what evidence?'

'She tried to undermine my authority by shouting in the street that the old crone was no witch, when I have ample evidence to the contrary.'

'We have not yet come to the old woman. Stick to the Stranger. What else have you against her?'

'A man from the crowd shouted that she was a witch.'

'Yes. I say she is a witch. She has bewitched my son.' Suddenly, Silas Markham, an imposing figure, rose from a seat at the side. 'And I have other evidence.' He looked round the crowd, and suddenly seeing the person he was looking for, pointed to her. 'You, there, the woman known as Sal. This witch caused your house to be burned down. Is that not right?'

Anna recognised the woman who had jumped from the window in the fire at the cottages in Schere Gate Alley. She was as pale as death and obviously petrified with fear. 'Aye, Master,' she said, her voice barely above a whisper. 'My house did catch fire, I can't say how, but this woman did live opposite.'

'And you there,' Silas pointed again. 'What have you to say? The woman has a familiar in the form of a cat?'

With a sinking heart Anna recognised Jenny, who looked as if she wished the ground would open up and swallow her.

'Aye, Master. I do believe she has a little cat. But . . .'

'That's enough.' Silas silenced her. 'What about you? The woman they call Lizzie?'

Lizzie shuffled forward, looking at the floor. 'I asked her if she had anything for my Letty's eyes,' she mumbled. 'They was all red and itchy. But somebody said not to take anything from her. They said she'd send my girl blind. I don't know if thass true.'

'There! You see? There's your evidence!' Silas Markham turned triumphantly to the magistrate. 'There can be no doubt of the woman's guilt. She should be hanged.'

The magistrate deliberated for several minutes. Then he nodded. 'Yes. The evidence is all there. Take her away. Back to her cell to await her sentence.'

'Swim her. Why don't you swim her. That'll settle it,' somebody called from the back.

The magistrate looked up. 'It's already settled. She'll hang. That's my final word.' He exchanged a swift, conspiratorial glance with Silas Markham.

Rough hands caught Anna and propelled her, half-fainting, back to the stinking dungeon.

Half an hour later Old Betty was flung in beside her.

'What's to become of you?' Anna whispered.

'Same as you,' Old Betty said.

'When?'

'Tomorrow. In the market place.'

'I didn't want to die, Betty,' Anna said in a flat voice. 'I had so much to live for. But it doesn't matter now. It was Paul's father who denounced me. He did it to make sure Paul would never marry me because I am a Stranger. Even if my life was spared Paul would never be allowed to marry me now and there's nobody else I care about.'

Old Betty groped for her hand. 'You're not done yet, my pretty. Don't give up hope. I'm not much for religion but it might help us both if we were to say a prayer together.'

'Thank you, Betty. At least I know I won't die alone.'

It was a very long night, yet the morning came all too soon. Once again the turnkey jangled his keys in the lock.

'No point in wastin' breakfast on you since you'll both be dead in an hour,' he said cheerfully. 'Come on, this way.' Once again he fastened them together and dragged them out of the cell.

Anna supported Betty, blinking in the dim light after the near darkness they had become used to. They were shoved unceremoniously along, up a flight of stone steps and out into the brightness of the summer day. Anna shaded her eyes with her arm, still holding on to Betty so that she shouldn't fall, and helped her to climb up into the tumbrel that was waiting to take them to the scaffold.

Then, rigid with terror, she stood beside the old woman, holding her up, as the cart began its journey. She couldn't believe that she was going to die, that she would never again see the sunshine, never again see Paul's smile and hear his voice, never again taste good bread and drink clear water. She couldn't imagine this world, which had suddenly become so beautiful, without her in it. She so desperately wanted to live. So desperately wanted to marry and have Paul's children, to grow old beside him.

Frantically, her eyes raked the crowd for a friendly face, but all around there was nothing but hostility. They were all shouting and hissing and running beside the tumbrel the better to pelt them with rotten fruit. There was nobody there who would save her.

The cart drew up beside the hastily built wooden platform outside the Moot Hall. Two ropes were looped ominously above it. She was bundled unceremoniously up on to this platform, with Old Betty close behind her. The crowd were still shouting

'Witch!' 'Witch!' 'Witch!' and throwing things at them. A rotten egg hit its target and the stinking mess ran down the side of Anna's face. She closed her eyes and hung her head. This was the end. There was no hope now. Quaking with terror she prayed that her fright wouldn't show and that she would die bravely. Summoning all her courage, she lifted her head and stared at the sky above the crowd.

Beside her, Old Betty appeared to have the same thought. All at once she seemed to grow taller as her old back straightened.

'Yes, you are right!' she cried and suddenly her voice was strong and powerful, carrying to the very edge of the crowd. 'I am

211

a witch. I cast spells. I can send folk mad or I can cure them of their ills. I have the evil eye . . .' her gaze swept the crowd, 'if I choose to I can turn it on you . . . And you . . . And you.' As she spoke she pointed at nobody in particular but the crowd were too gullible to notice this and fell back at her words, the jeering silenced. Some turned away, muttering that they had better things to do than watch a hanging; others suddenly remembered urgent business. But some remained, mesmerised by the old woman's words.

She leaned forward. 'You disbelieve me? Then listen to this. I put this woman under my spell when I saw her in the crowd.' She gave Anna a vicious poke. 'I gave her one look and made her shout out and speak up for me. I still have her under my power. She'll do whatever I want because she has no will of her own. Watch!' She turned to Anna and said loudly, 'Dance a jig, girl!' Then in a whisper, 'For the love of God, dance, my pretty!'

Hardly knowing what she was doing, Anna began to hop up and down.

'Faster, girl, faster!' Betty commanded, her voice ringing out loud and clear.

Anna jigged as fast as her failing strength would let her.

'Faster still!'

She jigged and spun round and hopped about as if her life depended on it. Which she dimly realised through the blood pounding in her head, it did.

'Now stop!'

She stumbled to a halt and fell to her knees. Betty bent over her and put her hands on her shoulders, saying in a sing-song voice, 'I release you from my spell. You are no longer in my power.' Her voice dropped to a whisper. 'There, my pretty, they'll believe that, stupid fools that they are. You'll walk free now. God go with you, my dear child.'

It was the last thing Anna heard before she fell forward in a dead faint.

She came to as someone threw water over her and she got shakily to her knees, realising that she had been released from the ropes that had tied her to Old Betty. Then she looked up and saw Old Betty's spindly legs and feet in their worn-out boots swinging gently to and fro four feet above her head. A sob caught in her throat but as she heard the superstitious mutterings among the crowd, and saw how gullible they were, how they had been completely taken in by her old friend's clever charade, she realised that she must keep up the pretence if she was to shake off any suspicion among them that she might have been tainted by Old Betty's witchcraft.

So she cringed away from the swinging corpse and slid off the platform, hiding her eyes from the lolling head of her old friend. Then she turned and ran, straight into the arms of Samuel Hegetorne.

He took her by the arm. 'I knew no good would come of your leaving my protection,' he said as he strode along, half-pulling, half-dragging her behind him. He turned briefly and looked her up and down in disgust. 'God, how you stink! And look at you! You're filthy! I don't know that I can bear to have you in the carriage with me.'

'I don't want . . .' she began.

'I don't care what you want or don't want. I'm taking you back to Garden House where I can look after you properly.' He pushed her into the carriage and they drove off, he swinging a pomander and with a scrap of lavender-scented lace held delicately to his nose.

'How did you know?' she asked, crouched in one corner whilst he sat in the other, as far away from her stench as he could get.

'Word gets round. Griete was at the market the day you were stupid enough to defend that old woman. I made enquiries and found out when the execution was to take place. Never fear, I would have rescued you if it had been necessary.'

She lifted her head. 'How?'

He held out his hand holding a bag of money. 'These people are always open to bribery,' he said shortly.

Anna had to admit that it was wonderful to lie in a tub of hot, rose-scented water, with Griete there to scrub her back and wash her hair, to remove every last trace of prison stench. The new little kitchen maid, who had to carry the buckets of scented water up to her room, was nearly worn out, because it took three changes of water before she felt she was really clean.

Then she allowed Griete to help her into one of the dresses she had left behind – was it only six months ago?

'So!' Samuel said later, when she was seated opposite to him at the long dining table, a plate of roast duck in front of her. 'I trust you've learned your lesson, my dear.'

She played with the food on her plate. It was some days since she had eaten properly and her stomach rebelled at the sight of this rich fare. She broke off a piece of manchet and put it in her mouth. It was sweet-tasting and smooth after the coarse, mouldy bread of the prison. She ate another piece, savouring it. Then she looked up at Samuel, who was looking very pleased with himself.

'Have I learned my lesson?' she repeated thoughtfully. 'I've learned that Old Betty was a true friend to me. She gave me back my life. No one could do more. I shall always remember her with affection and be grateful to her.'

'Be quiet, girl. Never let me hear you speak like that again!' He had turned quite pale at her words.

She smiled at him, surprised. 'You don't *really* believe she had me under her spell, Samuel, do you? She only spoke as she did to gain my release.'

'Whether or not it is true, many people believe it and it would be unwise to contradict them,' he said stiffly, annoyed at her mocking tone. 'Witchcraft is a powerful force.'

'Old Betty was no witch, I assure you. She was a very wise woman,' Anna said quietly.

'Well, I'll thank you to keep your opinion to yourself.' He jabbed his knife towards her plate. 'Aren't you going to eat your duck?'

'No. I'm afraid my stomach isn't yet ready for it.' She pushed back her chair. 'I'll go to bed now, if you don't mind. I haven't slept properly for . . .' she shook her head, 'I don't know how long it's been. It was impossible to tell one day from another in that place.'

'You were there for over a week,' he said more kindly. 'Yes, of course. You must be tired. You'll find your bed is ready. Your room is as you left it. The servants have orders to keep it so. Sleep well.'

For a week she was happy to let Samuel order her days, to let Griete pamper her. The experience in the castle prison had left her with terrible memories. She slept badly, afraid to blow out the candle because she couldn't bear the darkness, and when she did finally sleep she was plagued by bad dreams and nightmares, in which she was back in the stinking, rat-infested dungeon.

214

Realising just how close she had come to losing her life made her value everything she saw, everything she did. Life was good. Life was precious. For the moment that was enough; she was content to let everything else simply wash over her.

Inevitably, this apathy didn't last.

When she walked in the garden, savouring the bright sunshine, she could see that nothing at all had changed. The hedges were clipped to exactly the same shape, the borders carried exactly the same flowers, the knot garden was the same. Even the vegetables were grown where they had always been. She could close her eyes and go straight to the cabbage patch.

'I tell Mynheer Hegetorne that we should rotate the vegetables. It does no good to grow cabbages in the same place every year, they get the club root and wither,' the gardener told Anna. 'But he won't hear of anything being changed. Everything has to stay the same.' He sighed. 'I have ideas – good ideas, though I say it myself – but he won't even listen to what I plan.'

Anna hesitated, then decided to take Pieter into her confidence. 'Although he didn't know it at the time, because Samuel didn't tell him, my husband designed this garden as a memorial to Samuel's dead wife.' She spread her hands. 'Once it was done Samuel was so pleased with it that now he won't have anything altered.' She smiled at Pieter. 'I know how frustrating it must be for you, Pieter.'

He nodded. 'It is certainly beautifully designed. But not even to change where the cabbages grow . . .' He shook his head in despair.

'I know. And I'm sure it would be much better for it to grow and change rather than –' she hesitated, the word 'stagnate' had come into her mind but that wouldn't be fair to Pieter, who worked hard to keep everything alive and vibrant '– Rather than stay exactly the same,' she finished instead.

She went back into the house. Already the atmosphere was becoming claustrophobic. She felt she was being smothered in luxury, with nothing useful to do. And because she had nothing to do her thoughts turned more and more to Paul. She had lost him and with him her chance of happiness, his father had made sure of that. What Silas Markham had done was a cruel, spiteful way of making sure his son didn't marry a Stranger, she thought sadly.

She was not surprised that she had heard nothing from Paul. It

215

had been hard enough for him wanting to marry a Stranger in the first place, knowing his father's antipathy to the Dutch Congregation, but one with the stigma of witchcraft, however ill-founded, made it impossible. She doubted that she would ever see him again and she wept bitter tears into her pillow at night as she dwelt on what might have been.

To her surprise, Samuel expected her to resume the habits of the past, and to sit with him while he smoked his pipe after supper each night and talked on and on in his rather stentorian tone – which she had never noticed before – about nothing very much. But after a few weeks she began to fidget and long for the peace and freedom of her own little house.

'I think it's time I went back to my own cottage,' she said, cutting across his conversation one evening when she had been back at Garden House for well over a month. 'You've been very kind to me, Samuel, and I appreciate your hospitality but I am quite recovered now. I no longer have bad dreams and my appetite is restored so I think it's time I went home.'

He choked on his pipe. 'But this *is* your home, Anna. This is where you belong,' he said when he had recovered his breath. 'And this is where I want you to stay.'

She got up from her chair and began to pace up and down the room. 'No, Samuel,' she said at last. 'I don't belong here. Not any more. I have made a life for myself . . .'

'And nearly lost it in the process, I might remind you,' he said with only a hint of sarcasm.

'I was doing what I thought was right. I tried to save a dear, good friend from an unjust fate. I shall always have it on my conscience that I failed,' she said, on the verge of tears.

He waved his pipe, leaving a trail of smoke. 'Be that as it may. You are not capable of living alone. I indulged you once, but I shan't do it again. Let me remind you that it is only my generosity that enabled you to live in that cottage. If I hadn't sent money each week I've no doubt you would have starved.'

She swung round. 'I didn't touch a penny of the money you sent. I gave it all to the poor. But I didn't starve.' She stared at him, frowning. 'What do you think I am, Samuel? Some little milksop who can't boil water? I'm a grown woman. A widow. I am perfectly able to make my own way in the world and that's what I intend to do.'

216

'It's not what I intend for you, my dear. I intend to look after you. It's what Jan asked me to do before he took that fateful journey and I promised him that I would. I keep my promises, Anna.'

'Oh, Samuel, that was two years ago.'

'It makes no difference. A promise is a promise.'

She banged her fist on the table. 'But I don't *want* you to look after me, Samuel. I need to be independent. I shall go back to my cottage tomorrow.'

'You can't do that,' he said, unruffled.

'Why not?'

'Because I've got rid of it.'

She stared at him, open-mouthed. Then she sighed. 'Very well, then I shall have to find somewhere else to live.'

'No. I shan't let you go.'

'I'm afraid you can't stop me.' She went and sat down opposite to him again. 'I really don't want to quarrel with you, Samuel,' she said quietly. 'I have so much to be grateful to you for. And I *am* grateful. But if I want to leave you have no right to prevent me. In fact, you can't stop me.' She resumed her pacing up and down the room like a caged animal.

'Oh, I think, I can,' he said quietly.

She looked over her shoulder. 'How?'

'It's not what I would have chosen to do and it will of necessity be slightly unconventional.' He rubbed his hands together. 'Nevertheless, I'm sure we shall manage very well.'

She frowned. 'What are you talking about?'

He smiled triumphantly. 'I shall marry you.'

217

Chapter Twenty-Four

'No!' Anna said, horrified. Then, realising how rude she had sounded, she shook her head and said as gently as she could, 'I'm very flattered that you should wish to marry me, Samuel, but I don't think it would be at all a good idea.'

'Oh, it's not that I *wish* to marry you, my dear,' he said smoothly. 'I simply feel it is my duty, since I promised Jan I would look after you and since you seem incapable of looking after yourself.'

'That's not true. I'm perfectly capable of looking after myself,' she said indignantly. 'But leaving that aside, I'm sorry, I couldn't possibly marry you, Samuel.'

'Oh, and why not?' His eyebrows shot up.

'Because I am in love with somebody else.'

He was quiet for several minutes. 'And were you intending to marry this "somebody else"?' he asked at last.

'Yes, I was.'

'But now, after your recent – I think "disaster" wouldn't be too strong a word – you're not so sure.'

'There are problems,' she admitted.

He leaned back in his chair. 'I have never expected you to be in love with me, Anna,' he said, and she could detect a hint of regret in his voice. 'I know I'm old enough to be your father. But that needn't prevent a marriage between us.' His voice strengthened. 'And I don't intend that it should. I shall see the predikant tomorrow.' His expression softened. 'I can give you everything that money can buy, Anna,' he said. 'Many women would be glad to be in your position.'

'I know that, Samuel,' she said with a sigh. 'And I am

honoured, truly honoured, that you are prepared to take me as your wife.' She was quiet for several minutes, then she said, 'I'm sorry. I need to think very carefully about what you have said. Can we talk about it in the morning?'

He inclined his head. 'As you wish.'

She escaped and went to her room but she didn't sleep. She spent the night making plans and rejecting them. The only thing she was certain about was that she could not, would not marry Samuel Hegetorne, which left her no alternative but to leave his house immediately. But where could she go? She couldn't stay in Colchester, that much was certain, because he would search her out. Perhaps if she went to the predikant he would give her an introduction to somebody in London. No, that wouldn't do, the predikant would tell him where she had gone. She couldn't go to Paul – she couldn't ever go to Paul again, because she knew his father would have successfully poisoned his mind against her. She pressed her fingers to her throbbing temple. There must be somewhere safe! Think! Think!

As the new day slipped over the horizon, streaking the sky with blue and grey and yellow light she still had no idea where she could go, or what she could do. All she knew was that she must leave Garden House, now, before even the servants were awake.

She dressed quickly and crept down the back stairs and out through the back door, remembering that this was exactly the manner in which she had left her father's house what seemed like half a lifetime ago. Then as now, she had been escaping from an unwelcome marriage, but then she had had Jan to care for her. Now she was alone. Completely alone. Trying not to think about this, she hurried towards the town, half-walking, half-running, glancing over her shoulder every few steps in fear that she might be followed, desperate to escape from the house that she was beginning to regard as almost as much of a prison – albeit an elegant, comfortable prison – as the castle dungeon had been. As she hastened along, she tried to make her brain work, to think what she could do.

First she must go to her cottage. Samuel had told her he had got rid of it but there were things there that she belonged to her and that she needed, her herbal, what little money she possessed. Someone must have them. And there was Blackie, too. She needed to know what had happened to her little cat. Perhaps one of the women from the cottages was looking after her.

She sped along to Schere Gate just as the town was coming to life, workmen rubbing bleary eyes as they went off to do their day's work, women throwing out the rubbish.

There was no time to lose because the cottage was probably the first place Samuel would come to look for her.

A woman was emptying slops into the gutter when she arrived.

'I used to live in this cottage,' she said breathlessly. 'Do you know what happened to my possessions?'

'Aye. The woman from the cottage over there stole the lot,' the woman said with a sneer. 'They're a thieving lot over there. I shan't stay here long. I don't trust 'em.'

'Thank you.' Anna didn't wait to hear more but went across to Schere Gate Alley. Jenny was at her door, shaking a blanket. When she saw her she ran forward.

'Oh, Mistress, I'm that glad you were saved. I never meant to betray you,' she said, her face creased with worry. 'Honest to God, I never wanted to harm you, but Master Markham . . . I daren't go against him or he'd have turned us out . . .'

'I know, Jenny, I know. I understand. I don't blame you,' Anna said quickly. 'But you've got to help me. Do you know where the things from my cottage were taken? My herbal. A small purse of money. They are the important things. And do you know where Blackie is?'

A smile spread across Jenny's face. 'Oh, aye. I know where Blackie is, Mistress. My children have properly taken to her. They treat her like a baby.'

As if she knew they were talking about her, the cat suddenly appeared from inside the cottage, rubbing herself against Anna's skirt and purring loudly. Anna picked her up and stroked her silky fur.

'Oh, I've missed you, Blackie,' she said fondly. 'But I don't know what I'm going to do with you, because I've got to go away.'

As if she knew exactly what Anna was saying, Blackie scrambled up and sat on her shoulder.

'She thinks she's coming, too,' Jenny said, nodding.

Gently, Anna lifted her down. 'No, Blackie, you can't come. You must stay here, if Jenny will have you.'

220

'Oh, she can stay here. She's no trouble,' Jenny said.

'That's good. Thank you, Jenny. But the other things? Have you got them?'

'Oh, yes. Mistress. I've got several things. When they came to empty the place I told them you'd asked me to look after them. I've got your clothes . . .'

'Oh, I can't take clothes. You can have them. Just the herbal and my purse, that's all I need. Quickly, now. And if Mynheer Hegetorne comes and asks for me you must say you haven't seen me. Will you promise?'

'Aye, that I will. I shan't betray you again, Mistress. Not ever.' She hurried into the house and brought out a small basket. 'There. I've put all the small things in this. There were some brooches and a necklace; you'll be able to sell them if you need money. And I've put in a brooch that belonged to my mother. It's little enough compensation for what I did to you but it's the best I have to offer. And here's a loaf. I don't know where you're going but you'll need to eat.'

'Thank you, Jenny.' Impulsively, Anna kissed her cheek and hurried away, up Schere Gate steps and along Trinity Street. She knew now where she must go. It was the obvious place. She would go to Old Betty's cottage. It was empty now that the old woman was dead and far enough from Colchester to be sure that nobody who saw her there would recognise her. She could live out her days, just as Old Betty had hoped to do, in peace, with nobody to bother her.

But first she wanted to pay a last visit to her father's grave. She crossed the market place, trying not to look at the place in front of the Moot Hall where Old Betty had died, threading her way between the stallholders already putting out their wares and into Stockwell Street.

St Martin's churchyard was cool and quiet. She crouched down beside the grave and realised she was trembling.

'Goodbye, father,' she whispered, laying her head down on the green mound under which Henrick Tayspill lay. 'I wanted to reunite you with your Judith but it was not to be. When I am able, I shall let her know I found you. Rest in peace.'

Her eyes blurred with tears she turned to pick up her basket and saw that there was a dark shadow beside it. Puzzled, she wiped her eyes with her hand so that she could see what it was.

'Blackie! You followed me!' She bent down and stroked the purring cat. 'Oh, Blackie, you were determined not to lose me again, weren't you. Oh, very well, if you're so determined I'd better take you with me.' She straightened up and made Blackie comfortable in the basket. 'We've got a long way to go,' she warned. 'And if you jump out I'll never be able to find you again.' As if she understood, Blackie curled herself into a ball among the trinkets in the basket and went to sleep.

Anna, fearing she had already wasted too much time, hurried back to the market place, down East Hill towards the Harwich Road and the long walk to Old Betty's cottage.

Halfway down East Hill she slowed her step as she passed the house where Paul Markham lived with his parents. It was a large house with an archway leading through to the sheds where the wool and cloth were stored. Already carts were being loaded with finished cloth to be taken to the docks at Hythe. She couldn't see Paul as she went by and she daren't pause to look more carefully.

She sped on, keeping her mind busy by remembering the last time she was on this road. She had been with Jan then and they had been going in the opposite direction. They had been so full of hope, busily making plans for their future together, a future that had been all too brief for Jan. But they had been happy together while it lasted. A smile played about her lips as she remembered.

She was halfway to Manningtree, her feet and back aching from the pace she was keeping, when a cart loaded with bales of cloth drew up beside her.

'I'm making for Harwich, if that's any use to you,' the driver said, leaning down.

Gratefully, Anna climbed up beside him.

'Where are you bound for?' he asked, glad of somebody to talk to.

She hesitated. 'To visit a friend,' she said at last. 'The other side of Manningtree.'

'What you got in that basket? A cat?'

'Yes, that's right. It's for my friend.'

He turned to look at her but she tried to shield her face so he couldn't get a good view. 'You're a Stranger, ain't you?' he asked. 'I can tell by the way you speak.'

'I come from Flanders. Yes. But I've been here several years now.'

'This cloth is goin' to Calais, to the Staple. It could have gone from the Hythe but my master reckons it'll get there sooner if it goes from Harwich. I dunno if he's right but thass what he reckons.' He spat off the side of the cart. 'Don't make no difference to me whether I take it to Hythe or Harwich, long as I git paid.'

It was past midday when they passed Old Betty's cottage. The driver pointed to it with his whip. 'Thass where that owd witch lived what was hung a few weeks back,' he told her.

'Oh, is it? Then hurry past, driver. We don't want to be bewitched by looking at it,' she said, pretending to shudder.

'Ah, she's gone now. Can't do nobody no harm,' he said. 'Mind you, I try not to come past here after dark. Some say the place is haunted and you never know, her ghost might still be here.'

'Indeed it might.'

Anna let the cart rumble on for another mile, then she said, 'This will do me nicely, thank you, driver.'

'But there's naught but woodland here, Mistress,' he said in surprise.

'I know. My friend lives on the other side of the wood.' She climbed down from the cart and watched it trundle away. It was then she noticed the name painted across the back, MARKHAM & SON, and she cursed herself for not noticing it before she accepted his offer of a lift. But what harm could it do? She was never likely to see the man again. She put it out of her mind and struck off through the wood, waiting till the cart was well out of sight before making her way back to Old Betty's cottage.

It was much as she remembered. The sleeping loft with a straw bed and a tattered blanket, none too clean; a blackened pot hanging over the dead embers in the hearth; a rickety chair and table. A couple of chickens flew down from the rafters and ran for cover when they saw her. She smiled grimly. The place was just as squalid as she remembered from her last visit. But the garden had been well tilled. There were carrots and turnips, beans and peas ready for the picking, although now they were nearly choked with weeds. And the herb garden that Jan had made was flourishing.

'We shall do very well here, Blackie,' she said, putting down the basket so that Blackie could jump out. 'And if people think the place is haunted it's all to the good because that means they'll leave us alone.' She walked to the bottom of the garden and wound a bucket of clear fresh water up from the well and dipped herself a drink.

In the days that followed, Anna cleaned the cottage and made it habitable, although she was careful to leave the front of it looking derelict and unlived in. There were plenty of vegetables to eat and she found wild strawberries in the woods. And there were eggs. She discovered them in the most unlikely places and sometimes they were fit to eat and sometimes they weren't. There was also a tub of flour in the corner so that she could make bread once she had sifted out the weevils.

She was never lonely because there was plenty to do making the cottage habitable and she had Blackie for company. The little cat hardly left her side, following her wherever she went, whatever she did. It was as if she remembered the times her mistress had left her behind and was determined never to let her out of her sight again.

What she would do when the winter came and the flour and vegetables ran out Anna didn't dare to think, but for the moment she was happy, as happy that is, as she could ever expect to be again. But she was always watchful, always listening for the rumble of a cart or the hoofbeats of a horse. And when she heard the noise of anyone approaching she would take Blackie and hide in the woods until the danger was past. Not that anyone ever stopped at the cottage, in fact often hoofbeats quickened and carts rumbled faster because news had quickly spread that the place was haunted. In a few days, Anna's fear of discovery lessened and she ceased to run quite so far into the woods as the carts went by.

Anna's disappearance caused consternation at Garden House. Samuel paced up and down, cursing and blaming the servants for letting her escape, quite unfairly threatening dismissal if she wasn't found.

But since nobody had seen or heard her go, and not even Griete knew her plans, shouting and threatening did no good at all.

Finally, he sat down and tried to think rationally what was to be done. Part of him was inclined to leave her to her fate, whatever it might be. She had proved more trouble than he cared to admit since Jan died and in truth a wife was about the last thing he wanted. But he had made a promise to Jan that he would look after Anna and since she was proving so wayward he could see no other way of fulfilling that promise. With a sigh he realised where his duty lay; in a way he supposed it could be considered a just retribution for sending Jan to his death.

After four days spent searching the house, the garden and all the surrounding countryside he decided to visit the cottage where Anna had been living, although he didn't think it likely she had gone back there since he had told her he had sold it. But he was wrong. The woman who was now living there remembered seeing her and thought she had visited the cottages opposite. Reluctantly, Samuel went across to Schere Gate Alley and knocked on the door of the first cottage, without success. He tried each one in turn until he came to Jenny, in the last cottage. By this time his patience was wearing thin.

At first she denied having seen Anna, unwilling to betray her yet again.

'But what about her cat? She had a cat. Where is it?' he asked finally, his voice taking on a menacing tone.

'It's not here.' By this time Jenny was so intimidated she was nervously twisting her apron between her hands.

'Then where is it?'

'It went with her. It followed her and wouldn't come back when I called it,' she cried, hardly knowing what she was saying.

'Hah! So she *was* here!'

Jenny crumpled and put her hand to her mouth. Then, seeing there was no help but to tell him, she admitted, 'Yes, she was. Early in the morning three, perhaps four days ago. But I swear to God, sir, I don't know where she was making for. In fact, I don't think she knew herself, and that's the truth of it.'

'Pah!' Samuel leaped back on to his horse and galloped away, leaving Jenny weeping on her doorstep in case she had done Anna harm.

The predikant was his next call but Mynheer van Migrode was no help.

'It's hardly likely she'd come to me, Samuel,' he said. 'But come in and have some wine. You're looking quite distraught. Now,' when they were both settled with a glass of red wine, 'are you sure you want to find her?'

'Of course I'm sure, Abraham. You're already making arrangements for us to be married.' He finished his wine at a draught.

225

Abraham poured him more. 'An ill-advised match, as I've warned you, my friend. You should think carefully . . .'

'I have thought carefully,' he snapped. 'I am determined to marry her.'

'It seems she's equally determined not to marry you,' Abraham said, looking at him over the top of his wire-rimmed spectacles.

'Nonsense. She'll come round to the idea. When I can find her.' He drained the second glass and got to his feet. 'Well, if you can't help me I must look further.' He went off, his temper not improved by his talk with the predikant.

He turned his horse along Head Street and into the market place. He could think of only one other place where she might be. With that young Englishman, Paul Markham. Silas Markham wouldn't shelter her, of course, rumour had it that he was the man who had denounced her as a witch, so she was hardly likely to ask for help there. But he might have some idea where she had gone. But the idea of tackling Silas Markham was distasteful to him. He didn't like the man, never had, he was more trouble than anyone else at the Bay Hall, but needs must.

He gave a young boy a penny to hold his horse and went into the Bay Hall to find Silas Markham or better still, his son. A quick look round convinced him that neither of the Markhams was there, but having shown his face he found it difficult to get away because there were several problems to be solved and disputes settled. As Governor he was usually at the Bay Hall every day and four days' absence had left much unfinished business to attend to. It was past midday before he was able to reclaim his horse and make his way through the market place and down East Hill to Silas Markham's house.

The reception he received was less than cordial.

Silas Markham was in the yard overseeing the loading of bales of cloth on to a wagon. In another part of the yard Paul was watching the unloading of fleeces into the warehouse.

'What do you want, Stranger?' Silas asked curtly as Samuel cantered in. 'You're not welcome on my property.'

'I'm not looking for welcome. I'm looking for my future wife, Mevrouw Verlender.'

Silas's lip curled. 'The witch? Hasn't she been caught and hanged yet?' He laughed derisively. 'You're wasting your time. She's not likely to come here. I'd have her clapped in gaol as soon as look at her and she knows it. Thought she could marry my son! Well, she soon found out differently, didn't she! Your future wife, you say? Well, if I knew where she was I'd willingly help you to find her to keep my son out of her clutches. But I don't, so there's an end of it. Now I have work to do. I bid you good day, Stranger.' He turned back and resumed overseeing the loading on to the cart.

Furious at being so summarily dismissed, Samuel rode out of the yard and back up the hill.

It was very much later that day, when he had eaten a lonely supper and was sitting opposite the empty chair that Anna should have been occupying, going over the events of the recent past, that the idle thought came to him that she had always held that old woman – what was her name? Old Betty – in very high regard. Such high regard that she had landed herself in prison trying to help her. He frowned, remembering that Jan had once told him about the same old woman curing him of a snake bite when they first came off the boat from Flanders, on their journey from Harwich to Colchester. Was it possible that Anna had gone to ground in that old woman's hovel? He poured himself more wine. If that was so, it wouldn't be difficult to find her because there was only one road between the two places. He smiled as he drank the wine and poured more. It would keep till tomorrow. If she was there she would feel quite secure so there was no hurry.

He puffed out his cheeks. He was really getting too old for all this gallivanting about the countryside, but needs must if he wanted to complete the task he had set himself. And it would be worth it. Soon he would have her back where she belonged.

Chapter Twenty-Five

When Paul Markham saw Samuel Hegetorne ride into the yard he was busy counting fleeces off the cart into one of the sheds. He stayed out of the way, listening to the exchange between the Dutchman and his father, and heard the words, 'My future wife' spoken. His heart sank. So Anna was to marry this man, after all. He dragged another fleece off the cart and threw it into the warehouse. It was no more than might have been expected, of course. She was never again going to look at him, Paul, not after the dreadful thing his father had done to her.

He dragged another fleece off the cart. Then he stopped, frozen in the act of throwing it. It sounded as though Samuel Hegetorne was looking for her because he was asking if she had come here. Paul moved a little closer, making sure he couldn't be seen, so that he could hear better. He soon gathered that Anna had run away and Samuel didn't know where she had gone. That was why he had come here. Obviously, Samuel thought she had come to find Paul.

He felt a tugging at his sleeve. It was the driver of the cart.

'I can hear what that man is sayin', Master Paul,' he whispered. 'I reckon I seed that young woman the other day when I was takin' that cloth to Harwich. She was jest the other side o' Ardleigh, in a rare owd hurry, too. Said she was goin' to visit a friend out beyond Manningtree so I took her up on the cart with me to help 'er on 'er way. She'd got a little cat in a basket. I reckon that musta bin her, don't you, Master Paul? Do you reckon I oughta say suthin'?'

Paul stared at the man, realisation dawning. 'No!' he said in a fierce whisper. 'Keep your mouth shut, William. Say nothing to anybody. Just get on with your work. Wait a minute. Where did you put her down?'

'Jest past the witch's hovel. I remember it well, cause we talked about the place bein' haunted now th'owd witch is dead.'

'Thank you, William.' He patted him on the shoulder. 'Now, will you do something for me? If my father asks, tell him I had to go off on urgent business.' He waved his hand vaguely. 'Umm, tell him the fleeces were short. Or dirty. Oh, tell him anything, but if you value your life don't tell him or the Dutchman what you've just told me.'

As Samuel left the yard and rode up the hill, furious and disappointed, so Paul saddled Blaze, his horse, and rode off in the other direction. As soon as he got into open country he spurred his horse into a gallop. He knew it would only be a matter of time before Samuel found out where Anna had gone but he had got a head start and he didn't intend to lose it. He dug his spurs into his horse's side again.

As he galloped along the road he went over what William the carter had told him. She was making for a friend's house, he'd said. But Paul was certain that Anna had no friends that far from Colchester, so who or where could she have been making for? William said he had put her down about a mile past the witch's hovel. The witch's hovel. Old Betty's cottage. Could that be where she had gone? It made sense. Anna would feel safe there but she wouldn't have wanted the carter to know that was where she was making for, so she had got him to put her down well past and then doubled back. Poor sweet, she must be desperate.

In an hour he was there, but to his disappointment the cottage looked just as derelict as it had always done. The shutters were hanging crazily at the windows and the door was firmly shut with weeds and ivy growing up nearly to the latch. He left Blaze to graze on the sweet grass verge and went and banged on the door. There was no reply.

'Anna, for the love of God, are you in there?' he called. 'It's me, Paul. Anna, please, if you're hiding come out.'

Still there was no response. His heart sank. He had been so sure he would find her here but now he didn't know where to begin to look. Dejectedly, he turned away and went back to his horse. He mounted Blaze and gave one last look at the derelict little hovel.

Of course she wasn't there. The place wasn't fit for human habitation, he'd been a fool to think she might have come here.

Then he thought he heard a faint noise. He looked at the cottage again and saw a movement up on the roof beside the chimney. It was a little black cat.

He leaped off his horse and ran back to the cottage. 'Blackie!' he called softly.

The cat mewed and put a tentative paw out, afraid to come down.

'Where is she, Blackie? Where is Anna?' he asked excitedly, as if the cat could tell him.

Blackie mewed again.

'All right. I'll get you down in a minute.' He turned away. Anna was here, somewhere, if only he could find her. He went round to the back of the house. The door here was open and there were all the signs of recent occupation. There was water in the pitcher, the floor had been swept, the garden weeded. A dish of recently shelled peas had been spilled on the floor. He looked round the room and climbed to the sleeping loft but the place was empty.

He strode to the end of the garden and into the wood.

'Anna, for the love of God, where are you?' he called, striding through the undergrowth. 'It's me. Paul. Please don't hide from me.'

Then he saw her running through the trees towards him and the next minute she was in his arms, laughing and crying at the same time as he held her and smothered her with kisses.

'Samuel wants to marry me, Paul,' she said breathlessly. 'I couldn't. I couldn't marry him so I ran away and came here. I thought I'd be safe here and could live like my dear friend Old Betty. Because I knew you wouldn't want me . . .'

He cut her words off with another kiss. 'Oh, Anna. How could you think that! Of course I want you. But I didn't think you'd want me, not after the dreadful, wicked thing my father did to you.' He held her close again, then released her. 'But, my darling, we've no time to lose. Samuel is looking for you. It will only be a matter of time before he thinks of coming here . . .'

'Do you think he will, Paul?' she asked, fear in her eyes. 'I didn't think anyone would find me if I came here. How did you know I was here, Paul? Was it your carter? Did he tell you he'd seen me?'

'He said he'd given a lift to a young woman with a cat who was visiting a friend. I guessed it was you and I knew you hadn't got any friends this far from Colchester. But if I hadn't seen Blackie up on the roof . . .'

'Yes, I was afraid she would give me away. She's stuck up there and can't get down and I can't reach her.'

'Thank heaven for that. She deserves rescuing for leading me to you. I was on the verge of giving up, the place looked so dilapidated and empty.' He broke off a long branch from a sapling as they walked back through the wood. When they reached the cottage he climbed on the tree stump Betty had used as a chopping block and reached as far as he could up the roof with the branch. It fell several feet short of the cat.

He got down from the block. 'Come here, Anna. If I lift you up the extra length might do it,' he said. He swung her up in his arms and held her so that she could push the branch almost to where the frightened little cat sat, mewing piteously.

'Come on, Blackie,' she urged. 'There's no time to lose.'

Gingerly, Blackie put a dainty paw on the end of the branch. Then cautiously, with much persuasion from Anna, she crawled on to it and Anna gently dragged it towards her until she could reach the cat and take her in her arms.

'We're safe,' she said to Paul, and he lowered her and Blackie into his arms. 'I can't believe I've found you again,' he murmured into her hair, before he released them.

Carefully, Anna put Blackie down and watched as she stalked into the cottage and sat down in front of the hearth and began to wash herself as if nothing had happened.

They followed her in and Paul sat Anna down on the only chair, perching himself on the edge of the table and holding her hands in his as if he was afraid she might run away again.

'What are we going to do, Paul?' she asked, looking up at him with big, fearful eyes. 'We can't stay here, can we. Samuel is sure to find us and . . .' She shook her head. 'No, I won't marry him. There must be something we can do.'

He gave her hands a little shake. 'Well, as I see it, there's only one way to stop Samuel fetching you back and marrying you, Anna, and that's for me to marry you first,' he said firmly. 'Will you marry me, Anna? Can you forgive me for the dreadful thing my father did to you and consent to be my wife?'

'Oh, Paul.' She got to her feet and kissed him. 'You can't be held responsible for what your father did. Of course I want to marry you. More than anything in the world. But how can we marry? Samuel will find out when we go back to Colchester and I know he'll try to stop us.'

'I've already thought of that. We're not going back to Colchester. We'll go to Harwich and find a clergyman there who'll marry us.'

'When?'

'Now. As soon as my horse is watered and rested. Poor beast, I rode him hard to get here and he'll be carrying two of us for the rest of the journey.'

'Then we've time for a dish of broth before we start. I only light the fire under my cooking pot after dark so that the smoke can't be seen. The embers are still hot in the morning so the broth in the pot is hot, too.' She poured him a good helping.

'This is good,' he said as he drank it from the bowl. He grinned at her over its rim. 'I can see I shall never starve with you for my wife.'

Anna was too agitated to return his smile. She kept looking over her shoulder, expecting Samuel to appear at any moment. 'Old Betty's garden provided the vegetables and herbs. I have so much to be grateful to her for.' She drank a little from her own bowl but her stomach was tied in nervous knots and she had no appetite.

'Come, you must drink a little more than that,' he said, holding the bowl to her lips. 'I can't risk my bride fainting at the altar from lack of nourishment.' He smiled into her eyes and obediently she drank a little more.

'That's better,' he said, putting the bowl on the table. He stood up and drew her to her feet. 'It's time to go, now. I can see you are anxious and I shall not be happy until you are my lawful wife. Blaze has had a good drink and a rest and he's young and strong. He'll do the distance with energy to spare.'

When he was in the saddle he swung her up in front of him and they set off for Harwich. It seemed a long time to Anna before they reached the straggle of houses on the outskirts of the town and she kept looking back over Paul's shoulder, expecting to see Samuel in hot pursuit. But eventually, they came to a small church by the roadside.

As Paul reined in his horse they could see that a funeral was taking place in the churchyard.

'Couldn't be better,' he whispered in her ear.

He left Blaze tied to the lych gate where he could nibble at the grass and they went into the churchyard, keeping out of the way of the mourners as they left.

Then he took Anna by the hand and led her into the church, where the priest and the churchwardens were in the vestry, counting the money they had collected from the funeral party.

'I'll double what you have there if you will marry us,' Paul said.

The vicar looked up, frowning. 'Who are you? What do you want, barging in here without so much as a by-your-leave?' he asked, crossly.

'I'm sorry, sir. But we have no time to lose,' Paul said. 'I meant what I said. Marry me to this woman and I'll give you double what you have there. You have two churchwardens here who can act as witnesses. Come, man, it'll not take you above five minutes to read the marriage service over us.'

The vicar looked them both up and down. 'Run away, have you?'

'Ask no questions and you'll be told no lies. But I assure you there is no reason on God's earth why we should not be joined together in holy matrimony and this I'll swear on the good book. I ask you again. Will you marry us, sir?'

The vicar looked from Paul to Anna and back again and saw a responsible-looking, fresh-faced though rather anxious young man and a pretty young woman who had a look of suffering about her. They were obviously very much in love, the man had his arm protectively round her and she was holding tightly on to his other hand. He nodded. 'Aye,' he said. 'I'll marry you. I've just buried a man who'd been wed for nigh on forty years. His wife died and he followed her within a few days, dead of a broken heart. Marriages like that are made in heaven. I pray yours will be, too.'

He led them into the church and the churchwardens followed. At the altar they all watched as Paul took Anna's hand and said, 'I, Paul, take thee, Anna to my wedded wife, for better, for worse, and thereto I plight thee my troth.' He loosed her hand and she took his and repeated the words. Then he took off the gold ring he wore on his little finger and placed it on the fourth finger of her left hand. The vicar nodded and said, 'I now pronounce you man and wife' and they knelt while he gave them a blessing. It all took less than five minutes.

When it was done and Paul had kissed his wife he took the names of the vicar and the church wardens. 'Then, if anyone should doubt that we are legally married you will be our witnesses,' he explained.

'And gladly so,' both the churchwardens cried. They had rarely seen a marriage that seemed so clearly made in heaven.

Paul took his purse from his belt and emptied it on the table. The vicar began to count the money. Then he put it back into the purse. 'You may have more need of this than I, young man,' he said, handing it back.

'I think not, sir. I promised to pay for your services and pay I must if I would sleep easy in my bed, although the service you have done for us today is worth more than money could ever buy.'

He laid the purse on the table, took Anna's hand and left the church.

First they found a pie stall and bought hot pies. 'A poor wedding feast, but the best we can manage,' Paul said with a laugh. 'And the pies are tasty.'

'They are indeed,' Anna agreed, gravy running down her chin. 'Now that I am really your wife and I feel safe I am starving.'

'Then have another because I don't know where we shall rest our heads tonight, my love. Our first wedded night. I'm loath to ask Blaze to carry us back to Colchester because he's done more than his fair share of work today, but I've no money left for lodgings since I paid the vicar.'

'I've already thought of that. We'll go back to the cottage,' she said happily, smiling up at him. 'It's comfortable enough there and Blackie will be waiting for us.'

They walked along, hand in hand, with Blaze plodding obediently beside them in the late afternoon sunshine. Every now and then they stopped to pick daisies, which Anna made into daisy chains and Paul draped them round her neck and made a little coronet to twist into her hair. Then he picked her a bouquet of poppies and cornflowers and dog-roses from the hedgerow.

'Now, you really look like a bride on her wedding day, my love,' he said delightedly, kissing her again and again.

By the time they eventually reached the cottage the summer day was fading into a brilliant sunset that streaked the sky with red,

234

orange, purple and pink. They stood at the cottage door watching until the sun finally disappeared, taking the colours with it and leaving a soft, grey light that tipped slowly into darkness. Then they went indoors.

They spent the night in each other's arms in the sleeping loft, on a bed of straw that Anna had strewn with rosemary and lavender. They woke in the morning to love and delight in each other yet again until, long after the sun was up, they were disturbed by an insistent banging on the door.

A last kiss and Paul dragged on his breeches and went down the ladder to open the door. He was not at all surprised to see Samuel standing there and noticed with some amusement that the older man was, as always, fastidiously dressed, in purple velvet today, with the white lace at his collar and cuffs still looking clean and fresh even though he had ridden hard from Colchester.

But Samuel was astonished to see Paul. His jaw dropped and he took a step back. 'What in God's name are you doing here?' he demanded, his face reddening with annoyance.

'I might say the same to you,' Paul answered.

Samuel ignored that. 'Where's Anna?' he said. 'How did you know she was here? *Is* she here?'

'Oh, yes, she's here,' Paul answered.

'Then fetch her. Where is she? I've come to take her home with me.' He strode into the room. Then he halted. 'You! Have you . . .?' He took a step forward and glared at Paul menacingly. 'Have you come here and forced yourself on her? And she a defenceless woman?'

Paul smiled. 'Oh, no, Mynheer Hegetorne, I assure you I haven't forced myself on Anna. She was more than willing to take me to her bed.'

Samuel raised his arm as if to strike Paul but then Anna appeared and came down the ladder, tying the laces on her stomacher. She was rosy with sleep and love, her hair round her shoulders, her feet bare. She looked very happy. 'Good morning, Samuel,' she said.

Paul went over and took her by the hand. 'You can be the first to congratulate us, Mynheer Hegetorne. Anna has done me the honour of becoming my wife. We were married in Harwich yesterday.'

Samuel's eyes bulged in amazement and for a moment Anna

was afraid he was about to have a fit. But he recovered and composed himself.

'Is this how you repay me for my care, Anna?' he said, his voice low with fury. 'Going behind my back to marry an Englishman? An *Englishman* of all people! Have you no loyalty to your own countrymen? How could you desecrate your husband's memory by taking an *Englishman* to your bed? I'm saddened and disappointed in you, Anna. Jan would turn in his grave to know you had committed such a . . .' He clenched his hands, unable to go on.

'It is no sin to love, Samuel,' Anna said quietly, anticipating his words. She went over and stood in front of him. 'My Jan loved me too much to deny me the chance of happiness with a good man and to bear his children, any more than I would have wanted Jan to live the life of a monk if it had been me that had died.' She made to take his hand but he stepped back and put his hands behind him. 'But it's not just because Paul is English that you are so angry, is it. It's because I've found happiness with a man not of your choosing. That's what you can't forgive, isn't it?' She shook her head sadly. 'Can't you forgive me, Samuel?'

Paul stepped forward. 'There's nothing to forgive,' he said hotly. 'Why should you ask his forgiveness, Anna? Haven't you suffered enough? Why shouldn't you be happy again?'

She turned and put her finger on her husband's lips. 'You don't understand, my darling. Samuel may be misguided but I know he only has my interests at heart.'

'Then he has a funny way of showing it, that's all I can say.' He glowered at the older man, who was gazing round Old Betty's hovel in horrified fascination. He had obviously never been in such squalid surroundings ever before in his life.

'I can't understand it,' Samuel was muttering, as much to himself as to them. 'When I can give you so much, Anna, how can you prefer . . .?' he waved his hand, lost for words.

'We shan't be staying here, Samuel,' she said gently. 'Please don't be angry with us. I love Paul and he will look after me. Can't we remain friends?'

Samuel swallowed noisily. 'It's all wrong. It's me that should be caring for you. Not him.' He turned away and adjusted the purple hat that exactly matched his breeches. 'I have nothing more to say. To either of you.' With that he left.

Anna sat down at the table, her face woebegone. 'I wouldn't

have upset him like that for all the world,' she said sadly. 'He has been so good, so kind, first of all to Jan and me and then after Jan died, in caring for me, that now I feel guilty, I feel as if I've betrayed him.'

Paul looked at her, his face stony. 'Are you regretting our marriage already, Anna?' he asked coldly. 'Are you already wishing you had married that old man instead of me? That man, who could never give you the joy you shared with me last night, never give you children to love?'

She got to her feet and clung to him. 'No, Paul. Never think that. I love you more than life itself. And I could never have married Samuel, you must know that. Would I have run away from him if I'd wanted to marry him? No, it's just that I wish he had been more understanding, I wish he had realised he was only trying to keep me by his side because of his guilt over what happened to Jan, then he might have given us his blessing. That's all.'

'I fear he'll never do that, my darling.' He took her in his arms.

For the rest of the day they walked in the wood, picking berries and feeding them to each other; finding soft, grassy places where they could make love, or just sit and talk, simply delighting in each other's company. When darkness fell they returned to their straw nest under the eaves in Betty's cottage and slept again in each other's arms.

'Delightful though it is to lead this rustic life, I fear we must return to Colchester soon, my love,' Paul said one morning when they had been married nearly a week, as he leaned on one elbow and looked down at her as she lay naked beside him.

She pulled him down to her. 'Can't we stay here for ever, Paul?' she asked, kissing him hungrily.

'Would that we could, my love, but it isn't possible, is it?'

She made a face. 'No, I suppose not. But you've no money, you gave it all to the vicar who married us. So where shall we live? I've a little money left. Enough to buy bread and bacon to last us a few days, but that's all. And your father won't welcome us, you know that as well as I do.' She reached up and kissed the tip of his nose.

'No, but he needs me to help him run the business. He can't manage it alone, there's too much to do.' He kissed her soundly. 'Are you ready for a fight, sweetheart?'

237

'I'm ready for anything as long as we're together.'

'Then today we'll go back and face whatever Fate has in store for us.'

'Later,' she murmured.

He nuzzled her neck. 'Oh, I wasn't thinking of going just yet.'

Chapter Twenty-Six

'First we'll go and see my grandfather,' Paul announced as Blaze carried the two of them back to Colchester, ambling at a leisurely pace that Paul did nothing to discourage. 'I know we'll receive a welcome there.'

'And after that?' Anna asked, leaning back against him, totally trusting.

'After that, I suppose I shall have to go and see my father,' he said grimly. 'But let's not worry about that yet.' He bent and kissed the top of her head.

'Tell me about your grandfather,' she said.

'I'm very fond of him. We've always got on very well together. My grandmother says I'm like he was as a young man,' Paul said.

'Then I shall love him, I know it,' Anna said firmly. 'Your grandmother is still alive?'

'Oh, yes. Very much so. She nursed grandfather through his illness.' He laughed. 'He always says she refused to let him die. She's quite a forceful woman, my grandmother, for all she's so tiny.'

'Where do they live?'

'By St Botolph's Gate. You'll see. We'll be there before long.'

Josiah Markham's house was a tall, half-timbered building squashed between two others not far from the ruins of St Botolph's Priory. Inside, it was pleasantly welcoming, brightened by a large number of tapestries made by his wife, Margaret.

When Paul and Anna arrived they found Josiah and Margaret sitting in the garden under the shade of a large oak tree, Margaret busy with her needle, Josiah watching her contentedly. He had been a large man, like Paul, but his figure now was shrunken and

Anna noticed that one side of his face was slightly drawn down. Nevertheless, he still had a shock of pure white hair and his brown eyes were clear and warm and looked as if they missed nothing.

'Grandfather, grandmamma, may I present my wife, Anna.' With pride Paul led Anna forward.

Anna made a deep curtsey to Margaret, a tiny woman, with grey hair piled into a knot under a lavender cap that matched the colour of her gown, and shrewd grey eyes. She had been a beautiful woman in her youth and remnants of that beauty remained in her fine bone structure. She gave a slight smile and inclined her head in acknowledgement, then the smile faded as she looked up at Paul. 'You are married?' she asked and there was rebuke in her voice. 'Why were we not told? Your grandfather is not so infirm that we couldn't have attended your wedding.'

Paul dropped on one knee beside her. 'It wasn't like that, grandmamma. Indeed, you are the first to know. We were married in secret only a week ago, in the town of Harwich.'

'Why in such secrecy? Why did it have to be such a hole-in-a-corner affair?' She looked Anna up and down. 'There's no disgrace in taking your first-born to the altar with you. I'll wager most do.'

Paul shook his head. 'Anna isn't pregnant, grandmamma. She's a Stranger.'

'Ah.' The sound came from Josiah. It was hardly more than a long, drawn-out sigh. 'That won't please your father.' He spoke slowly and with some difficulty, giving Anna a lop-sided smile. He held out his hand. 'Welcome, my dear. Paul's grandmother and I have no such pre- prej-prejudices,' he had to make three attempts to pronounce the last word.

'That's what I hoped you'd say, grandfather,' Paul said with a grin. 'Because we have come to beg shelter from you.'

'We shan't refuse you, my boy, you know that.' Margaret said. 'First, though, you must eat. Have you broken your fast?' She didn't wait for an answer but leaned forward. 'And what's that you have in that basket?'

'My little cat.' Anna spoke for the first time and they could hear the foreign inflection in her voice. 'She has been through much with me.'

'Then you won't want to part with her. We must butter her feet to prevent her from straying.' Margaret struck the small bell by her side and soon a young maid came running. 'Bring food for my grandson and his wife. And milk for the cat to drink and butter for her paws.' She turned back to Paul. 'Now, tell us your story.'

Paul told them everything, Anna's widowhood, and Samuel's rather obsessive desire to protect her – which he touched on only lightly – his love for Anna and his father's refusal to accept her. He spoke reluctantly of Silas's disgraceful behaviour in denouncing her as a witch . . .

'Aye, we heard about that,' Josiah said, shaking his head. 'It was the talk of all Colchester.'

'It was unjust, grandfather,' Paul said vehemently.

'It was all wrong,' Anna added, equally vehemently. 'Old Betty should never have been put to death like that. She was no witch. She was old and poor, that was her only crime. She was a good friend to me. I owe my very life to her and I mourn her death every day.' She wiped away a tear.

'Your feelings do you credit, child,' Margaret said. 'Go on, boy.'

'Not much more to tell,' Paul said. 'Anna ran away – to Old Betty's cottage – where I found her and asked her to be my wife. She agreed, so we went to find a church with all speed. I gave all the money I had to the vicar who married us – he didn't want to take it but I insisted – then we went back to the cottage. But we knew we couldn't stay there so we came to you.'

'Quite right, too.' Josiah murmured.

'Have you told this, what's his name? Samuel? That you are married?' Margaret asked.

'He guessed Anna was at the cottage and came after her,' Paul said. He made a face. 'He wasn't pleased to find that Anna had married me.'

'I regret that,' Anna said, 'but he's a jealous man.'

'You'll make your peace with him.' It was a statement, not a question from Margaret.

'I hope so. In time,' Anna replied.

'Good. Now, eat the food Miriam has brought you while it is still hot.' She turned to the maid. 'See that the bedding from the second-best bed is aired and that the room is prepared for my grandson and his wife.' She turned back to Paul and Anna. 'You are very welcome to stay with us for as long as you wish,' she said, her smile taking the formality out of her words. 'We shall be glad of your company.'

The next day, with some trepidation, Paul went to see his father and resume work. He found Silas busy in the counting house, trying to make sense of the accounts that were normally Paul's responsibility.

'And where in the name of thunder have you been?' he asked, looking up from the ledger. 'Scallywagging off like that with never so much as a by-your-leave. Your mother has been beside herself with worry.'

'I'm sorry if she's been worried, father, but I'm back now. Shall I . . .?' he made to take the ledger.

'You will not. I want to know where you've been.' Silas put his hand down on the book.

'I've been getting married,' Paul said. 'In a church just outside Harwich.' Seeing the look on his father's face he added, 'Oh, it was all perfectly above board.'

His father frowned impatiently. 'Why? There was no need to go to such lengths, surely, my boy. You don't have to marry a wench just because you've put her in pod.'

Paul's face darkened. 'I didn't marry Anna because she was "in pod", as you so charmingly put it, I married her because I love her.'

Silas's head shot up. 'Anna? You don't mean to tell me you've wedded that Dutch wench!' he roared.

Paul didn't raise his voice. 'Yes. Anna has done me the honour of becoming my wife.'

Silas got to his feet, knocking over the stool he had been sitting on, his face purple with rage. 'How dare you come here and tell me you've married that woman! You know my feelings on the subject. I think it's high time the whole community was packed off, back to Flanders, or wherever it is they've come from! And you've had the bloody effrontery to marry one! Well, you're no son of mine!'

'I hope you don't mean that, father,' Paul said, trying to keep his temper. 'We work well together and it would be a pity to spoil a good business relationship because of this. I'll go and see mother. I'm sure she'll agree with me.' He went off, leaving his father to jab his quill into the ink pot so viciously that he knocked the point off and spilled ink all over the ledger.

242

Eleanor, Paul's mother, was alone, making bread in the kitchen, a task she enjoyed. The servants had been sent on other household duties. When she saw Paul her face lit up and she lifted her face for his kiss. 'Paul, you're back! Where have you been? I've been so worried about you.'

He bent and kissed her. 'There was no need. I'm perfectly well. Now, sit down, mother, I have something to tell you,' he said.

She sat down, wiping her floury hands on her apron. 'Yes?' she smiled at him eagerly, her dear boy, the light of her life, but her smile faded as he told her of his marriage and repeated his conversation with Silas.

'Oh, dear,' she said, her face creased with worry. 'You've married the girl! You shouldn't have gone against your father like that, Paul.'

'But I love Anna, mother. She means all the world to me.'

'I know, dear. But it makes Silas look so silly, after what he said in the market place, and Silas hates being made to look silly above all things.'

'Then he shouldn't have said what he did, mother, because he knew very well it wasn't true and it caused Anna a great deal of suffering.'

She nodded. 'I know. I told him so,' she said with a sigh. 'Where are you living, with your new wife?' she asked after a pause.

'With the grandparents. They welcomed Anna.'

'And so would I have done, given the choice,' she said wistfully. She looked up, startled, as Silas burst into the room.

'This stupid young puppy has told you what he's done?' he shouted. 'Yes, I can see he has.' he turned to Paul. 'I give you a choice. Either you get this marriage annulled or you can get out of my house and never come back.'

'No, Silas. You can't do that,' Eleanor pleaded. 'He's our only child. It would break my heart.'

'He should have thought of that before.' He glared at Paul. 'Well, sir, what is it to be?'

Paul bent and kissed his mother again. 'I'm sorry, mother, but I love Anna and I will never desert her. I hope you can understand.' He straightened up. 'You know where you can find us. I'd like you to meet her.'

'I'd like that, too, Paul.' Eleanor's eyes were wet with tears.

'I forbid it,' Silas said. 'Eleanor, you will have nothing more to do with this man. He is no longer our son.'

'Oh, Silas, how can you be so hard?' Eleanor said, the tears flowing freely now. 'I'm sure Anna is a lovely girl.'

'I had her denounced as a witch and I find no reason to change my opinion.' He turned to Paul and his lip curled. 'She's certainly bewitched you, you gullible little fool.'

Paul left, trying to put out of his mind the picture of his mother's ravaged face and his father's vitriolic words. He was shaking with fury at his father's bigoted ideas and he knew that if he hadn't left as he did he would have struck him. He went down the hill to the bridge and stood looking down at the water for a long time, trying to control his feelings. Then he went back to his grandfather's house, knowing he would have to tell him what had taken place.

Whilst Paul had gone to see his father, Anna went to the market. Since the terrible day of the hanging she had never managed to bring herself to do more than hurry through, as quickly as she could, on her way to somewhere else, but she knew she couldn't avoid it for ever. Without her having to explain, Margaret understood this and so that she shouldn't wander aimlessly gave her instructions to buy silk and wool of particular colours for her tapestry work.

Anna arrived at the market and tried to avoid looking at the spot where the hanging had taken place. But today there were so many stalls, so many entertainers of different kinds vying for the odd coppers from the crowd that it was difficult to remember exactly where it had happened. Indeed, it was hard to imagine that there had been enough space for the pandemonium that had taken place that day.

She wandered round for some time before she found the stall selling coloured thread, and after some deliberation bought what Margaret needed, then she found the wool stall to complete her purchases. She was preparing to leave when she felt her sleeve pulled and a voice said, 'Anna! Is it really you?'

It was Griete.

Anna's fact lit up. 'Oh, I'm so glad to see you, Griete. How are things at Garden House?'

'You may well ask!' Griete made a face. 'What happened to

you? You threw the complete household into uproar. You never heard such . . .'

Anna caught her arm. 'Wait a minute.' She called a passing pieman and quickly bought two pies. 'Let's go and sit on the grass in the castle bailey where we can talk,' she said, putting them safely in her basket.

'Where did you go? Where are you living?' Griete bombarded her with questions as they hurried through the crowd and out into the shadow of the great castle on the hill.

But Anna didn't answer her until they were sitting with their backs to the ancient castle where she had been incarcerated with Old Betty, on a knoll overlooking the tenter fields below, where lengths of cloth of all colours were pegged out on the tenter fames, like brightly coloured flags. Anna noticed a man moving among the frames and guessed that he was tightening the tenter pegs to keep the cloth that had been hung there after being fulled and thickened well stretched and taut.

'A pretty sight, don't you think?' she nodded towards the tenter fields as she handed Griete a pie.

Griete took a bite and nodded, her mouth full of pastry. After a minute, she said, 'My master has his cloth stretched in the fields beyond the house, as you well know. He says that Strangers' cloth gets spoiled if it's hung where the English hang theirs.'

Anna gave her an impish grin. 'Be careful what you say, Griete. I'm married to an Englishman.'

Griete's jaw dropped. 'You've married an *Englishman!*'

Anna nodded, her eyes shining. 'His name is Paul Markham. I'm very happy, Griete.'

But Griete didn't smile. 'Oh, Anna, you shouldn't have married an Englishman. Our people don't do that. We keep ourselves to ourselves because the English don't like us and we don't like them. We don't mix and it's better that way. Goodness knows what my master will say when he hears. He'll be furious.'

'He already knows, Griete.' Anna's smile faded. 'And you're right, he was furious. But it's time things changed. Our two communities should mix more with each other. How will we ever learn to live in harmony if we don't?'

'Well, I don't know.' Griete's sallow face was a picture of uncertainty. She munched her pie in silence. When she had finished she said, 'So that's why my master was in such a foul

245

mood when he came home the other day.' She turned to look at Anna. 'Do you know, he went to bed and stayed there for two days. Wouldn't speak to a soul. We thought he was ill. You've upset him very much, Anna.' Her voice dropped. 'I do believe he wanted to marry you himself. I know he's very fond of you.'

'And I'm very fond of him. But I could never have married him.' She hesitated, then added, 'I don't love him in a marrying way, if you know what I mean.'

Griete smiled. 'Yes, I think I know. You mean you're not *in* love with him.'

'That's about it.'

'I understand because I know what it's like to be in love, Anna.' Griete's face turned pink as she spoke. 'Do you remember Pieter, one of the new gardeners at Garden House?'

'Yes, I do. I remember speaking to him while I was there. He'd like to make changes but Samuel won't let him.'

'That's right.' She gave Anna a sidelong glance and said coyly. 'We're walking out.'

'Oh, Griete, that's wonderful,' Anna said. In truth, Griete, with her sallow skin and plain face, was not the kind of girl men looked twice at, although if they did they would see a kind and loving nature. 'Does Samuel know?'

Griete nodded. 'Oh, yes. He says Pieter is to be made head gardener soon because he is very knowledgeable and Pieter says when he is promoted he'll start saving for us to be married.'

Anna took Griete's hand. 'I'm very pleased for you, Griete.'

'You'll come to my wedding, won't you, Anna? Of course, it won't be until next year.'

'I will if I can,' Anna said soberly. 'But I'm not sure I would be very welcome at your master's house now.' Her expression lightened. 'But I'll come to church to see you married. And that's a promise.' She picked up her basket. 'And now I must go. My husband's grandmother will be waiting for the wool and silks for her tapestry.' She caught Griete's hands. 'It's been lovely to see you, Griete. I hope we'll meet in the market again, so that you can tell me all that's happening.'

They both got to their feet and turned to go their separate ways. But Anna had only gone a few steps when she heard Griete call.

'I nearly forgot to give you this, Anna,' she said, hurrying towards her, waving a letter. 'I've been carrying this around in my pocket ever since you left. It's a letter that was brought for you the very day you went. The master was so angry to think you'd gone that he screwed it up in fury and threw it away. But I rescued it and smoothed it out and I've kept it in my pocket because I was sure I would see you one day.' She handed a rather crumpled package to Anna. 'See, the seal isn't broken, it hasn't been tampered with. I hope it's not bad news, Anna. Letters usually are,' she added gloomily. 'Especially if they've had to travel across the German Sea.'

Anna took the letter and they parted. 'I shan't tell the master I've seen you, it might upset him further, and his temper is uncertain at the best of times,' Griete said over her shoulder as she disappeared into the crowd.

Anna went back to Josiah Markham's house. As she went in through the door she thought what a welcoming house it was, with its delicious smell of baking and its brightly coloured cushions and hangings. She gave Margaret her purchases and went up to the room she shared with Paul, a bright room overlooking the garden, hung with tapestries that Margaret had sewn, to open the letter. It was from her Aunt Dionis.

My Dear Niece (she read).

I passed on to your mother the last letter you sent but I don't think she ever received it because things are very unsettled in that part of the country.

I fear I have sad news for you. Your father, Cornelis, was killed some months ago at the hands of the Spanish barbarians. He was captured one day when he was at the Cloth Hall and taken to the square to be executed – to be made an example of, the Spanish troops said. It is said that he died bravely. Oh, why can't they leave us in peace to worship Our Lord as we choose and stop trying to force us into their Catholic ways?

Your mother is with me. When she was told what was happening to Cornelis she escaped with Bettris, her faithful servant, and they made their way here, to me, travelling mostly by night. Bettris cared for her on the way but by the time she reached my house she was exhausted and suffering from a fever.

She has expressed many times a wish to come to England so that she can be with you and also someone she referred to often in her delirium as Henrick. But this will not be for a long time yet, perhaps next summer, when the warm weather is here, because she has been very ill.

Bettris and I have been caring for her. We feared at one time she might die but she is recovering slowly.

I regret to burden you with such bad news but I know you would wish to be told and will look forward to seeing your dear mother again some time in the future.

Your affectionate aunt

Dionis Vanderplass

Anna read the letter three times and then sat staring into space. So Cornelis was dead. His death left her untouched although she grieved at his manner of dying. Too many good souls in her country had been put to death in the name of religion by the Spanish Catholics over the years. The irony was that she knew Cornelis had been careful to escape persecution over the years by the simple expedient of staying away from church and keeping his religious views, such as they were, to himself. Seemingly, this had not been enough and now he was dead.

Her thoughts turned to her mother and she thanked God that Judith was safe with Aunt Dionis. It would be wonderful to see her again when she was well enough to travel. But one thought troubled her. How was she going to break the news to Judith that her beloved Henrick was dead?

Chapter Twenty-Seven

Paul was back from his father's house in time for dinner, which was served at noon. It was with great difficulty that he held his temper in check as he told his grandfather of the morning's happenings. Josiah sat tight-lipped, not touching his food, as he listened, angry at Silas's high-handed treatment of his own son.

'The man may be my son but he's a fool and a knave,' he said, banging his fist on the table with what little strength he had. 'How does he ever think he's going to run that business without you, my boy? You were trained to it from the time you could walk. I can remember taking you round on my shoulders when you were a little boy, letting you handle the fleeces, run the yarn through your hands so you could tell a fine yarn from a coarse one, teaching you to know a good piece of cloth when you saw it.' In his anger his speech, never clear, became slurred. 'And in the counting house, you were always quicker with figures than your father. You seemed to have an aptitude for them. He added, 'I don't know where you got it from. Numbers were never Silas's strong point, even as a child.'

'That's very true,' Margaret agreed with a sigh. 'I remember spending hour after hour myself, trying to teach him to cast accounts but he could never add a column twice and reach the same answer.'

Josiah smiled, but only briefly. 'That's where you got your talent for figures from, then, my boy. Your grandmother.' His face resumed its thunderous expression.

Paul studied him, concerned at seeing him so upset and angry, afraid that he might be in danger of another seizure. He glanced at his grandmother, who although watchful, seemed unworried.

'I'm sure there's no need for concern. I've no doubt father will soon find someone to take my place,' Paul said lightly, trying to sound cheerful.

'Oh, yes,' Josiah roared, with more than a trace of bitterness. 'He'll find somebody. And that somebody will be able to rob him blind because his mathematics are too bad to check up on what's happening.' He shrugged his thin shoulders. 'I don't wish to speak ill of my son,' he said, a trace of weariness creeping into his voice. 'There is not another to better him in recognising a good fleece and knowing the best kind of cloth to make from it. He has an eye for quality and a flair for blending and matching colours that even the dyers envy. But that's where his skills lie, in his hand and eye, not, unfortunately in his head.'

'Except that he is headstrong,' Margaret remarked. She turned to Anna, who was looking upset and worried and only picking at her food. 'I'm sorry, my dear. This is very difficult and upsetting for you. But you mustn't take it personally. You are by no means the only Stranger in the town to be treated as badly as he has treated you, my dear. Given the opportunity he would pack the whole Congregation of Strangers back to where they came from. He simply cannot – or will not – see what an asset it has been to the town to have them here. It is a great pity. Silas is such a good man in other ways. He can be very kind-hearted,' she added a trifle wistfully.

'I shall speak to him,' Josiah said, his voice now slow and laboured. 'I have a right to say what I think. I still have an interest in the manufacture of Markham cloth and I've no wish to see the business I built up over so many years ruined and the family put in penury because of my son's stubborn pig-headedness.'

'You didn't have much success when he insisted on getting rid of Harry, the best weaver you'd ever had,' Margaret reminded him.

'That's true. But you may remember that it was at the time of my illness, when I had no energy to argue with him,' Josiah reminded her. 'And it may have been for the best, as it turned out. Harry is now a master weaver. He works for whoever he likes and makes a good living for himself.' He chuckled. 'And he still makes time to come and give me a game of chess most weeks. He tells me he has much to be grateful to Silas for, although he didn't think so at the time.' He paused, 'No, it's quite different this time.

Our fortune is at stake for one thing and for another, even more important, I will not have harmony in the family threatened. Silas is our only son and Paul is his only son; it's ridiculous that there should be antagonism between us.' He slumped in his chair, weak from the effort of talking so much, and passed his hand across his face.

'I think we've talked long enough on the subject. You've tired yourself, Josiah. Just eat your dinner quietly,' Margaret said soothingly. She looked across at Anna and a look of consternation crossed her face. 'Oh, I'm sorry my dear, we've been thoughtless and insensitive to speak of these things in your presence. I can see how much it has upset you. Look, you've eaten scarcely anything and your face has lost its colour.'

'No, please, you mustn't apologise on my account.' Anna shook her head. 'I am married to Paul. We both knew from the start that our marriage would cause difficulties and we agreed that we must face them together. But I am sad that it should be so.'

'Well said, sweetheart,' Paul said, reaching across the table to take her hand. Then he frowned. 'But something else is troubling you. I can see that. What is it?'

She bit her lip. 'It's about my mother,' she said, on the verge of tears. 'I saw Griete in the market place and she gave me a letter that had been sent to Mynheer Hegetorne's house for me. She had been carrying it around with her ever since I left in the hope that she would see me.' She took the letter out of her pocket and laid it on the table, smoothing the creases out. 'You can read it, if you like.' She looked up and then gave a slightly embarrassed smile. 'Ah, no. I forgot. You can't understand the language. Never mind, I'll read it to you.'

They listened in silence. Even when she had finished and folded the letter and put it back in her pocket nobody spoke.

'I had thought the Spanish Inquisition was over, the fighting and the torture all done, but it seems it still flares up from time to time,' she said in a flat voice, speaking half to herself. 'It's very odd. My father always prided himself on keeping out of trouble. I can't think why they should have chosen to make an example of him. It wasn't as if he was a particularly important man in the town, not like he used to be.'

Paul came to her side and put his arm round her. 'Oh, my poor sweet,' he said, stroking her hair. 'To think you'd been given such

251

dreadful news and we were so concerned with our little problems that we didn't even notice how upset you were. I'm sorry, Anna. Truly sorry.'

She smiled at him tremulously. 'You couldn't know, Paul. You didn't even know I'd received the letter.' She gave a little shrug. 'I was never very close to my father,' she said honestly. 'In fact, sometimes I felt that I hardly knew him at all, he was such a remote figure. It seemed to me that he spent nearly all his time at the Cloth Hall and very little of it at home with my mother and me.' She looked up at the faces round the table, all watching her, and added quickly, 'That's not to say I don't feel deeply shocked and sorry at what's happened – and very angry, too. Why should he have been put to death? What had he done? Were they simply making an example of him? I know that hanging is a merciful way to die compared with some of the tortures I've heard that the Spanish employ, but why did he have to die at all?' Her voice dropped. 'And what about my poor mother? That's what upsets me most of all, imagining what she must have suffered on her journey to my aunt's house. It's a long way to Amsterdam and she has led a pampered life. How will she have managed, hiding in barns and hedges by day and travelling on foot by night? It will have taxed her strength and resources to the limit, even though she had Bettris with her. It says in the letter she has been very ill.'

Margaret nodded sympathetically. 'There are many dangers lying in wait for two women travelling alone, aside from footpads and cutpurses. But at least you can rest happy in the knowledge that she arrived safely at your aunt's house. That must be a great consolation to you.' She pointed to the letter. 'But who is this Henrick your aunt speaks of? You have never mentioned him. Is he your brother?'

Anna licked her lips to give her time to think before she spoke. Now was not the time to reveal the circumstances of her birth. 'No, I have no brothers or sisters. Henrick is somebody my mother once knew who came to England to live,' she said vaguely. 'She thought I might meet him.' She smiled. 'I think she imagined England was not much bigger than a small village.'

'Clearly, she is hoping to see him when she comes to England,' Margaret said.

'A forlorn hope, I fear. When she is stronger I shall have to write and warn her that I fear he is dead. I believe it is his gravestone that I found in the graveyard at St Martin's Church.' She summoned up a smile. 'But I shan't tell her that yet. She's unlikely to be well enough to travel to England before next summer, so there's plenty of time.'

Margaret smiled at her. 'You are a brave girl, Anna.'

A little over a week later, on a sultry late August day when the air was so heavy that the sky seemed to rest on the rooftops, Josiah announced that he wished to see Silas, his son.

'Are you sure you are feeling strong enough to tackle him?' Margaret asked as she settled him in his favourite chair by the window. 'We don't want you making yourself ill again.'

'I am quite sure,' he said testily. 'Send one of the servants along to fetch him. Tell him to come this morning.'

'You can't order Silas about the way you order me, Josiah,' she said with more than a trace of humour as she straightened the round cap he wore on his white hair. 'Remember, he's a grown man with a business to look after.'

'He won't *have* a business much longer, if he doesn't stop this nonsense of keeping Paul away from his work.' He thumped the arm of his chair. 'That's what I want to see him about. I want an end to this nonsense. I was talking to Harry about it yesterday over our game of chess. He thinks I've left things long enough and that I should tackle him; talk to him, make him see sense.'

'You can talk to him. Whether he'll see sense is another matter,' Margaret said drily. 'I'll make sure Anna is out of the way when he comes. I wouldn't want him upsetting her with his horrible remarks about the Stranger community; he's embarrassed her quite enough.'

'You've quite taken to the girl, haven't you, Margaret.'

'Yes. I believe she's a sensible girl and a fine wife for Paul. They're clearly very much in love. It's a pity Silas can't see it. But there, he could never see any further than the end of his nose.'

'He will by the time I've finished with him.' He waved her away. 'Send somebody to fetch him. Now. While I'm in the mood.'

Silas received his father's message without enthusiasm, and he took his time in answering the summons, although in fact he wasn't very busy. But he suspected he knew what his father wanted so when he eventually arrived he breezed in, rubbing his hands together in a businesslike manner, saying, 'I can't stay long, father, I have a lot of work to do.'

Josiah nodded, recognising the charade. 'I'm sure you have, my boy. But you can sit down for five minutes, surely. I haven't seen you for several weeks. How's the business?'

'Oh, we've plenty of work. The agents are run off their feet taking the wool to the spinners and then collecting it from them, checking it and taking it on to the weavers. They're a crafty lot, those agents. I'm sure there's cheating going on but I can't seem to get to the bottom of it.' He sat down and rested one ankle on the other knee, trying to look relaxed.

'That's the sort of thing Paul is good at, isn't it,' Josiah said mildly, pulling the grograin gown he wore in the mornings more closely over his knees.

Silas's brow darkened. 'Ah, I thought it wouldn't be long before you started on that, father. But before you go any further let me put my case. How can I keep him on when he's had the effrontery to marry the same woman I denounced as a witch in the market place not much more than a month ago? It would have been bad enough if he'd taken her as his mistress, but to marry her! It's not to be borne. I'd be the laughing stock of Colchester if I kept him on.'

Josiah stroked his beard. 'You denounced her, but you didn't *really* believe she was a witch, did you, my boy?'

'Well, no, I think this witch-hunting business is going a bit far, to tell you the truth.' Silas shrugged dismissively. 'But that's hardly the point. It was a means to an end.'

'You denounced Anna simply to get her out of the way, so Paul couldn't marry her. Am I right?'

Silas nodded smugly. 'It seemed an excellent chance to get rid of her. Pity it didn't work.'

'That's a wicked thing to say. I'm ashamed a son of mine should even think such a thing,' Josiah said sternly. 'Have you any idea how much quite unnecessary suffering it caused the poor girl, being incarcerated in the castle dungeons for the best part of a week, terrified she would be dragged out and hanged at any moment. *For a crime she hadn't committed?*' Josiah sat back in his chair, breathing heavily.

Silas shrugged, but he had the grace to look sheepish.

Josiah continued, his voice calmer. 'Well, fortunately for Anna your despicable plan didn't work. She wasn't hanged for a witch, she was released, and now Paul has married her. And good for him I say. To my mind that's no more than justice.' He gave a chuckle, then he became serious again. 'But listen to me, Silas. Just because you didn't get your own way and your son has married a woman against your wishes there's no need to vent your spleen by throwing him out of the business, where, you know as well as I do, he's badly needed.' He leaned forward and tapped his chest. 'And don't forget it's my business, too. It's my money as well as yours that's at stake. I can't afford to see the business I took years building up fail because you're too pig-headed to admit you made a mistake.'

'I didn't make a mistake. The woman's a Stranger. I don't like Strangers. And I won't have them working for me, you know that,' Silas said, his mouth a thin, hard line.

Josiah looked surprised. 'Who said anything about Anna working for you? It's Paul I'm talking about. He's not a Stranger. He's your son.'

'He's married to one.' He glared at his father. 'I won't have her in my house.'

'Then you're a fool, because she's a fine woman, but that's your choice. But I'm not asking you to have her in your house. If she took my advice she wouldn't come if you did. Are you going to reinstate Paul?'

'Why should I? He's gone against my wishes. If he'll do it once he'll do it again.'

'He's a grown man. You can't expect to order his every move.'

'You're trying to order mine.'

'No, I'm not. I'm simply trying to make you see sense. I'm asking – not telling – you to reinstate Paul.'

'I don't suppose he'll come even if I ask him.'

'You won't know, if you don't give him the chance. But I think he will. For my sake, if not for yours.'

'Very well.' Silas spoke grudgingly. He stuck his head forward belligerently. 'But I won't acknowledge that woman.'

'That's your loss. But, as I said before, I'm not talking about Anna, I'm talking about Paul,' Josiah said tetchily. 'I'm sure Eleanor is unhappy that you dismissed him.'

'Eleanor knows nothing about the running of the business.'

'Maybe not, but she's not lacking in common sense and she can see through you without a lot of trouble. I'm sure she knows as well as I do that you dismissed Paul rather than admit that you might be in the wrong.'

'I'm not admitting I'm in the wrong, but I've said I'll take him back.'

'When?'

'He'd better start tomorrow. There's a big shipment of cloth due to go off and he can deal with the paperwork. Will that suit you?'

Josiah sighed heavily. 'As long as you don't vent your bad temper on him. You'll be doing yourself a mischief.' His tone changed now that he had got his way. 'You'll take a glass of wine with me before you go, son?'

'No, I haven't the time,' Silas said petulantly.

Josiah didn't argue. 'Very well. I know you're a busy man. Ask your mother to join me, then, on your way out.'

By the time Margaret entered the room, Josiah was looking smug.

'You could always twist him round your little finger,' she said giving him a sidelong glance as she handed him a glass of wine. 'When does Paul start work again?'

'Tomorrow.'

She settled herself with her tapestry, her own glass beside her. 'Now, tell me how you did it.'

With Paul back at work the time passed pleasantly enough for Anna. She helped Margaret to preserve the fruit and vegetables grown in the garden and as the brilliant summer days shortened and slipped into mellow, yellow and russet autumn days she went to the woods and gathered berries and herbs that she could dry or make into ointments and tinctures against winter ills. The afternoons were usually spent in Margaret's favourite room, a small room at the front of the house overlooking the street and known as the little parlour. Here they both worked on a section of a large tapestry depicting Rebecca at the well, which Margaret had designed and which would eventually hang in the hall.

Life seemed to have settled into an easy, uncomplicated routine. Almost too easy, too uncomplicated.

She said as much to Paul as they prepared for bed. Their room was on the first floor, overlooking the garden. It was panelled in dark oak and furnished very comfortably with a small oak table and two comfortable chairs, as well as a clothes press and the large trestle bed with green brocade hangings that matched the curtains at the two windows.

He climbed into bed beside her and kissed her, tangling his fingers in her hair. 'Are you quite happy, living here with the grandparents, Anna?' he asked. 'Sometimes you seem a little quiet and I wondered if perhaps you were not happy.'

'Oh, yes, Paul, I'm very happy,' she said quickly. 'I love them both as if they were my own and I believe they are fond of me, too.'

'Indeed, they are. Grandmamma is always singing your praises.'

'It's just that . . .' she hesitated and began again. 'At times I wonder if we've imposed on their hospitality for too long, dearest. Do you think they would prefer us to leave so that they could live out their lives in peace?'

He leaned over and kissed her again. 'No, I don't think that at all, sweetheart. In fact, I believe it would grieve them to hear you say such a thing. They would be very sad if they thought you wanted to leave this house.'

She settled in his arms. 'Then I'm happy to stay because I do love being here. It's just that I was afraid we had perhaps over-stayed our welcome.'

'Never think that, darling. Why, grandfather was saying only the other day that the house has come alive since we arrived.' He laid his cheek against hers and murmured wickedly, 'He was even saying that the rooms at the top of the house will make a good nursery when the time comes. Do you know, I think he's quite looking forward to becoming a great-grandfather.'

She gave a small sigh. 'I fear he'll have to wait a little longer for that.'

Paul sensed her unspoken disappointment and took her into his arms. 'We've only been married a few months,' he whispered. 'Don't be too impatient, my sweet.'

Some time later, when she was curled up sleepily in the crook of his arm she sensed that he was still awake and staring up into the darkness.

'Is something troubling you, Paul?' she asked softly.

He patted her arm as it lay across his chest. 'Of course not. Go to sleep, my love.'

257

'I think there is something, Paul. I confided my fears to you, you must do the same. I should hate to think we kept things from each other.'

He didn't answer.

She leaned up on one elbow and looked down at him in the dying flickers of the fire. 'Are you finding it difficult to work with your father, Paul, now that we're married?' she asked anxiously. 'Is he making life hard for you because you are married to a Stranger?

'What makes you think that?'

'Because I know your father. And because if it was anything else I'm sure you wouldn't hesitate to tell me.'

'My father has never been an easy man to work with, I've told you that, many times,' he answered vaguely.

'But it's worse now?'

'A little.' He could never tell her the constant derogatory remarks about the Stranger community that came from his father, and the vitriolic comments about people who betrayed their own people by marrying foreigners. It was like a dripping tap, wearing away his patience and taxing his temper until he wondered how much longer he could stand it without either walking out or doing his father a mischief.

Chapter Twenty-Eight

It was early in January. Outside the window snow was swirling like feathers from a plucked goose, to melt on the wet cobbles or to pile in drifts blown by the bitter north-east wind. Anna was sitting with Margaret in front of a large fire in the little parlour. Out in the street they could see passers-by, swathed in shawls and blankets, hats anchored by scarves and with rags wrapped over their boots, hurrying as best they could on the slippery paths, heads down, anxious to get indoors out of the icy weather. Safe in the warm room, the two women were busily at work on the tapestry of Rebecca at the well, Margaret on Rebecca's long golden tresses, Anna on part of her blue robe.

After a while Anna paused in her work and stared out of the window with a weary sigh.

'What's the matter, child?' Margaret looked up, immediately concerned.

With an effort, Anna smiled and resumed sewing. 'I am a little tired, that's all,' she said.

'Are you sure it's nothing more than that? You're looking very pale, my dear,' Margaret said. 'And I've noticed you've eaten hardly anything for the past week. Are you ill? Or worried?'

'I worry very much that I am the reason Paul is so unhappy in his work,' Anna admitted. 'I think that is why I have no appetite. But lately I find that even if I eat my stomach rejects the food.'

'I fear there is little you can do about that while Silas is so stubborn,' Margaret said sadly. 'Until he sees sense . . .' Frowning, she put her needle down and studied the girl. 'Are your courses regular?' she asked suddenly.

Anna shook her head. 'They have never been regular. Not since

'. . . not since the time I was kept in the castle dungeon.' She shuddered at the memory.

'Then had you considered that perhaps this sickness might be because you are with child, my dear?'

She looked up at Margaret, surprised. 'No. I hadn't.' A smile spread across her face. 'Do you really think it might be? Oh, I do hope you may be right. It could be the reason why I feel so sick and lethargic all the time, couldn't it?' She put her hand on her flat stomach. 'Oh, grandmamma Margaret, I can't tell you how happy it would make me if it was so. Paul, too. He would be overjoyed.'

'If it is so this will be your second child, will it not?' Margaret said, keeping her voice light.

'Yes, but it was very different last time. I didn't feel at all ill, except first thing in the morning. I suppose that's why I didn't think . . .' Her mood changed and she stared into the fire. 'I never saw her,' she said sadly. 'I never saw my baby. I don't believe she drew breath. I sometimes wonder what she would have been like if she had lived. They told me I nearly died too, but I knew nothing about that. At the time I would have welcomed death.' She brushed away a tear.

'I'm sorry, my dear. It was insensitive of me to remind you of such a sad time,' Margaret said, leaning forward and taking her hand. 'I only spoke of it so that I could reassure you that subsequent births are never as difficult as the first. I can promise that this birth will be easier. Have no fear. This time, if indeed you are pregnant, all will be well with you, I'm sure of it.'

Anna smiled at her, the tears gone. 'I'm quite sure I am to have a child,' she said firmly. 'There are other signs, now I come to think of it. My craving for apples, had you not noticed? And the fact that I can't bear the smell of boiling bones.' She shuddered. 'Even the thought of that makes me want to retch. Oh, yes, there is no doubt in my mind.' She got to her feet. 'Now I think I know what it is that ails me I'll make myself an infusion of camomile. I know that will help with this horrible nausea. I'll go to the still-room now, if you will excuse me, grandmamma Margaret.'

She pulled her shawl more closely round her and went along the passage that stretched the length of the house to the still-room beyond the kitchen where she kept her herbs and medicines. It was very cold there after the warmth of the parlour and she shivered a little as she mixed together meadowsweet and peppermint and put them to steep in boiled water ready to drink later. Then she made the camomile tea, looking out of the window at the garden and imagining in her mind's eye a child playing there as she sipped it. She laughed at herself for being silly as she brushed away a tear of sheer happiness and surveyed the scene as it was, with the snow falling even faster now, carpeting the grass and the flower beds and outlining the bare black branches of the trees and bushes.

She shivered in the cold and hurried back along the passage to the little parlour. As she passed Josiah's study, where he spent his afternoons, the door opened and a tall, grey-haired man emerged, pulling on a fur hat as he came.

'Yes, Josiah. I shall return next week, never fear,' the man was saying, a hint of laughter in his voice. 'Unless the snow keeps me confined to my house.'

'It will take more than snow to keep you from our game of chess, Harry. And it will be my turn to win, so don't be late,' Anna heard Josiah say firmly.

'I shall be on time. I'm always on time, you know that.' His tone changed as he nearly knocked into Anna. 'Oh, I beg your pardon, Mevrouw. The light is dim in this passage and I didn't see you there. Are you hurt?'

'No, not at all, thank you, sir.'

'Ah. You must be Anna, Paul's wife. I am right, yes? Josiah is always singing your praises.'

'He is very kind,' she said, glad of the lack of light because she felt herself turning pink at his words.

'Indeed, he is kind. He is a very good friend to me.' He inclined his head slightly as she reached the parlour door. 'Good day, Mevrouw.'

'Good day, Mynheer.'

She went back into the parlour and resumed her seat by the fire and took up her needle again.

'Are you feeling any better?' Margaret asked.

'Yes, I believe I am, thank you.'

'Could you manage a cup of wine and a piece of gingerbread?' She nodded. 'I think I might.'

Margaret fetched them herself, and Anna took a few bites of the gingerbread and a few sips of wine. 'I met Harry as I came from the stillroom,' she said, taking another tiny bite. 'It's the first time I've seen him to speak to.'

261

'He's a very shy man,' Margaret said. 'He comes and goes very quietly. You were lucky to see him. And even luckier that he spoke to you.'

'Why is he called Harry?'

Margaret looked up from her work in surprise. 'Because that's his name, of course.'

'No, it can't be his proper name, because he's a Stranger. I could tell that by the way he speaks English. It is not quite the way you English speak, his words are more ... umm, carefully formed, I suppose you might say. And he called me Mevrouw. Yet he has an English name.'

'You're very observant,' Margaret said admiringly. She shook her head. 'I don't know what his real name is, Anna, I've only ever known him as Harry.' She frowned. 'Come to think of it, I believe Josiah gave him that name when Silas took over the running of the weaving sheds in the hope he wouldn't notice he was employing a Stranger. It didn't work of course; Silas may be a stubborn, misguided man, but he's not stupid and he soon saw through it and threw Harry out, even though he was the best weaver they had. But somehow the name has stuck.'

'I wonder what his real name is,' Anna mused.

'I don't know. You must ask Josiah. Why do you want to know?'

'Just curiosity.' She was quiet for several minutes, then she said, 'I wonder if he ever knew my mother's friend, whose tombstone is in St Martin's graveyard.' She paused in the act of threading her needle and said wistfully, 'It would be so nice to talk to someone who might be able to tell me something about my ... him.'

Anna waited until they were curled up together in the big feather bed before she told Paul that she thought she might be pregnant. He was overjoyed.

'I just hope and pray everything goes well with you this time, my darling,' he whispered, stroking her hair. 'I couldn't bear ...'

She put her finger over his lips. 'Everything will go well, dearest, I'm convinced of it.'

He caught her hand and planted a kiss in the palm. 'You know you're everything in the world to me, don't you, Anna,' he said softly.

262

'Just as you are to me, Paul,' she replied.

'I only wish I could take you to meet my mother. I know she would love you, just as I do. But my father . . .'

'I know, Paul. I understand.'

The next evening, after they had all eaten the evening meal together and were sitting by the fire in the hall, Paul said, 'Mother is not at all well today. I think she is suffering from melancholia, which seems to have physical manifestations, keeping her to her bed, so I tried to cheer her up by telling her that Anna is with child.' He shook his head. 'She cried.'

'I would have thought she would be pleased,' Margaret said sharply.

'She was. She was delighted. I think that was why she cried. And because she would so dearly love to meet Anna.' He turned to Anna. 'It saddens her very much that she has never met you, sweetheart. She would so love to see you, and she keeps asking if I might be able to arrange something, although she knows it's impossible with my father as he is.' He sighed. 'I'm inclined to think the strain of keeping him in a good humour is telling on her, although of course she won't admit it.'

'Surely something can be arranged,' Margaret said thoughtfully.

'Yes, I'm sure it can. Anna can always visit when Silas is not there,' Josiah agreed. 'After all, he has to go to the Bay Hall; he has to buy fleeces; there must be a hundred and one things he has to do that take him from the house.'

'The trouble is, you can never tell when he'll be back,' Paul said gloomily. 'And I refuse to allow Anna to be subjected to his vitriolic tongue on the subject of her native people. Let me tell you, he can wax long and lyrical.' He spoke in the tone of one who had suffered.

'Nevertheless, you must be able to arrange something, Paul,' his grandmother said, with touching faith in her only grandson. Suddenly, she clapped her hands. 'I have it. When the snow has gone, Eleanor must come here to see Anna. Heaven knows, Silas visits his father seldom enough so it's hardly likely she'll encounter him here. And if she did there's no reason why a daughter-in-law shouldn't visit her mother-in-law, so he can hardly object.'

Paul shook his head. 'My father has even forbidden her to come to this house to see you, now. I think she might have disobeyed him but she lives in fear of his terrible tempers.'

'I can understand that. He always had difficulty in controlling his temper,' Margaret said sadly, 'even as a boy.'

'I think he's got worse as he's got older,' Paul said.

'He's not violent, is he, my boy?' Josiah asked, looking at him closely.

'Not with me. But perhaps that's because I'm bigger and stronger than he is.'

'With your mother?'

'Not that I'm aware of.' Paul's expression hardened. 'I'd thrash him within an inch of his life if I thought he'd laid a finger on her, even though he is my father.'

'I wouldn't blame you, Paul, even though he is my son,' Josiah said heavily.

The snow lingered for nearly a month but it soon lost its earlier pristine whiteness and became tired, covering the town with a horrible, frozen grey slush, with unmentionable things that would normally have been flushed away by the rain frozen fast in the gutters.

With the difficulty of transporting goods, business at the Bay Hall came almost to a standstill and at the market only a few of the more intrepid stallholders braved the cold to bring their goods to sell. Those that did come stamped up and down on icy feet behind their wares, blowing on their fingers and flapping their arms in an effort to keep the worst of the cold out, doing hardly enough business to make it worth their while because with no work being done there was precious little money to spend. Most people stayed at home and tried to keep warm as best they might, venturing out only to search the woods for twigs and dead branches to burn on the hearth, praying for an end to the snowy weather. Only the children enjoyed the snow and ice. They spent their time throwing snowballs and skating on any available piece of frozen water.

Paul struggled to his father's house most days even during the bad weather although there was little enough work to do with nearly everything in the town at a standstill.

Silas was not a bit grateful for this. He did nothing but grumble at the loss of earnings and the weakness of his workmen who couldn't brave a little ice and snow to come to work.

'But if they came there's no yarn for the weavers to work with,' Paul pointed out. 'And their fingers would be too frozen to work.'

'They could clean the looms,' Silas snapped.

'You wouldn't want to pay them for doing that all day.'

Silas turned away and gazed out of the window of the counting house and the lowering clouds. 'There's more snow to come,' he muttered.

'I think it's a little warmer. It may be rain in those clouds,' Paul remarked. He closed the ledger with a thump. 'Well, there's little more I can do here today. I'll go and see my lady mother. Is she any better?'

'I can't see there's anything wrong with her,' Silas said. 'But she's taken to her bed now. I've no patience with the woman.'

'Has the physician seen her?'

'What good would he do, except take money from my pocket?'

Paul didn't argue but went into the house and up the stairs to his mother's chamber.

'Paul,' she said, her face lighting up. She was lying propped up with pillows and swathed in shawls. A cloth soaked in vinegar was laid across her forehead. 'This is the best part of my day, when you come to visit me.'

'Are you feeling any better, mother?' he asked, kissing her.

'My head aches abominably and I have no strength, son. All my strength seems to be sapping away from me. I can't leave my bed now. My legs won't carry me even to the close stool.'

He frowned. 'Are they making you nourishing broth to help you regain your strength?'

She waved her hand listlessly. 'My maid Abigail brings me tasty morsels occasionally, when she's allowed into the kitchen, but I have no appetite.'

'You must eat, mother.' He stood looking down at her, pinching his lip. 'I'll talk to Anna about you. She's very good with remedies. Perhaps she has something that would help your recovery.'

That night, as Paul had predicted, the thaw came.

As the rain thundered on the roof and ran in rivers in the gutters, sweeping all the filth with it, Paul sat by the fire with his wife and grandparents, telling them of his mother's increased infirmity.

'I told her you might be able to give her a remedy, sweetheart,' he said when he had finished.

'I wouldn't like to do that without first seeing her,' Anna said doubtfully. 'Will you take me to her?'

'What about my father? Will you be prepared to risk encountering him?'

'Now that the thaw has come, surely he will be spending much of his time at the Bay Hall,' Josiah said. 'He'll have much to catch up with.'

Paul nodded. 'That's true. Very well, when I know he will not be there I will send for you, sweetheart.'

'And I shall come with you,' Margaret announced, when word came that it was safe for Anna to visit because Silas intended to spend the day at the Bay Hall. 'It's some time since I've seen my daughter-in-law and I've always been fond of her.'

The two women hurried along More Elms Lane, the quickest way from their house to Silas's house on East Hill, sheltered from a keen wind by the town wall that ran along beside it. The road was clean and dry now, having been thoroughly washed by the recent torrential rain and dried in the wind that followed, but it wouldn't be long before it was again cluttered with the usual stinking detritus of everyday life.

Paul was watching out for them and he hurried them up to Eleanor's rooms.

To everyone's surprise Eleanor was dressed and sitting in a chair by the fire, swathed in shawls.

'I refused to receive you both languishing in bed,' she said, obviously delighted to welcome them. 'My maid, Abigail, helped me to dress. She sighed. 'It took rather a long time and made me tired but I had a sleep and I'm now refreshed.' She took Anna's hand and her eyes filled with tears. 'Anna. I'm so very pleased you've come to see me.' She stretched out her other hand to Margaret. 'You, too, mother Margaret.'

'I wish we could come more often,' Margaret said, kissing her. She stood back and regarded her. 'Now, what is this illness you're suffering from? Anna, here, is very good with healing herbs. Paul has no doubt told you that.'

Eleanor smiled up at her. 'I think Paul has told me everything there is to tell about Anna,' she said. 'He never tires of talking to me about her and I never tire of listening. As to my illness, alas, I cannot put a name to it but it saps my strength. Ah, here is Abigail with refreshment for us. Will you take wine? And some of the delicious cakes that she makes? Even I can eat one of them although I have little appetite for much else.'

'You must eat,' Anna admonished her. 'You will lose all your strength if you don't.'

'I fear I've already lost most of it,' Eleanor said sadly. Then she smiled happily. 'But let's not talk about my illness. I feel much better today and there are much more interesting things to talk about. Tell me, now. I want to know everything. It's so long since I had such pleasant company.'

The three women sat for a long time talking companionably by the fire whilst Abigail sat sentinel by the window ready to warn them if Silas should happen to return unexpectedly.

'Although I don't believe he will,' Eleanor said happily. She was already looking much better; her face had lost its pallor and her eyes had regained a brightness that had been missing for several months. 'It is so long since he was at the Bay Hall that he will have much business to attend to. And he will want to catch up on all the news, too.' She stretched her arms above her head. 'It's quite a relief to have him out of the house. At least it's quiet for a while. When he's here it's like living with a whirlwind. He roars about, slamming doors and shouting. Nothing's ever right for him, these days.'

'So you stay in your chamber, out of the way,' Margaret remarked perceptively.

Eleanor gave a guilty smile. 'Well, I have to admit it's more peaceful here. I don't have to listen to him shouting at the servants and I don't have to worry about finding new ones when the old ones walk out because he's treated them so badly.'

'And if you feign illness Silas won't vent his temper on you?'

'I don't think mother Eleanor is feigning her illness,' Anna said gently. 'It may have been so to begin with, but now I fear her limbs may be withering through lack of use.' She turned to Eleanor. 'It's not too late, mother Eleanor. You can regain the use of your legs if you walk a little every day. Just to walk the length of your chamber each day would help. And I will send you some medicine and a salve to rub in to strengthen them.'

'And you must eat, Eleanor,' Margaret said sternly.

'But the food the servants cook is so unappetising,' Eleanor complained. 'And if I send Abigail to the kitchen she gets nothing

267

but abuse.' She smiled at the girl by the window. 'Abigail cooks very well, you've sampled her cakes today. But it's not often she gets the chance.'

'It's time you asserted yourself, Eleanor,' Margaret said briskly. 'You've let things go too far with that son of mine . . .'

'He's coming, ma'am. He's just ridden into the courtyard,' Abigail said quickly. 'The groom is just taking his horse . . .'

'Oh, my life, what shall we do?' Eleanor said, wringing her hands. 'If he finds you here . . .'

'If he finds me here he'll say nothing or he knows he'll get the length of my tongue,' Margaret said, taking charge. 'Abigail, take my granddaughter down the back stairs and out through the servants' entrance. Whatever you do make sure your master doesn't see her.'

'This way, ma'am.' Abigail caught Anna's hand and hurried her out of the door and along the passage. They reached the back stairs in time to hear Silas's heavy tread coming up the main staircase.

Chapter Twenty-Nine

By the time Margaret arrived home Anna had already made up the liniment for Eleanor.

'I wouldn't advise you to take it to her, my dear,' Margaret said grimly. 'I had a long talk with Silas – no, that's not quite right, I talked, he shouted. I'm sorry to have to say this but I'm afraid he has a hatred of you that goes beyond reason.'

Anna closed her eyes briefly. 'Oh, grandmamma Margaret, I am so very sorry to have brought this on your family,' she said, her voice aching with regret.

Margaret laid an arm round her shoulders. 'The fault doesn't lie with you, my child, it lies with Silas. He has always had this quite unreasonable hatred of the Stranger community, a hatred his father and I could neither understand nor share. The fact that you, a Stranger, thwarted him and made him look a fool was entirely his own fault, he shouldn't have behaved so despicably in the market place that day. He knows that and the knowledge only adds fuel to his hatred, a hatred that seems to be spilling over into the rest of his life. I almost wonder if he might be losing his mind . . .' She gave herself a mental shake and said briskly, 'But no, of course that isn't so. I suspect he's worried about the business not doing so well.'

'Oh, it's no wonder my poor Paul hates having to work with him,' Anna said.

'And it's also no wonder that Eleanor keeps to her rooms,' Margaret agreed. 'But if something isn't done soon she'll end up completely bedridden.'

'Paul can take this to her tomorrow. It should help,' Anna said, holding up the bottle of salve. 'I only wish I could go myself. She is such a sweet lady, I should like to get to know her better.'

'Better for all concerned that you don't, my dear,' Margaret said. 'Although I know she feels the same about you.'

So Anna had to content herself with sending messages to Eleanor by Paul and receiving replies by the same route. She learned that the salve, together with gentle exercise, was gradually strengthening Eleanor's limbs and that her appetite was improving, no little thanks to the broth that Margaret insisted on sending to her most days. It was little enough they could do for the poor entrapped woman but it was something.

One fine morning in the middle of March, Anna decided to take a trip to the market to buy ribbon for the cap she had been sewing for the coming baby. While she was there she looked around to see if there was a small gift she could take back for Margaret. Soon she found something suitable, a pin cushion in the shape of a cat, which she was sure Margaret would like. She paid for the pin cushion and just as she was turning away from the stall she felt a tug at her sleeve. Her face lit up when she saw who it was.

'Griete! How lovely to see you.'

'Oh, Anna, I'm so glad I've seen you,' she said excitedly, the words tumbling over each other in her eagerness. 'I wanted to tell you. It's all arranged. I am to be married next month. To my Pieter, you remember I told you about him? Well, my . . . our master has agreed that as Pieter is head gardener now we can be married and live in the cottage you and . . .' she hesitated, suddenly feeling awkward.

'The cottage Jan and I lived in,' Anna finished for her, beaming. She caught her hands. 'Oh, Griete, I hope you will both be as happy there as we were.'

'You don't mind, then?' Griete said uncertainly. 'I thought perhaps I was being tactless to speak of it.'

'Of course I don't mind, silly,' Anna said, giving her hands a little shake and then releasing them. 'Better that you should live there than that the cottage should stand empty. It will be a cosy little home for you.'

'But you and Jan . . .' she was still not convinced.

'Jan and I were very happy there. And no doubt we would be now if it hadn't been for . . . what happened. But that's in the past and I've been lucky enough to find love again, with my dear

English husband, Paul Markham. And at the end of the summer I shall have his child. My happiness is complete, Griete, and I hope yours will be, too.'

'Oh, I'm so glad to hear you say that, Anna,' Griete said, relieved. 'You will come to our wedding, won't you?'

'Of course I will. I'll be at the church, never fear.'

'And to the feast afterwards? My master is to provide it.'

Anna shook her head doubtfully. 'I'm not sure about that. Samuel Hegetorne might not wish to have me in his house, Griete. We didn't part on very good terms, remember.'

'Ah, no. I was forgetting. Your name is never mentioned in his presence now.' Her expression lightened. 'But you'll come to the church and see me wed. He can't object to that, can he? The second Thursday in April.'

'I'll be there. I promise.'

'You'll need a new gown if you're going to a wedding,' Margaret said when Anna spoke of her meeting with Griete as the four of them sat eating the evening meal at the big polished table in the hall. She turned to her son.

'It's time your wife had some new clothes, anyway, Paul. We can't have the wife of one of the most prominent clothiers in the town wearing the same skirt day after day, can we. I don't know why we didn't think of it before. Can you bring some cloth samples home for us to make choices from tomorrow?'

Paul speared a piece of meat carefully with his knife before he answered. 'I can bring home some samples, mother, but I'm not sure that they will be very suitable for Anna. I fear Markham's isn't quite the "prominent" clothiers it used to be. We have trouble keeping good weavers these days, unfortunately.'

'Why is that, my boy?' Josiah asked. Then he held up his hand. 'No, don't tell me,' he said with a sigh. 'Silas drives them away with his ill-tempered ways.'

'I fear you're right, grandfather,' Paul said. 'If there's the slightest blemish found in a piece of Markham's cloth at the Bay Hall, the weaver is held responsible and sent packing, whether or not the fault lies in the weaving. As you well know, it could be a fault in the way the yarn is spun that makes the weave irregular, and the weaver has no control over a discrepancy in the dye, but it makes no difference to father. It is a hard and unjust rule and naturally enough the weavers object to being blamed for other men's

271

faults. Of course, a good weaver can always find work elsewhere and I put in a word for them where I can, but that's no help to Markham's trade.' He turned to Anna and smiled. 'All the same, I'll see what I can find. I'm sorry, darling, I should have thought of it before. I'm sure there must be something that will be suitable.'

Anna laid her hand on her husband's arm. 'It really doesn't matter, Paul,' she insisted. 'This skirt is perfectly serviceable and unstained and the bodice is clean. I shall do very well as I am, although it was kind of grandmother Margaret to suggest a new gown.' She lowered her voice. 'I wouldn't want to cause you more trouble with your father, dearest. It grieves me knowing how much you have to suffer on my account as it is.'

'It's not simply on your account, sweetheart. My father finds fault with everything and everybody these days. I do believe even his poor horse cringes when he sees him at the stable door.'

'Oh, Paul!' Even his mother couldn't help laughing at such a wild statement. 'You exaggerate.'

'Well, just a little,' he admitted with a smile.

In the event, the matter of Anna's new gown was settled in an unexpected way.

It was less than a fortnight before Griete was to be married when Josiah presented Anna with a parcel.

'What is it?' she asked, intrigued.

'I don't know,' Josiah said. 'It's a present from Harry. He asked me to give it to you when he came to play chess this afternoon.'

'Harry?' A frown appeared between her eyebrows. 'Why should he give me a present?'

'Oh, do stop asking questions and open it,' Margaret said, impatient with excitement.

Anna carefully unwrapped the parcel and revealed a piece of soft velvet, a rich, deep blue in colour, shading almost to purple in the shadow of its folds. There was more than enough for a new gown.

Josiah leaned forward and rubbed the material between his thumb and forefinger. 'Harry wove this himself. I can tell. He's the only man I know who can produce such a smooth texture.'

Anna was still frowning. 'But why should he give me such a beautiful piece of velvet?' she asked. 'That's what I want to know.'

272

Margaret was looking at her husband intently. 'Did you tell Harry we'd spoken about a new gown for Anna?' she asked suspiciously.

'Me?' He gazed at her wide-eyed, a picture of innocence. 'What makes you think I would discuss such trivial matters when my mind is on an important game of chess?'

Margaret nodded and smiled. 'Just as I thought.'

'I only mentioned it in passing,' he protested. 'I wasn't even sure he was going to do it.'

'Oh, I'm sure,' Margaret said drily. 'How much did you pay him?'

'Nothing. He wouldn't let me pay for it, although of course I offered. Said it was something he'd wanted to do for some time.' He shrugged. 'Doesn't get much call for that class of work, I dare say.' He held out his plate. 'I'll have a little more of that pie, if you please, Margaret,' he said, putting an end to the conversation.

'I can't accept it, of course,' Anna said to Paul later, when they were in their own room. 'After all, I hardly know the man. I've only seen him as he's come and gone to his chess game with grandfather Josiah.'

'Perhaps he did it for you because you're both Dutch,' Paul suggested.

'That's hardly a reason, is it. Goodness me, there are hundreds more Dutch people in the town. No, it's more likely he did it as a favour to grandfather Josiah.'

'Well, whatever his reason, Anna, I think Harry might be offended if you tried to give it back to him,' he said. He ran his hand over the cloth. 'It's very fine velvet. I've never seen better. It will make up into a beautiful gown.' He held it up against her. 'Look, it almost matches your eyes. The colour suits you perfectly.' He kissed the tip of her nose. 'You must get it made up in time for Griete's wedding.'

'Do you really think I should?' She was still doubtful.

'Yes, sweetheart, I really think you should.' He kissed her again. 'Now, come to bed.'

The day of Griete's wedding the sun shone with perfect spring brightness. Although Anna would have liked Paul to accompany her she decided, after some discussion with him, that it might be best for her to go alone.

'You see, Paul, I want to keep as far in the background as I can,' she said. 'It shouldn't be difficult, there are sure to be a lot of people there, but if you come it might cause a bit of a stir, you being English.'

Paul burst out laughing. 'Never mind me being English, with your beauty and in that lovely gown you will never be able to make yourself inconspicuous,' he told her.

She looked down at herself. Margaret's dressmaker had made Harry's blue velvet material into a stylish gown, with enough fullness to accommodate Anna's swelling pregnancy. There had been enough material left to make a matching cap, dotted with the same tiny pearls that patterned the pale yellow silk stomacher. It was a beautiful gown, the velvet so soft and smooth that she couldn't resist running her hand over it every few minutes.

'Make sure Griete sees you, if nobody else,' Paul instructed her. 'She was so anxious that you should be there it would be a sin if she didn't see you.'

'I'll make sure,' Anna said with a smile. 'Though how I can conceal myself from Samuel Hegetorne while making sure I'm seen by Griete I don't know.'

She arrived at the wooden church in Head Street and positioned herself behind a pillar near the back. There were, as she had expected, a lot of people there, all with the bright gloves and scarves they kept especially for weddings, so she was confident no one would notice her.

Pieter, a stocky, handsome man, with a shock of black hair and a weatherbeaten face, came in wearing his best fustian coat and led by his three sisters as his bridesmaids, all carrying the traditional sprigs of rosemary. Griete followed soon after, her usually sallow complexion rosy with happiness as she came in on Samuel's arm, her russet skirt and bodice bedecked with the ribbons that the bride-men who were leading them in would capture later as bride-favours.

The ceremony, conducted by the predikant, Abraham van Migrode, was soon over, and Griete walked down the aisle on her husband's arm and everybody spilled out into the bright April sunshine. Anna hung back behind the crowd, intending to slip away as soon as she was able.

'Anna, my dear,' a voice said at her elbow. 'How very nice to see you.'

Her heart sank as she recognised Samuel's voice. She turned

274

and saw him standing there, looking his usual resplendent self in a ruby-coloured doublet and a matching grosgrain cloak trimmed with budge. She couldn't tell from his expression whether his words had been spoken in sincerity or sarcasm. She suspected the latter, since he was hardly likely to welcome her presence.

'Griete asked me to come and see her married,' she said quickly, 'just to the church, of course. I shall be going home shortly, as soon as the crowd has thinned.'

'No, no, no. You must come back to my house where the feast is prepared,' he said. 'I insist that you come.' He smiled at her, a smile that seemed genuinely delighted.

'I told Griete I would simply come and see her wed,' she said again. 'I don't want to intrude . . .'

'Nonsense. Of course you won't intrude. In any case, I want you to see the garden. It's looking beautiful. Pieter has worked very hard. He's a wonderful worker. I was lucky to find him.'

As he spoke he was propelling her towards his carriage and before she knew it she was inside it and following behind the crowd of guests who were capering along the road beside Griete and Pieter.

'Much more comfortable travelling by carriage,' Samuel said, leaning back and closing his eyes. 'At my age I must admit I find the customs attached to weddings a mite tedious.' He opened his eyes and smiled at her. 'I've provided the feast, so I don't feel obligated to take any further part in the proceedings.'

'Griete told me how kind you've been to her and Pieter,' Anna said carefully. She still wasn't quite sure of Samuel's motives. He seemed to have forgotten the acrimony of their last meeting but she was taking no chances.

They reached Garden House and Samuel handed her down. 'Welcome back to Garden House,' he said with a suspicion of a bow. 'Later, when you've eaten your fill I'll show you Alicia's garden.'

Her heart sank. She didn't want to see Alicia's garden, the garden that would bring back so many bitter-sweet memories of her all too brief life with Jan. Memories that were tucked safely in a corner of her heart, cherished and always there but allowing her to move forward and be happy in her life with Paul. 'I don't think . . .' she began.

'Eat first,' he said smoothly. 'Talk to Griete and Pieter. He's a

275

fine fellow. You'll like him, I'm sure. Just the man to take Jan's place. But I must make sure everything is running well, since I'm the host. Excuse me, won't you.' Another slight bow and he had gone, skirting the merry crowd that had already partaken too freely of the wine and sops provided at the end of the marriage ceremony.

There were a number of people milling about that Anna recognised. Henrick Crowbroke, the man she had once suspected might be her father, was standing by the window. Seeing him regarding the other guests with a faintly supercilious air, she felt nothing but relief that she had been wrong.

Griete, almost pretty in her excitement, came up to her, dragging her new husband by the hand.

'Anna, we're so very glad you've come, aren't we, Pieter.' She looked at him adoringly. 'I was disappointed when you said you would only come to the church because I knew Pieter would like to show you what he's done to the garden.'

'Samuel insisted that I should come,' Anna said. 'I was surprised when he asked me. I didn't think he'd want me here.'

'Well, never mind. You're here. That's what matters. Shall we take her into the garden, Pieter? She'll be surprised, won't she?'

'I hope you won't be disappointed, Mevrouw,' Pieter said seriously. 'Your husband . . . Jan . . .' he cleared his throat, slightly embarrassed, 'What I mean is . . .'

'If you love the garden as much as Jan did then I'm sure everything is looking quite lovely,' Anna said, putting him at his ease. 'And I should love to see it and walk in it again.' This was clearly what he wanted her to say although not at all what she wanted to do.

His weatherbeaten face broke into a smile. 'Then I shall be pleased to show it to you.' He put his arm round Griete. 'Come along, wife. You must come too.'

The three of them stepped outside. As they walked through the knot garden Anna was taken back to the time when it was planned, the stakes with rope stretched between them marking out the beds, Jan's strong arms digging out the soil, and his sense of achievement when the finished beds looked exactly as he'd planned. There were so many memories that she wondered if she could continue walking here.

She was so deep in her own thoughts that Griete had to take her by the hand and repeat what she had been saying.

'Pieter says the knot garden is so perfect that he persuaded Samuel not to have it altered,' she repeated.

'That's right,' Pieter agreed. 'It's quite a work of art. But as you can see he's given me a free hand with the rest of the garden.'

Anna looked up and saw that beyond the knot garden the vista was completely different. There was a fountain playing where rose beds had been, the borders were shaped differently, a yew tunnel, in its infancy now, ran the length of the garden at one side, gravel paths led to a central plinth on which stood a huge urn spilling over with flowers. Everything was different. Even the planting in the flower beds had been changed.

Anna simply stood and stared, her feelings jumbled. She didn't know whether she was glad to see that the garden had changed or whether she felt that Jan had been betrayed because it was no longer as he'd planned it.

'Well, what do you think?' Griete was asking impatiently.

She swallowed, her mouth suddenly dry. 'It's very beautiful,' she said at last. 'Not at all what I had expected.' She turned to Pieter. 'You've worked extremely hard.' Then, because she had to know, 'What does your master think of it?'

'He's delighted now it's finished,' he said, 'although I think he was a bit dubious at first. But when he saw what I had in mind and could see how things could be – not exactly improved but complemented – he became quite enthusiastic.'

'Yes. The two of them spent hours discussing what they would do next,' Griete said.

'That's right.' Pieter agreed, giving Griete a squeeze. 'In fact, I think Griete got a little jealous sometimes when we were working on some of the designs together.'

'Not me,' Griete said happily. 'I've got better things to do than moon after you all the time, husband.' But the took she gave him belied this.

Pieter grinned at her, then went on, 'Samuel's very artistic, you know. And he never minds rolling up his sleeves and giving me a hand. Especially with the weeding. He says it helps him to relax. Ah, here he comes. Good afternoon, sir.'

Samuel included them all in a broad beam. 'What do you think of the garden, Anna? Hasn't Pieter worked wonders?

He's a lazy lout but I manage to get him to do the odd job, here and there.'

They all laughed at Samuel's words. It was plain he and Pieter had such a good working relationship that it could withstand a little gentle teasing. Suddenly, a sense of profound relief washed over Anna. It was almost as if, with the advent of Pieter and the restructuring of the garden, Jan's ghost, and with it Samuel's misguided sense of responsibility towards her, Anna, Jan's widow, was at last laid to rest.

'. . . And next autumn I shall be sending Pieter to Amsterdam to bring back tulips for me,' Samuel was saying happily. 'I've made more enquiries . . .'

Anna smiled at him. 'I hope you'll have more success this time, Samuel.'

'Ah. Forgive me, Anna. That was insensitive of me,' he said, immediately contrite.

'It's all right, Samuel.' She reached up and kissed his cheek. 'I forgive you.'

'For everything?'

'Yes. For everything, Samuel.' She turned to Griete and Pieter. 'I must go home to my husband now. But before I go I want to drink a special toast to you and Pieter, to a long and happy life together.'

'Amen to that,' Samuel said. 'I'll join you.'

Chapter Thirty

Anna walked home from Griete's wedding deep in thought. She was relieved that her friendship with Samuel was back on its old footing and that their relationship was no longer acrimonious. After all his kindnesses to her – and she had endless cause to be grateful to him, a fact she had never forgotten – it had grieved her that they had parted on such bad terms that day at Old Betty's cottage. But it was almost as if, with the changes in his garden, Samuel had managed to begin to let go of the past, and with it his misguided guilt over Jan's death and his suffocating sense of responsibility towards her.

She walked on, then suddenly realising how late it was she hastened her step. Today was Harry's day for playing chess with Josiah and she had been confident she would be home from Griete's wedding in time to thank him for the piece of velvet and show him her new gown. But she hadn't anticipated being invited to the wedding feast and now she feared she would be too late to catch him.

She was right. By the time she arrived home he was long gone.

'Never mind. You can thank him next time he comes,' Margaret said, a trifle impatiently. 'Not that he'll say much. He's a very quiet man.' She caught Anna's hand and said excitedly, 'Now, come into the parlour and tell me all about this wedding . . .'

But Harry didn't come the next week, nor the week after and the week after that Anna was out so it was nearly a month before she had a chance to dress herself in the blue gown to go and thank him.

It was probably not the most opportune moment that she chose. The two men were hunched over the chess board intent on their game and Josiah at first didn't welcome the interruption. But he soon relented when he saw why Anna had come.

'You've lost none of your old skills, Harry,' he said, expertly fingering the velvet. 'It has made up well. And it looks good on my grandson's pretty little wife, don't you agree? Drapes well to show the variation in colour in the folds.'

Harry looked at Anna, and as his glance swept over her with a mixture of pride and admiration she couldn't tell whether it was herself or the velvet that had most caught his attention. 'The colour becomes you very well, Mevrouw,' he said with a slight smile. 'Just as I thought it would. You are pleased with the material?'

'I am, indeed.' She stroked the smoothness of the skirt. 'It has made me the most beautiful gown I have ever possessed. Thank you, Mynheer.'

'Then I am satisfied,' he said, and again he gave her his brief, rather shy smile.

Anxious to finish the conversation and get back to the game, Josiah leaned forward over the chess board again. 'Your move I think, Harry.'

'I'm sorry if I've upset your concentration by interrupting your game,' she said as she reached the door, 'but I was anxious for Harry to see . . .'

Josiah looked up and chuckled. 'You were anxious for Harry to see how beautiful you look in his velvet. We know.' He waved her away. 'Be off with you, baggage, and leave us to our game.'

Anna laughed too and left the room to the sound of the two men chuckling companionably.

It was almost two months after her wedding before Anna saw Griete again. It was at the market, where they usually met, and she was buying meat at the butchers' shambles. Anna noticed her as she finished putting her purchases in her basket and went over to her.

'I buy the best meat I can,' she confided to Anna after they had exchanged greetings. 'Good red meat keeps a man . . . you know, lusty. Not that my Pieter needs any help in that direction,' she added with a giggle and giving Anna a nudge.

'I must say you're looking very well, Griete,' Anna said with a smile. 'And I do believe you've put on weight.'

'Aye, that I have,' Griete said with a laugh. She leaned forward. 'I'm already with child,' she confided. 'What do you think of that! And us only wed these eight weeks!'

'I'm so glad you're happy, Griete,' Anna said.

'Oh, I am. We both are. And your cottage – I still think of it as your cottage, Anna – is wonderfully snug and comfortable. Just right for us. And Samuel – he's told us to call him Samuel – says if there's anything we want we've only to ask. He's a kind man, Anna.'

'He is, indeed,' Anna agreed. 'I'm sure he'll look after you well.'

Griete went off happily and Anna finished making her own purchases. As she was leaving the market she noticed a horse and rider out of the corner of her eye, the man on the horse cutting a swathe through the market crowd with his whip in his haste to get through. She was not surprised to see that it was Silas Markham; he always passed through the market as if he had sole right of way, and she quickly turned her head away so that he shouldn't recognise her.

But when he had passed, obviously on his way to the Bay Hall, an idea came to her. Silas had seemed in a great hurry today so presumably he had urgent business to attend to. With any luck this would occupy him for some time, at least long enough for her to sneak a quick visit to Eleanor. Of course, she wouldn't be able to stay long, but it was quite a long time since the day she went there with Margaret and she was quite anxious to see for herself that the medicine she had sent was effective and that her mother-in-law's health was improving.

She quickly bought a nosegay of flowers from the flower-seller and hurried out of the market and down East Hill to Markham House. She was quite breathless by the time she got there and banged on the door knocker. A rather dishevelled maid opened the door a crack.

'I wish to see your mistress,' Anna said briskly.

'She ain't seein' visitors.' The girl said laconically, picking her nose.

'She'll see me.' Anna pushed her aside and went up the stairs to Eleanor's room.

Eleanor, dressed in a blue cambric gown and with a lace cap on her greying curls, was standing by the window looking down into the yard below, where fleeces were being unloaded. As soon as Anna opened the door she came across the room, her hands outstretched. 'Oh, Anna, my dear,' she said, embracing her. 'You shouldn't have come, of course, but I'm so delighted to see you. Fetch us some wine, Abigail, as quickly as you can, then stand guard at the window,' she said over her shoulder. She turned back to Anna and took both hands in her own. 'You mustn't stay long, my dear. Silas has only gone to the Bay Hall so he'll be back before long.'

'I know. I saw him going there when I was in the market. That's what gave me the idea of coming to see you,' Anna said, her smile as broad as Eleanor's.

'Oh, I am so pleased you've come.' Eleanor clapped her hands. 'And see? I can walk. The salve you sent helped a lot. Abigail rubs my legs and arms with it and I walk every day, just as you said I should. Soon I shall be strong enough to go downstairs and take charge of the servants again, I'm sure of it, although the thought daunts me at the moment. But I'm prattling. What about you, sweeting? How are you? Has the sickness abated? Have you quickened? You look blooming.'

'I'm very well, now, thank you, mother Eleanor. And yes, I have felt the child move. Several times.'

'That's good.' Eleanor nodded. She went over to the window and looked out as Abigail came in with wine and biscuits. 'There's no sign of Silas yet. You can keep watch now, Abigail. Warn us at the first sign.'

'There's no need for alarm, mother Eleanor.' Anna said with a laugh. 'I know my way down the back stairs now so I can escape quickly.'

'Does Paul know you're here?' Eleanor asked, as they sat sipping wine and nibbling at the rather hard biscuits.

'I don't think so. I knew I hadn't much time so I came to the front door. The maid, I must say she looked a rather slovenly creature, didn't want to let me in. She said you weren't receiving visitors.'

Eleanor made a face. 'Would that I had any,' she said gloomily. 'Silas has managed to turn all my friends away by one means or another.' As she spoke her arm caught her wine glass and knocked it to the floor. 'Oh, that was careless of me. Abigail fetch a cloth, please. And another glass of wine. It's a particularly pleasant wine.'

As Abigail busied herself with the spilled wine Anna said, 'Grandmamma Margaret told me she'd had a long talk with him, hoping she could make him see reason, but he wouldn't listen. All he did was shout at her. She worries about him. And about you, mother Eleanor.'

Eleanor nodded. 'I know. And somehow I manage to put up with it all more easily now that I know I have my mother-in-law's sympathy. After all, Silas is her son so her loyalties must be divided. Ah, thank you, Abigail,' as Abigail placed another glass of wine at her elbow and went back to the window to resume her watch for Silas's return.

As they talked companionably together neither Eleanor nor Anna noticed the door opening behind them until an ominously quiet voice said, 'When the girl downstairs said you had a visitor I had an idea it might be the Dutch whore.' Silas advanced into the room, his horse whip in his hand.

Eleanor and Anna both got guiltily to their feet, surprise mingled with apprehension on their faces. They realised that by a stroke of ill-fortune he must have come back into the yard at the precise moment when Abigail was away from her post at the window, mopping up the wine.

His voice rose as he stood in the middle of the room with his feet planted firmly apart, slapping the stock of the whip against the palm of his other hand. 'How dare you come into my house, poisoning my wife's mind against me!' he said, his eyes bulging as he glared at Anna. 'Haven't you done enough damage to me and my family! Bewitching my son into marrying you against all my wishes and making me a laughing stock at the Bay Hall! They should have hanged you for the witch that you are when they had the chance!'

He began to advance on the two women, his face purple with rage, the veins in his forehead standing out in great purple knots. Eleanor instinctively reached out and took Anna's hand as they stood by the small table that held the remains of their little repast.

'Move out of the way, madam!' he ordered Eleanor, pointing with his whip. 'Stand over there, by the fireplace.'

'You have no right to order me about in my own chamber, Silas,' Eleanor said, standing her ground. 'And I'll thank you to put that whip down and speak more civilly when you address me.'

'Be quiet and do as I say,' he said dismissively. 'Unless you wish to share the thrashing I intend to give the Dutch whore.'

'You are not to touch Anna, Silas,' Eleanor said, trying to sound commanding whilst nervously clutching the frills at her neck. 'And don't call her by that dreadful name. She is our son's wife, remember.'

'I don't need reminding of *that!*' he spat. 'Now, do as I say, get over there, by the fireplace. Move, woman, or like I said, I'll thrash you, too!'

Eleanor looked imploringly at Anna as if for guidance.

'You had better do as he says, mother Eleanor,' Anna said. 'I don't think he'll touch me because of the child I'm carrying, but I wouldn't want to risk you getting hurt on my account.' She waited until Eleanor had moved over to the fireplace, then she turned her attention to Silas. 'I can only feel sorry for you, Master Markham,' she said quietly. 'I fear your prejudice and bigotry must make you a very unhappy man.'

He raised his whip. 'How dare you presume to speak to me in that manner, Stranger!' he shouted.

'Because it's true. I pity you, Master Markham. I pity you for the monster you have become in your hatred for my people. And especially your hatred for me. Because in truth I have never done you any harm. In fact, I have never, to my knowledge, done anybody harm. Nor would I.' She paused, then went on sadly, 'I bear you no grudge, Master Markham, for the evil thing you did to me that day in the market place but I cannot yet find it in my heart to forgive you. Your vindictiveness and lies have caused your family as well as me too much unnecessary suffering and misery for me to forgive you for what you have done. It was a cruel, evil thing you did to me that day, Silas Markham. And to Paul, your son, who loves me as I love him. Have you no regret? No remorse?'

'None whatever. My only regret is that they didn't hang you when they had the chance,' he said, narrowing his eyes. 'And by God, by the time I've finished with you you'll wish they had. It would have been a less painful death.' He flicked the whip so that the end of it caught Anna across the cheek.

With a cry, Eleanor ran forward and caught him by the arm raised to strike again. 'No, Silas! You'll scar her for life!'

He lowered his arm and smiled a slow, mirthless smile at Eleanor. 'Good. That's what I intend. When I've finished with her my son won't want to look at her, much less lie with her.' He shook her hand off his arm. 'There are more ways of killing a pig than choking it with strawberries, madam. I couldn't stop Paul from marrying the wench but I'll make damned sure he'll no longer want to keep her as his wife.'

Eleanor stared at him in horror. 'You're mad. You can't do this to Anna. I won't let you.' She caught his arm again. 'She's a dear girl, as dear to me as a daughter. Get out, Anna,' she called, over her shoulder. 'For the love of God, go, while you have the chance.'

But before Anna could reach the door he had thrust Eleanor aside and stepped in her way. 'No, not this time,' he said through gritted teeth. 'You escaped me the last time but you won't get the better of me now.' He dropped the whip and as he bent to pick it up he shook his head several times, as if to clear it.

'I think you should sit down, Master Markham,' Anna said, impatiently brushing away the blood that was running down her face from where the whip had cut it. She was amazed that her voice sounded so calm when she was so terrified inside. 'I believe you are not well.'

'I'm perfectly well!' he roared, staring at the whip in his hand as if he wasn't sure how it had got there. He raised it above his head, staggering a little. 'And I'm going to kill you,' he muttered.

'Don't be ridiculous, Silas,' Eleanor said, raising her voice. 'If you kill Anna you will kill your own grandchild. Paul's child.'

'Good. Then I'll have no Stranger bastard in my family,' he said. He peered round, frowning. 'Where is she? Where is the Dutch whore?' he said, waving the whip ineffectually in the air.

As Anna stood her ground, determined not to flinch, watching him, the door opened and a strong arm caught the whip and wrenched it out of his hand.

'Have you gone out of your mind, you stupid fool? You may be my father, but how dare you raise so much as a finger to my wife!' Paul, his face white with fury, pushed Silas aside and went across to Anna. 'He's hurt you, Anna. I can see that. Oh, sweetheart, what has he done?'

'He isn't well. He really isn't well,' Anna said weakly, brushing her hand across her face and leaning against him, faint with relief.

Silas moaned. 'It's my head. It's full of . . .' Suddenly, he turned deathly pale and fell to the floor in a dead faint.

Paul immediately knelt down beside him and listened at his chest. 'He still lives,' he said, looking up. 'We must get him to his bed.'

'Fetch the groom, Abigail,' Eleanor said, clapping her hands. 'And anyone else in the yard who can help to carry him. And send someone for the physician. And a hot brick to warm the bed.' Suddenly, she was in control, sending servants running to do her bidding, knowing exactly what needed to be done.

Before long Silas was made comfortable in his bed in a clean nightgown and cap and a fire burning in the grate. The physician came, shook his head and pronounced there was little he could do but he would come back in three days if the patient was still alive. Then he went away.

While this was going on Paul stayed with Anna, who was sitting by the fire in Eleanor's room. 'I can't stop shaking,' she said to him through chattering teeth.

'I'm not surprised, my love,' he said, putting his arm round her and holding her wine glass for her to sip. 'You've had a terrible fright. And so have I! If Abigail hadn't run to fetch me I dread to think what might have happened. He was like a madman.' He put his hand over hers. 'But what were you doing here in the first place, darling? You knew it wasn't safe for you to come.'

'I saw your father go to the Bay Hall and I thought I would have time to come and see mother Eleanor. Just briefly. I only intended to stay a few minutes, but she was so pleased to see me that I stayed longer than I realised.' She looked at him, her face still smudged with blood and said woefully, 'And he came back too soon.'

'But why didn't you come to the counting house and tell me you were here? I would at least have been warned and could have delayed him.' He lifted her off the chair and sat down himself, pulling her on to his knee. 'But it doesn't matter, sweetheart. As long as you're not harmed, nothing else matters.' He examined the cut on her cheek.

'It's only a scratch, Paul. It'll soon heal,' she said, gingerly putting her hand up to feel it.

'Come along, then. I'll get the groom to saddle my horse and I'll take you home. You need a posset and bed.' He tipped her face up to his. 'It won't be the first time you've travelled on Blaze with me, will it?' he said, smiling at her.

He was rewarded with a tremulous smile in return.

For three days Silas hovered between life and death. Eleanor was tireless in caring for him, and Margaret, his mother, came and sat by his bed to give her a little respite.

'I keep remembering how he was as a young man, mother Margaret,' Eleanor said sadly. 'He was such a fine man then, so kind, so good to me. We were very much in love, you know, those first years. I don't know what happened to him, I don't know why he became so obstinate and bad-tempered.'

'He always had a temper, even as a child, when things didn't go his way,' Margaret said. 'But it seems to have worsened as he's got older.' She smiled at Eleanor. 'Perhaps this illness will make him a little less impatient,' she said hopefully. She rummaged in her bag. 'Anna has sent this tincture for him. It may help, provided you don't tell him where it came from,' she added with a wry smile.

Eleanor took it. 'After the things he has done to her I wonder she took the trouble to send it,' she said, shaking her head sadly.

On the fourth day Silas opened his eyes but found himself unable to speak or move his right side.

'Ah, it's plain he has suffered a seizure, similar to the one Josiah suffered four years ago,' Margaret said sagely. 'Josiah has made a good recovery although there's still a weakness in his arm and leg and his speech is slow. There's no reason why Silas shouldn't do the same if he perseveres like his father did.'

Eleanor smiled. 'He will have to do as I say, won't he, mother Margaret. His recovery is in my hands. And the business is in Paul's care, which will be better for all concerned. Paul will manage much better without interference from his father.' She leaned over her husband and stroked his beard lovingly. 'We shall do very well, you and I, Silas, very well indeed,' she said softly.

As Silas looked up at her there were tears in his eyes, but he reached out with his good hand and grasped hers with surprising strength.

Chapter Thirty-One

Over the next days and weeks Markham House took on a very different look. Eleanor, totally recovered from her apathetic illness now that she had a purpose in life, immediately dismissed the slovenly servants Silas had been forced to employ because nobody else would work for him. With her kind face and pleasant, open manner she had no difficulty in replacing them with fresh-faced, hard-working girls, two of them from the Stranger community. A buxomly cheerful woman, the wife of one of the older grooms, was brought in to nurse Silas, and Eleanor made a point of sitting with him for some part of every day.

What Silas made of all the changes nobody knew since he had no way of telling them. Sometimes as she sat talking to him, telling him what she had done and what she intended to do, Eleanor thought she saw a flicker of something – was it remorse? – in his eyes and she wondered what, if anything, was going on in his mind, and whether he regretted his past behaviour. She liked to think this was so and she would smooth back his sparse hair and kiss his forehead, letting him know that in spite of everything she still cared for him.

In truth, Eleanor was happier than she had ever been. She had an independent spirit and had hated being ruled by her increasingly domineering husband. Now she was free. Free to organise her household, which she did with an efficiency that amazed everyone, free to do as she pleased. She blossomed.

Margaret noticed the change in her when she paid her weekly visits to sit with Silas. He, by contrast had shrunk from the strutting bully into helpless dependency.

'It's sad to see him thus,' Margaret said as she sat with Eleanor and Anna in the bright downstairs parlour where the sun streamed in at the windows, picking rainbow points of light in the dust motes dancing in the rays. 'But sometimes I think I see something of remorse in his eyes, and I wonder if he can think, if he can remember what his life has been these last years.'

'I wonder that, too, mother Margaret,' Eleanor said, pouring more wine into sparkling glasses and offering her guests another succulent biscuit. 'Like you, I seem to detect a sadness in him for the life he has led latterly. Perhaps one day he will speak again and we shall know.'

'His father made a good recovery, we must pray he does the same,' Margaret said. 'I predict that if he does recover he will be a changed man.'

'I hope you may be right,' Eleanor said, her words heart-felt. She turned and smiled at Anna. 'Perhaps the sight of his first grandchild will speed his recovery,' she said. 'You are blooming, Anna. Your pregnancy goes well, I can see it, I don't need to ask.' She laid her hand over Anna's. 'And it is so wonderful that you can visit me now without fear or hindrance. I value that above all else, my child.' She looked up at the ceiling to the room where her husband lay. 'It was almost worth . . .' She shook her head. 'No, it would be wicked even to think that.' She smiled and said again, 'It warms my heart that you are able to visit me so often, my dear.'

As Eleanor made improvements in the management of the house, so Paul improved the business, largely by renewing old contacts that Silas had lost through his unfair treatment of his employees and prejudice towards the Dutch community. As soon as he was able he provided the spinners with spinning wheels in their homes. This was a new innovation which the women regarded at first with some suspicion, but before long their distaffs were left to gather dust in favour of the new method which spun the yarn more evenly and quickly. This in turn pleased the weavers, who needed no second asking to return to their looms when they knew that Paul was now their master and would treat them well. Before long the business began to thrive again and Paul could hold his head high and know that the name of Markham was again respected at the Bay Hall.

One evening late in June, when the evening meal was cleared, Paul and Anna moved to the window seat by the open window to catch the evening breeze. Margaret and Josiah sat a little distance away by the fire that Josiah felt the need of even in the height of summer. After some minutes of companionable silence, Paul said thoughtfully, 'Do you think Harry might be persuaded to weave for us again, Father?'

Josiah stroked his beard. 'If you mean would he return to Markham's weaving sheds then I fear the answer is no. He is making a very good living doing work where he chooses and I may say he is very choosey these days. But he might be willing to execute – shall we say, special orders for us. Like the velvet he gave Anna, for instance. I feel sure he would be happy to help us on that basis.'

'His name isn't really Harry, is it, grandfather Josiah?' Anna asked.

Josiah chuckled. 'No, it isn't. But it seems to have stuck.'

'What is his real name?'

'Dear me. It's so long, I've nearly forgotten,' Josiah said, frowning. 'Henrick. That's it. Henrick Grenrice.' He beamed in triumph.

'Another Henrick!' Anna said. 'My mother's friend was called Henrick, too.'

'Anna was saying the other day that she wondered if Harry might have known her mother's friend, the one who is buried in St Martin's churchyard,' Margaret said, looking up from her embroidery. 'Would they have been about the same age, do you think, Anna?'

Anna shrugged. 'I've no way of knowing. My mother's Henrick was forty-nine when he died. It was on his gravestone. That's all I know.'

'You must come with me when I go to see Harry, Anna,' Paul said. 'You can ask him if he knew your Henrick.'

'My Henrick.' Anna smiled. 'I like that.'

Josiah was silent for several minutes, deep in thought. Then he said carefully, 'You must have a care when speaking to Harry about the past.'

They all turned to him, but it was Paul who spoke. 'Why, grandfather?'

Again Josiah didn't answer immediately but stared for some time into the small fire burning in the grate. 'Harry must have come to England some twenty . . .? twenty-two? years ago.' He shook his head. 'Perhaps longer than that. I don't really know. I didn't become acquainted with him till he'd been here for some time.'

'Where did he come from?' Margaret asked.

'I don't know that, either. Somewhere not very far from Ypres, I believe. But again, I'm not very sure.' He was silent again for several minutes. Then he went on, 'I only know what he's told me, of course but I've no reason to believe it's not the absolute truth. It seems that when he came to England he left his sweetheart behind in Flanders, and his plan was to work hard so that he could save enough money to bring her over here to him, presumably to marry her. Why she didn't come with him in the first place I don't know.'

'They couldn't afford the fare, I daresay.' Again it was Margaret who spoke.

'Or perhaps he wanted to find work and a place to settle before she came over,' Paul suggested.

Josiah nodded. 'Very likely. But whatever the reason he regretted leaving her behind. Being in a strange country, he was lonely; he missed his love. He missed her so much that he started going to the alehouse. Not often at first, just enough to help him cope with his loneliness. His entire life became a round of working, saving and when his day's work was done, going to the alehouse for a drink and a game of cards. But gradually he began to stay longer at the alehouse, to drink more and to gamble on the cards. Soon all the money he earned went to pay for his drinking and gambling, likewise all the money he had saved towards bringing his sweetheart across the German Sea. Not that he was earning much by this time because he couldn't find anyone to employ him for long, he was too unreliable.

'One morning he woke up after a hard night's drinking to the realisation that he was never going to save enough money to bring his love to England. As he looked round his squalid little room he realised that he didn't even want to bring her here because he was too ashamed of the man he had become.'

'You can't mean the Harry who comes here!' Anna said, shocked. 'Not the man who comes to play chess with you every week. Not the man who wove my beautiful velvet!'

Josiah nodded. 'The same man. But I haven't finished the story yet, have I.' He took a draught of the ale his wife had quietly called for whilst he was talking and went on, 'It was at that point

he resolved never to gamble again and only to drink in modera-
tion. He smartened himself up as well as his straightened circumstances would allow and went looking for work. But none of his
own people wanted him because of his reputation and the English
of course were unwilling to employ Strangers. However, when he
came to me I liked what I saw and took a chance on him. I never
regretted it. He turned out to be the finest weaver I had; he was
always reliable and he always worked hard. You've all seen the
quality of his work. It's second to none.'

'But when you gave up running things my father turned him
out. Simply because he was a Stranger,' Paul said bitterly.

'Yes.' Josiah chuckled. 'The idea of calling him Harry instead
of Henrick and trying to pretend he was English did no good at all,
of course. We never really thought it would, Silas is not that
stupid, but it was worth a try because Harry was – is such a good
weaver. And he's done very well for himself since Silas turned
him out, so perhaps it wasn't such a bad thing, after all.'

'Thank you for telling us, grandfather,' Paul said. 'We'll be
very careful what we say when we see him. Do you still want to
come with me, Anna?'

'Yes, please,' Anna said. 'I have a letter half-written to my
mother, telling her I've found my . . . her friend's gravestone. It
would soften the blow of his death if I could tell her something,
any small thing, about his life here.'

The evening Paul and Anna chose to visit Harry was cool. This
was fortunate because Anna had chosen to wear the blue velvet
gown in deference to the weaver of the velvet even though she
was getting very near her time.

Harry lived in a cottage in Lodder's Lane, not too far for Anna
in her advancing state of pregnancy to walk. It was a two-storey
cottage, the top storey glazed along its full length to catch all the
light. Anna guessed that the loom was on that floor. In the light of
what Josiah had told them a few nights ago she felt slightly apprehensive as Paul knocked on the door. They would have to be very
careful not to seem too intrusive about Harry's past when asking
about her father. She wouldn't want to offend him. She began to
rehearse in her mind how she could phrase her questions.

The door opened and Harry, a little surprised to see them,
invited them in. He couldn't have been expecting visitors yet he
was as neatly dressed as when he came to visit Josiah, his hair and

beard carefully combed. The cottage, too, reflected his person, with not a pin out of place. There was only one room, with a small bed in the corner, partly shielded from view by a clothes press. A table and chair stood by the small window overlooking the street, and an armchair by the fireplace with a bright woven cushion was the only other item of furniture. A rug, also woven in bright colours, lay before the hearth, and a shelf holding items of pewter and pottery stood above it.

'This is a great pleasure,' he said, offering Anna the armchair and Paul the chair by the table. He fetched a flagon of wine from the lean-to kitchen at the back and produced glasses. 'You will take a glass of wine with me?' he asked hospitably.

They thanked him and waited until he was seated on a small stool he had fetched from upstairs before Paul stated his business.

Harry considered the question for some time, stroking his beard in the way Anna had seen him when he was considering his next chess move. 'I should not want to work for a master again,' he said at last. 'But I shall be more than willing to weave cloth for you at an agreed price. And I will give your work precedence because I owe your grandfather a debt I can never repay.' He paused. 'I shall always be indebted to him for his kindness to me.'

Paul got up from his chair and shook him by the hand. 'I hope you will never regret your decision, Harry,' he said. He raised his glass. 'To a long and mutually profitable association.'

'I'll drink to that,' Harry said. 'I shall be more than happy to be doing work for Markham's again.' As he raised his glass Anna noticed that it had only been half filled.

There was a small companionable silence, then Paul said, 'My wife has something she would like to ask you, Harry. She wondered . . .' he turned to Anna and took her hand. 'No, I mustn't speak for you. You ask Harry, sweetheart.'

Anna flushed slightly. 'It's just that I wondered if you might have known a man called Henrick Tayspill. He's buried in St Martin's churchyard.'

Harry thought for several minutes. Then he shook his head. 'It's not a name I know,' he said at last. 'Is there any reason . . .?'

'It's just somebody I believe my mother might have known in the past,' she said. 'She spoke of him before I left my home to come to England, thinking I might meet him.' She pushed a strand of hair back under her cap nervously. 'I think she had no idea how

293

big England is. It's no matter.' Nevertheless she felt a stab of disappointment as she got up from her chair.

He put his hand out. 'No, please sit down. I think it might be possible that I can help,' he said quickly. 'May I know your mother's name?'

'Judith. Judith Fromenteel.' She watched him eagerly and saw several expressions cross his brow before he suddenly looked straight at her and she saw in his deep blue eyes a reflection of her own.

'So, you are my beautiful Judith's daughter?' he said softly. He smiled, a sweet, wondering smile. 'Do you know, I have always thought you had something of the look of her about you, but I thought it must be my imagination, a trick of the light . . .'

'And *you* are Henrick? The man she never stopped loving?' Anna said, an expression of delight crossing her face. She brushed away happy tears. 'And to think I was so sure that my father was Henrick Tayspill, the man buried in St Martin's churchyard, yet there you were, right under my nose . . .' She stopped as she saw his jaw drop.

'Your father?' he said incredulously.

'Your father?' Paul repeated, with an identical expression of incredulity on his face.

She nodded, smiling through her tears. 'Yes. If Harry is my mother's lost love then I am his daughter.' She turned to Harry. 'Just before I left to come to England my mother confessed to me that my father was not Cornelis Fromenteel, the man she was married to, but Henrick, her lost love.' She gave Harry a little, rather shy smile. 'I was the result of your stolen hours of love with my mother.'

He sat down heavily on his stool, consternation on his face. 'Oh, dear God. What she must have suffered. My poor darling. To think I brought her to . . .' He put his head in his hands. 'Oh, God, if I'd known I would never have . . .'

She got up and went to him. 'It's all right, Harry. You have no need to reproach yourself. My mother never suffered for it. Cornelis, her husband, the man I called father for eighteen years, had no idea I was not his child.'

His looked up at her and his face cleared. 'Thank you for that, my dear. I would never have willingly caused my Judith . . .' he gave half a smile, 'you see? I still think of her as my Judith . . . I would never have willingly caused her pain.'

'You didn't cause her pain, Harry. She told me that it was only the fact that I was your daughter that sustained her over the years,' Anna assured him. Her voice dropped. 'I believe she always regretted not coming to England with you.'

He got to his feet and stood looking at her, still with wonder on his face. 'You are my daughter,' he said softly, wonderingly. Very gently, he bent his head and kissed her cheek and she felt the wet tears on his face. 'I am not alone in the world after all.'

'Indeed you are not. And soon, very soon, as you see, you will have a grandchild.' She smiled at him through her own tears.

He shook his head. 'It is almost more happiness than I can bear,' he said. 'To think that I have a daughter is more than enough, but to find that she is married to the son of my greatest friend is beyond belief.'

'It's true, nonetheless,' Paul said happily, drawing Anna to his side and kissing her. 'Will you come back with us now, Harry, so that we can share the happy news with my father and mother?' he asked.

'I will. And gladly,' Harry said.

Back at the house by St Botolph's Gate there was great celebration when the news was told and Josiah called for more wine, which even in spite of everything Harry drank sparingly, as the full story was told.

'Now I can tear up the letter to my mother, which I had been so reluctant to send because it told of my father's death,' Anna said happily. 'When she knows I have found you, father, I am sure it will speed her recovery more than anything because she will be anxious to come to England to be with you again.'

Harry twirled the half-full wine glass he was holding in his hand. 'Perhaps you would allow me to write to her, Anna,' he said thoughtfully. He looked up, a smile spreading across his face. 'But no. I have no need to write. Now that her husband is no longer living there is no reason why I should not go to her in Amsterdam and bring her to England myself. I should like to do that.'

'That's a wonderful idea, Harry,' Josiah said. He cleared his throat awkwardly and said gruffly, 'Have you enough money? I could provide . . .'

Harry laughed aloud. 'My dear old friend, there's no need. I have money and to spare. Although I have worked hard and profitably, I have lived frugally these past years, from choice, not from necessity. But now I am glad, because when I bring my Judith to England I shall be able to provide her with a home that will satisfy all she could possibly want or need.'

'I think her needs will be amply satisfied when she sees you again, father,' Anna said.

Chapter Thirty-Two

There was great hustle and bustle preparing Harry for his trip to Amsterdam but at last he was gone, carrying letters and presents to Judith and Aunt Dionis and with promises to Anna that he would return as soon as possible with her mother.

A week after his departure Anna was brought to bed with a son after a speedy, trouble-free confinement. Some time later, as she lay in the big bed, the lusty baby in the crook of her arm and her husband beside her, she found her mind going back to her previous, sad confinement, when all the long hours of pain and suffering had ended with nothing. No baby, no husband. Even now she could remember the terrible desolation that had gripped her.

'You are very pensive, sweetheart,' Paul said, kissing her hair and bringing her back to the present. 'Is anything wrong? Are you not happy?'

'Oh, indeed I am, Paul.' She gave a sigh of contentment. 'I am so happy it almost frightens me. But my mind travels back to the last time . . .'

He kissed her again. 'That's understandable, my love. But do you not think that everything has a purpose? Without that time of unhappiness, and we both suffered in our different ways, perhaps we would appreciate less this precious life we have together now.'

'And this precious life, too.' She pulled the shawl aside to look at the sleeping child. 'What shall we call him, Paul? I declare he already has a look of you about him.'

'Nevertheless, I think we should call him Henrick, after your father,' he said firmly.

'Henrick Paul. I like that,' she said contentedly. 'After my father. I like that, too.'